HALFWAY HOME

BOOK YOUR PLACE ON OUR WEBSITE AND MAKE THE READING CONNECTION!

We've created a customized website just for our very special readers, where you can get the inside scoop on everything that's going on with Zebra, Pinnacle and Kensington books.

When you come online, you'll have the exciting opportunity to:

- View covers of upcoming books
- Read sample chapters
- Learn about our future publishing schedule (listed by publication month *and author*)
- Find out when your favorite authors will be visiting a city near you
- Search for and order backlist books from our online catalog
- Check out author bios and background information
- Send e-mail to your favorite authors
- Meet the Kensington staff online
- Join us in weekly chats with authors, readers and other guests
- Get writing guidelines
- AND MUCH MORE!

**Visit our website at
http://www.kensingtonbooks.com**

HALFWAY HOME

MARY SHELDON

KENSINGTON BOOKS
Kensington Publishing Corp.
http://www.kensingtonbooks.com

KENSINGTON BOOKS are published by

Kensington Publishing Corp.
850 Third Avenue
New York, NY 10022

Copyright © 2002 by Mary Sheldon

All Kensington Titles, Imprints, and Distributed Lines are available at special quantity discounts for bulk purchases for sales promotions, premiums, fund-raising, and educational or institutional use. Special book excerpts or customized printings can also be created to fit specific needs. For details, write or phone the office of the Kensington special sales manager: Kensington Publishing Corp., 850 Third Avenue, New York, NY 10022, attn: Special Sales Department, Phone: 1-800-221-2647.

Kensington and the K logo Reg. U.S. Pat. & TM Off.

First Kensington Books hardcover edition April 2002
First Kensington mass market printing: March 2003

10 9 8 7 6 5 4 3 2 1

Printed in the United States of America

For my mother,
Jorja Curtright Sheldon—
Until soon.

ACKNOWLEDGMENTS

The grateful author wishes to thank the following people:

My husband, Bob, and daughters Lizy and Rebecca. I love you beyond belief;

My agent and friend, Doris Halsey, who made this her mission;

Sidney and Alexandra Sheldon, Christopher Stone, Abigail Bok, and Rowana Trott for their patience and support;

Robert Stuckey and Judy Clark for sharing their expertise with me;

Michael and Deborah Viner, and Charlotte Chandler, who have been friends of this book from the very beginning;

All the people at Kensington, especially Laurie Parkin, Doug Mendini, Walter Zacharius, and Claire Gerus. And Ann LaFarge for her tireless and inspired editing;

And the memory of my friend Paul Rosenfield.

Prologue

First came the smack of thunder, intrusive and fierce. Then a pause, and then the hot, gritty New York City rain.

Alexis Donleavy peered out the streaked window of the taxi. The street torn up, the light broken—she'd never make it to the Cowleys' on time. And now with the rain, she couldn't simply abandon the taxi and walk—not in these heels.

"Driver," she said, leaning forward. "Could you please make a turn west here? Then go down the next block, and up Ninth Avenue. You can double back a couple of blocks farther north."

The driver, used to the commands of well-dressed women with briefcases, didn't bother to argue. He swung the car around and headed for Ninth Avenue.

That accomplished, Alexis began thinking about the day's next challenge. If she didn't bribe, threaten, or coerce the plasterers to finish the Cowleys' ceiling by Thursday, there was no way the painters could get to the—

Her thought stopped short along with the taxi.

Traffic had built up again.

"Can't you go around it?" she asked.

The driver took satisfaction in telling her no.

Alexis breathed deeply, made herself calm down. *In the scheme of things, what did it matter if she was fifteen minutes late? This wasn't about open-heart surgery; it was about redecorating a living room. Keep perspective; keep perspective.*

The cab was now stopped at a red light. Perspective was lost again.

Alexis forced herself to look outside the taxi. They were in the middle of the neighborhood known as "Hell's Kitchen." The heat and light were absorbed by nothing, were reflected off everything: the decaying structures, the starved weeds in the burned-out lots, the rusted chain-link fences.

Next to the taxi was a forbidding red brick building. There was a hand-painted sign on the front door. It said BRIAN HOUSE.

In front of the building, young boys were clustered. Some were black, some were Hispanic, a few were white. They looked to be about fifteen to seventeen years old. Their eyes were unreadable. Alexis felt herself thinking about the Hitchcock movie *The Birds*. That silent watching of eyes that did not belong to her own species. She looked at those eyes, and they looked at her.

And then there was a cry. Shrill, awful. Again, she thought of birds—there was nothing human about that sound. From around the corner came ten, twenty other boys, cresting the sidewalk in a sudden terrible wave.

Alexis sat frozen in the taxi, unable to look away. The boys made war. A tide of fists and screams and blood. And their faces. She would never forget their faces.

Without thinking, she rolled down her window and beat on the side of the car.

"Stop it! Stop it!" she began to scream.

Unbelievably, the tide did pause—and then it shifted. It shifted in her direction. All the boys, the ones from the building, and the others who had come, moved slowly toward her, united, and put their hands on the taxi. Pressed in, harder and harder. Began to rock the cab back and forth. Hands, black, brown, white, grasped for Alexis through the open window. She reared back—the hands reached in. Faces wild in the window. Voices screaming.

"Get out of here!" the driver shouted. "Goddam kids! Goddam kids!" He pressed the horn in frantic spasms. At last the light changed and the traffic cleared. The cab surged forward and away.

When Alexis reached her appointment, only five minutes late after all, she asked to use the bathroom. She sat on the edge of the bathtub and wept silently and bitterly. Then she splashed her face with water, and came out, calm. She did not tell the Cowleys what had happened in Hell's Kitchen, outside the red brick building. She did not tell her husband.

And later, she did not tell anyone about the dreams. Dreams of boys with glowing, angry faces. The hate, the fear, the rapture on those faces. It was the rapture that haunted her more than anything.

One

It was a day in mid-July. The city was sluggish and sulky with heat. The trees dripped grit onto the acrid, shimmering pavements as pedestrians moved silently and slowly down the avenues. The fruit on the vendors' stands looked dusty, the goods in shop windows dispirited. Steam rose clingingly from the gratings. Cabdrivers screamed.

Alexis was sitting in the courtyard of the Café des Artistes on the Upper West Side, waiting for an out-of-town client. She had come a few minutes early as she disliked the flutter of being the last to arrive. The waiter had brought her a Perrier and she drank it without enjoyment. She was feeling edgy and unwell, with a headache that jumped from her eyes to her temples. A brain tumor or the need for reading glasses? She supposed she should see a doctor; the headaches had been becoming more frequent of late.

* * *

A sudden frantic pink appearance at the entrance to the restaurant announced Mrs. Gollancz. When she saw Alexis, she waved a plump hand in relief, and hurried through the maze of tables toward her.

"Oh, that stupid cabdriver!" she wailed. "I told him he shouldn't have gone through the Park—am I very late?"

Alexis assured her that she wasn't.

Mrs. Gollancz settled herself in the chair. She was large and middle-aged, dressed for a day out in New York. She had evidently just come from the beauty shop, and her face glowed with cosmetics.

"This restaurant is supposed to be just absolutely wonderful," she told Alexis earnestly. "I'm so glad you suggested it."

Café des Artistes was ordinarily one of Alexis's favorites, too, but today as she looked around, the restaurant seemed overloud and overbright. The effect was oppressive, almost menacing.

Oh, God, she thought wearily. *What a mood I'm in.* She put it down to the heat. All her life, heat had depressed her. She forced thoughts of other things; she imagined a cool, solitary beach. Herself walking on wet, forgiving sand, a wind blowing her headache away.

The waiter came over and took their order. Alexis ordered a salad, and Mrs. Gollancz, after a great deal of consultation, decided on the special of the day. Then, as the waiter was turning to go, she amended it to the orange roughy.

Once the waiter had left, Mrs. Gollancz turned to Alexis with eager anxiety.

"Now, Mrs. Donleavy," she burst forth in bright,

fretful tones. "Let's get down to business. We haven't really tackled the foyer yet."

The beach went away. Alexis nodded, frowned; she reached under the table and brought out her portfolio. Then she and Mrs. Gollancz tackled the foyer.

The waiter brought their lunch. Mrs. Gollancz, exclaiming that the food was much too pretty to eat, ate it quickly. Alexis watched her with something that approached envy. Mrs. Gollancz was filled with such enthusiasm—about the designs, about the fish. She seemed to enter into each detail of life with satisfaction and pleasure. Alexis watched her eat, feeling emptier and emptier.

The waiter came by with the check, looked with surprise at Alexis's almost untouched salad, and asked if anything had been wrong with the meal.

Alexis shook her head, made herself smile.

She took the check quickly and presented her American Express Gold Card. Mrs. Gollancz was charmed. Much as she had liked the restaurant earlier, she became twice as expansive when she realized her meal was to be *gratis*. She told Alexis how much she had enjoyed the meeting, how brilliant Alexis's ideas were, how excited she was about the project. Alexis put away her portfolio. She felt exhausted by the praise.

Finally, they stood up to go.

"I'm headed over to the Met now," Mrs. Gollancz told her. "Can I drop you somewhere?"

"No," Alexis said. "No, thank you."

She put Mrs. Gollancz into her taxi, then went back into the restaurant. The headache had worsened, and she felt dizzy. She went into the ladies' room, took off her watch, filled a sink with cool water, and dipped her wrists in. Since the days of childhood, this had always made her feel better. But today the trick didn't work.

She took her hands out of the water and dried them carefully. She thought about canceling. It would be easy enough to do. It was so hot; she was so tired. She could go just as easily next week. Alexis glanced at her Hermès purse where her cell phone was, but she didn't make the call.

As she turned from the sink, she looked automatically at the woman in the mirror. This woman was elegant, almost intimidatingly well put-together—had Alexis seen herself as a stranger on the street, she would have approved. Everything worked, from the slim body in the beige silk suit to the sleekly cut blond hair above the finely powdered pale face. She looked sophisticated and confident and successful, exactly the way Alexis meant her to appear. She noticed that beyond these surface things, however, the reflection said little.

She strapped her watch back on and looked at it. Yes. It was time to go now.

Alexis found a taxi and slid onto the hot, patched leather seat. She was tempted to give the driver her home address. He would never know that that was not her original intention. But she gave him the other address instead.

The cab jerked down the avenue. Alexis opened the window and let the hot, used air breathe into her face. Usually, she was full of attention and opinions as she rode through the streets of New York. Dislike of a new building going up, interest in the opening of a store, appreciation for a window garden. But today she had no opinions. The cab hit a pothole, and Alexis came down hard on the seat. A nail underneath jabbed into her leg. She wondered wearily when she had had her last tetanus shot.

The cab slowed down. They were approaching Forty-eighth Street, Forty-seventh, Forty-fifth. Torn paper flapped on the streets, wrapped around lampposts. Homeless people, junkies, men with soiled eyes, lay in every doorway, collected on every corner. Alexis felt them see her, spot her color, draw a bead on it, follow it.

And then they were there.

Alexis paid the taxi driver, and got out of the car.

She stood for a few moments in front of Brian House. So she was actually here. Up until this moment, she hadn't been sure she would do it.

She had wondered how she would react to this moment—her return to this place. Her return to those teenagers, and their faces. As she stood there now, she felt obscurely disappointed. All her anxiety, all those dreams; they seemed silly now. There was no terror, no war, no rapture on the corner today. There was just a seedy building flanked by rusting bicycles. She felt annoyed at herself—what, after all, had she been looking for? Well, she was here; she had promised herself that she would do this; she might as well go through with it. She straightened, and entered through the stripped green door.

* * *

She found herself in a small anteroom. The floor was filthy, the paint on the walls a peeling brown. Discarded gum wrappers twinkled in the corners. The hallway beyond was choked with kids. Alexis watched them, sidelong. She was struck by their restlessness, their endless scuffling, twitching. They were not interested in her arrival, did not look up.

"May I help you?"

Alexis turned. A smooth-faced black woman, in her twenties but with prematurely white hair, was watching her from the desk.

"Yes," Alexis said. "My name is Alexis Donleavy. I have an appointment to see Mr. Wheelhouse at three."

The receptionist announced Alexis's name into an intercom.

"He'll be with you shortly," she told Alexis. "Please have a seat."

There was a broken couch available. Alexis remained standing. She watched the three kids nearest her—a Hispanic boy around sixteen years old wearing a dashiki, and two black girls, slightly younger, with heavy makeup. She couldn't understand what they were saying; it all appeared to be in some incomprehensible insider slang.

"Are you here as a volunteer?" the receptionist was asking.

Before she had a chance to answer, a voice spoke from behind her.

"Mrs. Donleavy? Please come in."

Steven Wheelhouse was at the door of his office. He was on the sliding side of fifty, black, tiredly dressed.

He led Alexis inside, and gestured her into a chair

across from his desk. She sat down and looked around the tiny room. It was determined to be cheerful; colorful posters were on the walls and displayed on the desk and bookshelves were various cards addressed to "Big Daddy Steve." It was odd to think of those sullen, shuffling kids sitting down to make such a card.

Steven Wheelhouse offered her coffee, which she refused.

He smiled at her.

"Well, Mrs. Donleavy," he said, "I've been looking forward to meeting you—I've been coming across your name a lot lately." He indicated some letters on his desk. "Judge Michaelson has written me about you and Sam Jacobson. I hadn't heard from Sam in ages. How's he doing? We used to co-host a yearly charity event together."

"Yes, he mentioned it. He's doing fine."

There was a pause. "So," Steven Wheelhouse asked, "what can I do for you?"

For a moment, Alexis thought of telling him—the incident in the taxi, the faces that had been in her dreams for the last month and a half. But that was out of the question. Instead, she was ready with her proper answer. It came out fluidly. She had not realized how often she must have practiced it in her head these last six weeks.

"Over the last month or so, I've been making inquiries about your program, and I've heard that you've accomplished some pretty wonderful things."

He nodded. "We certainly try."

"And I was wondering if I could be of any help to you."

He nodded and glanced at the letters again. "You're

a decorator, I see. Quite famous, according to these guys. I'm sorry I don't know your work. My wife loves that magazine—what is it? *House Beautiful?*"

Alexis thought about telling him that one of her rooms was being featured in that month's *House Beautiful* but decided not to.

"Yes—I am an interior decorator, but I also teach. Design and Art. That's where I thought I might be of help. I've taught several adult extension courses, and I thought I could do the same kind of thing here with some of the kids—a simplified version."

He looked a little skeptical. "You're proposing to teach them about interior decorating?"

"It would be more than that. It would be a course on design principles, on principles of art; we'd do interiors, certainly, but we'd also cover theory, painting, sculpture, architecture."

He nodded. "Kind of like a history of art course."

"Yes."

He smiled. "I took one of those my first year in college. One of the best classes I ever had, as a matter of fact. I especially loved those Greeks." He pointed to the bookcase behind him. On one of the shelves was a small statue of a discus thrower from the Hellenistic period.

"My dream is to get over to Greece someday," he said.

Alexis nodded. She did not mention that she had been to Athens last summer.

"I hope you make it."

"So," Steven Wheelhouse went on, "if I understand this correctly then, this would be a class teaching the kids about beautiful things."

Alexis liked the way that had been put.

"Exactly," she said.

He nodded. "That's so important. People some-times don't realize it—especially around here. We get so wrapped up in the practicalities of helping the kids that we miss some bigger issues."

"Well, I think it's an area in which I might do some good."

Alexis sat back, satisfied. It seemed that the deal had been made.

But Steven Wheelhouse was looking thoughtful.

"I'm not sure that we can take you up on your offer, though," he said.

Alexis flushed. "Why not?"

He indicated the letters again. "I appreciate the let-ters of introduction, certainly, and I'm sure you're a wonderful teacher, but teaching adult education courses and teaching these kids here are two very different things."

"I'm sure there are differences," she said, "but I have no doubt they can be worked out."

He looked at her. "Have you ever taught teenagers before?"

"Actually, no."

"Have you ever had any training in psychology?"

"Not really."

"Do you have any children of your own?"

She paused a moment before answering.

"No."

He sighed. "Mrs. Donleavy, let me tell you a little about my program. Fifteen years ago, my son Brian died from a drug overdose, and I started this place in his honor."

He looked up. Mentioning his son had made him, in that brief moment, very old.

"Yes," she said quietly, "I had heard that."

"My idea was to help other kids from ending up the way Brian did." He stood up and began to walk around the room. "Brian House is for kids who have problems—it's what we call a therapeutic school. A special school for kids with emotional disorders.

"We have kids here who have been on drugs since they were eight years old. Kids who have spent the last two years living in the back of a car. Kids who have been what we call 'relinquished.' Their father's in prison, their mother's in rehab; there's no one to look after them. Once they're past the cute age, they're too old to be adopted. So they live here."

He folded his arms. "Nearly everyone at Brian House is recovering from some form of drug abuse. Some of the boys have been pushers. Most of the girls have been prostitutes. They're very sophisticated in terms of being street smart, but emotionally they're incredibly vulnerable. They come from pasts that you and I cannot imagine."

I know about unimaginable pasts, Alexis thought.

"I see," she said.

"So you can understand how incredibly careful I have to be. Anyone who comes in contact with these kids has to be a trained professional. And I'm afraid that, as tempting as your offer is, I can't take that chance."

Alexis straightened.

"But it's really not taking such a chance. I'm not setting myself up as a staff member. We're just talking about a couple of hours a week."

Without warning, the door was suddenly jerked open, and a Hispanic girl jiggled frantically into the room.

"What is it, Romina?"

"Mr. Wheelhouse, Sarah's on detention, but she's watching TV and she won't stop!"

Steven Wheelhouse sighed.

"Tell her she's not getting a point today. And neither are you, for forgetting to knock."

"Fuck you," the girl said.

She slammed the door behind her.

"Seems like a normal kid to me," Alexis said.

Steven Wheelhouse smiled. Alexis felt encouraged by the smile.

"I wish you'd reconsider my offer," she said. "If you like, a member of your staff could oversee the class. And if I got into any difficulties, I would of course come to you for help immediately."

He said nothing.

"Couldn't you at least ask if the kids would be interested?"

"Oh, I'm sure they'd be interested," he admitted. "As a matter of fact, a few come to mind who would like nothing better."

Alexis leaned forward. "Then why not let me teach my class? Teach them about beautiful things, as you put it. If it doesn't work out, it doesn't work out. But, from what you've said about these kids, I doubt anything I could do or say would scar them too terribly, and who knows, it might just make a difference to one or two of them."

He let out a breath. "That's true," he admitted. "And it's also true that from time to time we've had people here, lecturers and so on, who weren't trained."

"Well, that's all I would be doing," she told him. "Lecturing and showing pictures."

He nodded, and was silent a moment longer. "I do tend to overreact sometimes, be a little overprotective."

"I completely understand."

"But, as you say, if anything came up, a staff member would be moments away. And it would only be for a few hours a week." His glance fell on the letter again. "Sam certainly thinks you're terrific, and he's never steered me wrong."

"So you'll let me teach the class?"

He sighed. "All right. For a month or two, at any rate. We'll have to see how it goes."

"That's all I'm asking."

"And not with a large group, either," he added hastily. "Just with a few kids."

"The ones you spoke about before. The ones you said would get a lot out of it."

"Would that be worth your time? Teaching just three kids?"

"Yes," she said.

He smiled slightly.

"You sound very sure. Okay, then. What kind of schedule were you proposing?"

"I could give you two hours, once a week."

He nodded.

"That would work. And when were you thinking about starting?"

She looked at her watch. Nothing until the dinner with Ron's clients at seven.

"Immediately," she said.

He laughed. He seemed much younger, lighter when he laughed.

He consulted a schedule.

"Well," he said, "as it turns out, those three kids I mentioned are all free now." He stood up. "I'll find you an empty classroom and bring them in." He smiled. "Let me know when you do Greek art. I might stop in for that class myself."

As he left the room, he pulled a form from one of the filing cabinets against the wall.

"Would you mind filling this out?" he asked. "We require it of anyone who does any work with us."

As he handed over the paper and a pen, he hesitated, but finally spoke.

"Pardon me for mentioning it, Mrs. Donleavy, but you're not exactly our usual volunteer."

"No," she said. "I imagine I'm not."

"Do you do this sort of thing often?"

"No," she said. "Actually, I'm quite selfish about my time."

He nodded.

"What made you decide to come to us?"

Alexis looked at Steven Wheelhouse.

Because my life is so rich that I feel guilty for having given nothing back.

Because my life is so empty that unless I put some meaning into it I will go mad.

Because I dream of those faces.

But what she said was, "I'm not entirely sure."

For some reason, this seemed to please him.

"I often operate from that place myself," he said. "I'll be back in a few minutes."

When he was gone, Alexis looked at the form.

It was the usual—name, address, occupation. She filled it all out automatically until she came to a question halfway down the page. "Father: living/deceased. Mother: living/deceased."

Alexis stared at the words. A flush came onto her face, and she put down the paper. Finally, she picked it up again, and after "Father," she circled "deceased." Then she paused, staring at the second half of the question. She found it hard to breathe. She put down the paper again and stood up. She made herself look around the room. She examined the posters, the postcard of the discus thrower; she tried to put herself back on the cool beach. Finally she came back to the chair and picked up the form again. After she circled the word "Mother," she circled "deceased" in a deliberate, dark parabola. The point of the pencil broke.

Two

When Alexis was a little girl, the story she loved most to hear was about her mother dying, giving birth to her.

They would be lying in Maggie's big bed on a Sunday morning. Maggie would be drinking coffee out of a cup that had a gold rim, and she would let Alexis have a sip. Alexis always liked to sip in the same spot her mother had drunk from.

"Mama," she would say, "tell me 'The Story.'"

"What story?" Maggie would tease, knowing perfectly well which one.

"The one where you died and came back for me."

"Well." Maggie would straighten up and her eyes would narrow with remembering. "It was right before you were born. I was so excited—no mother has ever been more excited. I had everything all ready for you—your pink room, all your dolls—and enough dresses to last you until you were three years old!"

Alexis loved this part. "You knew I was going to be a girl!"

"Yes." Maggie would laugh. "Daddy and Grandmother thought I was crazy, but I was absolutely sure. Well, the big night arrived. Daddy drove me to the hospital, and you started to come. And then something went wrong."

Alexis said eagerly, "Your heart stopped."

"Yes. The doctors couldn't figure out what happened, but they got me going again in a few minutes."

"But before they got you going again? Yes, yes?"

Her mother would look down dreamily.

"I felt myself floating up, out of my body. I could look down on the bed at myself. I looked so silly, so fat—like a big balloon!"

Alexis would always laugh at that part.

"And there I was at the bottom of a big golden tunnel. I started being pulled up through it. There was music playing, the most beautiful music. I kept going up; it was so lovely I never wanted to leave."

Alexis didn't like that part. "And then what?"

"And then I remembered you. I remembered that I was having a baby down on Earth. And as beautiful as that tunnel was, it was absolutely nothing, nothing compared to being with you. So I zoomed back down that tunnel, and the doctors got my heart started again, and the next thing I knew, I was holding you in my arms."

And she would grab Alexis in her arms now.

"And are you glad you stayed?" Alexis would always ask.

"Oh, yes, oh, yes, oh, yes," Maggie would murmur into her hair.

* * *

One of Alexis's favorite things to do was to set out playing cards and arrange them into her family. The Red King was her Father. Like her real daddy, he seemed quiet and handsome, not dangerous like the Black King. She herself was the Ace of Hearts, and just like in real life, her card-father read books to her, and taught her to swim. And just like Daddy, the King of Hearts was a banker and worked in New York City.

Grandmother was the Queen of Diamonds. This was because she had a diamond necklace that Grandfather had given her before he died. She was also, like the card, very grand. Alexis pretended that the card ran all kinds of charities, just like Grandmother did, and was always giving teas and luncheons. Jack the chauffeur was, of course, a Jack. Alexis let him be Jack of Diamonds, because he had been with her grandmother so long. Alex, the cook, was Jack of Spades, because Alexis thought the Jack of Spades was cute and so was Alex. And then she would lose interest a little, and randomly assign cards to Mary, the downstairs maid; Josie, the upstairs maid; Celia, the laundress; and the four gardeners. Nanny was easy. She was always the Ace of Spades, because that was the worst card in the deck.

"And what am I?" Maggie asked Alexis one day. But she had no answer. The Queen of Hearts was the obvious choice, but that seemed too dull, too ordinary for her mother.

"What card do you *want* to be?" Alexis asked.

"The Joker, of course," Maggie said instantly.

Alexis thought her mother must be kidding. The

Joker was a man, first of all, and he was ridiculous-looking, and he didn't have any points in the game. In the end, she painted a new card for Maggie, and called it the Queen of Everything.

Alexis spent a lot of time with her grandmother. She saw her every breakfast and dinner, and on Saturday afternoons she enjoyed a quiet hour in Grandmother's room. She would play with her dominoes while Grandmother went through papers. Sometimes the two of them would have tea. Grandmother would tell Alexis about the charities she was working for, how there were children who didn't have enough to eat. Alexis would feel very guilty. She would choke a little over her tea biscuits, but enjoy them all the more.

There was not as much time with her father. Weekdays, he was at work until late, and Alexis didn't see very much of him, but they always managed to spend a few hours together on weekends. He would read to her, boys' books that he had liked when he was her age. He taught her to play "Heart and Soul" and "Moon River" on the piano, and promised that she would have lessons when she was eight. Sometimes they went on walks, and she was amazed that he knew so much about flowers and leaves. She would tell him that he should be a gardener, not a banker, and he would laugh as if he was pleased.

There was too much time spent with Nanny, far, far too much time, and there was never enough time with her mother. No matter how many hours Alexis spent with Maggie, it was never enough.

For being with Maggie wasn't like being with a mother at all; she was more like a special magical friend, a genie. And she made everything so exciting. When Maggie suggested they play a game, it was never something ordinary like "Candyland" or "Old Maid." It might be a game of pretend, in which her mother would be Aladdin or Peter Pan, and they would go all over the house, pretending to fly away from evil magicians. Or there might be a treasure hunt, with Maggie leaving little clues in Alexis's shoes or on the windowsill, and a new doll at the end of the search. Or they might go on adventures—Maggie often took Alexis into New York, where they would go to the theater, or get ice cream at Serendipity, or visit a museum.

Sometimes they went to scary places—to parts of the city where men lay in the gutter, and people walked the streets in rags. When Alexis would complain about these outings, her mother would tell her, "You're not going to grow up narrow-minded; I want you to see everything there is to see." Alexis wasn't sure what narrow-minded was, but she went along with it because it was important to her mother—and as long as she was with her mother, who cared where she went anyway.

But even with all the outings, Alexis wanted still more time with Maggie. Especially at night. Every evening after she finished dinner with Nanny in the nursery, Alexis would rush into her mother's room.

"Are you staying home tonight?"

But most evenings, it seemed, Maggie would be sitting at her dressing table, wearing an evening gown, preparing to go out.

Alexis would cry, and Maggie would hold her, not minding the tears on her beaded or her crepe de chine dress.

"But why do you have to go?" Alexis would sob.

Sometimes it was a business meeting, sometimes it was a dinner party, sometimes it was a charity event. But whatever it was, Alexis could tell from Maggie's face that she didn't really want to go, that what she really wanted to do was stay home with her.

Alexis started to hate her mother's evening dresses. She decided that if her mother didn't have any more evening dresses, she wouldn't be able to go out anymore. One afternoon, she stole a pair of scissors from Nanny's sewing basket, sneaked into her mother's room, and began to cut up the gown that was hanging on the door.

Suddenly there was a cry—and a hand, Nanny's hand, swept down onto her shoulder. She seized Alexis and started to drag her down the long hallway toward her grandmother's room. Alexis clutched at everything she could reach; she knocked down a lamp, a Bedermeier table, and a Chagall print, but she could not get free.

When they reached Grandmother's room, Nanny announced in shaking tones what Alexis had done. Grandmother's face got very white.

"Alexis!" she said in a deep voice.

As she moved forward, her arm raised, Maggie rushed in from the hall and threw her arms around Alexis.

Alexis could feel the snap of her mother's heart. It was beating so fast that she was afraid it would stop again, the way it had in the hospital the day she was born. Then she looked up and saw the way her mother and her grandmother were staring at each other.

*   *   *

Somewhere inside her, Alexis had always known that her grandmother hated her mother. It was something she could just feel. Grandmother never said so, but Alexis was sure of it. She could see it in the looks Grandmother gave Maggie. She could hear it in the way Grandmother spoke about Maggie to friends on the phone.

And then there were the other things—things Alexis stored up like jigsaw puzzle pieces. One day, she overheard the chauffeur tell the cook that before Alexis was born, there had been a terrible fight. Grandmother had wanted a grand baby shower, with all the important people in the neighborhood invited. Maggie hadn't wanted that shower; she had wanted one with all her old friends from the theater. Then Daddy had stepped in. He had taken his mother's side, and Grandmother got her way. Alexis never quite understood this story. As long as she could remember, her mother had hated showers; baths were what she loved: hot, perfumed baths, that she would sometimes let Alexis join.

And then there was another story; she heard Alex the cook discussing it in the pantry. He said that, years ago, Grandmother hadn't wanted Daddy to marry Maggie at all. That she didn't want him being with someone who was an actress, and who came from California. But Daddy had married Maggie anyway. Alexis liked this story. She liked her daddy for being so brave. When he came home from work that night, she looked at him and tried to imagine him saying "Mother, I'm going to marry her!" But she couldn't do it. Her father was so quiet, and she had never seen him get excited about anything. So she decided that the cook's story had been a lie. And if it was a lie, then maybe they were all lies, and maybe that meant that her grandmother didn't hate her mother at all.

Except that Alexis knew better.

Alexis was going to be six. She was very excited about her birthday. She and Maggie talked about it a lot, those mornings when she would come into her mother's room and they would cuddle under the pink satin comforter. Maggie promised her that they would have a big party, with a magician and a puppet show and pony rides. They would even hire a vendor to sell hot dogs.

"I'm going to eat all the hot dogs!" Alexis cried.

"No! I am!" Maggie answered her.

"Me!"

"Me!"

"Says who?"

And Maggie fell on Alexis with tickles.

A few weeks later, Grandmother made an anouncement at breakfast.

"Your birthday's coming up, Alexis, and I wondered if you'd enjoy a party."

"Oh, yes! Yes!"

Grandmother smiled at her enthusiasm.

"I thought a tea party would be nice. We could invite some of the neighborhood children, and have the party on the lawn."

Alexis didn't know what to say. She didn't want to disappoint Grandmother, but she also didn't want that stuffy, silly party. She looked pleadingly at Maggie.

"Well, actually, Mother, Alexis and I had a little idea of our own." Maggie told about the plans for the party, but before she even got to the hot dogs, Grandmother was waving an irritated white hand.

"Maggie, dear, I don't really think that would be appropriate. It would be a little too showy."

Showy was one of the worst words Grandmother could say about anything, and it always hurt Alexis when she said it. Because her mother was always showy.

Maggie was very red. Her grandmother was very pale. Alexis didn't want there to be a fight.

"A tea party would be nice," she said quickly. Her grandmother's face grew a friendly pink again. But her mother's face didn't change.

It wasn't much fun getting ready for the party. Alexis wasn't allowed to choose the sandwiches, and she wasn't allowed to wear the dress she wanted. Instead, her grandmother bought her a new one, with babyish smocking on the front. When Alexis went to Maggie to complain, her mother only shrugged and didn't seem interested.

Maggie hadn't been interested in anything to do with the party. Since that morning at breakfast, she hadn't said a word about it. It made Alexis feel frightened that Maggie didn't seem to care. She was sorry she hadn't fought for the party with the clown and the hot dogs, but everyone knew that Grandmother was the boss. Maggie knew that, too. So what was the good of fighting? Still, it was no fun not having her mother care.

* * *

The day before the party, Maggie went out in the afternoon, and when she came back, she was carrying a huge donkey, all covered with bright bits of paper.

Alexis raced to hug her.

"What is it? What is it?"

"It's called a piñata. It's for your party." Maggie smiled. "It's filled with candy. We'll hang it up and you kids will take turns hitting it with a stick. Then, when it breaks, all the candy will fall out."

Alexis could picture it—the donkey swinging, the children yelling, and all that candy whooshing to the ground. But best of all, her mother had bought the piñata. Her mother was going to be part of the party, after all.

She hugged Maggie again, hard.

Grandmother walked in.

"Oh. A piñata," she said.

"Mama got it for the party!" Alexis cried. "Isn't it beautiful?"

Maggie's smile bubbled through the room.

The tea party was boring. The cake was good, and the presents looked interesting (Grandmother had said she wasn't allowed to open them until the guests left), but the day was nothing special. What would be great was the piñata. Finally, after tea, it was time.

The piñata had been set up on the patio; the children jumped around it.

"Alexis goes first," Maggie said, "since it's her birthday."

Alexis danced proudly up to her mother, and Maggie tied a soft scarf around her eyes. Alexis knew she would break the piñata with one try; she had practiced last night on a sock hung from the bedpost. She would break it, and then rip the blindfold off, and snatch up most of the candy.

She picked up the stick, swung hard, and there was a flat swish of air. She had missed.

Alexis pulled off the blindfold and stared at the untouched donkey. She felt her cheeks darkening. It was her birthday, and she had missed the piñata. She began to cry.

Maggie quickly came over to her, and put warm hands on Alexis's shoulder.

"Go again, baby," she said. "What the hell. It's your birthday."

Alexis grasped the stick again. As she raised it toward the plump donkey, she saw Grandmother dart forward. She looked so upset that Alexis stopped the stick in midair.

"No, Alexis," Grandmother said in a slow, low voice. "You've already had your turn. It's time to let the others have theirs."

Alexis looked up at Maggie. Maggie was staring at Grandmother. Her eyes were narrow and dark.

"Go again, baby," she said very quietly.

Alexis didn't know what to do. She looked at the red face and the white face above her. It made her think of Alice in Wonderland and the two queens. And then she looked at the donkey again. It was so cute, so fat, so full of candy. She lifted the stick again and began to hit wildly.

On her eleventh try, the donkey crashed to the ground. His head and tail fell off. The candy rushed out, and the children hollered and ran to get it. Alexis felt suddenly sick. She stood with the stick in her hand, staring at the donkey which had no head. She no longer wanted any candy, and she did not dare look up at her grandmother.

That night, Alexis was in her room, playing with her new birthday presents. She heard voices coming from the dining room; they sounded loud and dark. She went down to the bottom stair. She felt afraid to go any farther. The dining room door was open, and she could see the corner of the table. It was covered with silver plates, filled with cheeses and fat, purple grapes. They didn't seem to fit with these voices. Her father's was the loudest. Alexis had never known her father's voice could be so loud. She pretended he was saying that line, "Mother, I'm going to marry her!" but she couldn't do it. Because he was screaming at Maggie.

No one ever said anything, but Alexis always thought that it was because of the piñata that she was sent to the Willow Academy. This was a school her grandmother chose, and only girls went there. It was pretty on the outside, with brick paths and pussy willows growing in front, but Alexis hated the inside. It was always cold, and the floors smelled funny and the girls were mean. She had nightmares about it; she dreamed that she couldn't find the gymnasium, that she couldn't find her jacket, that the other girls sat on her during lunch.

Alexis would waken from the nightmares, screaming "Mama!" Maggie would come in, her red hair crumpled, and hold her. One night, Alexis had a nightmare about quicksand in the art room. Maggie came in and rocked her.

"Don't worry, baby," she kept saying. "I promise you. You'll have a good day tomorrow. I promise you."

The next morning, Alexis was sitting in class, when Mrs. Morton, the headmistress, came in.

"I'd like to see Alexis Avery, please."

All the girls stared as Alexis stood up. Even in her nightmares, she had never had to go to the headmistress's office. When she got there, she saw Maggie. Maggie was wearing her black coat, and she looked very sad.

"Your mother has come to get you, Alexis," Mrs. Morton said. "I'm afraid there's been a death in your family."

Alexis looked anxiously at her mother.

"No one you know, dear," Maggie said quickly. "A cousin." Quickly, she took Alexis away.

The moment they were in the car, Maggie undid the black coat. Underneath was a bright pink gingham dress. Then she reached into the backseat and brought forth Alexis's favorite blue jeans and top.

"I'm taking you to the circus," Maggie told her.

"But—"

"Oh, the cousin was just poetic license."

Alexis didn't know what poetic license was, but it was so wonderful to be rescued from school that she began to cry.

Maggie stroked her hair, so hard it almost hurt.

"I told you it would be a good day," she said grimly.

* * *

Alexis ate peanuts at the circus and screamed for the clowns to get away before they were run over by the car, and clapped for the tigers and fell in love with the lady with the spangles on her skirt. When it was over, she and Maggie swung clasped hands as they got back into the car.

Maggie was quiet on the drive home.

"I think, baby," she began.

Alexis knew what she was going to say.

"I won't tell," she told her mother.

Maggie smiled at her.

"It's not that we've done anything wrong," she said.

"I know," Alexis said. "But I still won't tell."

Grandmother found out anyway. Mrs. Morton had called to offer her condolences about the cousin. That night, Alexis heard shouting coming from the dining room again, and she knew there would be no more circuses.

Alexis didn't make any friends at school. At first she tried; she smiled at the girls, and asked their names, but no one was friendly. No one wanted to play with her during recess, no one clapped when she made a good shot at handball or won at tetherball. At lunch, no one wanted to trade sandwiches with her. And no one invited her over to play after school. Alexis didn't know why. She thought maybe she simply wasn't interesting enough. But one day, when she was passing a group of girls in the hallway, she heard them whispering. They stopped when she turned around. It made Alexis feel uneasy to think that there was something about her worth whispering about.

"They're just jealous," Maggie would tell her. "Or maybe they're shy. Anyway, give them time." Alexis gave them time, months and months, but no one became any friendlier.

The final school bell was the happiest moment of the day. The chauffeur would bring Alexis home and she would dash into her room, pull off her uniform, and change into her real clothes. Then she was herself again.

If her mother wasn't home, what Alexis liked most to do was go down to the stables and spend time with Molasses, her piebald pony. She was not a very good rider, but Molasses made her feel welcome on his back. As she rode slowly around, Alexis liked to imagine the way things would be when she was a grown-up. She would be tall and strong and no one would whisper about her. She would live somewhere out West, on her own farm. She would look after all the animals herself and make all her own meals. She wouldn't have any fancy furniture or any maids. And she would live there with her friend, Cody.

Cody was someone she knew now—he was a boy who lived in the oak tree by the stables. She had never told anyone about Cody, not even Maggie. She knew that Cody was invisible to everyone else but her, but that didn't mean that he wasn't real. Cody was very real. After Alexis finished riding Molasses, she would visit Cody. She would tell him about her day, and he would say that the girls at school sounded awful and stuck-up. He would tell her that he would always be her friend, and that he loved the idea of the farm. Sometimes Alexis stayed at the stables until dinner was called.

The following September, there was a new girl at school, Imogen Clark. Imogen was a year older than Alexis, tall, with a pert flip to her walk, and dark olive-green eyes. Imogen was very exciting. She was always talking about places she had visited, like Boston and even Las Vegas, and she wore her charm bracelet to school, even though it was forbidden. When she got into trouble with the teachers, she only rolled her eyes and sighed as if she was bored. All the girls wanted to be her special friend.

The second week of school, Imogen came up to Alexis in the lunch line.

"Your mother's Maggie Royal, right?"

Alexis tried to guess from Imogen's face if this was a good thing or a bad thing.

"Yes," she said cautiously.

Imogen smiled.

"Wow. She's pretty famous."

Alexis blushed with delight.

"I guess so."

Imogen stayed next to her in the lunch line and sat beside her at the table. They talked about how awful school was, and how much they hated it. By the end of the day, everyone knew that Imogen had chosen Alexis Avery to be her friend. A few girls even said good-bye to Alexis when she went home that day.

* * *

It took Alexis a few weeks to get up the courage to invite Imogen to her house.

"I'd love to come," Imogen said eagerly. "Will your mother be there?"

When Alexis said she thought so, Imogen hugged her.

"Grandmother, could I have a friend sleep over on Friday?" Alexis asked at dinner that night.

Grandmother seemed pleased. "Of course, dear."

Maggie was interested. "Who's coming?"

"Imogen. She's new. I think you're why she wants to come."

Grandmother seemed less pleased. Maggie looked delighted.

"We'll make sure she has a lovely time."

But Maggie wasn't at the house when Alexis and Imogen arrived the following Friday. The maid reminded Alexis that her parents and grandmother were in the city for an event at Lincoln Center and that they wouldn't be back until late. Alexis tried to put a happy spin on it, saying that now she and Imogen could have the house to themselves, but Imogen was clearly disappointed.

The hours until bedtime were dreary. Alexis tried to tempt Imogen with board games and gymnastics contests, but Imogen wasn't interested. Mercifully, bedtime came. The girls undressed in silence, and got into Alexis's carved four-poster. They lay there for several moments, and then they began to hear strange noises, bumps and rattles. The noises seemed to be coming from the corridor outside, and getting closer.

"What's that?" Imogen whispered, suddenly sounding not nearly so sophisticated.

"It's only the maid," Alexis told her uncertainly.

And then, from directly outside the bedroom, there came an unearthly moan.

The girls clutched each other, as the door opened slowly. A figure in a nightdress, staring in sightless horror, groped its way into the room.

"Out, damned spot! Out, I say! One; two; why, then 'tis time to do't. Hell is murky!" it shrieked.

Imogen shrieked back. The figure did not hear. It only wrung its hands and wailed. "Here's the smell of the blood still; all the perfumes of Arabia will not sweeten this little hand!"

Imogen turned a strange color, and fainted on the bed.

Maggie stopped wringing her hands and looked with interest at the toppled figure.

"One of my better performances," she said.

Alexis's friendship with Imogen cooled soon after that night, but she never blamed her mother. Seeing Maggie standing there in that room, saying those lines, had filled Alexis with a pride unlike any she had ever known. She wanted to tell Maggie how she had felt, but was too shy. It seemed incredible to her that, all her life, she had lived with this person—this famous, this amazing actress—and she had never really appreciated it. But after that night, Alexis started thinking of her mother not just as Mama, but as Maggie Royal. She started asking her mother questions about her career; when had she started acting, what were her favorite parts, what was her best performance?

One day, Maggie went over to her closet and pulled down a scrapbook Alexis had never seen. It wasn't anything like the books, tooled and covered in green leather, which held the family photographs. This book was bright scarlet, and beaten-up around the corners. Inside were all of Maggie's theater memories. There were reviews of plays she had done, still photographs of her onstage, and copies of theater programs. She went through the whole book with Alexis, page by page. Alexis especially loved the picture of her mother as Queen Elizabeth I, scornful in a blazing red wig, and the one of her as Rosalind, hands clasped, in love. Alexis wondered if her mother had looked like that when her father had said, "Mother, I'm going to marry her." When the book was finished, Maggie hugged Alexis very hard, and Alexis could tell that, behind the hug, she was crying. Then Maggie put the book back at the top of the closet. Alexis somehow knew that she shouldn't ask to see it again.

A few days later, Maggie showed her something else. It was a golden crown, covered in heavy jewels. Alexis stared at it; it was too beautiful even to covet.

"I wore this when I played Gertrude," Maggie told her. "I stole it when the show was finished."

She told Alexis about *Hamlet,* and what it was like playing Gertrude, and how awful it had been the night her taper had caught fire onstage. And then she put on the crown. Alexis's heart beat with surprise and joy, as it had beat the night her mother had come into her room as Lady Macbeth.

She didn't even ask to try the crown on herself.

Once, Alexis asked her mother why she didn't act anymore. Maggie was silent for a long, strange moment. Then she said with a little smile, "Because it isn't appropriate now."

Appropriate was a word Alexis knew well. Grandmother was always saying it; how this dress wasn't appropriate, or that hairstyle, or how it wasn't appropriate to spend so much time at the stables. Alexis guessed that Grandmother had told her mother that it wasn't appropriate for her to act anymore. But Maggie didn't say it as if she meant it, or believed in it. She said it as if it were a line in a play, and she were a bad actress who couldn't do the line in a way that was real.

That summer, Alexis, her parents, and her grandmother went to Nantucket for two weeks. It was the first family vacation Alexis could ever remember taking. She enjoyed the cozy beach house they rented, and getting to swim every day. It was fun going bicycling with her father and having ice cream with her mother every afternoon. And it was fabulous being without Nanny.

But on the whole, the vacation made Alexis nervous. It seemed to her that the grown-ups weren't having a very good time. They played cards and went to restaurants and shopped on the Main Street, but Alexis could tell they weren't really enjoying themselves. Her father kept calling the office; her grandmother took longer and longer naps during the afternoon; and Maggie would sometimes sit on the porch with a look that reminded Alexis of someone who was very hungry.

One morning on the beach, Alexis met a little girl called Katie. Katie was blond, with freckles, and she had a friendly laugh. She called herself "a local"—her father owned the tackle shop—and she said she had never been to New York. For some reason, that made Alexis like her even more. When Katie asked Alexis if she wanted to spend the night, Alexis said she would love to. It was the first time she had been invited to a sleep-over at another girl's home, but she didn't tell Katie that.

The next morning, when Alexis came back to her own house, she was very quiet. Maggie asked her if there was anything wrong, but Alexis shook her head. And there wasn't anything wrong—not exactly. It was just that, being at Katie's house, she had noticed things.

She had noticed that Katie's parents slept in the same bedroom, and she was wondering why her own parents had separate rooms. She had seen Katie's mother and father kiss each other in the hall, and she had never seen her parents do that. She had heard Katie's father ask his wife how her day had been, and she had sat down on the arm of his chair and told him all about it. He had seemed interested, asked questions. And Alexis wondered why her own mother didn't tell her father about her day like that, and why he never asked.

From then on, Alexis began to listen carefully to what her parents *did* talk about, and she realized that they didn't talk much at all. Her father would rise early, and be at the office before Maggie was even awake. When he came home at seven in the evening, it was time for dinner. He didn't have much to say during the meal; he was always tired from work, and after dinner, he went alone into his den to listen to opera records. Alexis would not see him again until the following morning, and so far as she knew, Maggie wouldn't either.

Her parents still went out a lot—to dinner, or to charity events or parties—but somehow she didn't suppose that her father was any different on those evenings. She imagined him driving silently along, Maggie silent beside him.

Alexis supposed her parents were happy, because all grown-ups were happy. Her parents were just different from Katie's, that was all. It was nothing to worry about.

One warm June afternoon, Alexis and Maggie went into New York. They visited the Metropolitan Museum, and played their usual game about which painting they most wanted to steal. They had lunch in the cafeteria, by the joyful fountains of dolphins and sprites, and Maggie gave Alexis a handful of pennies to throw in, so she could make as many wishes as she wanted. Then they went on to Bloomingdale's. They browsed through the evening dress department where Maggie tried on six gowns, the cosmetics department where she tried ten different scents, and finally, the toy department.

"Today's a buying day!" Maggie said with a smile,

and Alexis got the Tyrolean Madame Alexander doll she had been wanting.

After Bloomingdale's, Maggie said she would like to visit an antique store nearby. Alexis grumbled a little, but Maggie reminded her that the store was near Serendipity, their favorite ice cream place, and so Alexis was gracious about the errand.

As they were walking down Third Avenue, hand swinging in hand, Maggie stopped so suddenly that Alexis was thrown off balance. She looked up in surprise at her mother. Maggie's face was colorless, and her hand was clutching and cold. Alexis looked around, but she couldn't see anything out of the ordinary—only a tall, thin man walking toward them with a slight smile on his face.

"Maggie," he said.

Maggie introduced Alexis calmly, and said ordinary things, but Alexis could feel her mother's hand growing colder and colder. Finally, the man said he must be off, but that it had been wonderful seeing her.

"And wonderful to meet you," he told Alexis.

The man reminded Alexis of something. She finally decided that it was the King of Spades. After he had gone, she wanted to ask her mother about him, but she could tell, from Maggie's face, that she shouldn't.

The man was never mentioned again, but Alexis thought about him often. Because right after that day, everything changed. There began to be fights at home—loud and terrible fights between her parents. She could hear her father's voice, coming in bursting shouts. Then there would be her mother's voice, low and hard. Often Alexis would wake in the night, hearing noises.

She pretended they were from a storm outside, or branches blowing; but she knew it was those voices.

During the day, no one spoke about the fights. Grandmother said nothing, but she looked blue-white and spent a lot of time in her room. Her father came home from the office later and later. Only Maggie was full of gaiety, but it was a strange kind. She would take Alexis away from her homework, crying, "Come on, darling, let's get out of this crypt and go to a movie!" and she would drive too fast and laugh too much at the movie and Alexis didn't have a good time.

Alexis tried hard to find out what was going on. She was sneaky about it—she'd go downstairs to the kitchen on the pretext of being hungry, and she'd hang around the pantry, hoping that the cook or maid would say something that would explain why everything was suddenly so strange. But no one said anything.

She went out to the stables and asked Cody about it, but he only shrugged. And Molasses just looked at her with eyes that seemed anxious.

One wet Friday in October, Alexis came home from school and ran into the sitting room, calling for her mother. Her mother wasn't there. Alexis ran upstairs to Maggie's bedroom, but she wasn't there, either. There was something in the tidiness of the room that made Alexis feel uneasy. She finally found Josie sorting linens, and asked where her mother was. Josie drew in her breath. She said she didn't know, and looked away. Alexis ran into her own room, then stopped at the door. There, on her bed, were Maggie's red leather scrapbook, and Gertrude's jeweled crown.

Alexis stared at them from the doorway. It took her

a long time to cross the room and pick up the note that lay beside them.

"I want you to have these, baby," the note said. "I've gone away for the weekend and will be back on Monday. I love you. Until soon."

Alexis dropped the note. She put her hands over her mouth and screamed into them.

She knew she would never see her mother again.

Three

The plump young man with the dark beard checked his watch for the sixth time in as many minutes. He decided that if he walked very slowly, it could conceivably be construed as time to get going.

He opened his leather satchel and looked inside, making sure once again that his equipment was all there, and that he had a second package of batteries and an extra mike. He rubbed again at the small grease spot on his brown jacket, caused by a falling *frite* at lunch. He wished he had gone home to change, but on the other hand, this was his favorite jacket, the one he had worn for both the Shirley MacLaine and the Streisand interviews, and it always brought him luck.

He got up from the wrought-iron and wood bench, and walked toward the rue Dauphine, but he couldn't make himself walk as slowly as he would have liked. He tried to unflex his mind, grasping at his surroundings for sights of interest, but there were none. Paris had never been so devoid of distraction. Finally, he reached the corner of the rue de Fontan and turned up the street.

There it was—the fourth building in from the corner. He studied it intently. A three-story stone building like the others on the street—seventeenth century, eighteenth century? He would have to find out. He noticed that it was subtly different from its neighbors. The flowers in the tubs and the window boxes looked more expensive and exuberant (not that Paul Rosen knew anything about flowers) and the door was painted not the regulation black, but a bold fresh green.

He knocked on the door.

It was opened almost at once by an older man in a cream-colored linen jacket. As Paul was trying to assemble his French, the man spoke.

"Mr. Rosen?"

"Yes."

"Come right this way."

The man stepped aside; Paul entered the house. Instantly, as he looked around, his nervousness was gone, replaced by a sense of almost childish triumph and well-being. The hall, with its richness of antiques and rugs, was exactly the way he had imagined, no, willed, it to be. All that was missing was her portrait.

"This way, Monsieur."

The man led Paul into a sunny yellow parlor. And there she was, on the sofa, the portrait above her.

She was smaller than he had thought she would be, though he knew her measurements by heart and should not have been surprised, and older than even the latest stills made her appear, deep, soft-looking wrinkles around her mouth, bright red hair, daring, jade green caftan, chunky gold jewelry, amused eyes, also jade green.

Then, studying him, she laughed. The laugh unique. The illusion held, came together at the laugh.

"Miss Royal?"

"Mr. Rosen?"

Her voice was husky, sexy, wry.

"What an honor," Paul said.

She laughed again. "Call me Maggie."

She stayed on the sofa and watched as he unpacked the satchel. She nodded at the notebooks, tape recorder, and pencils laid out on the coffee table.

"How very professional-looking," she said with interest. Then she smiled. "I'm rather excited. *Vanity Fair*'s always been my favorite magazine. But I've never been in it before."

"Neither have I," he told her.

The penciled eyebrows rose.

"Oh? You're not one of their regular writers?"

Paul felt himself growing hot under his lucky jacket.

"No. I work for the *Los Angeles Times*. *Vanity Fair* came to me, asking if I'd do this interview."

She looked at him doubtfully.

"You look ridiculously young."

He thought about mentioning various awards and honors but said instead, "I should come right out and admit that I've always had a tremendous crush on you."

"Thank you," she said. She studied him for a moment more, then leaned back against the sofa. "Well, we have until six. Then I've got to get dressed for a deadly dull dinner party." She held out a Spode dish full of chocolate wafers. "Here. You must try one of these. My chef makes them himself."

"No, thank you," Paul said.

She shrugged. "Well, I certainly intend to have one. The Gavins' dinners are inedible. In fact, I think I'll have several." She took four. "All right—let's get this show on the road."

Paul cleared his suddenly dry throat, consulted his notebook, turned on the tape recorder.

"Well, let's start at the beginning. I was curious to find that there hasn't been much written about your childhood." He pushed a xeroxed article toward her. "As a matter of fact, you said in this 1974 interview with *Movietime* that you remembered absolutely nothing about it. Is that really the truth?"

Maggie made a dismissive gesture.

"Of course not. I remember everything. I probably didn't like the reporter. Anyway, my childhood isn't something I particularly enjoy talking about. Let's just say I grew up in the South, during the worst of the Depression, and leave it at that."

"Could we have any dates?"

She raised an eyebrow.

"You should know better than to ask an actress that. Anyway, I've always been terrible at math—if you want any dates, it's your job to figure them out."

"Could you at least tell me your first memory?"

She narrowed her eyes.

"All right," she said. "It's a good story."

She straightened and sat forward. Her voice was low and compelling.

"I was two years old. We lived in Arkansas—in a small town near Mena. It was the night of the big church Christmas social. I was absolutely beside myself with excitement. Mama put me in my new dress—

it was white with tatting on the edge—and my big sisters crowded around me, telling me I looked like an angel." Maggie smiled. "I liked that."

Paul also smiled. "I'm sure you did."

"We drove to the social in our big farm wagon, Papa, Mama, my three sisters, and me. The church was all lit up. There was a big Christmas tree—I remember how delicious it smelled. Music was playing, everyone was dancing. I wanted to run off and dance too, but Mama said I had to stay by her, and I started crying. Then the new schoolteacher came up—her name was Annie. She knelt down and hugged me and said how beautiful I looked in my little angel dress.

"I adored Annie. She was only—my God, she must have been only about seventeen—the sweetest girl. That night, she was wearing a dark green dress and she had a cameo at her throat. Isn't it odd, the way the mind works? I can still see her dress, but I can't for the life of me remember her last name.

"All the men asked Annie to dance, but she said no, she'd rather stay by her little angel. Finally, a man I liked—Mr. Brock, I think his name was—came up. Annie said she would dance with him, but only if I got to dance, too.

"So we danced together, the three of us. Annie holding me up against her shoulder, Mr. Brock with his arms around us both. Everyone around, clapping and laughing.

"And then suddenly everything got very cold. The door opened, and the snow blew in. A man I had never seen before walked into the room. He looked like an Indian—very tall and dark.

"The music and the dancing stopped—just like that.

"The man came toward Annie. I was still on her shoulder, trying to get her to keep dancing. But Mama ran over and pulled me away.

"The man kept walking. Then suddenly this gun was in his hand—this tiny little gun. I can still see it so clearly.

"Now here's where everything gets confused. You know how it is when you're told a story so many times; you're not sure how much you actually remember, and how much you're making up. But I know I remember this." Her voice was hard and bright. "I remember the sound of the shot, and I remember Annie's face being blasted away." Then she added more slowly, "And I also remember the way the blood looked on that beautiful green dress."

She glanced at Paul, her eyes as hard and bright as her voice.

"How's that for a first memory?"

He nodded, the reporter part of his mind busy. Get Annie's last name—a phone call to Bill Sorenson in Little Rock—check the records. How much of it was even true? And through it all, he worshiped Maggie for her perfect choice—whether fact or fiction—of a first memory.

"I found some old boxes not too long ago," she was saying, "and I came upon a photograph of that house we lived in then. It looked exactly like Tara."

Paul raised his head. "Tara? From *Gone with the Wind?* I was under the impression you were very poor."

Maggie looked at him coldly. "We weren't poor—we were starving. But my father was gentry, and he had inherited the house. His big dream was to turn it back into what it had been before the Civil War, but the Depression ended that."

She shook her head, almost with a shiver, seemingly lost in the memory. "What a strange place it was. This huge house, filled with the most beautiful furniture, draperies, rugs—but all rotting away. I remember the bed I slept in—a museum piece. No, I'm serious—this was a bed the Queen of England would have envied—but I didn't own a pair of shoes."

She was quiet.

"I wonder if that house is even there anymore. Probably it's been turned into a shopping center."

"I could check that for you."

She shook her head decisively.

"No. I'd rather not know. But thank you. Anyway, I didn't live there long; we had to move when I was five."

"Had to?"

"Yes." She laughed strangely. "I'm not sure how much of this is true, either, but it was the story I grew up with. Papa was—well, Papa liked the occasional drink. The story goes that one night he went into the local bar, and some strangers visiting from Texas were there. Papa stayed out all night, and the next morning he came home, blind drunk, and told Mama we were all moving. Apparently, he had traded our house for a pig farm in Amarillo, sight unseen."

Paul blinked. "That's hard to believe."

Maggie shrugged. "Perhaps. But in a way I've always understood it. It gets tiring being a failure."

"Do you remember any of this?"

"I remember Mama being very upset. I remember crying because she wouldn't let me bring my bed to

Texas. And I vaguely remember the trip. Papa bought a car—the first one he'd ever driven, I think, and it kept breaking down. According to my sister Mildred, we ran out of money, and we'd stop along the way and pick cotton to get more. But I don't really remember.

"Anyway, we finally arrived in Amarillo, at the pig farm. I certainly remember that. It was the most God-awful place—a shack, the worst thing you can imagine—the ground around it a sea of mud. And my mother turned to my father and said, 'Oh, Neil.' Just that. 'Oh, Neil.' But I'll never forget the way she said it. And then we all got out of the car, and started unpacking, and that was that."

She pressed her hands together hard, looked at them.

"I see those books—you know—those histories of the Depression. I look at those pictures, those children out in the fields, wearing rags, and I think, well, old girl, there you are. And you know something?" She looked up. Her eyes were misty. "There I still am.

"I think, if you don't mind, I'll have a cigarette." She lit the cigarette; he watched her smoke.

"Interviewers have always had their helpful little theories about how my childhood experiences have made me a richer actress," she said finally. "I just smile. Believe me, there is nothing, absolutely nothing, enriching about not knowing where your next meal is coming from.

"But that's enough of that. I'll give you something colorful for your article—and I don't think I've told this to too many reporters. When I was eight years old, my father went mad."

Check it out, Paul thought.

"Actually, mad might be too strong a word,"

Maggie amended. "Let's just say that his grip on reality got very weak."

"How so?"

"Well, Papa would sometimes forget that we weren't living in the old house anymore. He kept looking for it. He couldn't understand where the big lawn had gone to, and he kept wondering what had happened to his library. And he'd holler at Mama, telling her how she was keeping all his old friends away from him. Then he'd carry on about us girls, saying how he was going to set us up as debutantes, and send us to Europe to finishing school. The next day, he'd be completely normal again. For a week or two. Then one morning, he'd do something else crazy. I remember him coming down to breakfast once, dressed in his best white suit, with his opal stickpin in his tie, and a Panama hat and white gloves. Dressed like he was going to meet the governor. Then he went down to the barn and fed the pigs. He came back covered with mud, but Mama didn't say a word."

Bitterly, she laughed.

"He could also be quite a cruel man," she said. "I hope I haven't inherited that from him, but I probably have."

"How was he cruel?"

"He had a very black sense of humor. I remember when I was around eight, we had a part-time laundress working for us. She always brought her little boy with her; Rufe I think his name was. He was a sweet child, a bit backward. My father loved to torment him. One day, I've forgotten why, Papa had a telephone installed in the barn. Rufe had never seen a phone before, and Papa showed him how to use it. Then Papa went into town, and he called the line. When Rufe picked up,

Papa told him that he was the Devil, coming to get his soul. Rufe promptly went into an epileptic fit. Papa thought it was a great joke."

"That's pretty black, all right," Paul said.

"Isn't it?" She shook her head. "Papa was fascinated by anything like that—the occult, devil worship. And he had a big thing for death. When we still lived in Mena, he would take my sisters down to the morgue every week, to see all the new bodies that had come in."

"Oh, God."

She nodded. "I think he was terrified of dying. He'd never swim for fear he'd drown, and he absolutely hated thunderstorms. I remember this contraption he built—a sort of wooden throne—it was supposed to save him in case lightning hit the house. Whenever a storm came, Papa would rush off to his chair and strap himself in."

"What about the rest of you?"

She waved a hand. "Oh, the rest of us went about our business. Papa didn't bother making chairs for anyone but himself."

She smoked for a while in silence.

"How do you view your relationship with your father now?" Paul asked

Maggie thought for a moment before speaking.

"My father was the most exciting man I have ever known," she said. "It's hard to explain. In spite of everything, there was a grandeur about him—even a kind of greatness. No; that's too pompous. It was more of a sense of heritage—as if there were some family standard that, come hell or high water, Papa still had to follow."

She leaned forward, tapped the arm of the sofa with two slow, grave beats.

"And the important thing is—he gave me that standard, too. That's something I've always been grateful for. Do you understand? Papa made me believe that it didn't matter that I didn't have any shoes. It didn't matter that I had to pick up frozen manure in winter. All that mattered was that I was Maggie Royal—his daughter, the descendant of landed gentry. I was Somebody—and I was never to forget it."

She sighed.

"As I got older, part of me hated Papa—he was the most selfish man I've ever known. But at the same time, I would have killed for his attention."

"Which, by the way, I never got."

Again, she smoked.

"Well, enough about Papa. Let me tell you about my mother."

And Maggie's whole face changed into something suddenly gay and pleased.

"Mama!" She shook her head. "What a character! The total opposite of Papa. Nothing elegant about her. She was little and fat, she was "poor white trash," she was as mischievous as a monkey. Whenever she'd done something particularly awful, and someone would get mad at her, she'd throw up her hands and say, 'What do you want from me? I was just saving myself!'"

The voice sounded so old and Southern and outraged that Paul laughed aloud.

"One summer, she decided to raise rabbits to sell. The best-looking one in the bunch had no tail, so Mama remedied this by gluing on a puff of cotton. The rabbit was bought and taken away, and Mama would just go into gales of laughter, imagining the buyers' faces the day their bunny's tail fell off." Maggie laughed, a loud, inelegant shout.

"And one winter, when things got really bad, Mama put us girls together in one bedroom and she rented out the other rooms to boarders. The rooms were only a nickel a night, but even at those prices, boarders expected sheets on their beds, and Mama didn't have the money to buy them.

"The next day she took a job in a laundry. And every time a particularly desirable sheet came her way, Mama would sneak off into the bathroom. Each time she came out, she was a little bit fatter. At the end of the day she walked out of the job and never came back. And we had enough sheets to last out the winter."

Maggie paused, then said in a dry, bright voice, "Well, I'm starved. Absolutely starved. Isn't it funny how even thinking about those days makes me hungry."

She took a cookie. Paul noticed that her hand shook slightly. Embarrassed, he looked down at his notes.

"What were your schooldays like?" he asked her at last.

She waved a dismissive hand.

"Oh, horrendous. Papa didn't even want us to go to school in the first place. He said there were no children in town fit for us to associate with. But the local sheriff stepped in and we had to go. As it turned out, those other children didn't want to associate with us, either. I guess we weren't any too clean.

"If you'd like, I can show you a picture of me at school. I found it in that box of photos. Wait a second, and I'll go get it." She rose from the sofa and left the room.

Paul had a moment in which to sift, absorb, gather impressions, make decisions. But he did none of that. Instead, he watched the sun spread out luxuriously on the fine old carpet.

Maggie did not take long.

She brought the old photograph and pushed it toward him.

"Guess which is me."

"That one!" The hair.

"No. Try again."

"That one." The stance.

"No."

"I give up."

Wordlessly, she pointed.

Paul felt genuine shock. Seeing his face, she laughed delightedly.

"I can't believe it either."

Together they looked at the child in the photo, stringy-haired, mutinous, bedraggled.

"But I told you—she's still me," Maggie said.

"You don't look like you have much in common."

She waved a hand.

"The hair's better now."

Paul stared harder at the little girl in the picture, willing himself to go beyond her look of "No Trespassing Allowed." But he got nothing.

"What is the same?" he asked.

"The fears. The desires. And the acting, of course."

He was surprised. He had tracked Maggie's first performances back only to age nineteen.

"You acted when you were that young?"

"I've been acting since I was three," she told him. "My first performance was at a chautauqua."

Paul laughed. "Should I know what a chautauqua is?"

She was surprised. "Don't they have them anymore? Surely they must—down in rural areas? No? Well, it was a kind of traveling troupe show. The players would go around the South, and when they reached a likely town, they'd put on a play and invite the townspeople to be in it. Mama would have nothing to do with it, of course; she was very religious—but my sister Mildred, God bless her, decided that I should be in the show."

Maggie evidently liked telling this story. Her face was very vivid.

"She sneaked me in to see the manager, and he gave me the part of an angel. Once again, you see, an angel.

"Well! Was I in bliss! I loved my part—loved flitting around in my wings—but I guess, in the rehearsal, I mustn't have flitted terribly well. So the manager took away my wings and said I had to be a little brown seed instead. I cried all afternoon."

Slowly, the smile faded. Maggie leaned forward and looked into Paul's eyes.

"But what happened the night of the show," she told him quietly, "I'll never forget it.

"I sat on the steps of our town hall, facing the audience. Almost everyone in town—except Mama, of course—was there. I had the first words in the play. I said, 'I'm a little brown seed'—and suddenly, up from the audience, there came this wave of love. This wave of love. How can I possibly describe it to you? I knew in that instant that I had found what I wanted to do with my life—and everything changed forever."

And then she laughed.

"Well, maybe not everything," she amended. "After the chautauqua, Mildred sneaked me back to the house, hoping Mama wouldn't have heard about what we'd been up to—but she was waiting outside the house for us, strap in hand . . .

"My first bad review!" Maggie capped the story with a laugh.

Paul didn't laugh in return.

"Oh, come on; you can laugh!" she urged him.

But he was moved by the story of the little brown seed, didn't want it to end with a laugh. And meanwhile, the other voice in him was saying, *Check sources.*

"But of course, it didn't matter," Maggie went on. "From that moment on, from the moment I discovered that I was an actor, I was . . . free. The real world I lived in couldn't hurt me anymore. I had the power to be anyone or anything I wanted—just by making believe. It saved me, really.

"And who cared if it only lasted a few minutes?"

She paused for a long time, then looked at him oddly.

"You know, it has sometimes occurred to me, that when you get right down to it, maybe my acting wasn't all that different from my father going mad. Except with me, I was Cleopatra for five minutes, and then I went back to washing the dishes. But with Papa, it got to the point where he never stopped. The curtain just never came down on his performances."

It was a good line. Paul found himself wondering if she had used it before.

Maggie blinked, thinking over what she had just said.

"That's an awfully good line. Make sure you quote it exactly."

"I'll make sure."

"So," she went on briskly, "as I got older, acting became the most important thing in my life. But of course I couldn't tell anyone. You know how secretive young girls are. And besides, I knew Mama would have killed me if she ever found out.

"Anyway, that was my childhood. Do you know when your childhood ended?" she asked Paul.

"The day my voice changed?"

She shook her head as if she hadn't heard.

"My childhood ended the day I was twelve." She looked down. "It was on a Friday. My twelfth birthday. I raced home from school, and couldn't find anyone around. I thought maybe Mama had planned a surprise party for me, so I ran around looking. Well, I finally found everyone. They were in my father's room, sitting around his bed. He had died of a stroke while I was at school."

Maggie was quiet for a long time.

"Nothing was the same after that," she said at last. "Strange, isn't it, that that cold, selfish man should have been so important to me—but he was." She narrowed her eyes, remembering. "I guess Papa was the link—to that special heritage," she went on slowly. "When Papa was alive, I believed it when he said that I was Somebody. The Princess in disguise. With Papa gone, it became much harder to believe."

There were tears in her eyes.

"Since then," she said, "there've been plenty of other men in my life who have betrayed me, God only knows." Then she added with a rueful laugh, "But Papa is the only one whose white gloves I kept."

Four

Alexis sat in Steven Wheelhouse's office for fifteen minutes, but he did not return. She found herself increasingly uneasy.

Outside in the hall, the school bell shrilled. Alexis's nerves leaped in response.

And then Steven Wheelhouse was at the door.

"Are you finished?" he asked, gesturing toward the questionnaire.

In silence, she handed it over.

"Well, I was right," he told her easily. "The kids I had in mind would love to take your class. I told them to meet us in the counseling room in ten minutes, and we can get started."

"Fine," Alexis said.

"I'll give you a tour on the way."

Brian House was the saddest place Alexis had ever been to. She found it hard to know how to react. Had

Steven Wheelhouse seemed ashamed of the tiny, dank rooms and narrow, badly lit corridors, she could have responded with tact—but he was matter-of-fact about everything, expecting her acceptance.

"As I mentioned, we're a residence school," he said, rounding a corner. "Here are the kids' rooms. Girls in this corridor, boys in the next."

Alexis peered into the nearest room. The best scenic designer in Hollywood could not have come up with a more ingeniously heart-tugging set. The sagging single bed with its headboard of rusted iron and the carnival of faded plush animals on the coverlet. The walls patched, peeling, but covered with posters. Curtains decorated with little smiling apple faces at the windows, hiding the iron bars.

Alexis walked on to the next room. This one was worse. This one was jail. Nothing was here but a bed and a chest of drawers. Only yellowing strips of scotch tape showed that the walls had once been decorated.

"Why does it look like this?" Alexis asked sharply.

Steven Wheelhouse frowned.

"That was Jeanette's room," he said.

Alexis hurried by.

They passed a third room and Alexis looked in. A girl was sitting on the bed, staring dreamily into the corridor. She was dressed entirely in black, and her face, made up as elaborately as that of any Kabuki dancer, was completely white.

On the wall at the end of the corridor was a big eye-catching poster. On the top was printed HOW AM I FEEL-ING TODAY? and below were twenty yellow faces wearing different expressions. Choices included contented (smiling face), upset (glaring face), anxious (face with quivering mouth). Alexis stared at the poster. How was she feeling today? It was not a question she asked herself often.

"And here are the classrooms," Steven Wheelhouse told her.

Alexis looked in the glass pane of the nearest door. Kids were sitting at desks, and a teacher was drawing graphs on a blackboard. She was a little surprised to see such a normal-looking school environment.

"What do you teach here?" she asked.

He shrugged.

"The usual suspects. English, algebra, history. And for those who are interested, we've got a few APs."

"So this is a real high school?"

"Oh, absolutely. State licensed, with a board of directors. And all our standards—staffing patterns, payment rate, things like that—are determined by Social Services."

"But you run the place."

"I'm the director." He smiled. "I'm the one on hand for the crises."

They walked on.

"So if this is a regular high school, do the kids graduate?"

"Yes."

"And then what do they do?"

"Whatever they want. A good fifty percent of our kids go on to be gainfully employed, and a few go on to higher education—we had a boy last year who was accepted to NYU."

"And what about the other fifty percent?"

He paused a moment before answering.

"They end up where they were before."

They passed another classroom, and he pointed it out. "This is where our emancipation classes take place—that's probably the most valuable work that we do here."

"What's taught in those?"

"Survival skills. These kids could outlast you or me on the streets any day, but they don't have a clue when it comes to any other kind of life. So we teach them the things they'll need to know when they leave here—how to write a check, how to plan a budget, how to get a job. How to cover a tattoo. And we do work on self-care skills. We teach them how to improve their emotional pacing. How to ask for help. It's kind of a crash course in living in the real world."

"I'm sorry to be so nosy, but who pays for all this?"

"We're a nonprofit foundation. Since we have a 501-C3 status, we can get access to public monies. Most of our funding is through AFDC—Aid to Families with Dependent Children."

Alexis nodded.

They moved along.

"And here's the kitchen."

Alexis had always enjoyed industrial kitchens. There was something comforting about the huge institutional-sized cans of corn, the giant loaves of bread, the stove with its twelve burners. She was surprised, in this one, to see that, apart from one adult, the kids seemed to have taken over.

"The kids prepare the meals?"

"It's part of their schedule. Kitchen duty twice a week. All part of the plan to teach them self-sufficiency."

Alexis watched as a boy with dreadlocks and tattoos carefully measured salt into the big pot of boiling water.

She was then shown the dining room, the boys' bathroom, and the staff lounge.

"The staff wing is back there." Steven Wheelhouse pointed. "But I don't know that they'd like me to barge in."

"How many staff members do you have?"

"During the day, fourteen. At night, we have three on constant patrol—about a one to twenty-five ratio."

"Do they rotate?"

"No."

Alexis thought about what it would be like to live in this place full time.

"It's very important that we have a waking staff," he said. "With a coed school, certain issues arise."

"I can imagine. How do you keep the kids in their own rooms at night?"

"Well, if you noticed, there's a common room between the girls' and boys' wing. We make sure a staff member's always there. Also, we have strong expectations for the kids. We encourage them to stick to the rules."

"And if they don't?"

"There are punishments."

Alexis did not pursue this.

"Are they ever allowed to go out?"

"Of course. Our whole creed is 'discharge planning begins when you meet people.' So we get them into the community as much as possible—they help shop for food, buy things they need."

"They go by themselves?"

"No, that's not allowed. There's always a member of the staff with them."

"Do any kids run away?"

"Sure," he said slowly.

They stopped in front of a closed door.

"And here's our pride and joy," he told her. "Our new rec room. The kids get to come here when they've finished their classes for the day."

Steven Wheelhouse opened the door to a large room, vital with the smell of pale blue paint. It was very crowded. Three kids were sprawled on a sprung leather couch, watching a rerun of *Fantasy Island* on a small black-and-white television set. One girl was sitting on the arm of the sofa, carefully braiding a friend's hair. Alexis recognized her as Romina, the girl who had burst so angrily into Steven Wheelhouse's office earlier. She smiled up at him now, and gave a little wave. In one corner of the room was a vending machine, mostly sold out of its wares. In the other corner was a pinball machine, evidently the room's main attraction. A group of boys, three deep, hung over it. One tall boy wearing a thirties gangster hat was at the controls. His movements with the flippers were sinuous and beautiful.

He did not leave the machine, but when the other boys caught sight of Steven Wheelhouse, they surged over. Grinning, they feigned punches at his head, imprisoned his neck in a wrestling lock. They talked in unending, complaining shouts. Somebody had busted the radio. Somebody had unfair detention. Somebody hadn't shown up for bed duty. The girls also came up, but differently. They ran to Steven Wheelhouse, stroked his back, touched his sleeve, smiled up at him. Alexis was not noticed.

After a few minutes, Steven Wheelhouse looked at his watch.

"OK, you guys, that's enough," he said. "We'd better get moving," he told Alexis. "It's time for your class."

They left the recreation room and continued down the hall into a small inner office.

"This is ordinarily one of our counseling rooms," he told her. "Once a week, we try to have sessions with the kids' families."

"Do they come?"

Steven Wheelhouse shrugged slightly. "Not as often as we'd like."

Alexis looked around the room. It was furnished with a sectional couch made from three different sofas, and two broken dinette chairs. It was hellishly hot, and a tiny fan spat out at them. She found herself staring at a poster on the wall. It contained ten helpful suggestions to keep from hitting your children.

"This okay?" he asked briskly.

"It will be fine."

"Good," he said.

At that moment the door opened. Slowly, two teenagers came into the room.

"Well, here are two-thirds of them," Steven said. "Mrs. Donleavy, I'd like you to meet Tamara Morales and Greg Kirkwood."

Tamara was short, stocky, with inexpertly dyed blond hair. Her face was sodden-looking, hostile, uncurious.

Greg was African-American, slight and astonishingly delicate, his features the size of a child's. He had wire glasses, neatly subdued clothes, and wore his hair in a long, thin braid. He looked like a miniature rabbinical student.

Alexis found herself scrutinizing his hands. No—they were too childlike, too paw-like, ever to be an artist's hands. He would surely fail if he tried.

And then Alexis had the sudden heavy understanding that Greg was destined to fail at everything he ever tried.

"Mrs. Donleavy," Steven said, "has generously volunteered her time to teach you about art history and interior decorating."

How suddenly ridiculous it sounded.

Greg and Tamara looked blankly up at her.

"Well, I'll let you get acquainted," Steven said, rising to go. "I'm sure Linda will be here in a moment."

He closed the door behind him.

"Well," Alexis said.

The kids continued to stare.

"Why don't you sit down?" she suggested.

Looking at each other, they slowly sat.

"As Mr. Wheelhouse said, my name is Alexis Donleavy, and I'm an interior designer. Do you know what that is?"

Shrugs.

"Basically, it's someone who puts rooms and houses together. Like your new rec room. Somebody designed that—decided what material would look best, what kind of wallpaper to buy."

Greg snickered.

"Whatever was cheapest."

Alexis smiled.

"Well, yes, cost is always a consideration. Anyway,

behind what I do, and behind art in general, there are a lot of principles. Principles that have been around a long time—things like beauty, balance, order."

She could tell she was getting nowhere. The kids were looking restlessly around.

"And I'd like to teach you about some of those things."

There was another pause.

Alexis coughed to cover embarrassment. "I'm glad we're going to be a small class. I prefer it that way. Do you have any idea where our other member is?"

Tamara snorted.

"Linda? She's probably lost."

"Lost? Is she new here?"

"No. She's just . . ." Tamara tapped her head.

"Well," Alexis said dubiously, "I'm sure she'll show up eventually. But since we can't really start until she comes, why don't you two tell me something about yourselves."

Greg looked interested.

"You mean, why we're here?"

Alexis was a little taken aback.

"If you want to."

Greg beamed. "I got busted for heroin, and for doing time on the streets."

It took Alexis a moment to realize that he was talking about prostitution.

"Oh," she said as noncommittally as she could. "And how long have you been at Brian House?"

She knew that she was sounding false, like a talk show host, but Greg didn't notice. He seemed delighted with the attention.

"Six months," he said.

"Do you like it here?"

Greg shrugged. "It's not bad," he said. "I've done worse."

There was another pause.

"What about you?" Alexis asked Tamara.

"What about me?"

"Do you like it here?"

"No."

"Why not?"

The girl didn't answer.

"Don't bother with her," Greg told Alexis. "She's like that."

Tamara glared at him.

"I just don't need to talk all the time."

"Well, I wish you'd talk a little," Alexis told her. "I'm giving this class just for the three of you, and the more I know about your interests, the more helpful I can be."

Tamara was unimpressed.

Alexis turned back to Greg.

"Have you any idea what you'd like to do when you leave Brian House?"

He jumped up, illuminated by the question.

"Yes!" he cried. "I want to do comic strips! I love comic strips. My favorite's the superhero stuff—Pow! Bam!" He waved a diminutive arm. "But the stuff I do is a lot weirder than that. It's all about this place called 'Bugland,' and it's run by this freaky king bug, Mordread, and when he wants to punish his enemies, he just bites their head off. And they live in little bug beds and eat bug breakfasts."

His eyes were shining, delighted.

"Sounds very original," Alexis said slowly.

"Yeah," he agreed, "and when Mr. Wheelhouse

said you were teaching an art class, I thought it would really help."

Alexis tried to mask her certainty that it would not.

"I hope it does," she said. "And what about you?" she asked Tamara. "Why do you want to take this class?"

Tamara blinked at her.

"So I can make Level Four."

"What happens on Level Four?"

"I get time out; I get to see movies."

"Well, I guess that's a reason," Alexis said drily. "So you've no other interest in art?"

"No. When I get out of here, I want to be a flight attendant."

A flight attendant. Alexis winced at the incongruity of it.

"Why?" she asked.

"I want to travel."

She said it shyly, almost longingly.

"Where do you want to go?"

But the gleam was instantly gone. Tamara drew back in her chair.

"None of your business."

Alexis took a breath.

"No," she agreed, "but if I knew which countries were your favorites, we could make a point of studying their art."

"I don't want to know about their art," Tamara said flatly. "I just want to get to Level Four. And then I want to get out of here."

She looked at Alexis with experienced, expressionless eyes.

"Yes," Alexis said. "I can understand that." And then she added, "Why *are* you here?"

She didn't really expect an answer.

"I've been doing drugs since I was eleven," Tamara told her. "No big deal. But last year, I got into some bad shit."

Greg whistled.

"Yeah; she pushed drugs to Raff Hall." He punched her lightly on the arm. "You were pushing to five-year-olds, man!"

Tamara ignored him.

"So I got sent here."

"That must have been a difficult time for you." Stupid talk-show-host chatter again, but Alexis did not know how else to react.

"It was different when my father was around," Tamara said more softly. "He took care of me, he wouldn't let anyone do shit to me. But then he was put in jail, and I didn't get to see him."

"Is he still in jail?"

Tamara put her head down.

"No. He tried a break, and they shot him in the back." She took a weary breath. "What was so dumb was that he only had a month to go. You'd think he could have hung on for one more month."

No one said anything.

"I got to go to the funeral," she added. "That was nice."

"Is your mother still alive?"

"Yeah. I tried living with her a few months ago, but it didn't work out. She's with this new guy now, Presley"—Tamara twisted her mouth when she said the name—"and his little girl Janice. They didn't respect me; just because I was here, they acted like my stuff wasn't mine anymore. Like they'd let Janice into my room and she could take whatever she wanted. I had this great Barbie collection—I even had Oriental Barbie—and they'd just let her do anything she wanted with it. One day I came home and she'd trashed the whole thing." She spoke as if she still couldn't quite believe it. "Even Oriental Barbie."

She stared down at nail-chewed hands.

"Well," Alexis said, bidding other, better words to come. None did.

There was a soft, frantic knock and the door fluttered open.

"I'm so sorry I'm late!"

There stood the girl Alexis had seen in one of the rooms—the girl with the Kabuki makeup.

"I'm so sorry," the girl repeated in a tiny voice, appealing first to Alexis, then to Tamara and Greg. "Richard said I was supposed to go on shop duty for punishment, and I told him about this class, and we couldn't find Mr. Wheelhouse, and you know how Richard gets . . ."

"You must be Linda."

At first glance, Linda looked like a minor character from *The Beggar's Opera*. Tall and very thin, she was all in ragged black, even to the lace gloves that frayed from her fingertips. She wore high button shoes, stockings full of holes, a short dress, a man's sweater, a cloche hat, and a long veil. And underneath it, a chalk face, eyes elaborately outlined with kohl, and a mouth the color of poisonous berries.

Why on earth was it all being done? Alexis wondered. Then when she looked more closely, penetrating the exotic disguise, she realized. Underneath all the hoopla was a plump, rather ordinary little face.

Tamara and Greg rolled their eyes at each other, and Alexis understood that Linda was the outsider in the group.

"Well," Alexis said, "why don't we begin? As I've been telling Tamara and Greg, this is to be a class on principles of art. History of art. Design. Decorating." She remembered Steven Wheelhouse's words, "A class about beautiful things."

She could see Greg's eyes roll.

"People sometimes wonder, why bother with all that? These painters have been dead hundreds of years—why study them? And what does it matter what a room looks like? But it does matter," Alexis said. "People are drawn to beauty; it keeps us going. And hopefully this class will help educate your eyes, so that you can start determining for yourself what you respond to, and why."

Linda beamed. Tamara and Greg looked at Alexis slackly.

"Well, why don't we get started?" Alexis said.

For fifteen minutes, she talked about the emotional and historical importance of art and interior design. She tried her best not to sound pedantic, and endeavored to be humorous whenever possible, but pedantry came more easily to her than wit.

Tamara made no pretense at listening; she leaned back in her chair watching the fan, her pen moodily tapping her chin.

Greg wrote energetically in his notebook, but when Alexis leaned forward to see his notes, she found that he was working on a comic strip. From the quick glimpse she was afforded, it appeared that the main character was a dried-up, primly dressed bug-woman in her forties. Herself.

Only Linda was taking real notes—careful, eager notes that ran on and on. So to Linda alone, Alexis talked.

Finally, the bell rang. Steven Wheelhouse came back into the room.

"Well, that's enough for today," he said. "How did it go?"

"It was great, Mr. Wheelhouse," Linda said, smiling.

Tamara and Greg exchanged a look. Steven Wheelhouse saw it.

"And what about you two?" he asked. "Is this something you want to continue with?"

To Alexis's surprise, they nodded.

"Good," he said briskly.

Tamara and Greg rose and left without a word.

Linda gathered up all her things.

"Thank you so much, Mrs. Donleavy," she said. "I can't wait for next week."

Steven Wheelhouse leaned against the wall and looked at Alexis.

"So how do you think it went?"

She considered. The mismatched couch. Oriental Barbie. Greg's insufficient hands. Her comic-strip self. The fan from Hell. And Linda.

"I'm not sure," she said. Her glance fell on a pencil Linda had dropped. "Tell me about Linda."

He smiled.

"I thought you'd enjoy her. She's probably the most artistic kid we've got here. Her teachers think she's got a lot of talent. Not surprising, really. Her parents were both in the theater for a while, but then they got into a black magic cult. Turned their house into a coven. Linda couldn't take it, and moved onto the streets. Then she was picked up for cocaine and came here."

Alexis thought of Linda's eager face, the fluttering politeness, the innocence.

Steven Wheelhouse was looking down at her.

"Are you still up for teaching this class?"

"Yes."

He nodded, consulted the planner in his hand.

"Are Tuesdays good for you?"

"Yes."

"What about two-thirty?"

Alexis considered. She could not think of any activity that was particularly identified with Tuesdays at two-thirty.

"That'll be fine."

"Then we'll see you next week," he told her.

They walked together back down the hall. This time, Alexis did not notice the rooms they passed.

Five

It was a week before Thanksgiving. Alexis said good night to her father and grandmother, went upstairs to her room, and carefully locked the door. Then she walked over to her desk, opened the secret drawer, and pulled out the list.

She had started it nearly a month ago, on the Monday Maggie had promised she would return from her weekend trip. Alexis had waited all that day, sitting in her mother's closet, breathing in the scents of her clothes. *She's got to come back soon; she needs her dresses,* Alexis kept telling herself. She wouldn't leave the closet, wouldn't come out for lunch or dinner. Finally it grew late, and she had to go to bed. But Maggie still hadn't come home.

The next morning, Alexis came up with a plan. Maybe if she rode Molasses ten times around the field without stopping, that would make her mother come back. She felt better having something concrete to do, but Maggie still didn't return. The next day, she came up with another idea. Maybe if she walked around the whole house with her eyes closed, that would make her mother come back. On the third day, Alexis started keeping track, and writing everything down on a list. Every day she added an item. She would jump rope five hundred times without missing. She would brush her hair a thousand times. And one of the things on the list would surely be the right one. She would perform the action, never knowing that it was the spell-breaker, and the next day she would come home from school, and there would be her mother's scent in the hallway, and there would be her mother's suitcases in the bedroom, and there would be her mother, holding out her arms.

Alexis put the list away. She went to the closet and took down the scrapbook Maggie had left her. She sat with it on the bed and went through every picture, every review. She couldn't read all the words, but that didn't matter. Sometimes she played a game that there were little messages in the scrapbook, secret codes to herself. The photo from *School for Scandal,* where Maggie was blowing a kiss at the camera, was really a kiss for Alexis. And the review that said Maggie Royal was "piquant" was really referring to the games of peek-a-boo that Maggie used to play with her.

When she had read the scrapbook through, Alexis put it away and went to bed. She lay in the darkness and sent out thoughts to Maggie. She could see them, golden words, in the air. COME BACK. COME BACK. She was sure that her mother would see them also. That wherever Maggie was, they would suddenly appear, tiny topaz clouds, like miniature skywriting, in the air. And they would bring her back.

It would be easier if she knew where Maggie was,

but no one said anything. Her father and grandmother talked alone a great deal in the library, with low buzzing voices, but they stopped when Alexis came into the room. And the servants didn't say a word.

At the beginning of December, the Averys' cook retired to Florida and the new cook arrived. Jade was young and pert, and Alexis was eager to make friends with her. She came down to the kitchen one afternoon, before Jade started dinner.

"What are you making?"

"Veal cutlets."

"That's my mother's favorite," Alexis said with satisfaction. "You haven't met her yet. She's away for a little while, but I know she'll like to have your veal cutlets when she gets back."

Alexis enjoyed talking like that to Jade, as if her mother were going to come back the next day.

But Jade was looking at her strangely.

"Well, I guess I shouldn't say anything," she began, then stopped.

"Anything about what?" Alexis's neck felt suddenly wet.

"I guess I shouldn't tell you."

"Tell me what?"

Jade was starting to enjoy herself.

"Well, it's in all the papers. About your mother. How she ran off with some man."

Alexis ran over and hit Jade hard.

"How dare you!" she screamed. "How dare you! I'll have Grandmother fire you!"

But she did not tell her Grandmother what Jade had said. And the next afternoon, Jade came into Alexis's bedroom without knocking, and dumped a magazine on her bed. On the front page was a picture of Maggie, her head in a scarf, large sunglasses over her eyes. In the background was a man—the same tall, thin man they had run into that day in New York. MAGGIE FLEES TO FRANCE. Alexis crumpled up the magazine and threw it in the wastebasket.

After Jade left the room, Alexis pulled the magazine back out of the wastebasket. She smoothed the front page and looked closely at the photo of her mother. The scarf Maggie had on was the one she always wore with her rose-colored dress. And those sunglasses were the ones she had worn the day she had taken Alexis to the circus. Gently, Alexis touched the picture of Maggie's face. Then she tore the magazine into tiny pieces.

The girls at school whispered about her. Alexis knew what they were whispering about. She could only look at them as if she didn't care.

It was a few days before Christmas. Alexis came into the library and found her father sitting in his leather chair. He was crying into his hands. When he heard Alexis, he looked up but he did not stop weeping.

"Remember how much your mother loved Christmas?" he sobbed.

Alexis ran over and put her arms around him. She had never seen her father cry before. She could feel him panting beneath her, the way Molasses did when he had run beyond his strength.

She stroked his hair. She had never done that before, either. It had always been Maggie's hair that she had loved to brush, had loved to arrange in different styles.

"It'll be fine, Daddy," she said. "We'll have a great Christmas."

Astonishingly, he seemed to believe her. He patted her hand.

"We've got to spend more time together, you and me."

"That would be great."

"Do you like tennis? We'll play tennis."

Alexis thought of Maggie playing tennis. Red hair flying, laughing as she spun, and missing the ball.

Alexis deliberately lifted Maggie out of her mind.

"I'd love to," she told her father.

As she looked down at him, she thought of the name "Avery," how he was an Avery and how she was an Avery along with him. The name reminded her of Aviary. She saw them as proud birds, strong birds— birds who couldn't be wrecked, no matter what. There were birds, it was true, who flew away. But only one person had done that, and she wasn't an Avery. Not a real one, the way Alexis was.

Alexis still spent a lot of time out at the stables. But one day she went out to find Cody, and, no matter how many times she called, he wouldn't come out.

Alexis didn't like to mention Maggie's name to her father. Whenever she did, he looked as if he were in pain. From time to time, she brought the subject up to her grandmother; "Have you heard from my mother? Do you know where she is?" but Mrs. Avery would only purse her lips and talk about something else. Finally, Alexis stopped asking.

It took her longer to stop expecting a letter. Every day she would glance at the hall table where the mail was neatly laid out, looking for a letter addressed to her in Maggie's big, impatient scrawl. But no letter came.

Alexis's ninth birthday was in a week. She was sure that she would hear from her mother then. No matter where she was, no matter who she was with, Maggie wouldn't forget her birthday. Every afternoon, Alexis came home from school, expecting there to be a package or a card, postmarked France. Nothing came.

Finally, she asked her grandmother about it.

"Hasn't—hasn't my mother sent anything for my birthday?"

"No, dear," Mrs. Avery told her.

"Are you sure? Maybe it got mixed up with other mail."

"I'm sorry, dear," her grandmother said again.

Alexis shrugged, as if it didn't matter.

A few weeks later, her father came into her room. He sat on the edge of her bed and made little ridges in her bedspread with his pale fingers.

"I just wanted to tell you," he said, "that the—ah—divorce proceedings have started between your mother and myself."

Alexis tensed and looked out the window.

He went on awkwardly. "Of course your happiness is our most important concern. Because of the—situation—your grandmother and I feel—as do the lawyers—that it would be better for you to continue living here with us. In a stable environment, with no influences that would be, ah, harmful. You'll stay at your school, we'll carry on the way we have. Is that agreeable to you?"

Agreeable, bagreeable, cagreeable, dagreeable. She kicked at the covers restlessly.

He would not leave. "But when you're twelve, if you so choose, you may go live with your mother."

"Yes, yes, yes," she mouthed.

"Alexis, do you understand what I'm saying?"

"Yes, yes, yes," she gabbled more loudly.

"And you agree?"

Alexis pulled the covers over her head and waited for her father to leave the room.

She closed her eyes and imagined her mother. Maggie was standing, face flaming, hands on her hips.

"I will never let you have my baby. Never, never."

Never, bever, cever, dever.

Weeks and months went by. There began to be days when Alexis didn't think about her mother. Afternoons when she would help Grandmother with her charity teas, evenings when she and her father would play backgammon. Fourth grade ended. Fifth grade began. Alexis grew her hair long. It seemed sometimes that life had always gone on in this way, without Maggie. Sometimes it seemed that it had always been just the three of them, Averys together. And that was the way things would always continue.

It did not occur to Alexis that her father might start dating again.

* * *

One Friday evening, the phone rang. Alexis picked it up.

"Hello?"

"Oh, hello. Is Henry there?"

It was a female voice.

"No," Alexis said slowly. She did not offer information about when her father would be back.

That night at dinner, she told her father that a woman had called for him.

Mr. Avery looked at his mother. Mrs. Avery nodded.

"Ah, yes," he said to Alexis. His voice sounded unnatural. "That must have been Sylvia."

"Who's Sylvia?"

"A very nice lady I met a few months ago. She works for a company we deal with."

"Is she your girlfriend?"

"I guess you could say that. Yes."

Alexis turned very red.

"I—had meant to tell you about it. I was just waiting until an appropriate time came."

He looked foolish, a little proud. Alexis wanted to hit him.

"Would you like to meet her?"

She shook her head.

She met Sylvia the following Friday. She and her father went to a production of *Giselle* at Lincoln Center and there, waiting at the fountain, was a tall, blond woman wearing a camel's hair coat.

When the woman saw them, she gave a big smile in Alexis's direction.

"Well, I finally get to meet you!" she said. "I hear you forced the issue." And she hugged Alexis before she hugged Henry.

* * *

Sylvia turned out to be not bad. Alexis liked the way she paid attention to the ballet, and the way she handed Alexis a Kleenex at the sad ending. She liked it that Sylvia didn't try to hold her father's hand. And mostly she liked it that Sylvia didn't sound, or look, or act anything like Maggie.

After the ballet was finished, they stood on the sidewalk in front of the fountains.

"Anyone up for some ice cream?" Sylvia suggested.

"Me!" Alexis cried, doing a ballet spin.

In the middle of her twirl, she heard Sylvia say, "The best ice cream's at Serendipity. Why don't we go there?"

It was that June afternoon again, and she and Maggie were on their way to Serendipity. The tall, thin man was coming toward them, and Maggie's hand was growing colder and colder in her own.

Alexis stopped the twirl. She felt dizzy.

"No, thank you," she said. "I don't really feel like ice cream."

"What did you think of Sylvia?" her father asked too casually the next morning at breakfast.

Alexis thought carefully. If she said she liked Sylvia, her father would probably keep dating her, might even marry her. If she said she didn't, he might break off the relationship now. Alexis certainly didn't want a stepmother. She liked the extra time she'd been having with her father. She liked being his date to the movies, and his partner at tennis. If he got married, she'd go back to being just a plain daughter again. But of course she knew what she had to say.

"I liked her."

Her father's smile was huge, relieved.

"I like her, too," he confessed.

Alexis realized that nothing she could have said would have made any difference, anyway.

On the morning of her father's wedding day, Alexis woke up early, with a headache. She went downstairs and looked at all the gifts displayed on the dining room table. There were Lalique bowls and Spode platters, an antique clock, silver from Tiffany. All the cards wished Henry and Sylvia happiness, and years of joy. Mrs. Avery had given the couple a boat. They were going to honeymoon on it, though Sylvia made jokes about how she was such a bad sailor that Henry would end up pushing her overboard.

Alexis touched an angel on a Capidimonte lamp. She wondered about the day her father had married Maggie—*Mother, I'm marrying her.* Had there been similar cards and presents then? All these wishes for joy? Had Grandmother given a wonderful gift?

At ten o'clock, Sylvia came over. When she heard that Alexis had a headache, she hugged her and rubbed her head and gave her an aspirin. The headache went away.

It came back during the ceremony at the church. Alexis was a junior bridesmaid in yellow tulle, and she could see her father's and Sylvia's faces at the altar. They looked so happy together, complete.

When the ceremony was over, the guests came back to the house for the reception. Alexis did not join them. She ran upstairs to her room, opened up her desk drawer, grabbed her stationery, and started a letter:

"Dear Mama, Daddy has gotten married again. I miss you so terribly. Please could I come see you." She faltered, could not think what to say next. Finally, guiltily, she crumpled up the page.

On Alexis's twelfth birthday, her grandmother announced that, according to the terms of the divorce agreement, Alexis was now free, if she so desired, to communicate with, visit, even live with her mother again.

Alexis only nodded and said she would think about it.

She thought about it for a week. First, she decided she would write her mother, but she changed her mind. What could she say in a letter? It would all sound so flat and false. No, a visit would be much better. She imagined what it would be like, getting off the plane in Paris, and seeing Maggie rushing toward her. Feeling Maggie's arms tight around her neck. "At last, at last," Maggie would murmur. "My baby is here." Her visit would last the whole summer. She and Maggie would stay up late every night, talking. They would have little adventures, and find the best ice cream parlor in Paris. At the end of the visit, when it was time to go back home, Maggie would burst into tears and cry, "How could I have spent a single moment without you?" And Alexis would agree to stay. Living in Paris! What a change it would be. She would become a new Alexis. There would be a new house, a new bedroom, a new school. And there would be a new city outside her window.

On Friday, she went into her grandmother's room. "I've thought about what you said," she told her. "I think I'd like to try it—visiting my mother. Maybe I could go this summer."

Mrs. Avery nodded. Then she sighed slightly. "Are you sure?"

"What—do you mean?"

"Well, I'm a little concerned about how well it would work out." She coughed delicately, "The man your mother's involved with . . ."

"Philip Fredericks," Alexis said firmly. "I know his name."

Mrs. Avery blinked. "Do you? Oh, dear. I thought we'd managed to keep all that—unpleasantness away from you. Anyway, I don't know if such an—irregular household—would be the best influence for a young girl. And frankly I'm just not sure what your reception might be."

"Well, what does my mother say about it?" Alexis demanded.

"She hasn't said anything."

Alexis colored. "What do you mean?"

"She hasn't mentioned it." Her grandmother sounded surprised. "I thought you knew, dear. We haven't heard from your mother since you were eight years old."

Alexis looked down.

Her grandmother sighed softly. "I think it's safe to suppose that she's put that part of her life behind her."

Alexis went away. It crossed her mind that her grandmother might be lying, saying what she had to keep Alexis in New York. But she knew it wasn't true. The truth was, her mother hadn't loved her enough to stay for her. Her mother hadn't loved her enough to keep in touch with her. Her mother hadn't loved her enough to try and get her back. She thought about asking her father and asking his advice, but she didn't want to hear him say those same words: "We haven't heard from your mother since you were eight years old."

That night, Alexis came down with the flu. For a week, she was in bed with a high fever. She kept thinking Maggie was sitting next to her. She kept asking Maggie why she had left her. "Do you love me at all?" she kept screaming. Maggie only smiled and would not say a word. Alexis put her hot hands out to burn her mother. Maggie burned up and went away, cinders into the night.

A few days later, Alexis went down into the sitting room after dinner. Her grandmother was doing a jigsaw puzzle, and her father and Sylvia were playing chess.

"I've decided to stay here," she told her grandmother.

Mrs. Avery fit two pieces of the sky together.

"I think that's a very wise choice, dear."

When Alexis started the eighth grade, she made a new friend. Her name was Emily Howard and she came from Pittsburgh. Emily was heavy and pasty with a mass of shaggy black hair, and her IQ was the highest the school had ever recorded. Because she had polio when she was a child, she walked with a limp.

Alexis met Emily the second week of term. They were in Study Hall, taking a French test, and Emily sat beside her. "Mind if I cheat off you?" she asked Alexis.

"I was up watching *Wuthering Heights* last night and didn't get a chance to study."

"Sure," Alexis said.

Within a month, Alexis and Emily were inseparable. They ate lunch together every day, they cut gym class and hid behind the locker rooms, and on Friday nights they alternated sleepovers at each other's houses.

The ritual was the same, whichever house they were at. They would listen to Cat Stevens records, eat chocolate-covered pretzels, and play the Ouija board. Then they would get into bed, and five minutes later, one or the other would say, "I can't sleep." So they would sit up and talk for the next three hours.

They would talk about how much they hated school, and where they wanted to go to college (Emily, Yale; Alexis, undecided). They would talk about what they wanted to do with their lives (Emily, a psychiatrist; Alexis, an artist). Emily told Alexis all about Pittsburgh, and Alexis told Emily about Cody. Occasionally they talked about real boys, but these were the least interesting conversations, as neither of them knew any.

One night, Emily asked Alexis about her mother. Alexis swallowed.

"Oh, I don't really remember too much about her," she said. "She died when I was born."

Emily was silent. Alexis was not sure if she believed her, or if she had heard gossip at school. It didn't matter, in any case. Her mother was as good as dead.

One Study Hall, Alexis was in the school art room, finishing a pen and ink study she had been working on for the last two weeks. It was a copy of an old *Photo-*

play magazine cover. The woman on the cover rested a pointed chin on long, thin fingers. Her smile was mischievous and mysterious, her red hair scrappily cut.

The door opened and Emily came in.

"I've been looking all over for you!"

Alexis had no time to hide the picture. Emily caught sight of it immediately, and moved closer.

"Wow, that's fantastic. Who is it?"

Alexis felt herself turning pink.

"Some actress playing Peter Pan."

Emily looked from the portrait to Alexis.

"It's your mother."

Alexis nodded, scarlet.

Emily picked up the *Photoplay*.

"Maggie Royal."

Emily looked at the picture carefully. "You kind of have the same mouth." Then she added, "My father's been in love with her for years."

Now that Emily knew, Alexis showed her all the pictures of Maggie she had drawn in secret. One Friday night she even showed her friend the red leather scrapbook, and they went through it together, page by crumbling page.

"Don't you ever want to get in touch with her?" Emily asked.

"No," Alexis said. Her voice was tight. "She doesn't deserve it. She left me when I was eight years old. Without a word." There was a long pause and then she added, "Sometimes."

"Why don't you? I'll help you."

Alexis shook her head.

"No, that's okay," she told Emily. "Things are fine the way they are. Really. I've gotten used to not having her."

"That's sort of sad," Emily said. "I mean, she's your mother. If it were me, I'd want to at least talk to her."

In her head, Alexis could hear Maggie's husky voice speaking, but she could not imagine the words it was saying.

"No," she said again. "Not after all this time. It would just be too strange. Besides," she added, remembering her grandmother's words, "my mother's put that part of her life behind her."

In March, Emily's father was relocated to Cleveland, Ohio. Emily gave Alexis a gold bracelet as a farewell present, and Alexis hand-tinted a photograph of the two of them for Emily. They wrote to each other a great deal at first, then the letters grew more irregular. In one of the last letters Emily wrote, she said, "Caught your mother in an old movie last night. You've got her voice, too."

In her senior year, Alexis applied to colleges, sending applications and her portfolio to various art schools around the country.

Her grandmother could not understand.

"Why aren't you applying to Wellesley?" she asked. "We've always had an Avery woman at Wellesley."

"I know, Grandmother," Alexis told her. "But I want to go to a school that specializes in art."

"Just do me a favor," Grandmother told her. "Apply wherever else you like, but put Wellesley on the list."

Sighing, shaking her head, Alexis agreed.

The following April, the letters came. Alexis was

turned down by all the art schools. She was accepted to Wellesley.

After the initial disappointment, Alexis grew used to the idea, then finally excited. The last day of summer, she stood in front of her mirror for a long time, staring with wonder at the tall blond girl she saw there—the girl who was going off to Wellesley College the following morning and finally starting her life.

The suitcases had been unpacked, the dorm room was set up, and now the limousine was turned around, ready for the trip back to New York.

"Good-bye, dear," Alexis's grandmother said. As she kissed Alexis on the cheek, Alexis caught the scent of vanilla. She found she was close to tears. It was strange to think that tomorrow, for the first time ever, there would be no kiss, no scent of vanilla.

"Take care of yourself," Sylvia said. "Make sure you eat enough."

Henry Avery hugged her.

"We'll see you at Thanksgiving."

Alexis stood in the driveway long after the car had gone.

The October evening was misty and cold. Alexis was sitting at her desk, listening to Bach on the stereo and working on her "Adam Bede" essay. She finished a paragraph, and leaned back in her chair, smiling as she looked around the room. Everyone agreed that it was the prettiest room in the whole dorm, with its posters of French Impressionist exhibitions on the walls and colorful rugs on the floor. Jacey, her roommate, was always telling Alexis that when she finished college, she should be an interior decorator. It was an intriguing thought, even though she wasn't sure her grandmother would approve.

The door crashed open.

"Hey, Alexis!" Jacey, her dark hair misted with frost, came in. "Lisa and I are going into Boston to see a movie. Want to come?"

Alexis shook her head. "I can't. I've got to finish this essay."

Jacey sighed. " I'm getting worried about you. You haven't set a foot out of this place in two weeks!"

Alexis shrugged. "I like it here."

"I know. But it's not good for you." She sat down on her bed. "If you don't get out of here, how are you going to meet people?"

"I meet plenty of people."

"I mean boys."

Alexis flushed slightly.

"I don't want to meet boys."

"Oh, come on."

It was hard to explain, especially to someone like Jacey, who had been dating since she was twelve.

"Look, Jacey, I've just never been interested in going out with a different guy every week like you do. I'm sure I'll meet someone one day, but I'm not rushing it."

"I'm not saying be a tramp," Jacey told her, "I'm just saying have some fun. Lighten up. Get out a little."

She grabbed the college schedule and looked through it. "There's a dance next Friday. Why don't you go?"

"I'm really not interested."

"Do it as a favor to me," Jacey begged. "We'll go together—you'll keep me company. And who knows—maybe the boy of your dreams will show up!"

Alexis considered this.

"Okay," she said finally, surprising them both.

As the week went on, although she didn't let on to Jacey, Alexis started to grow more and more excited about the dance. Maybe it would be wonderful. Maybe she'd have a great time. And just maybe Jacey was right—maybe a special boy, the boy she'd dreamed about, the boy with ice-blond eyelashes and quirky crooked mouth, would be there. She imagined him scanning the crowd of girls, then tensing as he saw her. He could come up slowly and smile. "You have hair like a mermaid," he would say.

Jacey got to work. She took Alexis out shopping, and Alexis ended up with a long topaz-colored skirt, a lace top, dangly earrings, and a new haircut.

The night of the dance, all the girls helped her with her makeup.

"You look gorgeous," they told her. "Absolutely gorgeous."

But nobody asked her to dance. The band played song after song, couples moved fast or slowly, but Alexis remained motionless, unchosen, looking on. She stood by the refreshment table, telling herself that as long as she wasn't actually against a wall, then she couldn't be called a wallflower.

She studied all the young men who had come to the dance, the athletic types, the future businessmen, the ones who would be bald by age twenty-five. She saw that she had wasted her time. Her boy hadn't come after all.

"Don't worry—there's another dance in two weeks," Jacey said encouragingly.

But Alexis wouldn't go. She put the topaz skirt away in her suitcase, and gave the dangly earrings to Goodwill.

One Wednesday morning in November, Alexis set off for town to buy a gift for her grandmother's birthday. She tried "Lanz" and "The Stitchery" without success, then she crossed the street and went into the china shop.

"May I help you?" a voice asked.

Alexis looked up. Behind the counter was a boy. He was around nineteen, thin and pale, with thick gold hair and hands so delicate that they appeared translucent. He looked like Cody would have looked, had he ever grown up.

The boy smiled at Alexis, and she fell in love.

"I—I need to get something for my grandmother."

"That's nice," he said. His voice was soft and friendly. "Grannies usually get forgotten."

They talked about the gift for a while, and she chose the Lenox vase he brought out.

"What's your name?" he asked her as he wrapped the present.

"Alexis Avery."

"I'm Jimmy Craig. Are you at Wellesley?"

"Yes."

"You must be smart. I tried college a few years ago, but it wasn't for me."

He handed over the package. Now it was time to leave, and Alexis couldn't think of any excuse for remaining.

Then Jimmy looked at his watch and said, "I get my lunch break now. Can you join me, or do you have to be back at school?"

"I'm free," she told him.

Not counting a history class, a French review, and a geology lab.

They went to the little muffin shop across the street.

Alexis ached with nervousness, but Jimmy didn't seem to notice.

"Do you know what you're going to do when you finish college?" he asked her.

She told him she was going to be a painter, or maybe an interior designer. He told her he was going to be a missionary.

"A missionary!"

He laughed. "I was born to it. My parents were both missionaries. They worked in Hawaii—that's where they met. We lived there till I was twelve. Then we came here."

A missionary's wife. It was an intoxicating picture. Alexis guessed she would have to help him with his work, that would be only fair, but she would see to it that she still had plenty of time for her painting. She envisioned canvases full of jungle colors.

They finished their sandwiches and coffee, and Jimmy paid the check.

"Thank you so much," Alexis said. "I really enjoyed that." She laughed self-consciously. "A much-needed break from work."

He nodded. "If you're free on the weekend, maybe we could get together."

"All right."

They walked to the door of the restaurant, and he squeezed her hand.

"See you soon."

"Where on earth have you been?" Jacey asked, when Alexis came back to the room. Alexis smiled idiotically.

"I've met him," she said.

Jimmy asked her to a movie that weekend, and as they were sitting watching the show, he took her hand and held it. Afterward, when Jimmy asked her what she had thought of the film, she was embarrassed to find that she didn't have any opinion at all. She had been concentrating the whole time on the feel of her hand in his.

Afterward, he walked her back to the dorm. All the girls were waiting.

"Well?" Alexis asked when Jimmy had left.

"He seems sweet," Sarah said.

"Nice, but a little shy," was Jacey's verdict.

"I think he's cute," from Nora.

Alexis couldn't believe the blandness of the remarks. But all the girls agreed that they were very happy for her, and so glad that she had finally found her special boy.

*   *   *

Jimmy first kissed her on an afternoon in early December. He was walking her back to the campus after a date, and they stopped outside the gates.

"You've got something in your hair," he said, and removed a tiny dead leaf. Then he looked down at her, almost with surprise. She could see the idea of kissing her come into his face. He kissed her with great gentleness. It was not enough for Alexis; she pushed against him, wanting more. Then she pulled back, embarrassed.

She couldn't sleep that night, reliving the kiss.

The day Christmas vacation began, the family chauffeur picked Alexis up and brought her back home to Long Island. Her father and grandmother and Sylvia hugged her and asked how everything was going. Alexis said everything was wonderful, but she did not mention Jimmy Craig. It wasn't time yet.

Being without Jimmy for two weeks was torture. Christmas morning, Alexis opened in secret the little gift he had given her—a turquoise necklace—and she kissed it over and over.

The new semester began. Alexis started keeping a sketchpad on which she drew countless pictures of Jimmy—his eyes, the curve of his neck, the way his forearms came so smoothly down from his rolled shirtsleeves. And she kept a diary in which she recorded every detail of their dates. She looked forward to showing both the sketchpad and the diary to their children one day.

* * *

Alexis told Jimmy all her secrets. It was very important to her that he know absolutely everything. She told him about her evil nanny, and her friend Emily. She told him about the way she had felt when her father married Sylvia, and the way the Willow Academy had smelled. And finally, one day, she told him about Maggie. When she was finished, he had reached over and squeezed her hand. "I'm so sorry," he said.

It bothered Alexis a little that Jimmy never seemed to want to talk about himself in return.

"I wish you would," she would say. "Don't you see? I want to know everything about you—everything!"

But he would only smile uneasily. "I don't have that much to tell."

The one thing they never talked about was love. Alexis waited daily for Jimmy to say that he loved her. She waited throughout January, but he never spoke the words. Finally, it was February, and they were taking a walk by the train station.

"I've got to buy my Valentines tomorrow," she said.

"Do you still do that?" he asked her.

"Not for everyone. Just for the people I love. It's a pretty tiny list. You're on it," she added abruptly.

They walked on in silence.

"You should never have said that!" Jacey scolded when Alexis told her what had happened. "That's the quickest way in the world to scare off a boy—telling him you love him."

Alexis shook her head. "Not Jimmy."

"Of course Jimmy. Are you kidding? He's this local kid with no education. You've got all this money, and all this background, and then you go and tell him you love him! Poor guy!"

"Jacey, I had to be honest—he understands—"

"Just stop being so intense!" Jacey groaned. "Be casual, can't you? Just have fun with him. Don't start thinking about what you're going to name your children!"

"But I can't be casual! Don't you see? This isn't casual."

"Of course it's casual, Alexis; you're eighteen years old."

"Don't say that!" Alexis cried. "You don't understand!"

But it appeared that Jacey was right. For after that day, Jimmy seemed to change. He was less eager to see her, more uneasy in her presence. Alexis told herself she was imagining it, but she knew she wasn't. She could feel herself growing fainter and fainter in his life.

"I told you!" Jacey said. "He's terrified. You've got to back off."

Alexis tried. For two weeks, she managed to be casual, even standoffish. And she never once mentioned the word "love." But one Friday night, she couldn't stand it anymore. She and Jimmy had been to a movie, and he was walking her back to her dorm. He kissed her lightly, then turned to leave.

Alexis found that she was holding on to his arm. "Jacey's gone home for the weekend," she heard herself say. "We could spend the night together if you want."

Jimmy pulled back, startled.

"What?"

"In my room. Nobody would know."

"I don't think that's such a good idea."

She blushed. "I don't mean—what you think," she told him. "But we could just stay together. Sleep in the same bed. And we'll set the alarm for five. You'll be out before dawn. No one would ever find out." She swallowed, ashamed of herself. "Please, Jimmy. I think it would be good for us. And it would mean so much to me."

He was silent a long time.

"I'll have to call my folks," he said slowly, at last. "I guess I could tell them I'm at a friend's."

Alexis lay in her narrow bed, Jimmy's arms around her, heavenly warm. She concentrated on his breathing, matched her own to it. It would be like this every night when they were married, she told herself—the two of them off in South America or China. They would sleep in a brass bed in their little missionary hut. Thin white curtains would blow above them. They would lie tired, happy, relaxed in each other's embrace.

And then the room was filled with a keening screech.

"Fire!" she heard someone call.

Within seconds, the corridors were full of screaming girls.

"Hurry up!" the dorm president was shouting. "Onto the quad! Onto the quad!"

There was no escape for Jimmy. His descent was visible to everyone in the building.

The fire turned out to be a false alarm.

The phone in Alexis's room rang later that morning. She picked it up slowly.

"Alexis," her grandmother said, "I'd like you to come home for the weekend. The car will be there to pick you up at five."

On the four-and-a-half-hour drive back to New York, Alexis thought of every possible thing that her family could say. They would tell her she had embarrassed them all. She would say she was sorry. They would say she was too young to get involved. She would disagree. They would say she had hurt them by not telling them about Jimmy. This one was harder to answer. The truth was, she had been sure they wouldn't understand. He was poor, a local boy, a college dropout, not someone an Avery would fall in love with. But she was in love with him. She would never be in love with anybody else. She would make her family see that. And she would explain about what had happened last night. Surely her father and Sylvia would sympathize with wanting to be in the arms of someone you loved.

The car pulled into the driveway at last, and Alexis went inside. Her grandmother was in the library, having a glass of sherry.

"Alexis!" she said. "My dear, come on in. Join me, won't you?"

There seemed to be no anger whatsoever.

"No, no, thank you," Alexis stammered.

"Why, where's your young man?" Grandmother asked. "I assumed he'd be with you."

"I didn't think . . ."

Grandmother shook her head.

"Alexis, I'm not such a fuddy-duddy as all that. I admit, when your dorm president called me this morning, I was a little surprised—but you're a young woman now."

Alexis ran over and hugged her.

"Oh, Grandmother, I was so sure you'd be—well . . ."

Her grandmother smiled.

"You're my only grandchild, Alexis. I want everything for you that you want for yourself."

The foolish happy tears came. And the explanations about how wonderful Jimmy was, and how his background didn't matter, and how they would all love him.

"Well, one thing's clear," her grandmother said briskly. "We must meet this young man at once. Your father and Sylvia are in Maine this week, but they'll be back on Friday. Why don't you bring your Jimmy by then? We'll have a little dinner in his honor."

Alexis hesitated. "He's very shy."

Grandmother waved her hand. "I'm just talking about a family party," she said.

When Alexis got back to Wellesley on Sunday night, she called Jimmy at his house. Jimmy answered; he sounded guarded and strained. Alexis rushed to reassure him.

"The weekend went so well, Jimmy. I didn't see

Daddy and Sylvia, but I've told Grandmother everything. And she's dying for everyone to meet you. She's
setting up a little party this Friday."

"Alexis, I don't think—"

Tears came to her eyes.

"Don't you want to meet my family?"

He hesitated. "Alexis, I just don't think this is such
a good idea."

"Of course it is," she told him. "They're all lovely
people. I already told Grandmother that you didn't like
parties. It won't be anything elaborate; I promise you."

The following Friday, Jimmy, dressed in his best
blue suit, drove Alexis to Long Island. There was not
much conversation.

"Oh, my God!" he said, jerking on his brake as
they pulled into the driveway. The house was floodlit,
and a row of Mercedes and Cadillacs awaited the attention of tuxedoed valets. "What's going on?"

"I don't know," Alexis said. It was all she could do
to pull Jimmy from the car.

The hall was full of guests in black tie and evening
gowns. Waiters were circling with trays of food and
champagne. On the stairs was a trio, playing Brahms.
Grandmother, wearing all her pearls, came up to them
with a wide smile.

"Here you are," she said. And then, clapping her
hands, "Attention, everyone; here are the guests of
honor."

Jimmy fled into the library and locked the door. Alexis
pounded tearfully, but he would not emerge. She found
her grandmother.

"How could you?" she demanded.

Mrs. Avery opened her pale blue eyes wide.

"Oh, dear," she said regretfully, "I did so hope you'd enjoy the evening."

Finally, an hour later, Jimmy came out but would not speak to Alexis. He drove back to Wellesley.

The following day, he telephoned her.

"Alexis," he began.

She started to cry.

"Look, Alexis," he said stiffly, "I don't want to hurt you, but I think it's time we stopped seeing each other."

The thick, disbelieving tears choked her. She gripped the phone.

"Look, I know the party was awful, and I'm so sorry, but it was all just a horrible mistake. I won't let anything like that happen again. I swear."

He sighed. "It's not just the party, Alexis. It's everything."

She fought not to scream.

"But, Jimmy, I love you so much. You're everything in the world to me."

"Please, Alexis," he said sharply. "This whole thing is just getting way too emotional. I mean, you're a really nice girl, but my God. You—you seem to want so much."

His words echoed.

She flushed with shame.

"I see," she told him.

"I'm sorry. I really am."

She hung up the phone.

* * *

A few minutes later, she went into her grandmother's room.

"It's over," she said bitterly. "You must be very happy."

Mrs. Avery looked at her with reproach.

"I wouldn't say that, dear. But perhaps, all things considered, it's for the best."

Six

Maggie stood by the open window, staring out onto the street. The sunlight, spilling luxuriously onto the floor, looked like caramel.

"Do you like Paris?" she asked Paul.

The reporter smiled. "Who doesn't like Paris?"

She turned to face him.

"Oh, you'd be surprised. Are you here just for business?"

"I'm here just to see you, if that's what you mean."

Maggie appeared to like that.

"Well, don't forget to see the town. I can give you a list of marvelous places to visit."

Paul did not mention that he had been to Paris several times before. He wanted Maggie's list.

"Thank you," he said.

She took a last look at the street outside. Slowly she returned to the sofa and sat back down. She didn't speak for a long time.

"You were telling me about your father's death," he prompted her.

"I'm aware of that," she told him.

"I'm sorry," Paul said. She didn't appear to hear.

"My father's funeral was—unforgettable," she went on with a soft deadliness. "For one thing, the church was absolutely packed. It was astonishing to me. Papa was always so aloof—I never would have guessed that he had known so many people. Everyone was crying, carrying on like mad. Telling me what a gentleman he was. How kind and thoughtful. I thought surely I must be at the wrong funeral." She drew in a sharp breath.

"And then this woman came up to me. I'll never forget her face as long as I live. Fat, covered with thick white powder. She told me, "I don't know how my children and I could have made it through last year without your father. He paid all our doctor's bills. All our doctor's bills. He was a saint.""

Maggie's voice trembled with bitterness.

"I just looked at her. My father—the saint—was paying this woman's doctor bills and letting his own family starve. I butted her in the stomach with my head," she said with slow, ringing satisfaction, "and I ran out of the church. I didn't come home till nearly midnight.

"Mama was waiting up for me. I was sure she'd whip me, but she didn't. She didn't say a thing. I couldn't understand it. It didn't occur to me till much later that maybe she'd also heard what that fat woman had said."

Maggie shook her head. "When Mama came home from that funeral, she looked ten years older than when she had left for it. And she stayed that way for the rest of her life."

Paul let a few moments go by.

He put it awkwardly.

"How did your family handle—financially—and other-wise— your father's death?"

Maggie shrugged. "We handled it. What other choice did we have? Mama opened a little grocery store—that did quite well; my sister Mildred helped her run it, my oldest sister Cathy got married to a traveling salesman and moved to Salt Lake City."

"And what about you?"

"I started high school."

"What was that like?"

"A nightmare. Everyone hated me."

"Why?"

She considered this.

"I think it was partly because I was different. I still had that sense Papa had given me—that I was some sort of princess in disguise. I thought I was better than the rest of those other kids put together, and I'm sure I showed it."

Meditatively, she stroked a vein of silk embroidery on her caftan.

"I only had one dress. Mama made it—blue ging-ham with a white collar. It was all we could afford; I had to wear it every day. Every morning when I came to school, the kids would circle around me and flap their arms and say, "Here comes Blue Jay!" They would caw at me when I went down the hall." She crossed her arms in front of her. "But it didn't matter, not really. It couldn't change the fact that I was Somebody."

She smiled oddly.

"They were the reason I kept Maggie Royal as my

professional name, you know—those girls I went to high school with."

"Really?"

"Yes. I wanted to make sure that when they read their movie magazines and saw those pictures of that glamorous star out in Hollywood—wearing the most beautiful clothes—they would know, beyond a shadow of a doubt, that it was me." She laughed. "I can be very small sometimes.

"Anyway," she went on abruptly, "high school didn't last long. I quit when I was sixteen."

"Why?"

"Ah." Maggie took another cigarette. "That was Mrs. Shinn."

She smoked in silence for a few moments.

"She was the drama teacher. She was new—just come from Boston. Oh, I admired her. The way she dressed, in crisp little white shirts. The way she wore her hair. And I thought her accent was the most marvelous thing I'd ever heard.

"I couldn't wait for our first class. She started it off by having each one of us read a poem aloud. Five or six kids read. I could see her eyes glaze over at the incredible lack of talent on display. I was terrified that the bell would ring before I had a chance, but finally it was my turn.

"I read 'The Eagle' by Alfred, Lord Tennyson. When I finished, there was complete silence. Mrs. Shinn didn't say anything to me then. She just nodded and had the next girl read. But as soon as class was over, she came over. She said, 'I need to talk to you.'

"She took me to an empty classroom next door. She was pink with excitement. She said, 'My dear, you have talent. Real talent. You're an actress.'

"Well, it was quite simply one of the greatest moments of my life.

"She said we had to come up with a plan. I couldn't stay in West Texas, I was being wasted. She said I belonged in a drama school—somewhere where I could 'develop my gifts,' is how she put it. 'Have your parents come in to see me as soon as possible,' she said, 'and we'll discuss it.'"

Maggie put her head in her hands. It hurt Paul that the hands, under their long red nails, looked old.

"And then—this is hard to explain. But for that one moment, I suddenly saw what it all *could* have been like. If I had had money. If I had had other parents. If I had had another life. Yes, I could have gone to a famous drama school. Yes, I could have gone in beautiful clothes. Yes, I could have become a famous actress." She stubbed out the cigarette.

"Mrs. Shinn looked absolutely shocked when I began to cry. And then she looked down at my dress and at my shoes, and she got it. The pity that was in her eyes; I can't tell you. And I suddenly saw my whole future there in her face.

"I didn't have a chance."

Maggie fluffed her red hair away from her face.

"I left school that afternoon, and I never went back.

"I think that Mama was rather glad I quit. She had only had a second grade education herself, and didn't see much point in more. Besides, my sister Mildred was planning on moving to Denver, and so Mama needed my help running the grocery store."

Paul tried to be light.

"I somehow can't see you working at a grocery store."

"Oh, you'd be surprised," Maggie told him seriously. "I did a good job, actually. And I rather liked it. I could eat all the Butterfingers I wanted, and when the store was empty, I could rehearse monologues in the back room."

"So you were still acting?"

She gave him a look.

"Of course." Then the look faded. "Mrs. Shinn came in one day, to buy some groceries. She pretended she didn't see me. I pretended I didn't see her."

There was a pause. Paul looked down at his notes. "This must have been what—around '42? '43?"

"Somewhere around there."

"America was in the war by then?"

"Yes."

"How did that affect you?"

"To be honest, not very much," Maggie said. "I didn't lose anyone close to me. A few girls at school had brothers who died, but they weren't girls I spoke to."

Paul was silent for a moment. He cleared his throat and prepared for what he had to say next.

He knew he had to be careful.

"So," he began. "We have Maggie at what? Seventeen? Working at the store, busy with her acting. Any special friends? Any—boyfriends?"

She looked at him sharply.

"You're a very bad actor," she told him evenly. "I hope you have no aspirations in that area."

"No," he said.

"Good."

She sighed.

"What you're talking about—it's not something I particularly like to remember. And I don't talk about it in interviews."

"It could be off the record."

"Why should I tell you at all?"

"No reason. But I'd like to hear about it."

"Why? If it will be off the record?"

"I told you—I've had a crush on you all my life."

She thought about this.

"Yes. Well—what the hell. It was a long time ago." She stood up abruptly. "I think I'll have a drink first. Would you like anything?"

"No, thank you."

She went over to an inlaid Louis XV cabinet and opened it. Inside was a tiny bar, fitted out with liquors and glassware. She came back with some vodka in a Baccarat tumbler, and sat down. When she spoke again, her voice was a performing voice. Paul wondered if she was using it to distance herself from what she was saying—turning it into just another script.

"So. I had been working in Mama's store eight or nine months. One morning in June, a stranger came in. He was about fifty, very tall, very dark—arresting-looking."

"Stanley Pierson."

"Yes. He said 'Good Morning,' and smiled at me in a way no man had ever smiled at me before.

"I couldn't imagine what someone like this would be doing in our little grocery store. But he said that he had just bought the big Collins ranch on the outskirts of town, and that he needed to stock up on supplies.

"He stayed for a long time, talking to me. I couldn't for the life of me figure out why.

"Before he left, he asked if I would do him a favor. He said that he didn't know anyone in town yet, and asked if he could take me to dinner that night. I tried to be terribly grown-up about it, as though this sort of thing happened to me all the time. He told me he'd pick me up after work, in front of the store.

"I made up a story for Mama, saying I was spending the night with a friend. And that afternoon, I took all the money I'd been saving up for acting lessons, and bought myself a new dress."

She narrowed her eyes. "I've always thought that would make the most powerful scene in a movie. Can't you see it—this ambitious young girl is alone in her room; she's holding up her purse in one hand and a flier for an acting class in the other. Weighing them, and then letting the flier go; the camera follows it floating to the ground. Then the girl rushes off, to buy a frilly little red-and-white polka-dot dress. Sad in a way. But you know something?" Maggie admitted with a slight smile. "I can still see that dress.

"Stanley picked me up in a big black Ford coupe. It was terribly exciting—gangsterish-looking. I was scared to death someone would see us and tell Mama, so I made him take me clear out of town. We ended up at a roadside place. I'd never been anywhere like it.

"He asked me if I wanted something to drink, but I said no, I was a Baptist. He laughed and said he was, too. So I had my first drink that night." Maggie looked meditatively at her tumbler of vodka. "It's amazing to me now to think that there was actually a time when I had never had a drink.

"Stanley drank a lot," she went on briskly. "Whiskey. I was very impressed. He spent more money on drinks that evening than I had spent on my polka-dot dress.

"He told me all about himself that night. How, when he was just a little boy, his father died in prison. And how his stepfather used to whip him with a belt.

He showed me his arm, and you could still see the scars." She shook her head. "In my family, things like that were always hushed up. No one had ever talked to me this way before."

"It must have been very seductive."

"Yes. Especially when I touched that scar." Her laugh was a little embarrassed. "He told me that when he was fourteen years old, he ran away from home. Never went back. Somehow he got some money together, and by the time he was eighteen, he owned his own business." She shrugged. "I got the feeling that a few of his dealings weren't entirely on the up-and-up. But I didn't care. To be honest, I found it kind of exciting. He also said he'd been married, but that he had left his wife. I'd heard about things like that, but never actually met anyone who'd done it."

"Was that exciting, too?"

"Sure."

"Just before he dropped me back off at the store, he asked if he could see me the next evening—and then he kissed me."

"Your first kiss."

"Yes.

"And every night after that, I was with him."

"Didn't your mother get suspicious?"

"Heavens, no. She was so busy she didn't pay much attention. If I said I was going to a friend's house, she never checked up. She didn't even know that I didn't *have* friends.

"Well—" Maggie took a large gulp of her drink— "one night, about a month after we had met, Stanley said he had something to tell me. That he only had a year left to live."

She stared stonily at the glass.

"When I heard that, it felt like my father dying again. Does that sound very strange?"

"No," Paul told her.

"He asked me if I would make his last year on earth happy by marrying him. Of course I said I would.

"When I told Mama about Stanley and said we were getting married, she went absolutely to pieces. I'd never seen her so angry. She told me she'd kill herself before she'd let me. And then when she calmed down a little, she said the most extraordinary thing. She said, 'Maggie, I promise you one thing; if you marry this man, you'll never be an actress.'

"'You'll never be an actress.' Isn't that something? All those years, I thought it was my secret, that she had never guessed—and all that time, she knew. She knew."

She put a hand in front of her face. Paul jumped in quickly.

"How did that feel—getting married so young?"

"Are you kidding? I was scared to death. I couldn't cook, I couldn't clean, I couldn't keep a house to save my life. And I didn't know the first thing about men.

"But Stanley was dying, and he needed me. That's all I cared about. You know that line from the show *Oliver?* Slowly, she quoted, 'When you are lonely, then you will know—' "

Paul joined in. " 'When someone needs you, you love them so.' "

"Exactly," Maggie said. "It's that simple, isn't it? Anyway, we got married a few weeks later. The wedding was—understated, to say the least. We were married in the judge's office. There was no one Stanley wanted to invite, and my sisters refused to come. I wasn't expecting Mama either, but at the last minute she turned up, wearing her best flowered dress. She gave us Papa's mother's vase as a wedding gift. I'll never forget it.

"After the wedding, Stanley took me back to his ranch. I had wanted to go away somewhere on a honeymoon, but Stanley said he couldn't leave the ranch; there was too much work to do. I didn't really mind, though I did think it strange that a man who was dying would care so much about a ranch.

"I'd never been out to the Collins place before. Since Stanley spent so much on dinners and always told me how well he was doing, I'd expected it would be beautiful, but it was terrible. Filthy, absolutely filthy—mice droppings all over the place, and everything—the furniture, the carpets—covered in dust.

"The bedroom was the worst. Stained wallpaper, the most god-awful bed. I couldn't bear to think of Stanley dying there. I told him that I would make everything lovely—and that, when it was his time to go, he would go in a clean bed, in a beautiful room. And then—oh, God—he started to laugh."

Maggie's face contorted. "He laughed and he laughed. He said it had all been a joke; he had made the whole thing up, just to get me to marry him. He said, 'I'm not dying any more than you are.'

"I hit him. I screamed and kept hitting him. I said I was leaving him. He just kept on laughing. Then he pushed me down on the bed. I couldn't fight him off."

Very deliberately, Paul turned off the tape recorder.

"I hadn't heard that part of the story," he said stiffly.

"No," Maggie said. "And you probably wouldn't have heard it now if it hadn't been for the vodka." There was a spot of red hovering on each cheekbone.

They sat in silence for a long time.

"The next morning, I went back to Mama. She gave me all the money she had, and that afternoon, she took me to the train station. I can still see her, in her pink dress and straw hat, waving her little hand good-bye.

"The porter on the train asked me where I was going. I told him I was on my way to Hollywood to become a star."

Seven

A stalled van on Park Avenue caused a traffic jam, and by the time Alexis got home from Brian House, it was well past five o'clock.

She stepped out of the taxi. The aging, red-faced doorman hurried to help her.

"Hello, Mrs. Donleavy. Did you have a pleasant afternoon? Any packages?"

"Hello, McGruter. No packages, thank you."

Solicitously, he opened the door of the building for her.

"Horrible weather. I hope you haven't been out in the heat."

"No, I've been fine."

She found she was exhausted. Going into the lobby, she looked around at the marble floor, the glazed mirrors, the gilded molding. She compared it to that other lobby she had just been in.

* * *

Alexis rode up in the elevator, and let herself into her apartment. She switched the lights on, and saw her home almost with revelation. She went around the living room, paying attention to it in a way she hadn't in years. She fingered the heavy cream-colored draperies. She straightened the gilded frame of a Berthe Morisot etching. She looked at a small Battersea clock, noticing for the first time the bluebirds on the top panel. She knelt and touched the area rug that she had designed, enjoying the way the pale green lozenges formed such a gracious contrast to the flowers of pale yellow.

It was hard to believe that this orderliness, this summoned beauty, could even coexist in the same universe with Brian House. Alexis found herself recalling the rusty fan that had splashed air down on her during her class, and for a wry moment, she tried to picture that fan in the midst of her perfect living room.

Immediately, she stopped herself, disturbed. What a hateful little game. Why was she even playing it? A sickening possible answer came to her. That this was what her whole impulse to tutor at Brian House was about—simply a need to feel her own reality clean and secure around her by contrast. Had she really become so jaded that she needed to get her kicks by comparing her own life with that of children on drugs?

Alexis walked over to her built-in bar, and made herself a Scotch and soda.

She sat down on her deep blue silk sofa. She concentrated hard on the dusty New York sunset. She concentrated on her tiredness. She concentrated on the perfection of her living room. But the voices from Brian House kept intruding.

"I want to be a flight attendant . . ."

"It's all about this place called 'Bugland . . .' "

"One day I came home and she'd trashed the whole thing. Even Oriental Barbie . . ."

"Mother: living or deceased."

She heard the sound of Ron's key in the lock, and stood up quickly, grateful for the interruption.

From the hallway, she heard the rustlings of briefcase and papers, the jacket being folded.

"I'm in here, Ron," she called, eager to be distracted.

He came in, his footsteps flat, his blond looks dulled.

"How was your day?" Alexis asked.

A shadow was poured over his face.

"All right," he shrugged, and went toward the bathroom.

Alexis sighed. Whatever had made his day not all right, whether it was a case gone badly, or some overheard remark, or a long wait for a taxi, she, as usual, would never learn.

She sat back down on the sofa and concentrated again on the sunset. It had turned, by this time, blood-colored.

Ron seemed happier after his shower. He drank some wine, and told a story about the Rutledges, the couple they were going to dine with that evening. The husband was an industrialist from Dallas, and Ron badly wanted him as a client.

The story was a complicated one, full of legal intricacies, and Alexis had difficulty paying attention. Had it always been like this? she wondered. Or when they had first been married, had she been a better listener?

She couldn't remember. When Ron had finished the story, he was in a good mood again.

"So how was your day?" he asked.

Alexis started slightly.

"Fine," she said. "I had lunch with Mrs. Gollancz. That went well. I told you about her house—the one with the boxy little foyer. But I think we've solved it with a few mirrors."

Ron was nodding politely, in the same way that Alexis had listened to his story.

"That's great," he said.

He started to rise from the sofa. She stared at him, not knowing whether or not she was going to tell him about Brian House.

"Actually, something else happened," she said finally. "I've started tutoring."

He sat back down. "What?"

"Yes. At a place for underprivileged teenagers. I'm giving a kind of Art History/Decorating course for a few of them. Once a week for two hours."

He frowned. "I didn't know you were planning to do that."

She found she was breathing faster. "I've had it in mind for some time. I got some letters of recommendation together, but I didn't really decide until today."

Alexis wasn't sure what reaction she had expected from him. Approbation, perhaps—having a wife who tutored disadvantaged kids carried a certain éclat—or tolerant indifference. She was not prepared for the look of pity that took over her husband's face.

"You know why you're doing it, of course," he said at last.

"No," she said. "Tell me."

"For you," he said. "Because of your own child-hood."

She drew in a cold breath.

"All those abandonment issues," he went on. "Your mother leaving you. Your little escapade in Paris. It all fits in. You're not doing this to help those kids—you're doing it to help yourself. But don't get me wrong—I think it's great," he said dismissively.

"I'm so pleased that you think it's great," she told him, her voice crackling. But he was through with the subject by then, and was turning on the news.

The Rutledges were already waiting at the table when Ron and Alexis entered the restaurant.

The man stood up. "Alexis? I'm Bud, and this is my wife, Evie."

They were a couple in their late sixties. Bud wore a bolo tie and cowboy boots, but Evie was determinedly dressed as a New Yorker, complete with Chanel hand-bag.

"My wife's been talking about meeting you ever since we got to town. I think this dinner's the high point of the trip for her."

"I'm a big fan," Evie said. "That living room you did for *Better Homes and Gardens,* the one all in the Pompeii style? I've never seen anything so elegant."

"She tried to copy it in our house," Bud chortled. "Cost me a fortune to rip it out."

"Oh, Bud," his wife said. "But honestly, Alexis—I may call you that, may I? If we do relocate to New York, I hope you'll help me fix up our place."

"I'm sure Alexis would like nothing better," Ron cut in with a flourish.

Alexis ignored him.

"I'd be happy to help you," she told Evie quietly. Evie grabbed Alexis's hands and squeezed them. The drinks came and the talk turned to business.

"It's not that I have anything against the firm you're presently with," Ron was saying to Bud. "God knows, Marshall and I have been friends for years. But they've been having problems with their tax planning lately; they'd be the first ones to admit it—and given your situation, I do think that you need a special kind of handling."

How well he did it all, Alexis marveled. He was so affable, so knowledgable, so sensitively attentive. And the Rutledges had absolutely no idea how skillfully they were being trussed and prepared to join his client list.

The dinner order was taken, and the conversation waved back and forth. Then there came a pause.

"Well, I had a great little surprise waiting for me when I got home tonight," Alexis heard Ron say, and he put his arm around her shoulders. She wanted to pull away, but curiosity kept her fixed. She couldn't begin to imagine what this wonderful surprise had been.

"My wife has started tutoring underprivileged kids." In Ron's voice was just the right amount of tenderness and pride. Alexis felt her blood pressure rise.

"Oh, my!" Mrs. Rutledge turned eagerly toward her. "Where do you tutor?"

"I've just started," Alexis said shortly. "I don't know how long I'll be doing it. It's a place called Brian House."

"I think I've heard of that," Evie frowned. "Bud,

isn't that the place Cathy Grant was telling us about? That wonderful man whose son died?"

"Evie's really into the charities," Bud said to Ron.

"Well, I'll tell you what," Ron suggested with a big smile, "If you two do end up relocating, maybe Alexis and Evie could tutor together. Make it a weekly date. Lunch first somewhere, then on to Brian House."

Alexis wondered what would happen if she were suddenly to stand up and scream.

But at that moment, the waiter came with their dinner, and the talk turned to the latest scandal in the Senate.

"Well, that went well." Ron was exuberant as their taxi started off for home. "I think Rutledge is going to think very seriously about what I suggested."

Alexis nodded.

He looked over at her. "Thanks for all you did, by the way," he said. "I think your being there really made a difference. And I appreciate your offering to help Evie with their place."

"I liked the woman," Alexis said. "I'll be happy to help her."

She stared out the window for the remainder of the drive.

They arrived at their apartment, and Ron switched the lights on in silence. In silence they went into the bedroom; in silence they undressed.

Alexis lay in bed, her body cool in the sheets. She was walking along a windy beach, perhaps in Brittany.

There was a windmill just ahead and she would explore it.

"You mad at me?" she heard Ron ask from the other side of the bed.

It was too late to get into a fight.

"Not really," she told him wearily.

"I'm sorry if I upset you earlier. What I said about the tutoring. I was just a little surprised you were doing it."

"I understand. I'm a little surprised myself."

"I just don't want you to get hurt."

"I doubt if that's going to happen."

"You never know, with kids like that."

"They're just kids, Ron."

There was a shift in the bed, and she saw his shadow coming closer.

"What did you say you were tutoring them in?"

"Art History and Decorating."

"Hmmm . . . Not interested. What else do you teach?"

He was touching her leg.

The beach dried up. She watched as the windmill flapped its sails off into the blue sky.

She turned toward Ron.

One sultry Tuesday in September, Alexis got out of the taxi and walked into Brian House. She nodded at the receptionist.

"Hello, Dara."

"Oh, hi, Mrs. Donleavy," the young woman said casually.

As Alexis made her way to her classroom, a group of kids passed her. She knew all of their faces now, nearly all of their clothes, and most of their names. A

few waved. As she turned the final corner, she saw
Steven Wheelhouse coming from the rec room.

"Mrs. Donleavy! How's it going?"

She paused.

"We're doing the Renaissance now."

"I envy you." He smiled at her. "Well, your class
seems to be a big hit. The kids say they're getting a lot
out of it."

"Do they?"

"Yes. Enjoy the Renaissance." He waved and went
on.

Alexis entered the classroom and sat down on the
mismatched sofa. She thought about what Steven
Wheelhouse had said. Had he been lying to be polite,
or was it possible that he didn't know? The class was
not a big hit. The class was a disaster.

The frustrating thing was that she didn't know why.
She had been trying for nearly two months now—week
after week she gave her little presentations, and the
kids sat still and listened. But somehow nothing got
sparked. True, Linda was interested, but that was due
more to her own character than to anything Alexis was
giving her. The others were completely unmoved.

Alexis stood up impatiently and walked around the
room. She remembered the first time she had ever seen
Brian House. She thought about the passion and rapture on the kids' faces as they had attacked the taxi,
and the way she had felt, watching them. She had been
so sure that—how pompous it sounded—she had some
kind of mission here. It was curious that she could have
been so wrong.

Alexis could hear laughter coming down the hall—

Tamara and Greg. But the moment they opened the door and saw Alexis, they wrapped themselves in the usual sullen silence.

"Hi, Greg. Hi, Tamara."

They mumbled hellos, and sat down.

"Did you have a good week?"

Again, shrugs and monosyllables.

Alexis was starting to open her Janson's *History of Art*. Then, swamped by the pointlessness of it all, she let her hand drop. The book closed sharply.

She had no more to say.

She stared blankly at the kids. They looked at her. A full minute passed in silence.

At last, Alexis straightened. She looked at Greg.

"Your braids are crooked," she said.

He grinned.

"Oh, yeah? I suppose you could do better?"

"As a matter of fact, yes," Alexis returned. "I could do it a whole lot better."

"No white lady could do it a whole lot better!" Tamara challenged.

"This one can!"

Linda fluttered in then, and soon the three kids were excited, giggling, heated by the spectacle of Alexis doing Greg's hair.

Expertly, she untwisted the first braid and began to reseparate it into strands. But after a few twists, she faltered and suddenly stopped. The kids looked at her curiously. Alexis put her hands in front of her face and turned away.

"What's the matter?" Greg asked, looking up, his hair wild.

Alexis did not answer for a long time.

"It's just"—her voice shook—"it's just—I haven't braided anyone's hair since—my daughter died."

They stared at her in silence.

"I didn't know you had a daughter," Greg said at last.

"How did she die?"

"In an accident."

"How old was she?"

"Six. Her name was Elise."

They did not ask her more, did not say anything as she began to weep—but Linda came over, then Greg, then Tamara, and they each put a hand, one after the other, on Alexis's shoulder. The hands remained until the weeping stopped.

"I'm sorry about that," Alexis said.

But the kids were smiling at her in a way they had never smiled before.

"That's okay," Linda told her.

Greg reached over and gently put the *History of Art* back on Alexis's lap.

The following week, the whole atmosphere was different. The kids were there on time. And they had done their reading.

One Tuesday in early November, Alexis arrived early, carrying three totebags. When she got to the classroom, she went to work. She separated the sofa into its three original components, moved the coffee table from the corner of the room into the center, and arranged the sections of the couch around it. She took down the filthy curtains and stuffed them into her bag to be washed later at home. She pushed the filing cabinet into the corner where the coffee table had been, placed a rag rug on the floor and some geraniums on the desktop. Then finally, she brought out some Kilim cushions and arranged them on the sofa sections.

The bell rang and the kids came in.

"Oh, my God!" they shrieked, running around to look at the room.

Alexis tried not to show how pleased she felt.

The following week, as she was walking in, Steven Wheelhouse came out of his office.

"I understand you've been doing some decorating," he told her.

She raised an eyebrow. "And I won't even charge you."

When the kids came in to class, she had a big box waiting for them.

"What's that?"

She took it out of its casing. It was an empty bulletin board.

"This is a Board of Beauty," she explained, holding it up. "We're going to use it for anything we find beautiful or inspiring—art postcards, special photographs, pictures from magazines."

"Bugs?" Greg asked hopefully.

"A Board of Beauty." Dreamily, Linda repeated the words.

That week, to start the Board of Beauty off, Alexis went to the Modern Art Museum and the Public

Library. Since Tamara showed an interest in African art, she searched out a postcard of the African masks which had inspired Picasso. For Greg, she copied the book jacket of *Maus,* Art Spiegelman's graphic novel about the Holocaust. And for Linda, who loved tiny things, she brought in an art card of a Nicholas Hilliard miniature on vellum.

She tacked the items to the board before the kids arrived.

When they came in, they went over immediately, inspecting everything with cries of delight.

What pleased Alexis even more was that they had brought items of their own.

Tamara's fifteenth birthday was at the end of November, and Alexis planned on bringing cupcakes to school to celebrate the occasion. In the morning before her class, she went into a small antique shop on Second Avenue, looking for chairs for the Martins' dining room— and there she saw, propped on a table, a dusty doll in its original cardboard case. She went over to look at it. It was Oriental Barbie.

"How much is this?" she asked the store owner.

"A hundred dollars," she was told.

A hundred dollars was insane. She put the Barbie back and looked around the store a few moments more. Then she came back to the Barbie and picked it up again.

"How much is it to a decorator?"

"A hundred dollars," came the laconic answer.

Alexis sighed. "All right; I'll take it."

That afternoon, when Tamara came in to class, Alexis handed her a wrapped package.

"Happy Birthday."

Tamara opened the gift. When she saw what it was, she said nothing, but her hands trembled as she took the Barbie out.

Christmas was coming. Alexis was not particularly looking forward to the holidays; she always found herself fatigued and depressed around this time of year. Still, she did her best to be festive—she decided to use an all-white scheme in her Christmas decorating, and her apartment shimmered subtly with white linen stockings, a tree covered in antique white wooden ornaments, and silver dishes filled with all-white candy canes, imported from France.

One Tuesday in the middle of December, she came into Brian House to find the place awash with holiday spirit—the walls were covered in paper snowflakes, "Merry Christmas" and "Happy Chanukah" had been written in removable crayon on all the upper windowed portions of the classroom doors, the bulletin boards were covered in tinsel and holly, and a large tree, filled with homemade yarn and paper decorations, graced the reception area.

"The place looks wonderful," she told the kids when they came in for class.

"Did you see the cotton ball snow scene on the board by the Art Room?" Tamara asked proudly. "That was me."

"It was very nice," Alexis assured her. "What happens here at Christmas? Do you do anything special—caroling, parties?"

Greg shrugged. "Not really. We get a week off from school, but that's about it."

"Some of the kids are going home, but most people are just staying here."

"What about you?"

Tamara, Greg, and Linda said they would all be remaining at Brian House.

There was a pause.

"What are you going to do?" Linda asked finally.

Alexis hesitated a moment, not wanting to tell them about the cruise that she and Ron were going to take.

"Nothing too wonderful," she said lightly. "I'm going to visit my stepmother in Florida for a few days, then my husband and I are taking a little trip."

"Where?" Tamara demanded.

"The Bahamas," Alexis tried to say it casually.

All the kids gasped.

"That's the first place I want to go when I'm a flight attendant," Tamara told her.

They were all beaming at Alexis, thrilled by the thought of her holiday.

The following Tuesday, instead of having class, Alexis gave a surprise Christmas party for the kids. She went to Zabar's and bought bagels and cream cheese spreads and pasta salad and fruit juice. And for dessert, there were cupcakes and gingerbread cookies and a Kugelhof.

After they ate, she told the kids a story—O. Henry's *The Gift of the Magi*—and then they all sang Christmas carols.

"And here's a little something from Santa," Alexis said finally. She had filled a stocking for each of them—Tamara got tortoiseshell barrettes, rainbow mittens, and a makeup case; Greg had a selection of comic books, plastic spiders, and a pen and pencil set; and Linda got an origami kit and a black velvet hat.

"We have something for you, too," Tamara said triumphantly. It was a big bright card, signed by the three of them.

"It's beautiful," Alexis said. "I'll put it on my mantel, in the place of honor."

The card did indeed make a statement in the all-white room.

Alexis sent each of the kids a postcard from her trip to Florida and the Bahamas. And when she came back to Brian House at the beginning of January, she found that her postcards had all been tacked carefully onto the Board of Beauty.

The winter went on. The Board of Beauty had now become three Boards of Beauty, and the kids had reached Japanese art.

One Tuesday in February, Linda came in with something for the latest bulletin board. It was a pen and ink sketch of a heavy Byzantine bracelet.

"I saw it in a fashion magazine," she told Alexis, "and I thought it was so beautiful. I couldn't get the original," she apologized. "It was Nicole's magazine, and she wouldn't let me cut it up."

"Yes," Alexis said, "but where did you get this drawing?"

"Oh, I did it," Linda told her.

Alexis was startled, then pleased. The drawing was surprisingly good.

She told Ron about it at dinner.

"Her use of line was completely off balance, of course, but the way she inlaid the amber was quite amazing."

"She probably traced it," he said.

Alexis clenched at her fork.

"She didn't trace it."

"No, maybe not. But Alexis, don't lose perspective about these kids. "

"I beg your pardon," she said coldly.

"They're becoming much too important to you. You probably don't even realize it, but you talk about them constantly."

"I certainly don't."

"Yes, you do. 'What's her name' made this wonderful comment," he mimicked her, 'Gary was so funny in class today—' "

"His name is Greg, Ron."

He dismissed it. "Alexis, all I'm saying is that these aren't your kids."

The following Tuesday, Alexis arrived at Brian House to find her classroom empty. She waited fifteen minutes and was just about to leave, when Linda came breathlessly in.

"Oh, Mrs. Donleavy," she said, "Greg has a dentist appointment, and Tamara's on punishment, so they can't come today."

"Well," Alexis told Linda, "there's no point in having a class for one."

"Oh, please, Mrs. Donleavy," she begged. "Please."

"I'm afraid not," Alexis said. "We were going to start on the Impressionists today. I don't want to have to repeat the information for the others."

The girl slumped. She bit her lip, nodded, and looked away.

Alexis sighed. "Wait here a moment," she said, and left the room.

She walked down the hall to Steven Wheelhouse's office.

"Yes?" he called at her knock.

She opened the door.

"Ah, Mrs. Donleavy—how's it going?"

"Not terribly well," Alexis told him. "I arrived here today to find only one of my students able to attend class. In the future, if things like this come up, I wish you'd let me know in advance."

He was abashed, as she had meant him to be.

"Anyway," she went on, "since class isn't going to happen, I was wondering if I could have Linda for the afternoon."

Steven Wheelhouse was instantly alert.

"Why?"

"I want to take her to the Metropolitan Museum."

She could see Steven Wheelhouse's discomfort with the idea.

"Why do you need to do that?"

"I don't need to," Alexis told him, "but I think, as we're starting the Impressionists, it would be beneficial."

"Isn't this something that the whole class should go to?"

"If you'll remember, the whole class isn't here today," Alexis informed him. "I don't have the time next week, and I think Linda would get a great deal out of it."

"We usually don't let the kids go anywhere without a family member or someone from the staff as supervisor," he told her.

"I'll take full responsibility," Alexis assured him, "and I'll have her back no later than five."

"Well—I suppose it'll be all right," he said at last. And then added, with a half smile, "Have a good time."

Alexis's satisfaction at having gained her way lost some momentum as she made her way back to the classroom. She began thoroughly to regret her reckless impulse. Why on earth had she done it? Sheer ego, she decided. Because it had pleased her that Linda had been desolate at being told there would be no class today.

And what had she let herself in for? It would be an awkward few hours at best, trying to entertain a shy teenage girl.

She went back into the classroom and told Linda to get her coat—that she was taking her to the Metropolitan Museum of Art.

Linda clasped her hands together. And under her white makeup, she became even whiter.

Linda had never been to the museum before. She wanted to see everything, but Alexis insisted that they concentrate on the Impressionist wing. Linda moved slowly from painting to painting, her breathing shallow and intense.

"The water!" she whispered when they got to Monet's "Terrace at the Seaside, Sainte-Adresse." "You get seasick looking at the waves!"

She laughed at Degas's "Singer in Green," saying she looked like Charlotte from Brian House. And she lingered a long time before Renoir's "View of the Seacoast near Wargemont."

"I'd love to live in a place like that," she said. "In that little cottage there. Being by the sea. Having no one around."

Then, when she got to Van Gogh's "Cypresses," she gave a shocked little cry.

Alexis smiled. The "Cypresses" was one of the art postcards on their bulletin board, and she knew it was Linda's favorite.

When Linda looked up at her, Alexis was amazed to see that the girl's eyes were full of tears.

"Here it really is," she said.

As they walked back down the marble stairs, Alexis saw a couple remarking on them with amusement. Alexis supposed they did look odd, the perfectly groomed society woman with the punk-haired Kabuki-faced teenage girl.

"Well," Alexis said, "I don't know about you, but I would love a cup of tea."

A wary look came into the Linda's eyes—as if she suspected she was being set up for a trap.

"Don't worry," Alexis said. "You won't get into any trouble. I'll take full responsibility."

They ate at the museum cafeteria. Linda got a yogurt and, after nervously glancing at Alexis, some coffee.

"We're not really allowed to have caffeine," she admitted.

"Then you shouldn't have ordered it," Alexis said. "But I won't tell on you."

They found a table and sat down.

Alexis felt suddenly uneasy, now that there were no longer any paintings to talk about, but Linda did not seem to notice any awkwardness. She was looking around the room, scrutinizing the women's clothes, the decor, even the different meals, as minutely as she had gone over the Impressionists.

Then she turned to Alexis, smiling calmly and brightly.

"I'd like to work here one day. Buying paintings for the museum."

"You need to go to school for that."

Linda nodded vigorously.

"Oh, as soon as I get out of Brian House, I'm going to go to college. My cousin in New Jersey says I can live with her, and there's this dress shop I think I can get a job at."

"That sounds like a good start."

Linda looked embarrassedly at her empty yogurt container.

"What I'd really like," she blurted out in her shy, butterflying voice, "is to be like you."

"Why?" Alexis asked.

Linda looked up.

"It seems like nothing could ever go wrong in your life."

Alexis, taken aback, smiled.

"Well—how splendid to appear like that," she said lightly.

"Are you married?"

"Yes."

"What's your husband like?"

It had been a long time since anyone had asked Alexis to describe Ron.

"He's very bright," she said at last. "And we've been married for many years. Not that one necessarily has to do with the other."

Linda did not smile at the little joke.

"How many years?" she asked.

"Eighteen."

Linda nodded. Alexis could tell she liked that answer.

"I have a boyfriend," Linda told her suddenly, proudly.

Alexis was surprised. Linda, with her mannered delicacy, her androgynous clothes, and mask-like makeup, had seemed an almost asexual creature.

"Oh, really?" she said.

"Yes. He's at Brian House, too. Maybe you've seen him—Raoul?"

Again a surprise. Into Alexis's mind came the image of a boy—the boy in the gangster hat who had been playing the pinball machine so skillfully, the first day she had come to Brian House.

"Yes," she said. "I know which one he is."

Eagerly, Linda leaned forward.

"What did you think of him?"

"You would know best," Alexis answered carefully. Linda nodded.

"He seems tough, but he's not—not really."

How many times, since the beginning of the world, Alexis wondered, had that same sentence been repeated? How many delicate dreamy girls had found these secret depths that were or weren't there, in the men they loved?

"Do you two spend much time together?"

"Oh, no," Linda said. "We're on separation."

"Separation?"

"Yes. If Mr. Wheelhouse knows a boy and girl like each other, he separates them. We've been on separation for a month now. But we write notes," she added dreamily. "Our roommates pass them on. Mr. Wheelhouse doesn't know about those."

Then there was a sudden anxious look.

"Don't worry," Alexis said. "I won't tell about the notes. But I still don't understand," she added. "Aren't you allowed to talk? See each other at all?"

Linda shook her head.

"Yesterday, Raoul got caught smiling at me in class, and his privileges got taken away for two weeks."

Alexis's voice rose. "But that's ridiculous."

Into her mind came crashing the memory of Wellesley, Jimmy Craig, and herself at eighteen. The longing to be with the boy she loved. The secrecy, the night in her dormitory room. The shrilling of the fire alarm. She hadn't thought of that in years, but now it was more painful than she could believe. She did not trust herself to speak.

She took Linda into the museum book shop. A new book on Biedermeyer had recently come out, and

Alexis wanted to look at it. Linda stood quietly by while Alexis browsed. She did not look through any books on her own.

Afterward, they went into the gift shop. Here Linda came alive. She walked around reverently, tentatively touching scarves, postcards, sculptures.

In the jewelry case was a small gold-plated ring, a reproduction of one from the Cheops Dynasty. When Linda saw it, she stopped, drew in a breath, looked at it intently.

Alexis spoke to the salesman.

"We'd like to see this ring, please."

She had Linda try it on. The wide gold looked very pretty on the pale, narrow finger. Linda's hand trembled. Her eyes were dull with longing as she gazed at the ring.

"We'll take it," Alexis said.

Linda stared at her. Then she reached over with a little gasp and hugged Alexis hard around the neck. Alexis found herself near tears.

Eight

The June sky was sullen, and an occasional spray of rain spat down upon the event below. Alexis sat with the other graduates on the dais, damp in her black robes. She could see her family beneath, sitting in the first row of white wooden chairs. Her father was glancing at his watch; he had to be back in New York at four o'clock for a business meeting. Sylvia, discreet in beige, listened intently to the words of the college president. Grandmother sat at the end of the row, holding her silver-topped cane. Her eyes did not leave Alexis.

"And now it is my pleasure to present the graduating class."

The college president took up the list of names. Another shot of rain came down, and she read rapidly.

"Michele Janine Aarons." A freckled girl Alexis didn't know came forward, took the diploma, and was applauded.

"Barbara Stephanie Akron." A friend of Alexis's

from chemistry class rushed up and claimed her diploma.

Alexis tensed.

"Alexa Elizabeth Avery," the president intoned.

Alexa! Alexis's ears roared with embarrassment. Quickly, she rose, walked toward the podium, snatched the diploma, and raced back to her seat.

Her family came over the moment that the ceremony was finished.

"Oh, honey, we're so proud of you!" Sylvia told her.

"Yes, Alexa." Her father seemed to think it was some great joke.

Friends did, too. "Congratulations, Alexa."

Alexis laughed along with them, but it nonetheless was eerie. It was as if someone else had graduated from Wellesley, a stranger in her skin.

"Are you ready to go?" Grandmother asked.

"Yes." Her father carried the final suitcase from the empty dorm room. Alexis got into the limousine, and the car drove away.

She stood by her bedroom window that evening, staring out at the night. There was a tap at her door, and her father came in.

"I see you're all unpacked."

"I didn't have that much."

He sat down on the chair by the bed.

"So—no more school. How does it feel?"

"It's strange. I keep thinking I have art history class tomorrow."

"You'll get used to it." He smiled at her. "Any ideas on what comes next?"

She shook her head. "Nothing specific. Keep on with my painting. Maybe work at a gallery. I guess I should try for design school, but not right away."

"Do you have any plans for the summer?"

"No. Nothing at all."

He put his hands carefully together.

"Well, what do you think of this? Your grandmother and Sylvia and I have talked it over, and we'd like to send you to Europe for a few months as a graduation present."

"Oh, Daddy!" Alexis began to cry.

Art galleries. Museums. Ruined castles. And for three months, not having to wonder what she was going to do with the rest of her life.

She hugged and kissed her father. "Thank you! Thank you!"

"Your grandmother has one stipulation, though," her father told her. "She wants your cousin Daphne to come with you."

Alexis pulled back and made a face. "Daphne? Why her? We can't stand each other."

Her father laughed. "I know. But she's free this summer, and Grandmother doesn't want you going alone. You'll see; you two girls will have a great time. Okay?"

"Okay."

He squeezed her hand. "In the morning, we'll get you a passport."

Alexis sat down on her bed and sighed. *We'll get you a passport.* Surely the most romantic words ever spoken.

* * *

Alexis soon had the itinerary memorized. Start off in London. That meant the National Gallery, the Tate, and the Victoria and Albert Museum. Then the tour through England. That meant Jane Austen's house, Thomas Hardy country, and if Daphne was willing, a visit to Beatrix Potter's Lakeland. Then Paris, with the Louvre—Alexis guessed Daphne might want to see a few shops as well—then the south of France, with Renoir's house and the Picasso Museum. And then Rome! Florence! Germany!

It was all so wonderful—her eyes jumped from city to city on the itinerary. She didn't know which she was looking forward to most.

Possibly Florence, because of the "Birth of Venus"—or Paris, because of the Cluny Tapestries. But Paris was also where—Alexis straightened. No, she didn't want to think about that. And there was no reason to. All during the planning of the trip, Maggie's name had not even been mentioned.

Flight 12 to London was now boarding.

"Alexis, hurry! They're calling our section!" Daphne jumped up from her chair in the waiting area and clutched at her four carry-on bags.

"We'll be there in just a minute," Henry Avery told her. He took Alexis by the arm and walked with her to a quieter corner of the boarding lounge.

"I've got something for you," he said.

"Dramamine," Alexis guessed. She loved to tease her father for being a walking pharmaceutical.

"Actually, no." He pulled out a piece of paper from his pocket.

"This is your mother's address in Paris," he said diffidently. "Just in case you want it."

Alexis stiffened.

"I don't need it," she told him.

"Take it anyway. You never know."

She put the paper in her purse without looking at it.

Daphne was making huge gestures across the lounge.

"I think Daphne's on the verge of exploding," he told Alexis. "Have a safe trip, sweetheart. Call us."

She kissed him and got on the plane.

Paris in the rain made Alexis ache. The triumphant spires of churches, the solid cluster of hotels and shops were hidden by cloud. All that was left was a mean world of ground floors, dark cobbles, and the harsh drops on the hotel room window.

Alexis sat on her bed, staring at a book she was not reading.

"Alexis!"

"Yes?"

Daphne sat cross-legged on her bed, holding a French newspaper. She tapped it excitedly.

"Does *soldes* mean 'sale'?"

"I think so."

"Well, then, Printemps is having a shoe sale this afternoon. What are we waiting for?"

Alexis sighed. "Daphne, it's raining. And we went shopping all day yesterday."

Daphne looked affronted. "Well, we spent all Tuesday in the Louvre!"

"I know," Alexis told her hastily.

She did not want to get into another of these discussions. Throughout their three weeks in England, Daphne seemed to have an invisible chart in her head on which she listed all of the activities that were for Alexis, versus all the activities that were for herself. If the balance dipped even briefly in Alexis's favor, there was trouble.

"I'll tell you what," Alexis said. "I'm feeling a little tired, and I'd rather stay here. But why don't you go to the sale without me?"

"Oh, I couldn't," Daphne told her unconvincingly.

"Honestly. I want you to. Just be back by six. Maybe we'll have dinner in that little bistro again."

Daphne frowned. "Are you sure you'll be all right?"

Alexis laughed. "For three hours?"

"OK. Well, I'll see you later."

Daphne grabbed her raincoat and purse, and was gone.

Alexis sat in the stillness for a long moment. She went over to the window and gazed down at the charcoal streets below her. It was a strange sort of magic that Paris had. A disruptive, dark magic. She wasn't sure she entirely liked this city. She doubted it would be an easy place to live in. But—some people chose to do it.

Alexis found herself glancing over at her purse; deliberately, she glanced away. She walked away from the window and hung up a skirt and sweater. She tidied the desk. She tidied the bathroom counter. Then she went over to her purse, opened it, and slowly took out the folded piece of paper that her father had given her.

"Cent vingt-et-un, rue de Fontan," she told the taxi driver. He did not comment, did not say she should not go there. They passed through the rainy streets and finally arrived in front of a town house. It was different from the neighboring houses because its door had been painted a bright green. Alexis paid the driver and watched him pull away.

She stood in front of the door. She reached up and touched the smooth wood. On the count of three, she would knock. One, two, three. She knocked.

After a long moment, the door was opened by a tall man in a cream-colored linen coat. Alexis had taken two years of French in college, but they fled from her now.

"Bon après-midi," she faltered. *"Je pense*—I wonder—is this Maggie Royal's house?"

The man looked surprised, suspicious.

"Yes," he said in heavily accented English.

"Is she—at home?"

"No, Mademoiselle."

Relief and disappointment ran through Alexis in mingled streams.

"Will she be back soon, do you think?"

"Oui, Mademoiselle."

"May I—wait for her?"

"Does she expect you?"

"No," Alexis said. "She doesn't. It's sort of a surprise. I'm—a relative. I think she'll want to see me."

The butler seemed uncertain as to what to do. Finally, he moved aside and let Alexis enter.

"Will you please come to the drawing room," he asked her.

Alexis entered. The smell was what she noticed first—the smell of Maggie's perfume. The room smelled as her bedroom had, smelled as her pink satin quilt had, smelled as her nightgown had. Alexis found she couldn't breathe.

The butler was regarding her curiously.

"Can I get anything for you, Mademoiselle?"

"No, thank you."

He left the room.

Alexis walked slowly around. The room was gay and beautiful and filled with yellow. She went around slowly, touching the silk of a pillow, the polished curve of the sofa.

She paused before a table covered with framed photographs. There were professional stills of Maggie, candids of her at various ages. There were pictures taken in foreign locales Alexis could not identify, groups of laughing people she did not recognize, and many pictures of Philip Fredericks.

Alexis turned from the table abruptly. She felt suddenly uneasy in the room. Coming here had been a ridiculous idea—what on earth had she been thinking? Had she secretly imagined that, like the smell in the house, everything would be the same as it had been fifteen years before? How incredibly stupid. This was a room that belonged to a woman she no longer knew—a happy, successful woman who had a life Alexis did not share. A life filled with a lover and smiling friends, and memories of a past Alexis had not been part of.

And just suppose Maggie *were* to come in now—what then? She would be as unfamiliar as her room. After this many years, what could she and Alexis possibly have to say to each other? They would be strangers.

Alexis turned to go. And as she did, she saw, across the room in the bookcase, a framed photo of herself, taken when she was six years old. The shock of seeing it made her cry out. She hurried out of the drawing room and back into the hallway.

The butler was there. She guessed he had been keeping an eye on her during her entire visit.

"I've changed my mind," she said. "I've decided not to wait."

"Very well, Mademoiselle. Whom shall I say has called?"

"Please don't say anything," she told him. Then she stopped. "No. Just tell Miss Royal a fan of hers dropped by."

Alexis left the house and took a walk around the block. The rain was lighter now. She crossed the street to a park and sat down at an iron bench. She watched a young mother and her little girl, around six years old, going past. The child let go of her mother's hand and began to chase a pigeon. She tripped on a twig, and fell hard on the ground. She wailed loudly, holding up a grazed hand. The mother ran to her and held her, rocked her, murmured to her, until the crying stopped.

Alexis's eyes narrowed. She looked once more at

the house with the green door. Then she got up and walked away.

"Well, I'm broke for the next year!" Daphne crashed happily into the room, holding up her four bags of loot. "But it was worth it. I'm glad you didn't come, though; it was unbelievably crowded." She became aware of Alexis's silence. "You okay?"

"Sure," Alexis said.

"What did you do?"

"Just stayed in the room and read."

"You still want to go to that bistro?"

"That would be fine."

"Unless," Daphne paused, "you'd rather go to this cabaret. Someone on the street gave me a flier for it." She pulled the paper from her purse. "It looks kind of decadent," she said, pleased.

"Whatever you want."

They ended up at the cabaret. The place was small and dark and not particularly atmospheric.

Daphne was dismayed. "We could have done better in the West Village!"

But they ordered drinks and watched the band. Alexis rapidly drank three glasses of wine.

"Alexis! What are you doing?"

Alexis shrugged.

"You'll get sick—it's awful wine."

The green door seemed to shimmer and stretch, like an image seen underwater.

"I need some air," Alexis told Daphne. "I'll be right back."

* * *

As she made her way toward the door, she passed a table where a dark young man was sitting alone. He smiled, lifted his hand, and beckoned. Alexis paused for a moment, then found herself walking over.

"Vous êtes anglaise? English?"

"American."

"Ah, yes, American. You make vacation?"

"In a way."

"Lovely."

Alexis remembered the young men at the Wellesley dance, with their scrupulously clean shirts and conspicuously combed hair. This man looked nothing like that. He was in his late twenties, tousled, with deep lines in his forehead. The scarf knotted around his neck was a bleached blue, like his eyes. His voice was soft. She could feel a small ripple in her body.

"Sit down," he told her.

She sat.

"Comment—what are you called?"

She paused.

"Alexa."

"Alexa." He said it lingeringly, in a way that made Alexa into an exotic dancer or an exiled princess.

"And I am Armand. Armand, Alexa. They sound the same. Well, Alexa, you would like to dance with me?"

"All right."

They stood up. He took her to the dance floor. "Guantanamera" was playing. It wailed, full of longing. Tears came into Alexis's eyes. Armand put his arms around her. His hands grasped her hips, stroked up and down her sides. She did not stop him. They danced.

She could see Daphne staring at her from the table, mouth stunned open. Alexis looked away.

"Are you enjoying your time?"

Her head felt very heavy. She put it on his shoulder.

"No," she whispered.

"You don't like Paris?"

"It's made me sad."

He held her more closely.

"Come back with me for a little," he told her. "You would not be sad with me."

"I couldn't," she said.

"Why not? For a few hours."

"I guess I could for a few hours."

"Guantanamera" ended. Alexis went unsteadily back to her own table.

"Well!" said Daphne.

Alexis reached for her purse. "I'm going to be out a little while longer. Here's some money for the check."

"What are you talking about?" Daphne turned red. "You can't just leave!"

"I'm sorry," Alexis told her. "Go on back to the hotel. Go to sleep. I'll be back a little later. I promise. Don't worry."

Daphne half stood up. "Alexis, this is ridiculous. You can't do this. Look, they're bringing our food!"

Alexis hurried away from her.

They drove to Armand's apartment in the 18th Arrondissement. Alexis had never been on a motorcycle before. It made her dizzy, so she kept her eyes down and watched the splash of streetlights on the still-wet cobblestones. Her arms were around Armand, and she could feel the rise of his muscles as he drove.

His apartment was small and untidy, flooded with clothes and magazines, empty bottles and filled ash-trays.

"Viens dans mes bras que je te caline."

He held out his arms to her.

"I've never done—anything like this."

He said nothing, just kept holding out his arms.

Alexis woke up the next morning in the unmade bed that smelled of him, and of them.

She stared around the room. Oh, God. What had happened? It wasn't her. It hadn't been her.

Armand stretched, woke. She shook him.

"I've got to go back," she said. "Daphne's going to kill me."

"Then why go back?" he asked her, playing with her hair and pulling her toward him.

"At least I've got to call."

She called the hotel.

"I want to leave a message for Daphne Marshall in Room 404," she said. "You don't need to connect me. Just tell her that Alexis is fine. Do you have that? Alexis is fine—and she'll be back later."

She hung up the phone. Armand was smiling at her.

"Alexis, or Alexa?"

"Alexa," she said, and went back into his arms.

*   *   *

He fixed brunch for her, an omelet with chives. She asked him if he wanted her to make the bed and tidy up, but he said not to bother. She pretended she lived here with him. She looked out the window at their motorcycle, looked at the view of their street.

"What do you do?" she asked him.

"I work with cars. A mechanic. And you?"

"I don't know yet. I have no work."

To say that frightened her; she went on quickly. "That's one reason I'm here. In Europe. To help me decide what I want to do."

He laughed. "You American girls, always the need to know."

It depressed her, being just another American girl who needed to know.

"I'd better get back to the hotel," she said.

"Where are you staying?"

"Hotel de l'Université."

He whistled.

"Oh, rich, rich."

The wall of stereotypes rose.

He came over and rubbed her shoulder.

"I'm kidding with you," he said. "How much longer will you be in Paris?"

"A few more days."

"Will we see each other again?"

She knew they could not. She would never let herself be that person again.

"Armand," she said slowly, "before I go back, would you show me something?"

"What is that?"

"I don't know. You decide. Something special in Paris."

* * *

He took her to the Musée Grevin, a small wax museum housed in a red-velvet candy box of a building.

"I learned all my history from this place," he told her.

But the rooms were populated by the figures of people Alexis had never heard of. It gave her an eerie feeling; they were unfamiliar, she was unfamiliar; they had died, she would die.

The air felt tight around her; she needed to get out.

"Let me take you back to your hotel," he said when they were back on the street.

"No, no," she told him. "There's a taxi stand right over here. I'll be fine."

She did not want him at the hotel.

He kissed her good-bye, curiously formal.

"Au revoir, Mademoiselle," he said. *"Merci encore pour le plaisir de votre compagnie."*

Alexis arrived back at the hotel. She felt grimy, in need of a bath and cool white sheets. She took the elevator upstairs and went down the hall. She started to insert her key in the lock of her room, when the door was flung open, the key knocked away. Daphne, breathing hard, stood inside.

"So you've finally decided to show up," she said.

"I'm sorry," Alexis told her. "I called and left a message."

Harshly, Daphne laughed.

"How thoughtful—but you were about twelve hours too late. How could you?!" she burst out. "I was worried sick; you go off with a total stranger—he could have been a psychopath! You didn't say where you were going, I didn't have a clue where you were. I've been sitting on this bed waiting for you to come back since ten o'clock last night!" She put her hands in front of her face.

Alexis moved to her.

"Oh, Daphne, I'm sorry. It was terrible of me; I have no excuse. I just—I guess I was pretty drunk. But everything's okay, really. And I promise you, it'll never happen again."

Another laugh.

"You bet it won't."

A little pulse of dread.

"What do you mean?"

"You'd better call your father. He's waiting to talk to you."

Alexis sat down on the bed.

"Oh, Daphne! You did n't tell him!"

"What else was I supposed to do?" Daphne hissed. "You never came home."

Alexis made the call. When it was over, she hung up the receiver.

"The rest of my trip's been canceled," she said flatly. "I'm going back tomorrow."

"I'm sorry," Daphne said. "I'm going to stay on." She walked away from Alexis, and then turned back. "I think what's upset everyone the most is that it was just the sort of thing your mother would have done."

*   *   *

The following day, Alexis made her way down the aisle of the airplane and found her seat. Mechanically, she stowed her carry-on bag in the overhead compartment, sat down, and took the thin blanket out of its plastic case. She wrapped herself in it and closed her eyes. She pretended that she was in a little beach hut somewhere, maybe the Caribbean. The sun was soothing, the sand forgiving, and nobody was angry at her.

She felt a sudden jar. Someone was sitting down beside her, a sandy-haired young man wearing glasses and a business suit.

"Sorry for disturbing you," he said, "but I think take-off would have done it anyway."

"That's all right," she said. "The thing is, I'm not feeling very well. Maybe you should try to get another seat. So that I won't infect you."

"I never get sick," he told her comfortably.

After they were airborne, he turned to her again.

"I always feel better after take-off. They say that once you're past the first three minutes, you're okay until landing. Unless of course there's some guy with a bomb aboard."

"I'd like that."

He laughed. "What?"

"Never mind."

"No—tell me. I'm interested. Why do you want there to be a bomb?"

Alexis looked at him. It was appealing. A person you met for only a few hours, someone that you could tell everything to, and then never have to see again.

So she told him. Told him about the trip to Europe

and the night with Armand, and about being sent home. She did not tell him about going into the house with the green door.

"And I don't really even know why I did it," she finished. "That was the strange thing. It was as if some other person was hidden in me. It wasn't like me at all."

"What is like you?"

"It depends. But not that."

He extended his hand. "I'm Ron Donleavy, by the way."

"Alexis Avery."

He was startled.

"Henry Avery's daughter?"

"Yes."

"I know your father—we've been in on a few deals together. He's a good guy."

"Yes, he is."

"And he's pretty sophisticated. I'm sure he'll be able to understand what Paris can do to a young girl."

Alexis looked carefully at Ron. There was a relaxed competence about him that was attractive, an easy sense of taking charge.

"Is New York home for you?" she asked.

"Since I was sixteen. I grew up in the Midwest."

Alexis smiled. "When I was little, I always wanted to live in the Midwest. Have a farm all to myself."

"And what's the dream now?"

The way he was looking at her made her feel suddenly self-conscious.

The plane had started its descent. Inexorably, the lights of New York came closer. Alexis's hands were so cold that it hurt them to touch anything. She pulled the blanket tightly around her, and pushed her head into the tiny square of pillow. The plane touched ground, came to a stop. Passengers were rising, collecting their hand luggage. It was time to get off.

"Oh, God, this is it," Alexis said. She turned to Ron. "Well, thank you for listening to me. You made the trip much more bearable."

"I can't desert you now," he said. "Let me get you safely to the firing squad."

Her hands were too cold to open the overhead compartment. Ron opened it for her, and shouldered her carry-on bag. He 'helped her out of her seat and down the aisle of the plane.

Her father was waiting in the lounge, unsmiling. When Alexis saw him, her eyes filled with tears.

"Mr. Avery!" Ron came from behind her. "Ron Donleavy."

Henry turned to him in surprise. "Why, yes, of course."

They shook hands.

"I've had the pleasure of sitting by your very nervous daughter for the last six hours," Ron told him. "I've spent the entire trip assuring her that you couldn't possibly be any harder on her than she's been on herself. Please don't ruin my credibility, sir."

Henry said nothing.

"Well, good luck, Alexis."

Ron gave her back her carry-on bag, nodded at them both, and walked away.

Alexis turned to her father.

"Daddy, before you say anything—" she began.

Henry Avery patted her shoulder.

"We'll talk about it later," he told her. His voice was pale, remote.

The phone rang after dinner that evening. Alexis picked it up.

"Hello?"

It was Ron Donleavy.

"I just called to see how it went," he told her.

"It was grim. Pretty much what you'd expect."

"I'm sorry."

"But it seems to have blown itself out somewhat by now."

There was a pause.

"Would it be too soon to ask you to dinner?"

Alexis smiled. "No," she told him, "it wouldn't."

He took her to Lutèce for their first date. Their second date was to see a French film at the Plaza. Their third was a trip to the Frick, where Ron had never been, their fourth to a dinner at Le Ronde, their fifth to a football game. After that, Alexis lost count.

It was a clear, cold Saturday in December. Ron and Alexis were sitting at a café at Rockefeller Plaza, watching the skaters in the twilight.

Ron had seemed distracted throughout the evening. Now he was rolling his spoon relentlessly around in his coffee cup.

"Alexis," he began.

"Yes?"

"Well, you probably know what I'm about to ask you."

She did, but she wasn't going to let him off.

"I can't imagine."

"Well," he went on quickly, "we've been going out for six months now, and we haven't killed each other, not even once."

She smiled encouragingly.

"It seems to me we're a really good fit; I think we could be very happy together. What do you say we get married?"

This was the moment. This was the story she would be telling their children someday. Alexis knew that she must remember every detail—how the snow looked like a child's drawing, how the skaters swooped with such gallantry, how Ron took her hand.

"I think it's a great idea," she told him.

Her voice sounded strange to her own ears—it was friendly, but casual, lukewarm, as if getting married to Ron were no more important than arranging a doubles match at tennis. She tried again, this time with much more enthusiasm.

"Let's do it!"

He laughed and they became engaged.

Alexis came home to find her father, Grandmother, and Sylvia all watching television in the library. She stood in the doorway and smiled at them.

"I've got some news. Ron and I are getting married."

Grandmother, unsurprised, moved to kiss her.

"That's excellent, darling," she said mildly. "He's a very likable young man."

"Oh, Alexis," Sylvia said. "We couldn't be more delighted."

Henry Avery looked at her. "Are you sure?" he asked.

The two women laughed. "Oh, Henry, of course she's sure. We've all been sure."

"Then congratulations," he said to her.

That evening, Alexis heard her father's tap on her bedroom door. He came in and sat on the chair by her bed.

"So you're getting married."

"Pretty amazing, isn't it?"

"Well, you've certainly caused some excitement. Sylvia and your grandmother are already going through bridal magazines."

"Aren't you pleased, Daddy?"

He considered this. "Ron seems a good man. Very stable, predictable. He's got a solid future at his firm. Fathers like those qualities."

"But you don't?"

He was quiet for a long moment.

"Of course I do. But—you and I, Alexis—in many ways we're very traditional. But there's this—streak in both of us."

She looked away.

"I know."

"Do you think, in the long run, you'll be happy with Ron?"

"You're happy with Sylvia."

"Yes," he said. "Very happy. But I'm a lot older than you are."

She touched his hair affectionately. She found she was near tears.

"Daddy," she told him, "no one's older than I am."

The following week, Ron presented Alexis with a small black velvet box. She tensed as she opened it. It was another moment to remember, another moment to tell her children about. The ring was simple, tasteful, a diamond, of course. Alexis felt a small shock of disappointment. She wasn't sure what she had been hoping for, but somehow this wasn't it.

Alexis enjoyed planning the wedding. It was satisfying to draw up the guest list, and set a final date. It was fun to talk to caterers and discuss the pros and cons of beef teriyaki. She supervised every detail, from flowers to music to photography.

"Do you want candles in the church?" "Yes."

"Do you want Aunt Mildred to sing?" "No."

She was briefly flummoxed by the question of bridesmaids. She could not think of enough girls she really wanted. Finally, she chose Jacey, Sarah, another friend from college, and Ron's sister from Kansas City. She would have loved to have Emily from high school, but she had long since lost her address.

The day she got her wedding gown, she went into her father's study to model it for him.

"You're beautiful," he told her.

"Only three more weeks."

"You've done an incredible job."

"Thank you."

He rubbed the back of his neck.

"Alexis, have you thought about inviting your mother?"

Perspiration began to sting under the arms of the wedding dress.

"I don't think that would be appropriate," she said. "I haven't seen her in fifteen years."

"Still—shouldn't she be here for your wedding day?"

Her voice trembled.

"I don't see why. She wasn't here for any of the other days." She paused, took a breath. "I don't mean to sound harsh. It's just that she'd be a complete stranger—there's nothing between us anymore."

She thought of the day in Paris, in the yellow drawing room that smelled of Maggie.

He came over and patted her arm.

"Perhaps so, but she's still your mother."

"Sylvia's my mother now." But even as Alexis said it, it felt false.

He sighed. "Honey, you know how much Sylvia loves you. But no matter what you may tell yourself, you're still Maggie's daughter." More slowly, he added, "One day you've got to come to terms with that. It's important, Alexis. See her again."

She swallowed, nodded. "I will. One day. I promise. But not now. I'm just not up to it now. Can it wait till I'm older—till I'm nine?"

This had always been her query as a small child, when she wanted to put off a shot or a dentist appointment.

He smiled. "Sure it can. I just want this wedding to be perfect for you."

She gulped back tears. "It will be."

*   *   *

The morning of her wedding day, Alexis woke early with the awareness that she had been dreaming of her mother. She put the dream out of her mind.

The wedding was beautiful—everything she had wanted it to be.

Alexis and Ron were leaving on their honeymoon. The taxi was waiting to drive them to the airport.

Ron shook Henry's hand, kissed Sylvia and Mrs. Avery.

"Take care of our girl," Henry Avery said.

He hugged Alexis gently.

"Be very happy," he told her.

Nine

This was the part during which Paul, in all his celebrity interviews, grew oddly nostalgic. Nostalgic for a past and a place that he had never even seen.

He leaned forward, asked the question.

"What was it like— Hollywood, in the forties?"

Maggie smiled at him. With that question, she seemed to throw away all the sadness of the moments before.

"I'll never forget the moment my train pulled into Los Angeles," she told him. "I stepped down from the Super Chief, and there, hitting me over the head, coming from absolutely everywhere, was the scent of orange blossoms."

"Ah," Paul said. Time and again, he had heard about the orange blossoms.

Maggie's eyes were bright with remembering.

"You've seen all those dreary black-and-white pictures of old Hollywood. Well, forget them—that's not how it looked at all. It was the most enchanting place imaginable—the colors of Paradise—the sky, the flowers, I can't tell you. Oh, that magical aching green.

"And I found it a terribly exciting city. There was such a sense of possibility—and yet everything was very casual. In those days, back East, men never went out on the streets without wearing a coat and tie. But in Los Angeles, they walked around in their shirtsleeves."

She smiled. "And believe it or not, there weren't too many automobiles. We rode everywhere by streetcar."

Paul nodded. "The 'big red cars.' "

"Such a civilized way to travel."

"Did you ever go to Clifton's Pacific Seas? That was supposed to be incredible."

"It was utterly adorable. The food wasn't anything special—just your basic cafeteria food—but the restaurant was made to look like a tropical island. It had palm trees and hula girls and ice cream coming down from a volcano on a conveyor belt. And singing waiters, believe it or not. And if you couldn't pay, they still let you eat."

"Did you ever eat for free?"

Maggie stiffened. "Never," she said coldly.

Hastily, Paul changed the subject.

"And what about nightlife? Did you ever go to the Cocoanut Grove?"

She relaxed. "Only once—it cost a fortune. About a year after I came to Hollywood, a young actor who had a crush on me took me there. I didn't care anything about him, but I would have done anything to go to the Grove. It was just lovely—so elegant. Nothing like nightclubs nowadays. Jack Smith performed there that evening—I'll never forget it."

Then she shook her head.

"I just had a curious thought. You're a young man—you've got another—what?—fifty years to go. Yet no matter how long you live, you'll never see the things I've seen. And you know something?" she added with a challenging little smile, "I don't think I'd trade you."

"No," Paul said.

"When I got to Los Angeles, one of the first things I did was to take a tour of the movie stars' homes. Do people still do that?"

"Sure."

"But I bet it's a very different tour. In those days, people with money lived mainly in Hollywood, and only a few in Beverly Hills. Bel Air wasn't much, and Malibu was just a beach."

She tapped the sofa. "There was one house I'll never forget. It was a big pink mansion up in the Hollywood Hills. The lady in the seat next to me pointed it out. She said, 'Oh, isn't that lovely? I wonder who lives there.' And I told her, 'I don't know—but I can tell you who's going to be living there in five years—me!'"

Delightedly, Maggie laughed. "Can you believe that self-confidence? Pretty crazy! But I was right—I ended up making it big, didn't I?"

"Did you really buy the house?"

"No. I did look at it, years later, but the kitchen and bathrooms were a disgrace.

"Anyway, there I was, new to Hollywood, not knowing a soul. But I got my bearings right away. For the first few days, I stayed at a cheap little hotel on Hollywood Boulevard, and I started learning my way around. Within a week, I'd found a job and a place to live."

"The Courtyard, off Vine Street," Paul said.

Maggie was impressed. "Did you actually go see it?"

"I couldn't. It had been torn down."

"I'm sure. It was falling apart even then. In the forties, Hollywood was absolutely filled with those little boardinghouses. They were all pretty much the same—just slapped together and given a bright coat of paint. All the would-be young actresses in town lived in them—the rent was practically nothing."

She smiled. "I can't tell you how much I loved that dreadful little apartment. There's something very satisfying about one's first place, don't you think? I went a little crazy decorating it. I got some books from the library, and I tried out all their techniques—trompe l'oeil, marbelizing, you name it. Can you imagine? The main hall of Versailles, copied in an eight-foot-square living room by someone with no artistic talent whatsoever! All I can say is, Thank God no photos exist!"

Paul laughed, wishing they did.

"To pay my rent, I got a job as hamburger chef in a little restaurant down the street. I ended up as the best short order cook in the place. I'm still proud of that! I should make you my grilled cheese sandwich sometime—it's the best in the world. Do you cook?" she asked him.

"No."

She frowned. "Every man should know how to cook. I'll have Pierre give you a few simple recipes on your way out."

"I'd rather have your grilled cheese sandwich," he told her.

She laughed.

"Was it frustrating, cooking when you wanted to be acting?"

"Not at all. I looked at it as a means to an end. And isn't it the same way now? All those young actors in New York waiting tables? Besides, I was acting in my head all the time. And all the money I made went to drama lessons."

"Irma Hoffman coached you, I know."

"Oh, that was years later—when I didn't really need it. When I needed it, all I could afford was Miss Fitch. Miss Hermione Fitch."

She drew out the name with delicate irony.

"Probably the worst drama coach that ever was. No talent whatsoever. But I'm grateful to her for one thing. She got rid of my Texas accent."

"How did she do that?"

"She had me come up with a list of phrases I used every day. Then she wrote all the words down phonetically, the way I should be saying them. I swear, Henry Higgins was nothing to this woman. She had me going around sounding like the Queen of England. "Would you like some toe-mahto cah-chup on your hahm-burger?""

Paul laughed.

"But I speak beautifully now—don't you think so?"

She didn't wait for him to agree.

"Those were good days," Maggie went on. "I like looking back on them. And I like the girl I was then. Eighteen years old, free, full of passion, doing exactly what she wanted to do. It was one of the happiest times of my life."

Then a spasm passed over her face, and she reached for another cigarette.

"Do you want to hear about Kelly?" she asked.

Kelly. In none of his research had Paul come upon a Kelly.

"Yes," he said.

Maggie smoked in silence for a moment.

"Kelly was my best friend. For some reason, I've never had many friends in my life."

"Why do you think that is?"

"Oh, I don't know. Jealousy certainly is a factor—especially when I've been doing well. But I'm sure it's more than that. I imagine I'm a rather difficult friend. I can be very demanding; I expect a great deal from the people I love. If they don't deliver, they're out of my life. But I give a great deal in return."

"They say that if you have three true friends, you've done very well."

"I've had one," she said shortly. She smoked some more.

"Back in Texas, I'd never had anything in common with the girls I grew up with. I thought that once I reached Hollywood, it would be different—I mean, good heavens, everyone in town was here for the same reason. But of course, that was the problem."

"Competition."

"Exactly. I'm sure the girls were nice enough, but they were out for themselves, trying to get a career going. Friendship just wasn't that important—unless, of course, you met someone who had an 'in' with a casting director. Then it was a good idea to be friends. Or maybe that's just the way it seemed to me.

"Anyway, I was very lonely.

"About four months after I moved to town, I met Kelly Donnelly. Kelly was one of the most naturally beautiful girls I've ever known. Curly black hair, that moist Irish skin, those blue, blue eyes. I've never seen anyone else with eyes quite like hers." The spasm passed across her face again. "I don't think I believe in reincarnation—no, I'm sure I don't—but it's odd. Almost every time I see a baby, I look into its eyes to see if they're Kelly's eyes. They never are."

She cleared her throat.

"Kelly was from Florida—she needed a little work in the toemahto/hahm-burger realm herself—but she was going to be a dancer, not an actor, so it didn't matter very much what kind of accent she had."

She was silent a moment.

"How did you meet her?"

"In a casting office. One morning, I read in *Variety* that Columbia was having an open casting call for a musical, so I rushed over. There were about four hundred girls there, waiting. We were kept there, hour after hour; I started talking to the girl next to me—that was Kelly. She was screamingly funny. Finally, we gave up on the call and went for a bite to eat. We stayed there all afternoon at that crummy little restaurant, comparing lousy childhoods. We ended up crying like idiots.

"When it was time to go home, I just—didn't want to let Kelly go. I told her I'd been looking for a roommate—untrue—and asked if she was interested. She moved in a week later.

"We had some wonderful times," Maggie went on softly. "Kelly had a gift for making everything into a big adventure. We'd stay up until four in the morning, talking. We'd see movies. We'd give each other facials. We'd try out recipes from gourmet magazines. And we'd do crazy things. We'd go to the ostrich farms out in Pasadena and ride the ostriches. Or we'd drive down to Venice—it was quite a place back then; they had real gondolas in the canals. Or we'd go downtown to China City. That was splendid—everyone was in costume, and you could get a rickshaw ride. And of course, there were the amusement parks. We went to those every chance we got."

"Did you ever go on 'The Pike' in Long Beach?"

"Sure. It was heaven! And nearly every Friday night we'd go roller-skating at Ocean Park Pier. And then on Sunday—that was my day off—we had our special tradition—we'd go down to Bullocks Wilshire, and window-shop. Discuss all the beautiful dresses we'd buy one day. And then we'd go to Musso and Franks and eat flannel cakes.

"We had our futures all planned out. Kelly would be the new Cyd Charisse, I would be the next Garbo. We'd marry divine men—they couldn't be actors or dancers—and we'd be godmothers to each other's children. Such fun. For the first time in my life, I felt—well, I felt young." Paul had never heard so much tenderness in her voice—not even in her films.

"Kelly was such a good person—not saccharine, but she believed in the best of everyone, and somehow that made you want to *be* that best. And there was such sweetness about her—the total opposite of me. No"— Maggie instantly held up a hand—"I'm not looking for a compliment. Everyone who knew her felt it about Kelly.

"And another thing about her—we all knew she'd be a star someday. She'd only been in Hollywood a few months, but already she'd gotten some attention. She was a good dancer—she worked very hard at it, took class every day—and of course, there were those looks.

"Sure enough, she got a feature film. Just a chorus role, but it was for a big Fred Astaire movie. When she first told me the news, I'll be honest with you—I wanted to strangle her!" Maggie laughed. "But only for a day or two. She deserved success. And she was so generous about it. She promised me that as soon as she had any clout, she'd take me with her into MGM, storm Louis Mayer's office, and demand that they give me a contract!" Maggie smiled and shook her head. Then the smile went away.

"Well, that never happened," she said.

"Two days into the shooting, Kelly sprained her shoulder. She knew that if anyone found out, she'd be replaced. She went into an absolute panic; I'd never seen her that way before." Maggie shifted uneasily in her chair. "Of course, I should have said to hell with the movie—just get well; but in those days, that isn't the way we thought."

"No."

Her voice clicked on, in a sharp monotone.

"Kelly ended up going to the wrong people. One of the dancers she knew told her about this doctor who gave these magic vitamin shots. They were supposed to take all the pain away. Kelly went to him and got the shot. She was able to do her scene, but she hurt her arm again. Afterward, she was in worse pain than ever. She wanted to go back to the doctor, but I told her not to do it. I knew there had to be some funny business with those shots."

Maggie stood up, paced, her caftan blowing.

"She kept going back to the doctor. She swore up and down that she wasn't, but I knew she was lying. She was so nervous. And she had lost so much weight. Her wrist looked like a chicken bone. Then one day I came home and she was sobbing on the couch. She said she had been taking the shots all along, but now she had run out of money to pay for them, and she didn't know what to do."

Maggie stood still, and faced Paul levelly.

"I had the money, but I wouldn't give it to her. Instead I gave her a lecture. She left the house and was gone half the night. When she finally came back, I asked her where she had been—and she started to laugh. I can still hear that laugh," Maggie said blankly. "She told me she'd seen the doctor, and that everything was fine now. She said, 'There are other ways of paying besides money.'

"I couldn't believe it. I told her—" Maggie put her hands over her face, and shook her head. When she took her hands away again, her eyes were sharply bright with tears. She looked hard at Paul.

"Words kill. Never, never forget that.

"When I came home from work the next night, I found Kelly dead on her bed."

Paul found himself groping for the button to turn the tape recorder off.

"She left a note," Maggie said, "asking me to forgive her. She said how much she loved me, and that she knew I would be a big star someday.

"And that's all I have left of Kelly." Her voice was flat. "That note, a locket, and those fifteen seconds in the Fred Astaire movie."

She and Paul stared at each other.

"Well, let's move along, shall we?"

Paul turned the tape recorder on again.

"No," Maggie said. "Just another moment, I think."

He pushed the off switch again.

She sat on the sofa, looking out the window, her face withdrawn, saying nothing. Finally she sighed.

"It's awful, getting old," she told him.

Then she nodded at the tape recorder.

"I'm ready. You can turn that thing on."

She smiled a set smile.

"Well," she said. "On to happier times.

"My second year in Los Angeles, things started to pick up. I finally got some work in little theater. A few parts in Equity Waiver productions, some good reviews." The smile grew more real. "I can't tell you what fun it was, telling my boss at the restaurant that I had to leave early because I had a show to do. I loved every moment—going to the theater, getting into costume, putting on my makeup, doing the play. And then, of course, I couldn't sleep a wink when I got home; I'd be reliving every line."

"Did you ever suffer from stage fright?"

"Me? Never! Not unless you call throwing up ten times a night 'stage fright'!"

They laughed.

"Do you remember the names of any of the plays you were in?" He knew a few of the titles, wondered if there were others.

"No. Only my first lead. That was in a play called *Heartbreak.*"

Paul nodded. He recalled a line or two from the review, the critic enjoying his dismissive attacks on the fledgling actress.

"Stinking review," Maggie said meditatively, as if reading his thoughts. "But the play was rather a success. I even invited Mama to come out for that one— but she couldn't leave the grocery store."

Maggie gave a sudden, unamused laugh. "Which reminds me of a story. When I asked Mama to come see *Heartbreak,* she told me that her sister Billie was going to be in Pasadena that week, and that I should invite *her* to my play.

"I never could stand my aunt Billie. She was a strict Baptist, very dour, but after all, she was family. I called her and she said she would come. I got her a complimentary seat, I rushed around buying her little presents, I arranged for us to go to dinner at a nice restaurant afterward. Cost me a week's salary.

"Well, I'll never forget it. Two minutes before curtain, a note arrived backstage for me. It was from Aunt Billie, saying she wasn't coming. Apparently, she'd talked to her minister, and he'd forbidden her to go. She wrote me that actors—let me get this right—actors were 'the Devil's puppets' and that, according to the minister, I could plan on spending the rest of eternity in Hell." Maggie's laugh was high and false. "Mama was furious, bless her heart. I don't think she ever spoke to Aunt Billie again.

"But I got my revenge!" she smiled. "Oh, yes. Years later, one of Billie's daughters moved out to California and got in touch with me. She called to ask if I could get her an invitation to an Academy Awards party. I had a great time planning ways to turn her down. And then I decided it would be much more fun to invite her. She turned out to be a fat girl with very bad skin; she got completely smashed and necked with the bartender!" This time, Maggie's laugh rang absolutely true.

"Was the rest of your family supportive of your acting?"

"Not really. That same year, my sister Cathy came out with her daughter. I saw quite a bit of them, took them all over town, but they wouldn't come to my play, either. It was curious—it seemed like the more successful I became, the less my family wanted anything to do with me.

"You'd think that they would have"—she made a sharp defensive gesture with her hands—"well, never mind. I hope you never experience anything like it.

"Only Mama stayed in touch," she went on more softly. "Always. Bless her heart. How I looked forward to getting those little notes, one on Monday, one on Thursday. She always wrote in pencil on yellow lined paper. They were marvelous letters. Full of gossip and mischief, and then she'd get guilty, and throw in something about Jesus."

She smiled.

"It's funny, but I think I only really started knowing my mother in those years I was away from her.

"When I'd been in California about two and a half years, I landed the lead in a wonderful play—you know Henry James's *The Heiress?* Good, good show. Well, I invited Mama out for a two-week visit, to come and see it. She called me up and said that she had gotten a neighbor to mind the store, and that she was coming. I couldn't believe it. She hadn't been out of Texas in over fifteen years.

"I booked her on the Super Chief, and I was in agony for the whole three days, wondering if she was getting along all right. Well, I needn't have worried."

Maggie's face was bright.

"I got to the station an hour early to meet her, and as long as I live, I'll never forget the sight of that fat little figure in the flowered hat stepping down from the train. Surrounding her was the entire flock of passengers and porters—shouting good-bye, helping her down, taking her suitcase, handing her flowers. My little Mama."

Paul felt warm with enjoyment at her enjoyment.

"Oh, what a visit we had. It was one of the happiest two weeks of my life. I'd saved up all my money, and I took Mama everywhere. To the hottest matinee in town, on a studio tour, to the most glamorous restaurants. She adored it all. Those little black eyes sparkling at everything. Then, I got really daring and took her on a tour of Hollywood's darker side—I pointed out a few prostitutes, and what I'd heard was the best whorehouse in town." Maggie giggled. "She enjoyed that part most of all!

"On the last day I took her into Bullocks Wilshire, and I bought her her first designer outfit. It was a Lanz dress, soft blue cotton with little pink flowers. Took me six months to pay it off! But it was the best thing I ever bought."

She shook her head.

"How Mama loved that dress. That night, I caught her at two in the morning, trying it on once again before the mirror.

"It was very hard, putting her on the train back to Texas."

Then she looked down.

"Mama died the next year. I came backstage after a performance and there was a telegram on my dressing table.

"She had been sitting on her front porch, doing some tatting. Then she had a stroke and was gone."

When she looked up again, her face was calm and set.

"I think that's rather lovely, don't you?" she asked.

"Sitting there peacefully, making something beautiful, and suddenly death comes. And you're taken off without the chance to dread it."

She caught Paul's ironic expression.

"Don't look at me like that," she said sharply. "You don't know the years it's taken me to get to this point. If I can think my mother's death is lovely, kindly let me do it."

He took pity, swallowed, smiled.

"I went back to Texas for the funeral," she said after a moment. "It was the first time I'd been home in almost five years."

Her eyes narrowed.

"I had always imagined coming back in victory. And it *was* a victory. I had escaped; I had made it; I was Somebody now. But it was the damndest thing— the moment the train pulled into the depot, and I saw those same old houses and those same old people, I turned right back into the same old Maggie. I didn't even speak with my beautiful accent anymore."

She shivered.

"The funeral was awful. All that Baptist horror. But Mama looked like an angel. And I saw to it that she was buried in her blue Lanz dress."

She waved her hand, as if to deny the memory admittance.

"I left to go back to Los Angeles the next day. As I was getting on the train, a man came up to me. For a moment, I didn't even know who he was; then I realized it was Stanley. He looked terrible. He said he'd heard how well I was doing in Hollywood, and how happy he was for me. Things hadn't been going so great for him—his business had folded and he had to give up the ranch—but he'd met this nice woman, a waitress, and he wanted to get married. I said I'd be happy to give him a divorce.

"Then I left Texas and I've never been back."

She lit another cigarette, smoked in silence.

"It took me a long time to get over Mama's death," she said flatly. "If we ever truly do get over something like that."

She pulled at a loose thread on the brocade of the sofa.

"The next year was rough. It looked like I was going to get Sol Lehman as an agent, but he changed his mind at the last minute. I was up for a few movies; they fell through. I wasn't even getting parts in little theater anymore. The whole timing was off.

"And I was very lonely. After Kelly, I didn't want any more roommates—or any more girlfriends, for that matter. There were a few men interested in me, but they were actors—and not as talented as I was.

"To top it off, the owner of the restaurant I worked at decided to retire, and I was out of a job. By autumn, I was completely broke.

"I had to do something. I decided to become a receptionist. I'd known a girl who did that—she was the receptionist for a local radio show—and I'd filled in for her one day when she was sick. I'd rather enjoyed myself. I figured I'd try for a job at a production company—I'd be closer to the theater than I had been frying hamburgers, and at least I'd get a chance to use my voice. So I sent out eighteen resumés, and waited. I only got one letter back—from a new production company called Thespis. They asked me to come in for an interview."

Paul's heart began to beat in fast anticipation.

"I dressed up in my best beige suit, and went down

to Hollywood Boulevard where the office was. I waited in the lobby for an hour and a half.

"Finally, a man came to the door. Very tall, thin, elegant. He said, "Miss Royal? I'm Philip Fredericks."

She laughed.

"I think I was in love before I'd risen to my feet."

Ten

It was five o'clock. Dusk had gentled and depressed the sky, and the buildings near the Metropolitan Museum looked drained in the fading pink light. Crosstown traffic was slow, and the taxi driver cursed continually as he hit one red light after another.

Finally, the taxi pulled to a stop in front of Brian House. One of the counselors was waiting out in front.

Linda cleared her throat and looked over at Alexis.

"Mrs. Donleavy," she began formally, as though she'd been rehearsing these words all during the ride, "I had the most wonderful time at the museum. I want to thank you so much for—"

"Do me a favor and don't thank me," Alexis laughed. "This man's meter's running, and I still have to go thirty blocks back uptown. Anyway, it was a pleasure."

Linda smiled back. She got out of the taxi and walked with the counselor into the dark brick building. The heavy door opened to her, then closed.

* * *

Alexis arrived home tired. She and Ron had a party to go to that night, a housewarming for some clients of hers, but there was time for a bath before she got dressed, and maybe a glass of wine.

She was in the bath when Ron came home.

"Ron? How did it go?"

He came in, smiling.

"We finally closed," he said.

"Congratulations!"

He sat down on the ottoman.

"Yeah. It was a bear, but Nesbitt came around to my way of thinking at the end. And listen to this— when we were leaving the office, I think he was actually putting out feelers about my joining his in-house counsel!"

"Oh, Ron, that's wonderful."

He bent down and kissed her briefly. "Hey, I got you something on the way home."

He reached into his briefcase and pulled out a wrapped package from Oggetti.

Alexis smiled. "This looks interesting."

Drying her hands on a face towel, she opened the package. Inside was a small address book, covered in marbleized Venetian paper.

"You said you needed a new one."

"Ron! How very thoughtful of you."

"Did I get the right color?" he asked.

"Absolutely," she told him, although it was untrue. "It's perfect. Thank you so much."

He stood up, satisfied by her reaction. "Well, I want to catch some of the pregame." He started out of the room.

"Don't forget, we have to leave in half an hour."

He turned and frowned.

"Leave for what?"

"The Lipscombs' party."

He groaned. "Oh, God, that housewarming thing. But the game's on tonight!"

"I know, I know," she told him. "But I said we'd go weeks ago."

"Can't *you* go? Do you really need me?"

"I'm afraid so. Myra Lipscomb's cousin is going to be there; he's applying to law schools, and I said you'd talk to him. I promise we won't stay long."

Ron sighed. "Well," he said flatly, "anything for business."

He left to get dressed. Alexis was relieved that he hadn't made more of a fuss about the party. And then there was the address book; that had really been terribly sweet of him.

While she was dressing, the phone rang. Alexis picked up the receiver.

"Hello—hello? Mrs. Donleavy?"

The voice was breathless.

"It's—it's Linda."

"Why, hello, Linda," Alexis said, not showing her surprise.

"I hope you don't mind my calling,"

"No, but how did you get my number?"

There was a pause.

"Well, I asked Steven Wheelhouse but he wouldn't give it to me. Then I went by his office later. Well, the door was open, and Dara wasn't around . . . I found it on his desk. I guess I shouldn't have taken it."

"Probably not," Alexis said.

"But I had to call you. I just had to thank you again. I'm wearing the Egyptian ring you bought me. It's the most beautiful thing anyone's ever given me. In my whole life."

"Well, I'm glad," Alexis said. "I enjoyed the afternoon, too." She saw the way Ron was looking at her, and broke off. "Linda, I have to go now. I'll see you on Tuesday." She hung up the phone.

"Who was that?"

"Linda—one of the kids I tutor."

He frowned. "They call you at home?"

"Only this once."

He paused, straightened, and Alexis felt the mental sensation of mounting the stairs to the witness box.

"I don't like this," Ron said slowly. "Those kids shouldn't have our number."

Alexis shrugged. "I wouldn't make too much of it."

He coughed, then spoke very distinctly.

"Alexis, keep in mind what kind of children these are. I know you're trying to help them, but . . ." he shook his head.

"Ron, honestly—this was a one-time thing."

"How can you be so sure? Think about it a minute. One of these kids has your home number now—what if they all get hold of it? Crank calls could be the least of our concerns!"

"All right," she said. "I'll make sure Linda throws it away."

But Ron's eyes widened at a new thought.

"And what if they ever get hold of our address?" he demanded. "Do you have any idea what that could mean? Some punk breaks in, and there goes the Chagall; how would you feel about that? Or suppose we come home late some night, and end up with our throats slit!"

"Oh, Ron!" she said wearily. "You're being ridiculous. I know these kids."

"I'm not saying one of the kids you know would do it," he told her, "but they have friends, don't they? Other kids in the place? People on the street? Word gets around."

"They have absolutely no way of getting this address," she told him. "When I filled in the application, I gave them my address at the office."

She was a little ashamed saying this, admitting that she, too, had her tendencies to paranoia. But Ron was gratified by the admission.

"Good," he said. "That was using your head."

Then he frowned again.

"You've never brought any of these kids to the apartment, have you?"

"Of course not."

"Good. Well, I want you to promise me that you never will. Under any circumstances."

Resenting being made to promise, she promised.

Ron went back to getting dressed.

He was absolutely charming to Myra Lipscomb's cousin.

The following Tuesday, Alexis arrived at Brian House a few minutes later than usual. The bell had rung between classes, and the corridor was filled with students. As she was going into the classroom, Alexis noticed Linda coming along the hall.

The girl's graceful isolation struck Alexis afresh. Linda seemed to have no part whatsoever in the shrilling jostle around her. She walked slowly, delicately, with a private smile on her face. Then all at once, she saw something or someone, and everything changed. She stopped walking. She tensed. And her expression switched to a look of longing so naked that Alexis drew in a breath.

She followed the girl's glance. And there, sprawled against a doorjamb, was a lanky, auburn-haired boy, laughing boisterously with a friend. Raoul.

Then Raoul looked up and saw Linda. In an instant, his own look became a faithful reflection of hers—and the two stood there, poised across the hall from each other, staring and in love.

Watching them, an unexpected stinging loneliness pooled up inside Alexis.

The following Tuesday, Linda was late to class. This had never happened before. Alexis asked Tamara and Greg where she was, but they only shrugged and said that, as far as they knew, she wasn't sick or on detention. Finally, fifteen minutes into the class, Linda arrived.

At first, Alexis pretended not to notice anything was wrong, but it was hard to ignore Linda's blotched face and red eyes. Alexis continued to talk about Paul Klee, but it was clear that no one was listening to her. Every time she turned her back, she could hear the whispering and the passing of notes. Finally she gave up.

"Would someone please tell me what's going on?" she asked.

Tamara and Greg looked uneasily at Linda. Linda bent her head and shrugged.

"It's okay," she whispered. "You can tell her."

"It's Samantha!" Tamara said finally.

"Who's Samantha?"

"One of the girls here. You've probably seen her. She's got really fat hips."

"And she dresses like a slut."

"Well, what about her?"

"She thinks she can get away with anything!"

Linda was saying nothing. She just sat, miserable, like stone.

"Well, what happened was, Linda made this little box," Tamara hurried on. "For her hairclips and stuff. Samantha saw it in her room and she asked if Linda could make her one, too. She said she'd pay her."

At this, Linda put her face in her hands.

"And?"

"I made her the box," Linda whispered. "I had to pay for the materials, but I thought it would be all right—I figured I'd get the money back when Samantha paid me. But—but—I gave the box to her this morning, and—she said she liked it, but—she didn't have the money to buy it anymore."

Linda burst into tears.

"How much was she supposed to pay you?" Alexis asked.

She barely caught Linda's sobbed answer.

"Six dollars."

Alexis stared at her. Six dollars. *Six dollars*. A rapid parade zoomed into her mind—last night's two-hundred-dollar dinner. Mrs. Kolby and her four-thousand-dollar jade lamp. The Termots and their twenty-five-thousand-dollar bathroom.

Linda continued to sob. Alexis watched her in perplexity.

"Don't cry," she said. "That isn't going to help. Did you give Samantha the box?"

Linda shook her head in a spasm.

"I couldn't. She said she'd give me two dollars for it, but it cost more than three dollars to make."

"So you still have it?"

Linda nodded.

Alexis found herself needing to see this box. This tragic little six-dollar box.

Linda reached into her purse, and brought it out.

Alexis looked at the box carefully.

It was charming. Naive, cleverly made of lacquered cardboard, and painted with a motif of angels.

"It's very well done," she said at last. She put the box on the table.

The three watched her in silence. She knew they expected wisdom from her, and she felt angry because she had none to give.

Finally she turned to the pale and trembling Linda.

"Look," she said. "I can imagine what a disappointment this is for you. I'm truly sorry it happened. But I think you've learned a valuable lesson here—and next time you want to sell something, make sure to get the agreement down in writing first."

Linda bowed her head, nodded.

"Now, can we get back to Paul Klee?"

At last the bell rang, and the kids left in silence. It wasn't until Alexis was closing the classroom door that she realized Linda had forgotten her box. She started to

call after the girl, but stopped. Instead, she picked up
the little box and put it in her purse.

She walked down the hall to Steven Wheelhouse's
office.

"Come in!" he called.

He was doing paperwork, and looked harassed.

"Ah, Mrs. Donleavy," he said when he saw her.

"I'm sorry to interrupt you," she said, "but I wanted
to bring something to your attention. It concerns Linda.
Apparently one of the other girls here, Samantha, com-
missioned her to make a box, and promised to pay her
six dollars. Then, when the work was done, and Linda
had already paid for the materials, Samantha went
back on her word."

Steven Wheelhouse looked uncertain.

"And what is it you wish me to do?"

"I assumed *you* would wish to do something. Talk
to Samantha, for a start."

He sighed.

"Mrs. Donleavy, it's not really my business. And I
can't take sides like that with the kids. This is something Linda needs to work out with Samantha—maybe
in a therapy session."

"I see," she said. "Well, thank you."

Later that afternoon, Alexis had an appointment
with Miriam Lawson, a wealthy widow. Mrs. Lawson,
sated with a lifetime of luxury, had decided, à la Marie
Antoinette, that in her latest redecorating extrava-
ganza, she would go the purely pastoral route.

"I've brought you some samples," Alexis told her, pulling fabrics and wallpapers from her briefcase. "The gold Toile de Jouy for the powder room, as we discussed, and I found a rather interesting panorama by Zuber—it's a scene of Naples, and it's done with hand-carved printing blocks. I thought it might be effective in the dining room."

"It's beautiful," Mrs. Lawson said. "They'll both be perfect."

Alexis made a note.

Mrs. Lawson sighed. "I can't wait until all this is done. It'll be such a restful look." She indicated with displeasure the fashionable room around her. "All this clutter has such a jangling effect." She frowned especially at a heavy Lalique crystal on her coffee table. "I feel it's weighing me down."

"We'll concentrate on lighter accessories. I found some *papier mâché* candlesticks that might work over the fireplace, and"—Alexis hesitated for a moment—"what do you think of this for the end table?"

From her purse, she pulled out Linda's box.

"How charming," Mrs. Lawson said. "Is it French?"

"No. It was made by someone local—a young artist."

Mrs. Lawson frowned thoughtfully. "Is it available in any other patterns? I have a real phobia about angels—too many years at Catholic school, I guess. But if it could be done as a floral—with pansies? Are pansies French?"

Alexis considered.

"I think there are pansies in France. If not, we could do lavender instead. And I'm sure the artist could be persuaded to work on commission. But of course, I'd have to ask."

"Please do!" Mrs. Lawson beamed.

The following week after class, Alexis took Linda privately aside. She gave her back her box.

"Oh, and by the way," she said, "a client of mine is commissioning you to do a similar one for her."

Linda gaped. Alexis pretended not to notice her astonishment.

"But she wants pansies, not angels."

From her totebag, she drew out a huge book on watercolor flowers.

"This is from the library. You'd better not lose it."

Linda twisted her hands. "Oh, Mrs. Donleavy!"

"Don't get too excited," Alexis cautioned. "My client will only accept the box if she likes it."

"She'll like it." The girl's face was dogged, flushed. "I'll make sure she will. I'll do the best job I've ever done."

Alexis smiled. "I'll buy the supplies for you," she said. "And I'll get you some better paint than what you've been using. Then it's up to you. Oh, one thing more," she said. "I wouldn't mention this to anyone until it's finished."

"No, no," Linda assured her. "I won't say a single word."

When Alexis entered Brian House the next Tuesday, Steven Wheelhouse was waiting for her.

"Mrs. Donleavy," he said. "I understand that Linda has been asked to paint a box for a client of yours."

Alexis sighed.

"That's right," she said.

He smiled a shadowed smile.

"Great," he said. "Things like that can do a lot to boost these kids' self-esteem. Oh, incidentally," he added, "will Linda be paid for this box?"

"Yes."

"Do you know how much?"

"We haven't discussed price yet."

"Well," Steven Wheelhouse went on, "my only ground rule is that you don't give her more than twenty dollars. I'm sure you can understand—putting more than that in these kids' pockets would be very unwise."

"But what," Alexis asked, "if my client is willing to pay more?"

Steven Wheelhouse gave a strained little laugh.

"Well! If you need anywhere to park the excess, Brian House could always find a use for it!"

"I'll keep that in mind." Alexis moved away.

She went into the classroom. Linda was there, beaming at her.

"Please stay after class, Linda," Alexis said. "I want to talk to you."

After class, Linda came nervously up to Alexis.

"You wanted to see me?"

"I understand that you told about the project—after I asked you not to."

Linda looked down.

"I'm sorry, Mrs. Donleavy," she said pleadingly. "I

didn't mean to. It just slipped out. I was so excited I couldn't help it."

Looking at her, Alexis had a sudden memory of what it was like to be a teenager. Of course Linda hadn't been able to help it. Of course it had slipped out. What else could have been expected?

"Well," she said, "I guess there's no harm done."

She reached into her satchel and pulled out a bag from Grumbacher. "Here are the supplies I promised you. You should be able to do a good job with these."

Reverently, Linda took up the tubes of paint and touched the virgin palette.

"Thank you, Mrs. Donleavy," she whispered.

The following Tuesday, when Alexis came into class, the finished box was waiting for her in the center of the big table.

The three kids were crowding around, discussing it excitedly. When they saw Alexis, they drew back and waited eagerly for her reaction.

When Alexis looked at the box, an involuntary smile came to her face. And then, in domino effect, Tamara started to smile—then Greg—then Linda—and finally all four were beaming at the box and at one another.

Alexis nodded.

"Excellent work, Linda," she said.

Mrs. Lawson was enchanted with the box.

"What an original!" she said. "It'll be perfect on the end table. I'll take it."

Alexis coughed. "I don't think we ever discussed price."

"How much?"

"Eighty dollars."

Mrs. Lawson waved a hand.

Alexis thought briefly about giving all the money to Linda, but she didn't. She gave her only the permitted twenty.

"I'm very proud of you," Alexis told her.

She handed the remaining sixty dollars over to Steven Wheelhouse.

"You might consider using this to buy a new fan for our classroom," she told him. "The one we've got is a disaster."

The new fan was there the following week, and Alexis pointed it out to the class.

"We have Linda to thank for this," she said.

Tamara and Greg applauded. Alexis was gratified to see that, under her kabuki makeup, Linda was pink with pleasure.

"Jacey!" Alexis opened the door. She took her friend in her arms and hugged her.

"God, it's good to be here," Jacey said. She looked tired, and there were lines around her mouth that Alexis didn't remember from her last visit in the autumn. "I keep forgetting how loud New York is. But your place is an oasis of peace, as usual." She gazed around and pointed to the hall table. "Is that new?"

"No, I just had it refinished."

"It looks great." She walked into the living room

and sat heavily down on the sofa. "Well, I'm absolutely exhausted. Where's this alleged tea you promised me?"

"Coming right up," Alexis assured her.

An hour later, the sun had set. The tea was down to the dregs, the biscuits were eaten. Alexis and Jacey sat on the drawing room sofa, emptied of talk. Jacey twisted the fringe of a pillow in her fingers. Alexis had a final sip of cold chamomile. They smiled at each other lazily, looked at the sky.

"You haven't mentioned Sylvia," Jacey said suddenly. "How's she doing?"

"She's all right. I talked to her on Sunday. She's liking the retirement home a little better, but I don't really think she's happy in Florida. I wish she'd stayed here and let me look after her."

Jacey shook her head. "She wouldn't have been happy here, either. With your dad gone, she won't be happy anywhere. It was the same with my mother."

"I guess you're right." Alexis said. "You know, it's funny—to this day, some little thing will happen, and I still find myself thinking, 'I must tell Daddy.' And then I remember. It's crazy. I mean, it'll be three years in March."

Jacey squeezed Alexis's hand.

"It's the same with me and my dad," she said. "It's a weird feeling."

"Yeah."

"Especially when you think that we're the next in line."

Alexis shook her head. "Not me. My grandmother's still going strong, thank you very much."

"You're kidding."

"No. Ninety-four years old—she'll bury us all."

Jacey wrinkled her nose. "She always terrified me."

"She can be pretty intimidating. But she's amazing—she had a stroke last July, and within a month she was back on her feet, giving a fund-raiser. She never seems to lose interest."

"That's incredible," Jacey said. "I can't imagine never losing interest. I certainly have," she added abruptly.

Alexis thought about it. "Me, too."

"Have you? That's a relief to hear. I get so depressed sometimes when you tell me about all the great things going on with you."

Alexis shrugged. "I'm not saying my life's not wonderful, but there are those moments. Sure. When you wonder what the point is. Or if there's any point at all."

Jacey sighed. "There never used to be moments like that."

"Of course not. It's a special gift reserved for our forties."

They laughed.

"Is Simon afflicted?"

"He doesn't seem to be. Or if he is, he certainly doesn't tell me."

"Neither does Ron." Alexis's voice sounded cold to her own ears. "But of course I haven't seen much of him lately," she added hastily. "He's had three big back-to-back deals."

Jacey nodded glumly. "And Simon spends half his time in Tokyo. It isn't what we thought it would be like, is it?"

"No," Alexis admitted. "I mean, it's fine. Ron and I are happier than most of the couples we know, I suppose. It's just that—well, I sometimes wonder how much is really still there. You know what I mean? It's like each year that goes by puts more—junk—between us. We race around, doing all these things, and somehow we get more and more separated." She shook her head. "I found a photo the other day of us on our honeymoon, sailing in Acapulco. I can't tell you how sad it made me feel. But then again, last week Ron bought me a lovely little address book out of the blue. So I don't know."

"Oh, who does?" Jacey asked impatiently. "Is it too early for a drink? What time is it, anyway?"

"Five-thirty."

"Oh, God, I've got to go. My train's in an hour."

"Can't you stay? Ron and I have his firm dinner tonight, but I could make up the guest room for you. It would only take a minute."

"No, I've got to get back. I've got a committee meeting tomorrow morning."

She stood up. "Sweetie, it's always so wonderful seeing you. And don't worry about anything—all this stuff—it's just normal. Anyway, I think you're fabulous. The most fabulous woman I know."

There were tears behind Alexis's eyes. "The feeling is mutual."

They hugged each other hard.

The firm dinner was being held at the Tavern on the Green. Ron went straight from work, Alexis met him there. The Tavern on the Green was her favorite restaurant, touching her as no other place did. It brought back childhood Christmas—the twinkling fairy lights on the trees outside, the crystal and jewel colors, the bronze reindeer, and gay music.

Tonight's party seemed to go on forever. Most of the wives she knew, and with these she could maintain a friendly silence, interspersed with occasional comments about children or office news. But there were also several wives of associates new to the firm, and Alexis must be attentive and friendly to those.

It was fatiguing work.

She was also depressed by Ron, seeing his face shine at the jokes of the senior partners, seeing him assiduously ask all the right wives to dance. He moved constantly, laughed all the time. He seemed such a little man.

They did not talk much in the taxi going home. As they were undressing for bed, Ron turned to her.

"If you want to know the truth, I think maybe I'm getting too old for these evenings."

Alexis was brushing her hair. She paused. "Why do you say that?"

"Oh, I don't know." He sounded like a disappointed little boy. "It just seems to me they used to be a lot more fun."

She put down the brush, went over, and took him in her arms.

"I guess it's seeing those same people year after year," he said into her hair. "Having the same damned meal. I feel like I'm caught in some trap. And all those guys—they look so old. Do I look that old?"

"No, you don't," she said firmly. He was silent in her arms.

*   *   *

They made love. Afterward, while Ron slept, Alexis went into the living room. She did not turn the lights on, but found her way to the couch where Jacey had sat earlier that afternoon. She stared into the darkness.

Eleven

Alexis removed the cake from its cardboard box and arranged it on a porcelain platter. The message on the frosting read *Happy First Anniversary*. It was incredible to think that she and Ron had been married an entire year.

It was six-thirty—only half an hour before Ron was due to come home. Alexis checked the roast in the oven and got the salad started. Then she hurried into the bedroom and changed into the silk maroon dress Ron said made her look like a flamenco dancer. She put on makeup, did her hair, and she was ready.

She came back into the living room, and sat down on the sofa. The sunset came and went, leaving a charcoal sky. The apartment darkened slowly, and Alexis felt a rising sadness settle around her. She sighed impatiently. She hated it when these moments of depression came. And it was so senseless—there was really no reason at all for them.

Everything in her life was going so well. She must

keep hold of that thought. Everything was going so well.

The apartment, for instance. How she loved it. Everyone agreed that she and Ron had been extraordinarily lucky to be living in Greenwich Village in the first place—and then, on top of that, to have found this lovely flat right on Ninth Street, with its gracious, blurred lines, tall ceilings, and Art Deco windows. It had been a joy to fix up, decorating the rooms in keeping with their aura of faded splendor.

And then there was the design course she was taking at NYU. That was a lot of fun. She wasn't sure where it would lead, but in the meantime she was enjoying it tremendously.

And her social life was pleasant—mainly she spent time with Ron's friends, but they were nice enough, and there were also a few women from class that she had coffee with from time to time.

Of course Ron was the biggest blessing of all. After a year of marriage, she still got a thrill every morning, waking up, looking over at him, and thinking, "My husband." Maybe, to be honest, they weren't quite as close, as all-in-all to each other, as she had hoped they would be, but that would come in time.

Really, everything was wonderful.

So what was wrong? What was wrong with her?

Alexis only knew that sometimes this senseless sadness caught at her so hard she couldn't breathe. Sometimes, when she was looking at the newspapers, she could see an obituary with her name at the top.

Then lately, too, she had been feeling unwell. There had been the sudden lethargy that had come over her during class the day before—and this afternoon, walking home from Balducci's, she had been hit by such a wave of giddiness that she had to put down the grocery bags and sit on the pavement until it passed.

It was seven o'clock—Ron would be here any moment. Resolutely, Alexis snapped on the lights; the last thing she wanted was to be in this kind of mood for their anniversary. She finished dressing the salad, and put a vase of flowers on the table.

A few minutes later, she could hear his key in the lock.

"Happy Anniversary!" Alexis cried before the door was even fully open. She ran across the room into Ron's arms, colliding with his briefcase.

Gently, with a tinge of annoyance, he pushed her off.

Alexis gave a sob and ran into the bedroom.

Ron came in a few minutes later. She was sitting on the edge of the bed, staring out the window. He went over to her.

"You do this to yourself, you know," he told her reasonably. "You don't give me time to unwind, and then you come rushing at me. Let me relax a few minutes first. Then I'll be more in the mood." He bent down and hugged her taut shoulders. "You just expect too much from me." He kissed her hair and sighed. "Well, anyway, Happy Anniversary."

"Happy Anniversary," she told him.

The following Monday, Alexis had a doctor's appointment. The next morning, she sat down at the kitchen table and called for the results.

"Just a moment," said the nurse.

Alexis stared out the window. She made herself breathe.

The nurse came back on the line.

"Congratulations," she said.

Alexis walked slowly up Madison Avenue. She could barely hear the sounds of traffic, could barely see the rushing crowds. She, Alexis Avery Donleavy, was going to have a baby.

It was absolutely impossible.

A young mother passed by, pushing an infant in a stroller. Alexis looked with trepidation at the pair. The woman looked so confident, the baby so content. How did you keep a baby content? What did you do if it started screaming? Her glance went to the stroller. And how did you know which kind of stroller to buy? What were the best toys to string along the top? She had heard somewhere that babies liked black and white— was that true? But this baby had yellow ducks. Were yellow ducks better? And that big bag hanging from the handle—what on earth was it filled with? Alexis began to perspire.

Who was she kidding? The truth was, she simply wasn't ready to be a parent, and neither was Ron. Oh, yes, sometime in the future, when they were older and more settled, a baby would be wonderful—but not now. It would be impossible now. Was Ron supposed to stay home from business dinners to play with the baby? Would she have to quit her design classes? Would she be up all night, giving feedings every few hours? What if the baby had colic? What if the baby never stopped crying? And what if she didn't like the baby? What if the baby didn't like her?

Alexis began to hyperventilate. She leaned against the door of a building and panted.

When she straightened up at last, she saw that the building she had been leaning against was a shop—a shop that sold children's clothes. The window display was full of little manikins holding butterfly nets and wearing bright summer outfits; and there, in the center of the display, was a tiny pink-and-white checked dress smocked with roses. Alexis stood electrified, staring at it. Into her mind came the sudden image of a little girl running barefoot across a lawn, and wearing that dress—a pale little girl with her own blond hair and Ron's blue eyes.

She began to cry.

The proprietor of the shop saw Alexis through the window. He came to the door and opened it.

"Are you all right?" he asked.

"I'm fine," Alexis whispered. "It's just—I've found out I'm going to have a baby."

The man beamed at her and patted her shoulder.

"That's wonderful," he told her. "I have four myself. Believe me, that's good news."

"Yes," Alexis said, wiping her eyes. "Isn't it the best?"

She bought the little dress.

Ron came home early that night.

"I'm in the mood for an old movie," he said, flipping open the newspaper. "If we hurry, we can catch *Lola Montes* at the Village Gate. Sound good to you?"

"Sure," Alexis said, "but there's something I wanted to tell you first." She touched his arm. "Put the paper down."

He put the paper down.

"We're going to have a baby."

Ron stared at her. Alexis smiled, recognizing in his eyes the same terrified thoughts that she had been having that afternoon.

"Are you sure?"

She held his arm more tightly.

"Yes. It'll be fine, Ron. It'll be wonderful."

He dropped down on the armchair.

"My dad will go crazy," he said. "He's always wanted to be a grandfather." He shook his head. "Which will make me—"

"A father."

"I can't believe it." Tears came to his eyes.

"I had no idea we were planning this," he said.

Alexis started to cry also. "I had no idea, either."

They held each other.

"Lucky little baby," he said, "to have you as a mother."

"Oh, I don't know," she told him. "I've been in a total panic all day, wondering what sort of stroller you're supposed to get."

"You'll be great," he said. "God, I hope it's a boy. We'll go sailing together."

Alexis did not tell Ron that the baby was going to be a little blond girl who would be wearing the pink-and-white smocked dress.

"You two will have a great time together. You'll be a wonderful father."

Dreamily, he nodded.

"Yeah; I think I will." He patted her arm. "Good job, Alexis."

Then his glance fell on the newspaper.

"We can still catch that movie," he told her.

* * *

"A baby!" Sylvia cried, rushing to hug first Alexis, and then Ron. "I'm so happy!"

"We couldn't be more delighted," Grandmother told them, nodding with satisfaction. "Congratulations to you both."

Henry Avery said nothing. He embraced Alexis and then gently reached down and touched her stomach. The gesture made Alexis want to weep.

They all had a glass of champagne—except for Alexis, who had fruit juice—and toasted the baby. Sylvia offered to give Alexis a shower at 21 Club. Mrs. Avery announced she would give her diamond and emerald brooch to the baby, should it be a girl, or her husband's coin collection, should it be a boy. They talked about doctors and due dates, schools and types of childbirth. Happily, Alexis listened to herself talk—she sounded like a real mother.

"Well, I just can't get over it," Sylvia said. "A grandmother! I'm going to be a grandmother."

Alexis felt a sudden dizziness. She was six years old again, lying on Maggie's pink satin quilt.

"I can't wait to be a grandmother," Maggie was saying. "I'm going to spoil your children to pieces!"

"More than you spoil me?"

"Oh, never that—but next to you, I'll love them more than anything in the world."

Alexis swallowed.

"You'll be a wonderful grandmother, Sylvia."

"I don't believe it!" Jacey shrieked, staring in shock at Alexis's burgeoning stomach, "Why didn't you tell me?"

"I wanted it to be a surprise. I wanted to see the look on your face."

"Well, was it satisfactory?"

"Completely."

Jacey shook her head. "I can't get over it. You, of all people. You always said you hated children!"

Alexis laughed. "Not this one."

Jacey hugged her. "Not mine, either, I hope."

Alexis looked down at Kevin, the little boy asleep in Jacey's carrier. She touched the powder-soft hand; the minuteness of the fingernails made her mouth tremble.

"No; he's wonderful," she said. "Oh, Jacey."

The two women settled themselves and the baby in the booth of Wolf's restaurant. They talked about college friends, and Jacey's life in Boston, and the business which had brought her and her husband to New York for a few days. But Alexis found that her eyes kept moving to Kevin. Greedily, she watched his eyelashes and the way his mouth made soft munching movements as he slept. Then he woke and sleepily reached for his mother.

Casually, still talking about the renovations she was doing on their apartment, Jacey pulled her dress down, unhooked her bra, and gave her breast to the baby. Alexis felt herself redden. Even when they were roommates in college, Alexis could not recall seeing her friend naked. The baby took the nipple, and the waitress came by for their order. The red gradually left Alexis's face. She wondered if, in another few months, she would be doing it, too, having lunch with a friend and airily exposing herself to the world.

"I can just imagine what your pregnancy's been like," Jacey was saying. "Stop me if I'm wrong. You've read every book ever written, and you know more than the doctors. You've comparison-shopped every crib and stroller and you've got the nursery completely decorated."

"Notice I'm not stopping you," Alexis said.

"And you've already hired your nanny."

"Ah," Alexis said. "You're wrong there. I'm going to take care of this baby myself."

Jacey's astonished face made them both laugh.

"I can't believe it," she said finally, "but I'm so happy for you. You'll see," she added. "It'll be the greatest love of your life."

Alexis touched her stomach. The greatest love of her life. She felt a small kick.

It was the night she and Ron were going to choose the baby's name. They went to their favorite Italian restaurant on Bleeker Street, and when they were seated, Alexis pulled the book of names from her purse.

"If it's a girl," she began, "I have a very definite first choice. It's been my favorite name since I was eight years old—it's from Hans Christian Andersen's 'The Wild Swans.' "

"So what is it?"

"Elise."

Ron wrinkled his nose. "No," he said. "Too prissy. I hate those little princess names. I want something with a little more zip in it—let's call her Donna. Or what about Cheryl? If you don't mind that I once had a girlfriend called Cheryl."

Alexis's voice trembled. "I don't like either one, actually. Please—won't you think about Elise?"

Ron sighed. "Alexis, I hate 'Elise.' It's an absolutely idiotic name."

Alexis reddened. "Okay, let's not do girls' names now. Let's start with boys' names." She flipped through the book. "What about Michael?"

"Too ordinary."

"Alexander?"

"Oh, come on. That's a French chef."

"Brian?"

"Please." He grabbed the book.

He flipped through to the R's, and a plump smile came onto his face.

"Actually," he said, "I don't think we have to look further than this. Ron Donleavy Junior," he said, savoring it.

Alexis felt the blood race through her face.

"No!" she said.

Ron looked shocked.

"I didn't mean it like that," she said quickly. "I agree—Ron is a perfect name—for you. But I just think the baby should have something different—a fresh start."

They went through the entire book, unable to agree on any names, and hating each other's suggestions. Finally, there were no more suggestions. The waiter brought their coffees.

"I have an idea," Alexis said carefully, "if it's a boy, we'll call him Ron. And if it's a girl, we'll call her Elise."

Ron thought about it a moment. Then, "All right," he said.

Alexis knew he was sure the baby was going to be a boy.

* * *

Elise Anne Donleavy was born on February ninth, at seven fifty-five in the morning. She was the little girl in the smocked dress, pale, delicate, with hair of Rumpelstiltskin gold.

It was feeding time, and the nurse brought in the sleeping baby. Alexis held her close. She could not believe Elise's softness, her fragility. She stroked the warm powdery head, memorized the way the tiny ears curled secretively in on themselves. She watched the tiny chest move with miniature breaths, and breathed with her.

"Elise," Alexis whispered at last.

The baby's eyes opened and she and Alexis looked at each other.

This is the love of my life, Alexis thought.

It was visiting hour. The door opened, and Ron, Henry, and Sylvia came softly in.

"We just saw the baby in the nursery," Sylvia said. "Oh, Alexis, she's absolutely exquisite. And I love the name 'Elise.' So unusual. Is it a family name?" she asked Ron.

"No," he said.

Alexis's father came over and kissed her. "I'm proud of you," he whispered. "You did a great job. She looks exactly like you did the day you were born."

The day Maggie had died and then came back because she couldn't bear to leave her baby.

"Where's Grandmother?" Alexis asked quickly.

"She wasn't feeling too well, and we didn't think she ought to come. But she sends her love."

Sylvia sat down on the bed. "We've brought a few things for the Little Princess."

There was a Steiff teddy bear, a Christian Dior jumpsuit, and a silver teething ring, engraved with *Elise*.

"That was quick," Ron said.

Sylvia laughed. "I know. I told the jewelry store I had a taxi double-parked outside, and I stood over them while they engraved it!"

Alexis didn't quite like the teething ring. Elise's name being on it made the baby more public somehow, more her own person, and not so much Alexis's.

"It's beautiful," she told Sylvia.

After her family left, Alexis decided she would read a little—or better yet, start filling out the birth announcements. She sat up slowly and tried to pull herself out of bed, but the effort was too painful. It was astonishing how weak she felt. She waited a moment, and tried again. This time, she managed to stand up. Painfully, she crab-walked over to her suitcase on the chair, pulled out the box of announcements and her address book, then got gratefully back into bed.

She began to fill out the cards. She sent them to everyone she could think of—friends from college, colleagues in her design class, cousins of Ron's, the manager of their apartment building. With every card she filled out, Elise seemed more established, more familiar, more real.

Finally, there were only two cards left in the box.

Alexis took the top one and filled in the information about Elise's birth. Then, along the top of the card, she wrote, "Dear Mama, You are a grandmother."

She paused, crumpled the note, and took a fresh one. "Dear Maggie, You are a grandmother," she wrote. She crumpled this one as well.

Here is the grandchild you said you would spoil, but not as much as you spoiled me.

She threw both cards into the wastebasket.

Three days later, Alexis brought Elise home from the hospital. Ron had offered to stay home from work and help them get settled, but Alexis had told him she could manage. The truth was, she wanted this moment alone with Elise.

She brought the baby up the stairs, and into the apartment. She took Elise all around; she showed her everything.

She showed Elise her favorite view from the window, and held up some lilac before her face. She took Elise on a tour of all her art posters and let her feel her velvet coat. She put some Mozart on the stereo, held Elise in her arms, and swayed with her to the music.

"These are all things I love," she whispered, "but not as much as I love you."

It was a cold evening in early April. Alexis and Ron stepped out of the cab and hurried into the noisy warmth of the Chinese restaurant. To Alexis, who had hardly been out of the apartment in two months, the small place seemed overwhelming.

"There they are!" Ron said, waving to a young couple in a booth near the back. He stalked toward them, smiling. Alexis followed more slowly.

The man stood up when he saw Alexis.

"I'm Chad Parker," he said, shaking her hand, "and this is my wife, Sara."

Sara smiled with anxious brightness. Alexis guessed that this was the first time her husband had included her in a business dinner.

"It's really great that you could come," Chad told Alexis. "I understand you've got a new baby who's keeping you pretty busy."

"Not so new now," Ron told him. "She's two months old—old enough to start paying her way. I've given her some paralegal work to cut her teeth on."

The Parkers laughed at the little joke. Alexis did not appear to have heard it.

"Actually, it's the first night we've ever left Elise with a sitter," she told Sara. "If you don't mind, I'd like to call home—just to make sure she's all right."

Ron laughed shortly. "Alexis, can't you at least wait till we've ordered?"

"No," she said. "I'd really like to call now."

A few minutes later, she came back into the dining room.

"Everything's fine," she smiled. "Elise is asleep."

Ron sighed. "What did you expect?" he asked.

"It must be incredible, being a mother," Sara said quickly. "I don't think I could handle it at all. The patience it must take."

"Well, it has its moments," Alexis confessed. "And as Ron has no doubt told you, I'm completely obsessed." She shook her head. "Today I thought I'd gone around the bend completely."

"Why? What happened?" Sara asked.

Clad and Ron were also listening now.

Alexis looked a little embarrassed.

"Well, Elise was invited to a birthday party. I spent

the whole morning getting her ready. I gave her a bath. I washed her hair. I put on her diaper. I put on her undershirt. I put on her tights. I got her in her party dress. I brushed her hair. I put on her sweater. I put on her leggings. I put on her coat.

"Finally she was ready. I put her in the stroller and we left the apartment. I opened the front door to go onto the street, and I suddenly noticed that I was very, very cold. I looked down and I saw that I was still wearing my nightgown."

Chad and Sara laughed and laughed. When Alexis glanced over at Ron, she saw that he was not laughing at all.

In the taxi going home, Ron sighed.

"Well, it was sure good to get out. I hope we'll start doing it a lot more often."

Alexis, counting the blocks until she could be with Elise again, fought panic.

"Didn't you miss the baby?" she asked.

He stared at her. "Alexis, it was for two and a half hours."

They did not speak for the rest of the ride.

"Sweetheart, stand still!" Alexis held out the pink silk kimono. "It's time to get you dressed!"

Elise slowed her dance. "Is that for the pageant?"

"Yes. It's your special costume—it's called a kimono."

The little girl's lip began to tremble. "It's silly. I don't want to wear it. It looks like a nightgown."

"It's made of silk," Alexis said quickly. "Pure silk. Feel how soft it is." Elise felt.

"And look at the dragons embroidered on it."

The dragons were cross-eyed, and they made Elise laugh. Alexis was able to get her arm into the kimono.

"And when you're wearing this costume," she said, "you have to behave in a very special way."

"Like this?" Elise did a handstand, and crashed on the floor, the kimono wrapped around her head.

Alexis rescued her. "No, not like that. You're pretending to be a Japanese girl who lived hundreds of years ago. You need to be very quiet, very gentle. Take tiny little steps."

"Like this?" Elise jumped around the room with giant leaps.

Alexis laughed and groaned.

Mrs. Avery wasn't feeling well enough to attend the pageant, and Ron had a meeting, but when Alexis arrived at Elise's nursery school, her father and Sylvia were already in their seats.

They kissed, and Alexis sat beside them.

"When does Elise come on?"

"She's in the first scene—the story of Little Peach."

"Is she excited?"

"That hardly describes it. The last I saw of her, she was doing cartwheels off the scenery."

The lights went down, and the pageant began. A little girl came onstage. Her head was held demurely down, a fan fluttered delicately in her hand, and her footsteps were shy and small. It took Alexis a moment to realize that it was her daughter.

Elise knelt on the stage and began to sing. As she

listened, Alexis's cheeks began to redden, and her throat began to close. It was the angle of the head, perhaps the lighting on the cheekbones, something in the voice. It was her mother singing on that stage.

After the show, everyone came over to congratulate Elise and Alexis.

"You were just wonderful," the principal told Elise. And to Alexis, "She's a born actress."

Alexis struggled to nod.

"Come here, baby." Alexis took Elise onto her lap. "Mama has something to tell you. I went to see the doctor today."

"Did you get a shot?" Elise asked.

"No, I was lucky. But he did tell me something interesting. He said that it looks like you're going to be having a little brother or sister."

Elise tried to jump off her lap. Alexis held on.

"Honey, you'll love it," she urged the struggling little girl. "You're going to have so much fun. And since you're five years older, you'll be the boss. It'll be like having your own baby."

Elise quieted.

"But will I still be your favorite?" she asked in a low voice.

Alexis hugged her. "Of course you will be, but just don't tell the baby. We don't want to hurt its feelings."

Elise nodded thoughtfully.

"And will I be Daddy's favorite?"

"I'm sure of it."

"Even if it's a boy?"

Ron Donleavy Junior.

"Even if it's a boy," Alexis told her hastily. "Boys

are great, but haven't you heard the phrase 'Daddy's girl'?"

Relief washed over Elise's face.

"I'm Daddy's girl, Daddy's girl."

"Yes, and Mama's girl," Alexis broke in. "You're Mama's girl, too."

Elise ignored the addition. "Daddy's girl! Daddy's girl!"

A few weeks later, Alexis took Elise on her lap again.

"I'm afraid the baby's gone away, sweetheart."

Elise began to cry, and Alexis rocked her in her arms.

"I'm sorry. I'm so sorry, darling."

"If it was a little sister, I was going to give her my charm bracelet," Elise wept.

Alexis's lips trembled.

"That was very generous of you," she said at last. "Well, I'll tell you what—whenever you wear that bracelet, we'll both think of her."

Then she began to cry also, and Elise stroked her hair.

"But don't forget, Mama," she whispered, "you've still got your favorite."

Alexis kissed her again and again.

It was the night before Elise's sixth birthday, and Alexis came into the little girl's room to tuck her in. Elise was sitting up in bed, surrounded by dolls, a veterinary set, and coloring books.

"It's time to get to bed now," Alexis told her, removing the toys. "You've got a big day tomorrow."

"Is my party starting the minute I get up?"

Alexis put Elise under the covers, and sat beside her.

"No, but you'll be getting presents at breakfast, and then the party starts at ten."

"Will the clown be there right away?"

"Yes, and the magician will be coming at ten-thirty. And at eleven, we'll have the cake."

Elise sighed with happiness.

"Did you have birthday parties when you were a little girl?"

Into Alexis's mind came the image of a tea party, and her mother buying a piñata. And being allowed to hit it until it burst, and the whiteness of her grandmother's face. Even after all these years, she felt cold.

"Only one," she told Elise hastily. "But it wasn't nearly as much fun as yours will be."

Elise considered this.

"Did Grandma Sylvia make you the party?"

"No. Great-Grandma did—and my mother," she added.

Elise frowned.

"You had a mother?"

"Sure."

"What was her name?"

"Maggie."

Elise laughed.

"Maggie! That's funny. Listen—I'm being a parrot—Maggie!" she squawked. "Maggie!"

Alexis smiled. "You're a great parrot."

The little girl settled back onto the pillows.

"When I'm a grown-up, I'm going to grow flowers and sell them to stores."

"That sounds lovely."

Elise looked at her with suspicion.

"You don't sound like it does."

"Oh, baby," Alexis said hastily, "It's just kind of strange thinking of you being a grown-up."

Elise patted Alexis's arm.

"Well," she said judiciously, "You can sell flowers with me."

Alexis smiled.

"It's a deal," she said.

While Elise held the chair for her, Alexis reached into the hall closet and pulled the suitcases down from the highest shelf.

"Will these be enough?" the little girl asked anxiously.

Alexis laughed. "We're only going away for the weekend."

"But all my animals want to come."

"I wouldn't bring too many. You've got all kinds of things to play with at Grandma and Grandpa's."

"But Grey Elephant's going to come."

"Of course Grey Elephant's going to come. I won't come if Grey Elephant doesn't come."

Elise smiled. "Can we have tea in my playhouse?"

"Every single day. And maybe Grandma Sylvia will find some horses for us to ride."

"And can we go into town and get ice cream?"

"Sure."

"And can I go in the boat? Please?"

"No, honey." Alexis said firmly. "You know you can't."

Elise stamped a foot.

"But we've got the Fourth of July parade to look forward to," Alexis told her quickly, "and the fireworks and the picnic. Grey Elephant will like that."

Elise nodded. "I'd better get his hat."

The family was sitting in the library when the butler came in.

"Dinner is served," he announced.

The best Meissen china had been put out, and a vase of roses was before every place.

"You didn't have to go to this trouble for us," Alexis told Sylvia, touched.

"Are you kidding? We've been looking forward to this visit for weeks!"

Ron sighed with pleasure as the first course, carrot and ginger soup, was served.

"God, it's good to be here," he said. "The city's just getting crazier and crazier—you don't know how great it is to get away."

"Well, we're thrilled to have you," Sylvia told him. She leaned over and hugged Elise, who was sitting next to her. "Especially you, young lady."

"You kids have any special plans?" Henry Avery asked.

Alexis shook her head. "Not really. Just being with you two."

"I want to go sailing," Ron said.

"Me, too," Elise cried.

Alexis sighed. Why on earth had Ron brought it up? She didn't want to go through this again.

"Honey, you know you can't," she told Elise. "Not till you learn to swim."

"What's happening with that?" Sylvia asked.

"The doctor said she should wait another year. Her ear canals are still very tiny apparently, and every time she gets water in them, she gets an earache."

"But I want to swim!" Elise cried. "I want to go sailing with Daddy!"

"Well, I want to go sailing with you, too," Ron smiled at her. "So tell your ears to hurry up and grow so they won't get earaches. Then you'll learn to swim and we'll go out on the boat every day."

"Can Grey Elephant come?"

"Grey Elephant can be the captain."

When Alexis woke up the next morning, she knew from the strength of the sunshine that it was late. Ron was already up and gone. It was wonderful to stretch in the linen sheets and plan the day. No breakfast to make, no apartment to tidy. She'd take a long walk before it got too hot. Then maybe she'd take Elise into town and see if there was anything cute in that new children's store Sylvia had told her about.

Alexis stretched, got out of bed, and put on her robe. She went down the hall to Elise's room.

"Hey, baby!" she called, stepping inside. Then she stopped. The bed was empty.

"Elise?" There was no answer. She checked the bathroom, but the little girl wasn't there either.

She went downstairs into the dining room.

"Elise?"

There was no one at the table.

She went back upstairs to the master bedroom. Sylvia was sitting at her dressing table, talking on the phone. She waved to Alexis.

"Good morning," she mouthed. "Have you had breakfast yet?"

Alexis shook her head.

"I was wondering if you'd seen Elise."

Sylvia held up a finger.

"Amy," she said into the phone, "Alexis is up now, and I've got to get going. I'll see you on the thirteenth. Yes. Right. 'Bye."

She hung up.

"Did you try the kitchen? She said she wanted to help Mattie bake brownies for the picnic."

Alexis smiled.

"Of course. She's been talking about it all week."

But only the cook was in the kitchen.

"Has Elise been here?" Alexis asked.

Mattie shook her head.

"I haven't seen her since last night."

Alexis grew suddenly very cold.

They all began to look. They searched the house, the grounds, the sheds, the stables.

"Elise! Elise!"

The cries coming from everywhere, louder and louder, were met with silence.

Alexis was in Elise's little playhouse. She was kneeling on the floor. Her hands were in front of her face, her eyes were closed. She sent out little golden letters into the air. COME BACK. COME BACK.

She waited. It grew very quiet, and then she heard voices outside. She rose quickly.

Sylvia came into the playhouse. Her eyes were red.

Alexis could see figures moving on the lawn, and she started to go toward them.

Sylvia stopped her.

"Don't, dear," she said.

Alexis did not move.

"They've found Elise."

Alexis was silent for a long time.

"Where?" she asked.

"In the swimming pool."

That evening the housekeeper discovered the little note on the table by the back door. "I am gong to swim for Dady."

"We'll have a lovely night, my angel," Alexis told Elise. She dressed her in her favorite Tinkerbell nightgown and put her in bed.

Henry and Ron and her grandmother kept knocking on the door, but she had locked it and would not let them in.

"Alexis," Sylvia called gently. "Dear, this isn't right. Arrangements have to be made. The doctor says—"

"I don't care what he says," Alexis told her.

Alexis carefully arranged Grey Elephant in Elise's arms. Then she got *The Blue Fairy Book* from the shelf and pulled up a chair beside the bed. Ordinarily, she read Elise one story every night. This night, she read her the entire book. By the time she had finished, her voice was so hoarse she could hardly speak.

Dawn had come. Alexis kissed Elise on her forehead.

"Sleep well, my baby," she whispered. "Until soon."

And she unlocked the door.

Twelve

There was a soft knock on the heavy beveled drawing room door. Pierre, the houseman, came in.

"Madame, there is a phone call for you," he said.

Maggie seemed relieved by the interruption. "Who is it?"

"A Mr. Walters."

Maggie stood up.

"It's business," she told Paul. "This man stands to make me a fortune. I'll be back in a few minutes."

She strode from the room.

Paul was left to himself. He walked over to the piano and studied the silver-framed photographs atop it. There was a still of Maggie as Viola, candids taken with Fellini and Picasso, a comic shot of her in a "Spaghetti Western," trying to ride a horse, and a beautiful portrait of her in a costume he did not recognize; it looked classical—possibly she was playing Medea.

Then he walked over to the bookshelves and looked at the photographs there. In the center was a studio portrait of a little girl whom Paul assumed was Alexis. She was wearing a velvet dress and sitting on a wicker chair. She looked around six years old, with a timid, rather weary smile.

Scattered around were many photographs of Philip. Paul looked at these with special interest. Other than those pictures in the tabloids, which, as always, made their subject look grotesque, he had seen few photographs of Philip Fredericks. Philip as a young man was very much a type—Noël Coward, Cole Porter, with the heavy eyelids, the heavy overcoat, the slicked-black hair, the chic, knotted tie. But in later pictures—ones taken when he first came to Paris with Maggie?—the air of guardedness, of irony, was gone. He seemed luminous, generous. Then, in his final years, the face changed again. It became gentler, more expectant of sorrow. He looked fragile and insubstantial next to Maggie, almost as if his strength had gone to her, to lend her radiance.

Maggie returned.

"So sorry to have kept you waiting," she said.

"I hope he made you that fortune."

She stiffened slightly. Paul sensed that his remark had overstepped a boundary.

"I've been looking at photographs," he changed the subject quickly. "Is that all right?"

"Of course," she said. "I assume you managed to figure out who everyone was."

"Everyone except you in the toga."

"I was Antigone."

"I wish I could have seen that."

"Yes," Maggie said meditatively. "I was brilliant."

She sat down, flipped her caftan out of the way.

"Well, let's get on with this. I won't ask where we were," she told him. "I know where we were. Philip."

She grimaced. "As I was walking back here, I was thinking how I was going to handle this—deciding what to tell you, and what not to tell you."

"Why don't you just tell me what you want to," Paul said.

She smiled dryly.

"That's what I intended to do anyway."

She lit another cigarette.

"First of all, you've got to understand what Hollywood was like in those days. Now, of course, anything goes. Actors can be completely honest about themselves. Nobody's shocked if this one's gay, or that one's on drugs, or if somebody runs away with someone else's wife. They go on talk shows and the audience loves them. A much healthier attitude, I think—don't you?"

Paul agreed.

"But back in the forties, it was utter hypocrisy. Actors were under contract, and you had to sign morality clauses. The studio heads ran this town—the most dreadful little men—and such terrible prudes."

"I've heard that in their personal lives, those men were anything but," Paul said.

"You're right. Most of them were absolute satyrs. But that didn't matter in the least. Their actors had to be lily-white." She laughed shortly. "Of course, in secret . . . In secret, everything you can imagine went on. Much, much more so than today, I think. And that was all right—the studios turned a blind eye, as long as it stayed secret. If you made friends with Hedda and Louella, if you kept on the right side of the Hays office—they were the ones who made up that ridiculous code of moral conduct—you could do anything you wanted in private. But of course, the strain was terrible. It completely ruined lives. Look at poor Rock Hudson and all those others, having to live those lies. But they had no choice. If you didn't play the game, you were out, out, out."

She shook her head. "Get me started on the subject, and you see what happens? I climb right onto my soapbox. Well, that's enough of that; let's get back to me." She laughed. "Where we belong!"

"You had just met Philip Fredericks."

"Yes. He said, 'I understand you want to be our receptionist.' I followed him back to his office and he offered me a chair across from him. He asked me questions, and I must have answered them—I don't remember a thing. I was in a complete daze. I couldn't keep my eyes off his hands," she added softly. "They were the most delicate hands—an artist's hands. At the end of the interview he told me, 'If you want the job, it's yours.'

"I was utterly thrilled. I went home, terribly excited, and called a girl I knew—someone I thought was a friend. I told her I'd just met the man I was going to marry." Maggie paused. "She couldn't wait to tell me that Philip was married already."

"What did you do?"

"I cried for an hour and decided to turn the job down. But in the end, I took it. Of course. You can't run away from your destiny."

Maggie narrowed her eyes.

"And as it turned out, I ended up being a wonderful receptionist. I learned the secret early—make every client who calls think that his or her call is the most important one of the whole day."

"It sounds as if your receptionist work was equal to your grilled cheese sandwiches," Paul offered.

"Even better. I threw myself completely into the part. So help me, it was an Academy Award performance."

"And with—Mr. Fredericks?"

She raised her eyebrows.

"I was totally professional. Receptionist to Boss, and nothing more. Another Academy Award performance, I might add! That whole first year, I stayed as far away from Philip as possible. But I found out everything I could about him. And of course, that made me love him even more," she added with a painful little laugh.

Paul nodded. He thought of the stories he had uncovered in his own research, and how poignant they would seem to a young woman, hungry for love.

"Philip's father apparently was a lot like mine. Gentry, but with absolutely no grip on reality. He got into some political trouble back in Hungary and the family had to flee to America when Philip was a little boy. They lost everything they had."

She shook her head.

"At the end, when Philip was dying, he told me a story I'll never forget.

"His father loved classical music. Back in Hungary, he had a wonderful collection of records, and every night he and Philip would play a special game.

His father would put a record on the gramophone, and Philip would have to guess what piece it was. When they got to America, they were penniless—they had had to leave everything behind. But every night, they would still play the game. Except now, since they no longer had their gramophone, Philip's father would whistle the music instead."

"Wow," Paul said.

"Yes."

Maggie put her head in her hands. The jewels in her rings caught the light.

Then she lifted her head again. "Philip was the most urbane, charming man you could ever meet. But his demons were always there. He took great care not to let anybody know, but I knew. I could always see that frightened little boy in him.

"And he could always see Maggie." Her voice rang, ragged. "The real Maggie. The hungry little girl with no shoes, trying her damndest to believe that she was Somebody."

Distractedly, she stubbed out the cigarette. They both stared at the smoking remains.

"If I had known then, how it would all end," she went on in a curious voice, "I sometimes wonder if I would have behaved differently." She stopped. "Well, maybe it was better that I didn't know. It usually is, isn't it?"

She did not wait for an answer.

"It was a hard year for me. Going into the office every day, and seeing Philip. Being so madly in love, and having to hide it."

Paul waited a discreet moment.

"And Philip? Did you know what he felt?"

"Oh, he was completely professional. But of course, I knew. I had known that since the day we met.

"But during that whole first year, nothing. I'm proud of us both for that."

"Did you ever meet—his wife?"

She made a face. "Lenore. Only once. But I heard all the office gossip. Philip had married her back in Boston, right after he graduated from law school; she was very rich, I gather. When he decided to come to Hollywood, apparently she fought it tooth and nail. Felt the film industry was beneath her.

"She wasn't terribly liked at the office.

"When I met her, I was just stunned. She wasn't what I was expecting at all. She looked—let's see— like a high school history teacher—no, worse; a math teacher—a math teacher who enjoys flunking the kids.

"Of course, when the magazines printed all those stories about us, they managed to find pictures of her when she was very young and innocent-looking But I'm sure you've seen all those."

She did not look toward Paul's nod.

Then, unexpectedly, a much lighter note came into her voice.

"I did make friends with Philip's son, though. His name was Richard—he was about four. An absolutely darling little boy. His nanny used to bring him to the office sometimes. He would always steal my memo pad and hide it in one of the filing cabinets—that was our little game."

A sad silence fell. Maggie seemed trapped within it. Paul changed the subject.

"Did you do any acting during that time?"

Slowly, she refocused.

"No, not at all. I didn't even audition. I simply didn't have the energy. Sometimes at night I would dream that I was onstage, but that was it."

Knowing what story was coming next, he waited in patience.

"And then, one day"—a tiny smile—"a messenger put a script on my desk.

"Usually, I just passed scripts back to the Executive Office without even looking at them, but the title of this one caught my eye. It was called *Green Flame.*"

She acknowledged his grin. "You know all this," she said.

"I want to hear it from you."

She arranged the caftan fussily.

"Well, just by chance, this script happened to arrive on my lunch break, when I had nothing to do. I picked it up, and started to read it. Then, when I got to page four, and the character Fran came in that barroom, I *knew*. I knew that this was it—that this part was meant for me."

Her whole face shone.

"From that moment on, it took over my life. I went about as Fran from morning to night."

"Considering the character, that's a little scary," Paul said.

Maggie shrugged. "Not if you understand her— and I understood her completely. I knew exactly why she had to kill Dale.

"Anyway, I made myself a copy of the script, and I worked on it every chance I got. By the end of the week, I had put a complete performance together—but I couldn't do a damn thing about it. I just had to wait. Weeks went by. Philip's company bought the project. I took all the calls. The deal went through, and the movie was ready to be cast.

"Day after day, I had to sit there at my desk and watch a parade of actresses—all of them completely wrong—come and read for my part. I wished every kind of voodoo known to man upon them. And it worked! Only two weeks before shooting, and Fran still wasn't cast.

"One day a girl I knew walked into the office—a little Miss No-Talent who lived down the block from me. She was terribly amused to find me working as a receptionist, and told me all about this wonderful part her agent had sent her to read for—Fran.

"Well, that was it. I'd had enough. She went into the conference room where all the producers were, and did her audition, and I sat there and seethed. A few minutes later, Philip showed her out.

"Now here's where the story gets wonderful," Maggie said softly. She showed Paul her lightly freckled arm. "Look—even after all these years, I still get goose bumps.

"I followed Philip back to the conference room, closed the door, and locked it behind me. No one had any idea of what was going on, of course—they all looked scared to death at being held hostage by the receptionist!

"I said, 'I want to read the part of Fran for you.'

"I read for them—her big speech to the mother—and as long as I live, I will never forget the moment that followed.

"Whenever I can't sleep," she said simply, "I relive that moment.

"There was complete silence at first. And then one of the producers began to applaud. And then they all applauded. And then Philip said, 'I think we've found Fran.'"

She wiped her eyes.

"It must have been quite an experience. Your first movie—and debuting in that part."

"It was fantastic. I loved making that movie. At first, I was a little nervous about working with George Raft—I'd heard awful things about him—but he was always terribly kind to me during the shooting."

"Was working with him the high point of the film?"

Maggie considered. "No. I think my favorite part was having my hair done every morning. I've always had ghastly hair—it's baby thin, and does precisely what it wants to—but that hairdresser was a genius. He made me look absolutely beautiful."

The smile broadened. "And I loved the clothes. I've always adored those 1860s' costumes. And Wardrobe let me wear the locket that Kelly gave me. If you look closely, you can see it in every scene."

She leaned back.

"I knew, with everything in me, that the movie would be a smash—and that it would make me a star. Every night before I went to sleep, I would imagine newspaper headlines: RECEPTIONIST SCORES IN DEBUT. MAGGIE ROYAL—HEADED FOR OSCAR. I made up something different every night, and do you know something? Nearly every one of those headlines came true.

"It changed my life completely, of course. Suddenly I was famous—I was on the front page of *Variety,* and every magazine in town wanted to do a story on me."

"I know. I've read them all. They called you the Cinderella girl."

"Yes. Except for the ones that called me a cold-blooded manipulator."

"Which was the truth?"

"I guess they both were."

She paused, shook her head.

"What a time that was. All the dreams coming true." Then she added briskly, "And I took it pretty well, I think. During the years I'd been in Hollywood, I'd thought a lot about how I'd handle fame when I finally got it. I had everything figured out—the way I'd treat the press, whether or not I'd give autographs, which advertisements I'd do."

Maggie tapped the arm of her chair and gave a shrewd little smile. "I like that about me. I like myself for worrying about those things, instead of where next month's rent was coming from. And who knows? Maybe that's the reason I made it.

"And I'll tell you something else. When I did become famous, I ended up sticking with every decision I made."

"Is that why you answer every fan letter personally?"

"Yes," she said. "I simply can't understand the Garbos of the world. I adored everyone knowing who I was—being Somebody at last. The day after *Green Flame* premiered, twenty-seven scripts arrived at the office. Only now, I wasn't the receptionist whose job was to sign for them. Now those scripts were coming for *me.*"

Tears glittered in her eyes.

"It was fantastic.

"And I've got to tell you about the clothes! The shoes I bought! My first Chanel blouse!"

There was a pause and Maggie looked at Paul keenly.

"But this isn't what you want to hear about, is it?"

She took a breath.

"I don't think any woman sets out to have an affair with a married man," she said flatly. "And I don't think any woman sets out to break up a marriage. We tell ourselves all those clichés—that no one can break up a good marriage, that the feeling was just too strong for us.

"A few days after I had signed to do *Green Flame,* Philip came over to my desk and handed me a book. It was that Hans Andersen story, *The Steadfast Tin Soldier.* You know it, I'm sure—the toy soldier falls in love with a paper ballerina, but fate comes between them and they can't be together. So at the end, the two of them jump into the fire.

"When I read the story, I knew it was Philip's way of finally telling me he loved me."

She paused speculatively.

"When *Green Flame* was shot, Philip was always on the set. During my scenes, I would see his shadow come up from behind the lights. I knew he was watching me.

"But we never spoke.

"The night of the premiere, his wife and son were away in Europe. The studio thought it would be good publicity if the star of the picture came to the premiere on the arm of the producer. So Philip was my escort.

"We sat side by side. When the lights went down, he took my hand. After the movie was over, he took me back to my apartment—he didn't need to say a word.

"We were together the entire time his wife was away."

Paul breathed as quietly as he could, wanting her to forget his presence.

"It was an enchanted summer. We didn't go out much. We just stayed in my apartment. I remember I made Philip go around and touch everything in it—so ridiculous—the cups, the pillowcases, the picture of Mama. So that no matter what happened, he would always be a part of everything."

The voice grew more and more offhand.

"In September, his wife came back. Philip asked for a divorce the day she returned. But she wouldn't give it to him. Instead, she went around Hollywood saying her husband had betrayed her with a whore.

"But I'm sure you know all about that," she told Paul.

Yes, he knew all about that.

"Sometimes, I wonder how I kept my sanity.

"Philip said we would ride it out together. He said it would all blow over, that by the time my next picture was released, no one in Hollywood, including me, would even remember those headlines.

"Well, I, for one, can still recite them word for word."

She shook her head in a little spasm.

"Philip was very, very dear during it all. He didn't say much, but it must have been terrible for him as well. After all, his name was in the gossip columns, too. But it's different for a man, isn't it?

"He rented an apartment in the Hollywood Hills, and we moved in there together. It was a strange time. Philip still worked, of course, but it was harder for the deals to get made. No one called it a boycott, but of course that's what it was. And everywhere I went, there were reporters. It got to the point where I didn't want to go outside. I stayed at home, reading—I got through the entire works of Dickens—and waiting for Philip to come home."

"What about acting?"

"Are you kidding? No studio would touch me. And I didn't want Philip's company to take that kind of chance. We could have left Hollywood, of course, gone back East, but Philip wouldn't do that. He wanted to face them all down."

"It must have been very difficult."

"Yes. But Philip was completely determined. He said we would get married the following Christmas Eve, and that every studio head in town would be invited. And he did the most touching thing. He had the man who had done my clothes for *Green Flame* design me an 1860s wedding dress. I put the sketch on the bedroom wall, and I looked at it all the time—but it's funny—I always knew I would never wear that dress."

The sun was starting to set, and extravagant color washed over Maggie from the windows.

"I had put the book Philip had given me, *The Steadfast Tin Soldier,* in the den. Every so often I'd come upon it, and read about the soldier and the ballerina jumping into the fire. *That* was the ending I believed in.

"But you know something—Philip was right. By spring, the gossip did begin to die out. And we heard nothing more from his wife. Philip said that was a good sign. But then early one morning the phone rang. Philip went to get it. When he came back, he looked absolutely gray. He said, 'That was St. John's Hospital. Lenore tried to kill herself.'"

Maggie rose, stood behind the sofa, the sunset fierce around her.

"It all started up again—the headlines, the hue and cry—but this time, it was worse than before. I don't know how much all that had to do with Philip's decision. Whether the strain was too great. Or whether it was just the guilt.

"But he left me and went back to her."

Thirteen

Miriam Lawson fluttered anxious hands. "Oh, Mrs. Donleavy—it's utter chaos here. Thank you a thousand times for coming over."

"It's quite all right," Alexis told her. "I live just around the corner."

She glanced into the living room where a man in white, obviously the caterer, was arguing vehemently with Mrs. Lawson's cook. Plumbers went back and forth from the bathroom, and banging sounds issued from the kitchen.

"I couldn't believe it!" Mrs. Lawson told her. "All I did was flush, and the water just kept coming up and coming up—and look what it's done to the wallpaper!" She led Alexis into the guest bathroom, and showed her where the brownish stain drowned the toile shepherdess. "And the kitchen stove—the caterer says it simply isn't sufficient to handle the party tomorrow. I don't know how we're going to manage!"

She gripped Alexis's hands. "And when I think—when I think that all we ever intended was simplicity!"

Alexis squeezed the white hands. "Don't worry," she said. "Everything will be fine. I'll have a word with the caterer; I'm sure it can be worked out. Believe me, there are many restaurants in this city that operate with smaller stoves than you've got. And I've already called my plumber. He promised he'd be right over. I think the wallpaper will dry without any problem, but if bad comes to worse, I'll be over before the party with some paste, and I'll glue it back myself."

Mrs. Lawson sighed. "Thank you," she said. Then she frowned. "Has Nadine shown you the guest list? I keep having this terrible feeling that there's someone I've forgotten to invite. Nadine! Nadine!"

The young anxious-looking secretary hurried from the office. "Please show Mrs. Donleavy the list for tomorrow's party."

The list was brought and Alexis looked at it. Every society matron in town was included, as well as an ambassador or two, the editor of a decorating magazine, and herself.

"I can't think of anyone you've left out," she said.

"Are you sure there's no one you'd like to bring?" Mrs. Lawson asked.

Alexis shook her head.

"Well, if you change your mind, it's a buffet, and there'll be plenty."

"Honestly, no." Alexis wondered if that was a little sad, that she had nobody she wanted to invite. But Ron would be at work, and she wasn't in the habit of lunching with women friends.

The doorbell rang. It was the plumber.

"Thank God!" Mrs. Lawson said fervently. "All I can say is, thank God."

Alexis smiled. "Well, I think you'll be all right now."

As Alexis walked home, she could almost sense the evening pressing upon the city. Although it was May, it did not feel like spring. The sky was heavy and airless, and even the trees seemed to be straining to keep the weary weight off.

Weary weight. That described what Alexis was feeling exactly. Weary weight from a too-full, too-empty day.

She reached her apartment building.

"Hello, Mrs. Donleavy," said the doorman. She strove to echo his smile.

When she got up to her apartment, she could see that the light on the answering machine was blinking. She hit the button, hoping that it wasn't Mrs. Lawson with another emergency.

"I just called to say that the meeting's running late," came Ron's voice. "So I won't be home for dinner. See you when I see you."

Alexis stood by the phone, uncertain of what to do now. She had planned on making a chicken dish that night, but she didn't feel like going to the trouble if Ron wouldn't be home.

She ended up fixing herself some cream of tomato soup. She put it on a tray, added a festive napkin from Mexico, and brought it into the living room. Dinner and a good book; that would be pleasant. She picked up the new best-seller that Ron had left lying on the ottoman, and began to read it. It was an espionage novel, not very well written, and at page nineteen she put the book down. She picked up the remote control instead and turned on the television. There might be something good on the movie channel.

She was taking the empty soup plate back to the kitchen, so it was the voice rather than the face which struck her first. She froze, the dish rigid in her hands. The voice went on and on—husky, laughing—the voice of her mother.

Alexis put the tray on the kitchen counter and went back to the living room.

There was Maggie, in the old black-and-white movie. Young, eager. And so beautiful. It had been years since Alexis had watched one of her mother's films. Whenever she saw in the *TV Guide* that one was on, she made a point of avoiding it. But tonight, she watched, her eyes and her head hot and aching.

She watched the movie until it ended. She had trouble following the plot—she only saw her mother. Some of the gestures she remembered so well—some of the inflections. She watched, awed and sorrowful.

The key slid in the lock, and Ron was home. He came into the living room.

He did not say anything, just watched the final minutes of the film with Alexis. He put his arm around her.

"She's really good," he said.

Near tears, Alexis nodded.

"I didn't know you watched her movies."

"I don't. This one just happened to be on."

He shook his head. "It must be so strange, seeing her like that."

"Yes."

"Is that the way she looked when you—knew her?"

"No. She was much younger in this. I never saw her act."

Except as Lady Macbeth, in my bedroom.

Alexis stood up abruptly. She went into the kitchen and started cleaning up, but she paid no attention to what she was doing. Instead, images from the movie kept coming into her mind. Maggie telling the factory owner to get out of her workroom. The way she held her head. The pointing gesture she had used. And her voice. That voice.

I wonder if it's still the same.

Alexis wrenched her thoughts away.

She would not think about her mother. She would think about something else.

She concentrated on tomorrow's schedule. There was the morning meeting with the Fergusons' architect, a hairdresser's appointment, Mrs. Lawson's luncheon, and in the afternoon, a visit to Scalamandré to scout out some fabrics.

It would be a busy day. A pleasantly busy day. But Alexis found herself growing exhausted at the very thought of it. What on earth was wrong? she wondered. Five years ago, even two, she would have looked forward to such a schedule. She would have relished the discussion with the architect, loved going to choose new fabrics; she would have enjoyed talking with the guests at the luncheon, possibly gaining a new client or two. But lately, more and more, it seemed, there was this lethargy. Was it that she was simply spoiled, or was she getting old?

The thought of the luncheon, especially, filled Alexis with weariness. It would be the same crowd of people, the same discussions, even the same compliments on her decorating. She briefly considered canceling, but recalling Mrs. Lawson's panic that afternoon, Alexis knew there was no way she could let the woman down.

She thought again about Mrs. Lawson's invitation to bring a guest to the party. It was a pity Jacey didn't live closer; she would have loved to come, but she wasn't due to visit New York for another month. And all the other women Alexis knew were so involved with their own lives.

Then she drew in a sudden sharp breath. She dropped the soup bowl into the pan of soapy water, dried her hands, and went into the den. She looked up Mrs. Lawson's telephone number, and dialed.

"Hello?" said a breathless voice.

"Mrs. Lawson, this is Alexis Donleavy. I hope I haven't called too late. I was just wondering—may I still take you up on your offer of bringing a guest tomorrow?"

The next afternoon, at twelve-thirty, Alexis was standing on the corner of Sixty-seventh Street, willing a taxi to come. One appeared promptly from around the corner, and she got inside. The driver glanced back at her balefully in his rearview mirror.

"Where to?"

Alexis gave the address of Brian House.

The driver hit his steering wheel, cursing at having to go back downtown on such a muggy day.

When they reached Brian House, Alexis told the driver to wait. She dashed inside, and there was Linda, standing, as instructed, by the front desk, pale with excitement.

"If you'll just sign her out, Mrs. Donleavy," Dara said.

Alexis did so, and then she and Linda made their way back to the taxi.

"We're now going back uptown, to Forty-five East Eighty-second Street," Alexis informed the driver.

He punched his foot down on the gas pedal.

With the motion, Linda's attempt at calmness dissolved.

"Oh, Mrs. Donleavy, I'm so nervous," she burst out. "Please tell me what the surprise is! Steven Wheelhouse only said that you wanted to take me somewhere. But he wouldn't say where we were going."

Alexis smiled.

"That's because I asked him not to."

Linda looked impressed.

It hadn't been quite as easy as all that, however. Steven Wheelhouse had sounded very unsure over the phone, when Alexis had called to request Linda for a few hours that afternoon.

"What is this in reference to?" he asked.

"To the box Linda designed for my client."

"Could it wait until the weekend?" She could hear him rustling papers. "Linda's got class until three."

"I'm afraid it has to be today," she said. "I'm sorry

about her missing school, but it's a very special opportunity for her to see her work on display. I think it would do wonders"—she used his own words, "for her self-esteem."

He had finally agreed.

"Just make sure to have her back by four o'clock," he said.

Alexis promised that she would. "And please don't tell her why I want to see her—I'd like it to be a surprise."

He promised in return.

"Will you tell me now?" Linda asked eagerly.

"I'm taking you to Mrs. Lawson's apartment," Alexis told her. "That's the lady you made the box for. She's having a luncheon —and we thought you might enjoy going."

Linda's face flashed pink and white in turn. And then suddenly she looked wretched.

"But, Mrs. Donleavy," she said. "I can't."

"Why not?" Alexis asked.

Embarrassedly, Linda indicated her appearance.

She was dressed that day in black leather shorts, a black lace top, black boots, and elbow-length gloves.

Alexis took in the sight.

"So?"

"Well . . ." Linda said in a low voice, "I won't look like anyone else there."

"Of course you won't," Alexis told her crisply. "And there's no reason you should."

They rang the doorbell. Mrs. Lawson's maid opened the door, and Alexis walked inside the apartment, Linda following timidly behind her.

"Here you are at last!" Mrs. Lawson cried.

Alexis had been a little apprehensive as to what the woman's reaction would be when she discovered that Linda was only fifteen years old, but Mrs. Lawson was enchanted.

"So this is the little artist!" she cried. "She's adorable! Wherever did you find her?"

Linda and Alexis only smiled mysteriously. They had both agreed that it would perhaps be wiser not to mention anything about Brian House, or the circumstances under which the two of them had met.

Mrs. Lawson led them into the living room, which was full of guests.

"This is Alexis Donleavy," she announced, "the genius behind the redecoration. And this is—what was your name again, dear?—this is Linda, who made that charming box on the end table."

There were murmurs and compliments. Alexis did indeed know nearly all the women in the room, and they exchanged greetings. Then the editor of the decorating magazine hurried up and asked if Alexis would agree to do an interview for their October issue.

"Is that your daughter?" he asked, pointing at Linda.

"No," Alexis said.

"Oh, sorry; I somehow got the idea she was."

Alexis went over to Linda, who was standing self-consciously behind the sofa.

"Look, Linda," she said.

She took the girl's hand and led her over to the coffee table. On it was an antique Venetian paperweight, a small Victorian watercolor on an easel, and the box.

"What do you think?"

Linda only fluttered her hands and said nothing.

"Did you really make this?"

Maddie Patterson, a woman Alexis knew slightly, came up to them.

"How old are you? Fifteen? Well, I tell you, I have a daughter just about your age, and believe me, she could never in a million years . . ."

Alexis watched the two of them, listened to Linda's responses. The girl was both gracious and curiously dignified—Alexis was impressed by the way she was handling herself. Then another woman came up to join the conversation, and Alexis decided it was safe to leave Linda alone with them for a few minutes.

She went off into another room, to discuss an architectural change with Peggy Havens, a current client; when she came back, most of the guests had gone to the buffet. She found Linda in the dining room, sitting on a footstool, and working her way through a plate of pasta. On the floor beside her were four chocolate chip cookies and the remains of a large cup of coffee.

"I thought you weren't supposed to have caffeine," Alexis observed.

Linda blushed.

The caterer came up to them, the silver coffeepot extended.

"May I offer you some more?" he asked.

Linda looked apprehensively at Alexis.

"Oh, go ahead," Alexis said. "Since it is a special occasion. And then she added, "I won't tell on you."

She remembered saying that before.

When she and Linda had finished their lunch, Alexis found Mrs. Lawson.

"It was a wonderful party," she said. "Thank you so much for having us."

"Surely you're not going?"

"I'm afraid we have to," Alexis said. "I need to get Linda back to school."

Mrs. Lawson kissed Alexis on the cheek and extended her hand to Linda. "It was such a pleasure to meet you," she said. "I'm sure you'll be a famous artist when you grow up."

Linda thanked her with graceful decorum, but the moment she and Alexis were in the elevator, the calmness dropped.

"Oh, Mrs. Donleavy!" she jerked out. "That was the greatest thing that's ever happened to me! Her place was so beautiful! And seeing my box on the table!"

Alexis smiled. "Well, it belonged there," she said.

She loved the look on Linda's face. She knew that feeling of triumph, and she wanted to expand the moment, let Linda savor it as long as possible.

Self-consciously, she coughed. "Would you like to go for a walk in the park?" she asked.

"Can we?" Linda asked eagerly. "You told Mrs. Lawson I needed to be back at school."

"That was a convenient lie," Alexis confessed. "I get bored at luncheons." She checked her watch. "Actually, we have an hour and a half."

Linda clasped her hands together.

But as they stepped out of the elevator into the lobby, they saw that the muggy weather had coalesced at last. Dirty New York rain was assaulting the pavement.

"Oh, no!" Linda breathed.

"Well, that cancels the park," Alexis said.

Linda looked like she was about to cry.

"Listen," Alexis told her suddenly. "I live only a block from here. Why don't we make a dash for it, and go to my apartment?"

As Alexis opened her front door, she remembered the promise Ron had extracted from her—never to let one of the kids from Brian House into their home.

Well, it was too late now.

Linda came into the apartment and stood by the doorway.

"Oh, my God," she whispered, looking around. She walked slowly, trancelike, through the living room, examining everything. When she spotted Alexis's collection of Limoges boxes, she gave a little cry.

Alexis made a mental note to get her one for her birthday.

"Sometimes they have designs inside," she told Linda.

One by one, Linda carefully opened the boxes, exclaiming with delight when she found a flower or a flourish painted under the lid.

"I'm going to do that with my boxes, too," she breathed.

Then Alexis took her around the rest of the apartment. Linda looked with care at all the paintings, scrutinized all the items on the bookshelves, felt the fabrics of the bedspread and the draperies, even noticed the brass frog on the tiebacks.

Alexis tried to make the visit educational, and pointed out to Linda the various mistakes she felt she had made in the decorating. But Linda could see no mistakes anywhere.

They sat down at last in the living room.

"I'll make us some tea," Alexis said. "Do you like chamomile?"

"I've never tried it."

"Well, you should. There's no caffeine in it."

Linda loved the tea, and Alexis noted, yet again, the satisfaction she felt at introducing the girl to new experiences.

"So how are things going with you?" Alexis asked her.

"Oh, all right."

"School okay?"

Linda shrugged.

"You and Samantha getting along?"

"Actually, she left Brian House last week. She moved back in with her parents."

She said it wistfully.

Alexis remembered what Steven Wheelhouse had told her about Linda's own family.

"How's Raoul?" she asked quickly, looking for a happy change of subject.

It was the wrong thing to have said. Linda's head went down.

"We're on punishment," she said in a small voice. "We can't see each other for a month."

"Why not?"

"Mr. Wheelhouse caught us in the dining room together. We were holding hands."

Tears started to darken Linda's eyelashes.

Alexis watched her; and as it had happened before, at the same time she was seeing another girl—herself as a teenager, so desperately in love with Jimmy Craig.

Alexis gulped the rest of her chamomile tea. It seared the roof of her mouth.

"Damn!" she said.

Linda looked startled.

"Are you okay, Mrs. Donleavy?"

Alexis put the cup down.

"I'm sorry," she said. "It's just—you made me remember something I haven't thought of for a long time."

Linda waited. Alexis went on self-consciously.

"Back when I was in college, there was a boy—and we couldn't be together. That's all. Looking back, I can see it was nothing," she tried to sound light, "but at the time it was very painful."

"Didn't you ever get to be with him?" Linda asked in a low voice.

Alexis thought of Jimmy locking himself in the Avery library, and her beating on the door.

"No."

"That's so sad," Linda said.

"No, it isn't," Alexis told her briskly. "Everything turned out the way it should have. And believe me, the right thing will happen with you and Raoul as well."

"But what is that?"

"I don't know," Alexis admitted. "When you get a little older—"

"But we love each other now!"

Alexis sighed.

"Is there no way you and Raoul could find a quiet place just to talk?" she asked. As she said the words, she knew she shouldn't be asking, shouldn't be getting involved in this.

Linda shook her head.

"There are monitors all over the place. And we're never allowed to close doors, so people are always coming in and out."

Then her face brightened slightly.

"But this week's been better," she said. "I've been making some more boxes with the money you gave me. And Raoul's okay, too. His older brother's in town, and Mr. Wheelhouse is letting them spend the afternoon together. Leo's in sales. He's taken Raoul to a really good restaurant today."

Alexis smiled at the naive importance in the girl's voice.

"And what restaurant's that?"

Linda named a place, and Alexis nodded. Just the sort of place an out-of-towner in sales would choose.

"Do you know it?" Linda asked anxiously. "Is it really good?"

"Yes, I know it well," Alexis told her, avoiding the second question. "It's just around the corner from here."

Linda drew in a breath and looked at her.

"Oh, Mrs. Donleavy," she whispered.

Alexis always wondered later what strange bend her mind took then. Whether it was the force of Linda's expression at that moment—or was it that memory of herself at eighteen? But even as she was dialing Information to get the number of the restaurant, she was very clearly aware that she should not be doing this.

But really, what harm can it do? They've probably left already.

No, the gentlemen hadn't left, she was told by the maitre d'; and a few moments later, another voice came onto the telephone.

"Raoul," Alexis said, and she could feel Linda stiffen on the couch behind her. "Raoul, this is Alexis Donleavy. I tutor at Brian House, and Linda's one of the girls in my class."

There was a confused pause.

"Is she all right?" Raoul asked.

"Yes," Alexis said. "She's here with me now. We're having tea, as a matter of fact—right around the corner from you. I wondered if you and your brother would like to join us?"

It was unadulterated insanity. She entertained visions of Ron coming home early to find not one but three "hoodlums" in his living room. Fervently she hoped Raoul would say they could not come.

"Sure. We'll be there in five minutes," he said.

Alexis gave the address and hung up.

Linda was pale with ecstasy. She fluttered, got up from the sofa, sat back down again, reached for her purse, and drew out a broken plastic comb. In a nervous, jerky motion, unlike any Alexis had ever seen from her before, she began frantically to comb her hair.

Alexis reached out finally, stopped Linda's hand, and took the comb away. Then, for several seconds, she held the girl by her anxious, agitated shoulders until she was once more calm.

"Now come here," Alexis told her.

She led Linda to the bathroom, and opened the top

drawer of her dresser. The girl drew in a breath when she saw the array—antique tortoiseshell combs, boar bristle brushes, silver pins, barrettes from France, rosewood clips—all lying on a nest of scented Ralph Lauren drawer liners.

"Use these," Alexis said.

Slowly, Linda picked up an ivory brush and drew it through her hair. Alexis watched the pale brush and the paler hands, the red nails, and the black hair.

At last Linda was finished. She put down the brush and waited obediently.

Next, Alexis indicated the row of Lalique perfume decanters.

"Put some on," she said.

Linda hesitated.

"Which one do *you* use?"

Alexis pointed to the Chanel.

"May I use that?"

Alexis nodded. Linda timidly opened the bottle, touched her finger to the neck, and applied one drop.

Alexis laughed.

"That's no way to treat Chanel."

A sudden sharp memory of Maggie—putting on perfume, dousing Alexis, laughing. "*That's* the way you put on perfume, baby. With a liberal hand! A liberal hand! And don't you ever forget it."

She put the scent briskly all over Linda's arms and hair.

A few minutes later, the doorbell rang. Alexis opened the door. There was Raoul, all dressed up in a stiffly cheap suit, looking off-balance and oddly vulnerable. He greeted Alexis shyly. She found herself rather touched by him in this new, unexpected mode.

"Hi, Alexis—I'm Leo."

Behind Raoul stood the older brother. Alexis read him quickly as a sharp little opportunist. She disliked the way his moist brown eyes flicked around her apartment, appraising her possessions. She also disliked the overstrong pressure of his hand on hers, and the feeling he put forth that somehow the two of them were in cahoots.

"Nice thing you're doing for the kids," he told her with what amounted to a leer. Alexis felt like groaning. It wasn't a nice thing at all—it was sheer idiocy.

But when she brought Raoul and Leo into the living room, and Raoul and Linda saw each other, she was glad she had done it.

Leo grinned at her, and again she resented the complicity in his smile.

"What can I offer you?" Alexis went on automatic hostess. "Tea? Cookies? Perrier?"

Nobody wanted anything. Alexis knew that Linda and Raoul were longing, dying, to be left alone. She wondered with one part of her mind if she should permit this; with the other part, she knew that it had already been decided.

She turned abruptly.

"Leo," she said, "Why don't you come into the kitchen with me?"

She led Leo into her kitchen. He looked around appreciatively.

"Next time you're in Chicago, you really ought to come see our store," he told her. "We've got stuff just like this. Really high-class. I know you'd appreciate it."

During the next few minutes, Alexis said a variety of things; but all she could really think about was Linda and Raoul—Linda and Raoul, and how much she hated the gel Leo wore on his thick, shining hair.

Ten minutes passed.

"I think it's time we went back in," she said finally. She strode ahead of Leo, back to the living room.

Linda and Raoul looked very beautiful. The sun through the venetian blinds sent a confetti of light onto their faces. They were kissing, their faces serene and reverent under the whips of sunlight. Alexis watched them in silence for a moment.

Behind her, Leo came up. He saw the two entwined, and chuckled suggestively. At the sound he made, Linda and Raoul sprang apart.

Alexis felt a rush of pity for Linda, who was blinking with embarrassment and bewilderment in the sunlight.

"We were just—we were just—" she began pleadingly.

"That's all right," said Alexis.

The sight of these two hungrily kissing, the expression on their faces, filled her with memory, with pleasure, with envy. And she wondered again at her stupidity in allowing this meeting. She had known—of course she had—what would happen if she left them alone.

Alexis could just imagine what Steven Wheelhouse would say if he ever found out. *But it was his fault to begin with,* she told herself. *None of this would have happened if it hadn't been for his ridiculous restrictions.* Besides, what *had* happened? Nothing. Just a kiss.

"It's three-thirty," she told Linda. "I'd better get you back to Brian House."

"And I'd better get *you* back," Leo said to Raoul. "Separately."

Again, that leer of complicity. Alexis stiffened.

"Yes. Well, why don't you two go there first. We'll follow in a few minutes. I'm sure Linda will want some time to get ready."

She walked Leo and Raoul to the door, marched firmly through farewell small-talk, and led them out. When she went back to the living room, Linda was sitting stiffly on the sofa.

"I'm so sorry," she burst out. "We didn't mean to. You won't tell, will you?"

Again, the web of cover-up. Alexis felt uncomfortable, and said nothing for a moment. Linda misunderstood her silence.

"Oh, Mrs. Donleavy," she wailed, "if they find out, we'll be expelled. Please. Please!"

"Of course I won't tell," Alexis said firmly. "You know that. But that was the last time. We can't do anything like that again."

"Of course not," Linda said.

But there was an odd look in her eyes; and Alexis was filled with a sense of being helplessly swept away.

Fourteen

"Why don't I light a fire?" Maggie said.

It was a strange suggestion, given the heat of the afternoon and the fact that she had to get dressed for her dinner party soon. But Paul understood that the fire was meant as a sort of comic relief—a harmless intermission from Philip Fredericks.

She went over to the marble fireplace, and began arranging logs, twigs, newspaper. Her expertise impressed Paul.

"Were you a Girl Scout?" he asked.

"Are you kidding? Mama couldn't afford the uniform. No, my sister Mildred taught me. We used to camp out when I was little. We'd go off somewhere quiet and make a fire and sleep under the stars."

"Your mother didn't mind?"

Maggie laughed. "She didn't know."

She returned to the sofa.

"That was silly of me," she said suddenly. "I have

to be going in a few minutes. Oh, well—we'll have a few minutes of a beautiful fire."

She settled herself.

"I've made some enemies over the years," she began, as though she had been silently rehearsing this all during the building of the fire. "And there've been some things in my life I've regretted doing. But what can I tell you? As my mama always used to say, you have to save yourself. After Philip left me, I—saved myself."

She spoke softly to the fire.

"I believe that we create our own destinies—and that we can make whatever we want of our lives. So even at the time—and I'm very proud of this—I didn't go around whining about what had happened. So the man I loved had left me and I was the laughingstock of Hollywood; the question was"—she looked from the fire and into Paul's face—"what was I going to do next?

"I couldn't stay in town. I'm sure you know how much Hollywood loves to punish—and after what had happened, I knew I wasn't going to be offered any parts for a long, long time."

"Was it really so—organized as all that?"

"Oh, yes. No one came right out and said that was the reason you weren't working, but everyone knew." She paused. "Besides, it hurt too much to stay—Philip's wife was going all over town saying that their marriage had never been better." A spasm crossed her face. "I needed a fresh start.

"I decided to move back East—to New York. In those days, it took a long time to get across the country, and you didn't feel that New York was just around the corner, the way you do now. Also, New Yorkers are notorious for looking down on the West Coast—I figured that no one there would care in the least what had happened to me back in Hollywood.

"The apartment had been rented in Philip's name, so I didn't have any red tape to go through. I got in touch with his business manager and told him I was going. Then I packed my clothes, sold a few things, and was ready to leave. And the day before my train ride east, wouldn't you know it—I had to make my big dramatic gesture.

"I decided to take the bus tour of the city—the same one I had taken six years before, the first day I had arrived in Los Angeles. Nothing had changed. The bus was full of would-be young actresses, and the driver pointed out all the same sights." Maggie shook her head. "But everything we passed now—every street, every corner—had some memory for me. Kelly. Mama. Philip."

"That must have been hard."

Harshly, she laughed. "Hard? Halfway through the tour, I got off the bus and walked home.

"The next day, I took the Super Chief to New York. I did nothing on the whole trip but eat Planters peanuts and read mystery stories. Didn't even look out the window.

"I arrived in New York during the middle of a taxi strike, on the hottest day of the year. I got off the train, and the first thing I saw was a man exposing himself right outside the donut shop in Grand Central Station."

"What a beginning."

Maggie was silent for a long time. She stretched her hands before the fire, and gazed at them intently.

"I've dined out many a time on stories from my first few months in New York. The time I found the dead rat in my bed, and the crazy neighbor with the macaw and getting caught on the fire escape. Great stories. And I tell them very well." She looked up at Paul. "I like myself for that. For making those times seem so Auntie Mame-ish and gay. When they weren't."

The hands still waved slowly back and forth before the fire.

"It was a dreadful year. I had thought getting started again would be easier than it had been in Hollywood, but it wasn't. I was auditioning all over the place, for Broadway, off-Broadway, even little theater, but never getting any parts. Very hard on the ego, let me tell you. And my money was running out. That November, it got so cold that I had to sell the garnet necklace Philip had given me, to buy a coat."

She took her hands from before the fire and put them over her eyes.

"I can still see that horrible coat. It was dark green wool. I've loathed that color ever since."

She straightened up.

"But I kept hanging in there. Doing what I could to save myself. I finally got a job tending bar at a little restaurant on East Eighty-sixth Street. I made a fortune in tips. Actually," she added reflectively, "if I hadn't needed to act, I think I could have been quite happy tending bar. I enjoyed meeting all the people—and hearing all the stories."

Paul's reporter antennae almost waved in her face.

"What was the most interesting story you heard?"

Maggie put back her head and roared with laughter. "Oh, come on! You know it already."

He grinned. "But only other people's versions."

"All right, all right," she said. She arranged herself gracefully. "One rainy Friday night, right before I was about to get off work, a fellow came into the bar. He had the sweetest face and the biggest, most ridiculous mustache I'd ever laid eyes on. He looked absolutely tragic. He ordered a drink, and we started talking. He told me his name was Marty Klein, and said he was a writer/director—he'd written this play called *Tools of the Trade*, which he'd been trying to get produced for two years. Finally it had opened at a little off-off-Broadway theater, but the reviews were terrible—I'd seen them—and the show was about to close. That night, Marty and his leading lady got into a terrible fight, and she quit on him—with one performance left to go. She didn't have an understudy, and Marty was absolutely beside himself."

Maggie sat forward. She looked very animated, very young.

"I don't know what on earth possessed me—certainly it wasn't goodness of heart, no matter what the movie magazines may have said. I think it was simply that I hadn't acted in such a long time, and I was desperate to be onstage again. Any stage. But whatever it was, to my horror I heard myself telling Marty that tomorrow was my night off, and that I would be happy to go on for him in his play."

She beamed at Paul.

"Can you imagine? It was total insanity. I hadn't even seen the script! For all I knew, I could have a five-page monologue staring me in the face!

"Well, Marty all but fell to his knees. And the more grateful he was, the more I wished I'd never gotten myself into the damned thing in the first place! He raced off to get the script, and I found my fears had been wrong. The monologue was *ten* pages!"

They both laughed.

"So. I had less than twenty-four hours to memorize an entire play and come up with a performance. Looking back, I don't know which of us was the crazier—me for making the promise, or Marty for accepting it.

"Mercifully, I don't remember too much about the next night. All I can say is, thank God no one told me at the time that Robert Marshall was in the audience—or I don't think I would have had the courage to go on at all.

"I woke up the next morning to a phone call from Marty. I couldn't understand a word he was saying, he was so excited, but finally, I gathered that I was supposed to get up, get out, and buy the *Morning Post.*"

Her voice held a trace of unsteadiness.

"So I did. I still have Robert Marshall's review. It's one of the few I've kept."

Paul quoted the first line. She bowed her head in acknowledgment.

"Well, *Tools of the Trade* was held over one week, then a month, and then it went on to become a smash. At first we couldn't believe it, and we kept having farewell parties every week; but a year and a half later, we were still running.

"It was a good run. Except for a few battles with Frank Bosce—but that's a whole subject unto itself!—I enjoyed working with the cast, and I loved the play."

Maggie did her gesture, now familiar to Paul, of narrowing her eyes and tapping on the arm of the sofa, in some secret, unguessed-at code.

"There's a lot of depth in Marty's work. I don't think the critics give him enough credit—well, maybe he lays himself open to that because he's so flamboyant—but all I know is, during that whole year and a half, I never once felt I'd squeezed everything I could out of my part.

"And as much as I hate to admit it, I never did get that damned monologue word-perfect!"

The animation ceased. The story was over. Paul had enjoyed the performance, even though he suspected that it was a set piece, repeated over and over for various reporters throughout the years.

"Finally the play closed," Maggie said. And now she was no longer performing. "There's such a sadness about those nights. It's like nothing else on earth. And if you're an actor, it's especially awful—because of course you're absolutely sure that you'll never work again." Her laugh was rueful.

"But actually, it turned out pretty well for all of us. It was the start of old Frank Bosce's career, and Estelle Linder—she played my mother—has made a fortune doing commercials. Marty, of course, went on to win the Tony for *Boomtown,* and I ended up signing with Irwin Jacobson, the best agent in New York.

"Those were good years," her voice rose firmly. "Good to remember. I did three plays—put in quite a few decent performances. And," she added wryly, "I was even forgiven by Hollywood.

"One day my agent called to say that MGM was doing a film about Napoleon. And they wanted me for Josephine."

She took another cigarette, looked at it meditatively.

"God, I love to smoke," she told Paul. "But I don't smoke them all the way down," she added.

"I noticed," he said.

"Of course I was scared to death, coming back to Hollywood. But it couldn't have been more pleasant. I flew back this time, and when we landed, all these fans were waiting at the airport. The studio had booked me into a beautiful suite at the Beverly Hills Hotel—it was filled with big baskets of flowers and fruits. Reporters kept coming by, as friendly as could be. And you know something?"

She smiled at Paul behind the cigarette smoke. It was a strange smile, remote and almost cruelly knowing.

"All those same people were still there. All those people who had dropped me four years before. Now they wanted to see me again—but I didn't take their calls."

She smoked her cigarette with great concentration.

"Philip had moved to Europe," she said almost offhandedly. "I found that out the first day I got to town. He had gone back to France with his family, and was making movies there. So that was that.

"I made the film—it was a hit—I was offered another, then another."

She shrugged.

"And suddenly—it was so odd—I was a star again."

"Was it the same as before?"

She considered. "No. This time I took things a little more—well, less naively perhaps."

She did not go on.

"Meaning what?" he asked.

"Meaning that this time around, I bought fewer

clothes and more jewelry. Meaning that this time I let more people pick up the check at restaurants. Meaning that I stopped telling reporters all my secrets."

She looked at Paul, and he felt slapped. He made his next question purposefully banal.

"Did it live up to your expectations, being a star in Hollywood again?"

"Not particularly," she answered crisply. "The work aside, it wasn't my happiest time. I stayed several years, made five or six movies—a few of them were quite good, actually—but somehow it wasn't much fun. It all seemed rather pointless.

"Or maybe it was just me.

"And of course, those were the Joe McCarthy years—not the greatest time to be in Hollywood."

"Did you have any trouble with the Un-American Activities committee?"

"No, though I've always been a Democrat. But I had friends whose lives were ruined. It was a nightmare."

Then she looked at Paul as a person again, not as a reporter.

"And there were still all the memories of Philip. Everywhere I looked. Nothing made them go away. So eventually, I went back to New York."

"Was that a difficult adjustment?"

"Not this time. Right off the bat, I was offered the new Desiree Kaufman play—great part—and I found the most enchanting town house on East Thirty-ninth Street. There were two darling priests who lived upstairs from me—gay, naturally; we became great friends. We used to do everything together. I even took them on a cruise to the Bahamas."

Paul phrased the next question carefully.

"You weren't open to more—romantic—relationships?"

"No," she answered flatly. "No, not at all. After Philip, that—died in me."

Then she smiled a little sourly at him. "You're good," she said. "Yes, it was around that time that I met Henry."

"You don't have to talk about it if you don't want to," he told her.

"It's all right," she shrugged. "It's all part of the story."

She sighed and looked into the fire.

"I'd been doing the play about four months. One night, I came into my dressing room and found a dozen roses on the makeup table. I was used to getting flowers, but this was the first time I had ever seen sterling silver roses. Do you know them?"

"No."

"The minute you leave here, you must go to a florist and buy yourself one. They're absolutely magical—a pale, pale lavender.

"There was a little card attached to the flowers. It said, 'May I come around to see you after the Saturday matinee?' And it was signed 'Henry Avery.' Well, I didn't know Henry Avery from Adam, and I was very careful who I let into my dressing room.

"He left his telephone number, but I never called.

"Well, the flowers kept coming. Every performance, a dozen sterling silver roses. I admit, I was starting to get a little curious. So one night, I had the stage manager leave a message for Henry, saying that he could come backstage after that night's performance. When I gave her the name, she said, 'Oh, my God, is he one of *the* Averys?' I told her I had no idea."

Paul looked skeptical.

"It's true," she said. "I'd never followed the society pages. At that point, I really did have no idea.

"Henry turned out to be quite attractive. Very Leslie Howard-ish—that silver-blond look. And with a lovely low, soft voice.

"He took me for supper at the Athletic Club—I'd never been there before. It was very old-money, very understated. My father would have adored it.

"I asked Henry if he sent roses to all the leading ladies on Broadway. He just laughed. He said he wasn't much of a theatergoer, but that he'd happened to see my play with some business associates and enjoyed my performance so much that he'd gone back six or seven more times.

"That was very flattering. 'I'd love to take you out,' he told me. Most of the men I knew wouldn't have used such an old-fashioned expression, and I found it charming. I told him I wasn't interested in anything serious, but that I would be happy to have him 'take me out.'

"So we started seeing each other. I liked Henry more and more. He was a sweet man—courteous—extremely bright—he'd gone to Harvard—and he could be very funny when he wanted.

"The relationship wasn't perfect, naturally. Henry had no interest in theater, and of course that was my whole life. And I confess, I wasn't exactly excited by what went on during his day at the office. So we didn't have a whole lot in common. Also, I didn't think much of his friends. They were deadly dull, and they treated me as if I was a chorus girl, for heaven's sake.

"But I liked Henry—I found him an intriguing man. He had this curious *wrapped* quality about him. It was like getting a box from Tiffany's. You're not sure what's inside, but you know from the box and the ribbon that *whatever* it is has value.

"About six weeks after we met, we went on a picnic. That was my idea. I'd had it to here with all the black-tie dinners he took me to, and I thought this would be fun. Well, it was a disaster. I'd forgotten to pack anything to drink, the ants got us, and it started to rain. I was very impressed with Henry—he just laughed and laughed, and said he was enjoying every moment. He told me that meeting me had been the best thing that ever happened to him, and that he never wanted to lose me. He asked me to marry him. And I accepted."

Maggie held up an imperious hand, forestalling Paul's reaction.

"I knew that he wasn't the right man, but then, love with the right man had nearly killed me. So there you are.

"We were married that fall.

"Of course everyone assumed I married Henry for his money. That's only partly true," she said bluntly.

Paul felt uneasy.

"Oh, come on." Maggie looked at him, annoyed. "Why shouldn't the money have meant something to me? Growing up the way I did—not knowing where my next meal was coming from? Of course it meant something. It meant a lot. But the thing to remember," she said emphatically, "the thing to remember is that the money wasn't the only reason I married him. No—I really did marry Henry for Henry.

"But the problems started right away. A few days after we got engaged, Henry took me to meet his mother. That should have warned me, but at the time I thought it was a good sign.

"Henry had told me how close he and his mother were—after his father had died, he had given up his apartment and moved back in with her, so she wouldn't have to be alone. I wasn't so sure that she'd be thrilled to be getting a daughter-in-law, but Henry said she'd love me. So I got dressed in my best blue suit, and off we went.

"The house was on Long Island—right by Old Westbury. Do you know the area?"

"I was there once," Paul said. He had gone on a pilgrimage when he was seventeen, trying to get a glimpse of the house Maggie had lived in. But he did not mention this.

"It took about an hour and a half to get there, and I was getting more nervous by the second. Finally, we turned off the road onto this endless driveway—and there was the house.

"It was absolutely enormous. We're talking Manderley here. Stables, guesthouses, a garden the size of the town I grew up in. And the whole family out in force to meet me." Maggie shook her head with rueful remembrance.

"Henry's mother was standing at the top of the steps. She was straight out of a Shaw play—the Withering Dowager. She had her sisters with her, these terribly proper ladies in their pearls and their cashmere sweaters. Henry's brother was also there—he had flown in from Chicago. He was quite taken with me, I could tell, but that mother—oh, my God. From the instant she clapped eyes on me, it was pure hatred.

" 'Henry tells me you're an actress,' she said to me. 'Is this actually true?'

"Well, it went on from there. A complete disaster. After it was over, when we were driving back to New York, I said to Henry that his mother and I were never going to get along, and maybe it would be better if we didn't get married.

"Well, he was just wonderful about it. He had a talk with the woman, said he was marrying me no matter what, and told her to shape up or else. Well, she shaped up. At least for the moment."

Maggie shrugged. "Of course I understood her point of view completely. I mean, if I'd been Henry's mother, I wouldn't have wanted me for a daughter-in-law either. An actress with my background? Come on. It was a ridiculous match." Then she gave Paul a quizzical smile. "But aren't the ridiculous matches the ones you always root for?"

"I don't see that it was so ridiculous."

"Oh, come on. Of course you do." She sat back musingly. "But in some ways, maybe it wasn't. We really did have a lot to give each other. Henry had always been so protected; he'd never known any Real Life—and that was me all over. And by marrying Henry, I could get my whole glorious heritage back—just like that." She paused and added softly, "I always used to think how proud Papa would have been to see me in that big house.

"Anyway, crazy or not, we got married.

"The wedding was very grand. Everyone came. And you should have seen my dress—Princess Grace's was nothing in comparison."

"I totally agree," Paul said.

Maggie looked at him, suddenly grave. "I felt very lucky to be marrying Henry," she said, "and I truly wanted things to work out between us."

Pain crossed her face. "And perhaps they could have. If Henry had been a little stronger. Or if I hadn't been who I am."

She shrugged. "But it started to fall apart almost from the beginning. I'd been so proud of Henry for marrying me against his mother's wishes, but he never stood up to her about anything ever again. From the moment we were married, I watched him turn right back into a little boy.

"I knew it would be a disaster if we kept on living with her—I begged Henry to get us a place of our own. He promised me he would—but somehow it never happened. Old Mrs. Avery saw to that. The emotional blackmail that went on—you wouldn't believe it. Every time Henry would talk about moving out, there would be some crisis with the estate—something only Henry could deal with. Or she'd get sick. That woman had more things wrong with her than anyone I've ever known—but only when Henry talked about leaving her. Other than that, she was perfectly fine.

"We had a terrible fight about it, our first Christmas together. Finally Henry came right out and admitted he didn't want to move—he said he'd feel too guilty leaving his mother alone. She didn't have that much more time left, he told me, and once she was gone, we could have the rest of our lives together, just the two of us." Maggie snorted. "Well, that day never came. In fact, I'll bet you any amount of money that that woman is still alive—she'll outlast us all.

"Henry died a few years ago," she added, more softly. "I got a letter from the lawyers. I was sorry to hear it. He was a good man."

There was a pause. "So life went on. I tried to make the best of it, but I didn't do terribly well—I guess I wasn't used to playing second fiddle." She flipped back her hair with an uncomfortable gesture. "I know things would have gone a lot more smoothly if I could have just done the dutiful daughter-in-law bit—that's all the woman wanted, really—but I simply couldn't." She looked at Paul. "Don't you see—I couldn't?"

"Yes," Paul said.

"And it just got worse. About a year after we were married, I was offered Hedda on Broadway. I was very excited. I was all set to sign the contracts, when old Mrs. Avery informed me that she preferred I didn't do the show. It was an indignity, she said—an indignity, mind you!—for an Avery—even one by marriage, to continue acting when she didn't have to. And Henry stood there and didn't say a word.

"Afterward, he apologized. He said that he didn't agree with his mother, and that he loved my being an actor. But when I asked him if he wanted me to do Hedda, he hemmed and hawed. He said that maybe it wasn't such a good idea, that it would mean a lot of time away from home, that I had certain responsibilities as his wife. So I knew that really he felt the same way she did."

"What did you do?"

"I almost left him over it. I packed my bags, and took them down to the car. And then I sat there in the driver's seat," she added in a low voice. "Just sat there for over an hour, thinking."

She fixed her green eyes on Paul.

"Do you have any idea what it is to be an actor?" she demanded. "Even when you're on top? It's only a matter of time. Especially for a woman. And then what?"

Paul felt helpless.

"I was nearing thirty. I wanted to forget Philip. I wanted a life. I wanted a child. Is that so hard to understand?

"So I took my bags back to the house."

Her gaze faltered, fluttered down.

"Maybe it was selfish of me," she said. "Maybe it would have been better for everyone if I had left. I don't know."

Then she straightened.

"But I do know this—if I hadn't stayed, I wouldn't have had Alexis."

Paul looked toward the bookshelf, at the photograph of the little girl in the velvet dress.

"I saw her picture earlier—she's very lovely."

Warmth flooded Maggie's face.

"Oh, yes—she was beautiful. From the moment she was born. The most beautiful baby you ever saw. Yes, yes"—she caught sight of Paul's smile and dismissed it—"I know all mothers feel that way. But in this case it was true.

"She wasn't beautiful in that cutesy baby way. She was a person—right from the beginning. I took one look at her, and there was this—sense of recognition. This feeling of, oh, of course—it's you. At last."

Her eyes filled with tears.

She put her head in her hands and began to weep.

Fifteen

Alexis came into her apartment and tossed her gym bag on the floor. She felt irritated and tired. Usually, an hour of aerobics helped her mood, but today the panacea had failed. The meeting with the Stadlers' architect had not gone well, and unless they found a way of changing the configuration for the new office . . .

Alexis sighed. She didn't want to think about it now. What she wanted was something pleasant and soothing to do, to take her mind off everything. Her glance fell on the new leather photograph album she had bought the day before—just the thing. She pulled down a big box of pictures from the closet, sat on the floor, and began to sort them into piles. She was halfway through, when the phone rang.

"Mrs. Donleavy? It's Nora Maloney—"

For an instant, the name meant nothing.

"Mrs. Avery's housekeeper."

Alexis dropped the photographs.

"Yes, Nora—is everything all right?"

"Well, your grandmother had a fall this afternoon. She was trying to pick up her dressing gown, and she slipped. It's nothing very serious—the doctor doesn't think anything's broken, but he's taken her in for some X rays, just in case. I thought you would want to know."

"Yes, of course. Thank you so much," Alexis said mechanically. "I appreciate your calling." She got the doctor's number from the housekeeper. "Give Grandmother my love, and tell her that Ron and I will come visit her this weekend."

"I'm sure that will make her very happy."

Alexis hung up the phone. Numbly, she went through the pile of photographs until she found one of her grandmother. She held it carefully, looked at it a long time. Mrs. Avery was standing in her garden, wearing the green striped silk dress Alexis remembered from her childhood. A faint scent of vanilla seemed to permeate the room, and tears came into Alexis's eyes. Her grandmother looked so strong and powerful in the picture, a woman who would never slip picking up her dressing gown.

Mrs. Avery was still upstairs when Alexis and Ron arrived at the house.

"She's been a little tired this morning," Nora told them. "But she wants to come down and see you. Perhaps you'd like to wait in the library for a few minutes."

"I'll be watching the tournament," Ron said, and moved off.

"I'll be right there," Alexis told him.

She stood alone for a moment in the large hallway. It had been a month or two since she had visited her grandmother, and she walked slowly around. When she came to the small oil painting of the vase of peonies which hung above the settee, she stopped. That had been her favorite painting when she was a little girl— she used to beg her grandmother to let her have it for her own. Looking at it now, it made her sad to realize that it was really quite a bad picture.

She joined Ron in the library. After a few moments, Nora came in.

"Mrs. Avery's feeling a little too tired to come downstairs," she told them. "Perhaps you could visit her in her room instead."

Alexis told herself that this meant nothing; it did not mean her grandmother was going to die.

"Alexis, darling." Mrs. Avery lay in bed, white against the white pillows. Alexis was shocked by how translucent her face was.

"Hello, Grandmother," she gulped, and kissed the cool cheek. "How are you feeling?"

"Oh, the doctor says these things are to be expected," Mrs. Avery shrugged. "But I'm glad it made you come out. I don't get to see enough of you."

Gently, Alexis squeezed her hand.

"It's perfectly understandable," her grandmother said briskly. "You have your own life; the last thing you'd want to do is to visit an old woman."

"Don't be ridiculous," Alexis told her.

A shadow crossed Mrs. Avery's face. "Have I been good to you, dear?" she asked.

"Good to me? Better than good!" Alexis cried in bewilderment. "You know you have!"

Her grandmother shook her head restlessly. "I *don't* know," she said. There were some things, perhaps . . ." She frowned. "Things I might have done differently. I'm afraid I didn't always behave as—generously as I could have." She looked up. "But at the time—you must believe me, Alexis, I was only doing what I thought was best for you."

Alexis stroked her arm.

"I don't know what you're talking about," she said. "but I do know this—you've always been the best grandmother in the world."

Mrs. Avery patted her hand.

"I've tried to be, dear."

Alexis cried on the drive home.

"She's going to go soon, Ron," she kept saying. "I know it. I know it."

He tried comforting her, but she would not be comforted. Finally he gave up and turned on the radio.

The next day, Alexis called the house and was told by Nora that her grandmother was in the garden, pruning roses. She wept and wept, with sheer relief.

The following Tuesday morning, Alexis was reading the paper in the breakfast room when Ron came in.

"We should be getting the proofs of the spread today," he said.

"The spread?"

"For *Architectural Digest*."

Alexis had completely forgotten. In fact, it was

rather a coup—an article featuring her work in general and their apartment in particular.

"Harrison is sick about it," Ron laughed. "I found out from his secretary that he all but bribed *Architectural Digest* for a mention of his new house in the Hamptons—but he couldn't get a line. And here you get a whole spread." He shook his head solemnly. "You must be very excited."

Alexis thought about this.

No, she wasn't particularly. It was an honor, of course, and it would bring in more clients and more money. But she didn't really need more money and she didn't really need more clients.

What she did need, she realized, was an example of trompe d'oeuil to show the kids in her class—and the article in the magazine would provide it.

But she did not tell this to Ron.

"Of course," she said, "I'm thrilled."

The traffic going downtown was heavy that afternoon, and Alexis arrived at Brian House a few minutes late. When she got to the classroom, Tamara, Greg, and Linda were not there. She waited until the warning bell rang, then, when they still did not appear, she went out into the corridor to look for them.

The halls were empty—then all at once, they were filled with a loud surge of students. The kids were laughing, excited, more animated than Alexis had ever seen them. Strange, she thought; only when they were happy did they look like children.

In the middle of the crowd, she saw her three students. They waved at her, and hurried toward the classroom.

"What's going on?" Alexis asked as they burst in.

"Oh, Mrs. Donleavy—there's a movie producer here!" Linda told her.

"From Hollywood," Greg broke in.

"He's going to make me a star!" Tamara wiggled her hips.

"He does documentaries," Linda explained. "And he's making one about places like Brian House. He's going to film some of it here, using us!"

"Using me!" Tamara crowed.

"Well, that's certainly exciting," Alexis said.

"Dara said he called like a week ago, but she thought he was putting her on when he said he was from Hollywood."

"But it's true?"

"It sure is," Greg said importantly. "I saw him right before morning break."

"Oh, my God!" Tamara cried. "Where?"

"In the dining room."

She jumped up and started for the door.

Alexis laughed. "I'm sure he's left there by now."

Tamara turned back. "What was he like?"

"Normal. But he was taking Polaroids."

"You can't make a movie with Polaroids!" Tamara scoffed.

"I think it's standard procedure," Alexis told them. "So when he gets back to California, he can remember the layout of the rooms and plan his shots."

"Did he get a picture of Busby?"

Busby was the overweight dining room helper, the local joke and legend.

"Yes," Greg said recklessly. "He shot the whole pack on Busby!"

"Oh, my God! Busby in a movie?"

"Busby in a movie!!"

Their excitement was beginning to go over the edge.

"Okay," Alexis said. "Let's try to settle down now."

They stopped laughing and looked at her reproachfully.

"I agree—this is all very thrilling," she told them. "And it'll be a lot of fun to see what happens. But presumably this producer isn't coming in here to film us at this moment—so why don't we get some work done?" She smiled at them. "You want to look good when he *does* come to film you, don't you?"

Grudgingly, they settled down to their notebooks.

"We're going to do some more painting analysis today," Alexis said. "I think you'll like this one." She reached into her satchel and brought out an art card. "This is an oil painting of Sarah Moulton, otherwise known as 'Pinkie.' "

They stared at the portrait of the little girl standing on the windblown hillside.

"That's a funky name."

"No, it isn't look at her hat; it's pink." Tamara said triumphantly.

"Well, actually," Alexis amended, "it's believed that the nickname wasn't because of the color—she was called 'Pinkie' because it means 'small'—like your pinkie finger. Anyway, it was painted by an Englishman, Sir Thomas Lawrence, in 1794, and it's located at the Huntington Gallery, in San Marino, California."

"California!" Tamara picked up on this instantly. "Is San Marino anywhere near Hollywood?"

"I think actually it is quite near."

"Oh, my God," Greg said reverently. "Do you think the producer ever went and saw 'Pinkie'?"

"I'm sure he did," Alexis told him. "Now, what strikes you first about this picture?"

"She's a babe," Greg said.

"Her hair's not moving," Tamara frowned. "I mean, it's a windy day, and her hat's blowing. But her hair's just like—sticking there. She must have a ton of gel on it."

"It's sort of mysterious," Linda said. "The way she's holding her hand—like she's trying to say something."

Alexis smiled. "Perhaps she is. The portrait was painted for her grandmother, and critics wonder if the way Pinkie's posing her arm might be like a little secret code between them."

Greg glowed. "In my new comic strip, this big cockroach from another planet cracks the Bugland code, and he's about to take over!"

"Well, I'm sure Mordeath will be able to stop him," Alexis said. "But for now, why don't we get back to Pinkie?"

After class, Alexis was walking down the corridor to the lobby, when Steven Wheelhouse's door opened.

"Mrs. Donleavy," he called. "Could you come in here a moment?"

She went into his office, and saw a man seated on the sofa. He was in his early fifties, dark-haired, and olive-skinned. He was casually dressed, but there was a giveaway Polo logo and an elegance in the easy way he rose from the sofa to shake her hand. This could only be the Hollywood producer.

"Mrs. Donleavy, may I present Mr. Fredericks."

"Richard," the man amended, smiling.

Alexis was taken aback by the intentness of his scrutiny of her.

"It's a pleasure meeting you," she told him. "Even though it wasn't a pleasure trying to teach my class today. I'm afraid your arrival totally eclipsed the glories of 'Pinkie.' "

Alexis was surprised at herself. She didn't usually try this hard, even with clients, and especially with men.

Richard smiled, used to charm.

"Well, I hope you don't hold it against me," he said. "Because I'd love to interview you for this documentary I'm doing."

"But I'm not a teacher," she told him.

He nodded. "I realize that. Steven was telling me about your volunteer work, and I think it would make an interesting angle."

Alexis dismissed it.

"You'll find I'm a pretty dull subject," she said, but she was surprised at how flattered she felt.

Then she thought of Ron, and wondered, uncomfortably, what he would have to say about all this. She could already hear the legalistic questions and objections, in that tense, pitched-slightly-higher-than-usual voice, and she felt weary in advance.

"I'd be happy to do it," she said.

He nodded, unsurprised. Then he smiled at her. "Are you free for a few minutes now?" he asked.

Alexis was taken aback.

"Now?"

"I don't mean to film. But I'm flying back to L.A. on Thursday, and I'd like to do as much groundwork as possible before I leave. I was wondering if we could go somewhere and talk over a few preliminaries."

* * *

They went to a coffee shop a few blocks away. Alexis was self-conscious, walking in with Richard Fredericks, and she was aware of how odd it was that she should react this way. In her work, meetings were constant events, and her clientele included as many men as women, quite a few of whom, she knew, were attracted to her. Yet there was something about this man that put her on the edge. *Of what?* she asked herself. *Would you perhaps care to elaborate, Alexis?* She would not. He had said nothing personal, had given no signals of any kind. Still, some undeniable instant something had happened.

They sat down at a booth, on seats that were covered with red ripped upholstery.

"One of the things I miss most about New York are the coffee shops," Richard told her. "I've gotten some of my best ideas for movies sitting at a counter and eavesdropping."

Alexis laughed. "Don't they have good eavesdropping in Los Angeles?"

"The people aren't as interesting."

"I had always imagined it would be just the opposite."

"You've obviously never been to L.A."

She paused. "No, I haven't. I love San Francisco, but somehow the idea of Los Angeles has never appealed to me."

He nodded thoughtfully.

The red-haired waitress came over. She made no secret of her admiration for Richard—even when taking Alexis's order, her eyes remained on him. Alexis was reminded again of what an attractive man he was.

Richard turned to Alexis again.

"I'm well acquainted with your work," he told her. "As a matter of fact, when my wife—my ex-wife, I should say—and I were thinking of moving to New York a few years ago, I wanted to ask you to decorate for us. But she assured me we couldn't afford you."

"Well, that's very flattering," Alexis said, making her voice deliberately professional. "I'm afraid I can't return the compliment, though—I don't see too many documentaries."

"Oh, this is my first attempt at one of those," he said. "Up till now, I've been involved in so-called art films. You wouldn't have seen any of those either," he added hastily, with a smile she liked. "But the theater's in my blood, I suppose."

And then, after a beat, he added, "What about you?"

Alexis thought it a very odd question.

"There's nothing theatrical about me," she told him. "My father was in banking."

But her answer did not dilute the strangeness.

"And what about your mother?" he asked.

She stared at him, a feeling of uneasiness rising in her chest.

"My mother?" she repeated. Then she said, as lightly as she could, "What an unusual line of questioning."

He looked at her a moment more, then finally said, "I'm sorry. I told you, I'm an inveterate snoop." He reached under the booth and pulled his briefcase onto the table. Snapping it open, he pulled out a yellow tablet.

"Well. So tell me about your work at Brian House.

When you started, why you started, what it is you teach . . ."

She told him, and as she spoke, the strange earlier questions faded from her mind. He was a flattering audience, listening with interest as she told him about the kids and all the strategies she used to keep them interested in her class.

"And are they working?"

"I think so," she said. "Tamara actually went out and bought a Picasso poster last week, and Greg has added a new cockroach called 'Bug-icelli' to his comic strip. Believe me, these are victories."

He nodded. "I'm glad," he said.

And then suddenly he leaned forward and put his hands over Alexis's.

"I've wanted to meet you for thirty-five years," he told her softly.

Alexis's throat closed.

"What?" she whispered.

His voice was light. "I think that was the real reason my ex-wife didn't want you decorating our apartment."

Alexis stared at him.

"What—are you talking about?"

"Can't you guess who I am?" he asked her.

"No," she said sharply. "I can't."

"Let me show you a picture of my father."

He pulled out a black Mark Cross wallet, and withdrew a photograph, protected with plastic. Alexis stared at the sepia snapshot. She grew numb as she looked at the picture—and the whole restaurant started to scream silently around her.

*   *   *

Eight years old. Walking down Third Avenue on a hot June day. Swinging hands with Maggie. And then Maggie stopping, her hand suddenly cold, then colder, then unbearably cold. And a man coming toward them.

Rage, shock, rocked Alexis. She thrust the photo back at Richard Fredericks. She could not speak.

Richard also said nothing for a moment. He took the picture but did not put it back in his wallet. He leaned it instead against his water glass, so the man in the photograph remained a part of the scene, smiling courteously at the tumbled plastic tablecloth.

"He was a wonderful man," Richard said at last, and again, louder, "A wonderful man." And then, to her, "They had a great love."

Alexis started to rise, but she found she could not stand up.

Richard leaned forward.

"There was a picture of you in the bookcase," he said. "Sitting on a wicker chair, wearing a red velvet dress. When I was a little boy, I'd visit them in Paris. That picture was the first thing I'd go look at, every time. I've never forgotten it."

Alexis stared numbly down at the table.

"And there was this special room that was always kept for you, filled with the most wonderful toys. I'd go in there when no one was around, and play with them. Once I broke a music box." He shook his head. "It was the only time I ever saw Maggie angry. She said those toys were meant for you, when you came to live with her. She told me she missed you every day of her life.

"I've often wondered what it must be like to have someone love you that much," he added slowly.

Tears were running down Alexis's face.

Richard made a motion toward her. She backed away.

"You bastard. What a foul thing to do."

He looked distressed.

"Alexis—I'm sorry. I had hoped this would be such a fortunate meeting."

Alexis stared at him. "A fortunate meeting?" Her voice rose. "How can you possibly think it would be a fortunate meeting? And how dare you sit there and tell me how much my mother loved me—you don't know anything about it at all!"

The couple at the next table turned around to look at her.

"I'm sorry," Richard said quickly.

" *'Let's have some coffee and talk about the documentary,'* " she mimicked him furiously. "And then you dare to show me that man's picture. You dare tell me—"

"Alexis," he said, "my father's been dead for fifteen years. This all happened a long time ago."

The words echoed.

This all happened a long time ago. Yes; of course it had. Alexis's breath slowed. She had embarrassed herself. She had behaved ridiculously. She had screamed about something that had been over and done with for a lifetime.

She waited several moments more.

"You're quite right," she said coolly. "It was a long time ago."

"Please don't be angry," he told her. "I never thought we'd meet. Why should we? In all these years, I've never tried to get in touch with you. And until this afternoon, I didn't have any idea that you worked at Brian House. But when Steven mentioned your name, I knew it was an opportunity that couldn't be passed up."

"Well, as you can see, you were wrong," she said. "And if you had told me who you were from the beginning, I could have saved you the trouble. The past is not something I'm interested in."

"I'm sorry," he said again.

She rose. "It's getting late. I need to be going." Briskly, she shook Richard's hand and rose from the booth. "I wish you luck with your documentary."

"Will you still be part of it?"

"No," she said.

She left the restaurant.

Alexis walked through the city all afternoon. She could not bear a moment's slackness, a moment's silence, a moment's solitude. Even waiting at a red light to cross the street made her want to scream. She walked until she was exhausted. Then she went back to her apartment.

The doorman looked concerned when he saw her.

"Good afternoon, Mrs. Donleavy—are you all right?"

"I'm fine," she said.

But when she saw herself reflected in the tall pier glass in the lobby, she understood why he had asked. She looked wrecked.

The apartment was empty and silent. Alexis went into the bathroom, drew a bath, and lay down in it. Her body remained stiff in the hot water. She closed her eyes. All right, she thought. All right. It was time to face what had happened.

She waited for the emotion to come. It did come, but it was feebler, and much more trivial than she had expected it would be.

She felt a great relief.

And really—after all was said and done, what actually *had* happened? Nothing. Meeting Philip's son didn't change anything. It didn't change the past, nor the present, nor the future. It reminded her of certain things, yes, but those things could be resubmerged with ease.

It had only been that first moment of shock—of seeing that photograph, of being forced to remember. And that would have happened to anyone. But now it was done—and she congratulated herself on how quickly she had moved past it.

But that strange thing he had said about the room in Paris—the room full of toys that were being saved for her . . . What had he meant?

Alexis shook her head and took a deep breath. She imagined she was in the English countryside. She was standing by a gray stone cottage, watching the ruffling waters of a cool blue pond.

Ron came home at eight.

"Alexis!" he called. "I got the proofs on the article! They sent them to me at work."

Alexis came in from the bedroom, and he handed the manila envelope to her. She noted that he had already opened it.

"Well, how is it?" she asked.

Ron put on his lawyer face.

"I've made a few notations on things that have to be changed."

Alexis glanced at the proofs of the article, and saw that he had marked it up completely. She wondered how the editors of *Architectural Digest* would like that.

She concentrated instead on the photographs. They were excellent—a nice blend of wide-angled impressions and intimate close-ups.

Looking at them, Alexis tried to be impersonal. She studied the shots as if she were walking into the apartment of a new client. Gathering in her impressions of the occupants. What did these photographed rooms tell her?

Oh, they were impeccably decorated, certainly. Only Alexis Donleavy could have done them. But what else did they say? They said nothing. There was nothing else. No emotion whatsoever came off the pages.

She frowned, a little chilled by this, and looked more closely at the pictures. It seemed to her that there was almost too much perfection in those rooms. Not sterility, but rather a terribly self-conscious attempt at the opposite. The gay clutter of so-artfully arranged objects, the basket of magazines displayed with such homey casualness.

What void are they hiding? she wondered.

Nonsense, she answered herself. *The only reason I'm not impressed is because I know my own tricks so well.*

On the final page was a picture she was surprised the editors had chosen—the last shot the photographer had snapped, in fact. It was a shot of herself and Ron in the dining room.

Alexis studied their faces and figures with detachment. They looked handsome—a classic couple—but the same absence that was in the apartment seemed to be in their faces. *No*, thought Alexis. *The truth is, it's quite simply the most flattering photograph of me that's ever been taken. And I'm having a hard time handling it.*

She went to bed early.

She was screaming for Maggie, but she couldn't find her. Maggie wasn't in her room. Maggie wasn't in the house. Maggie wasn't anywhere.

She ran into her bedroom. There on the pillow was Maggie's scrapbook. And on top of the book was Maggie's crown. And on the top of the crown was Maggie's note.

She reached toward the note. It started to grow and grow until it was filling the room and it was suffocating her and she couldn't breathe. The words on the note were huge. Good-bye, they said. Good-bye, good-bye.

She screamed and screamed and screamed.

Ron was shaking her.

"Alexis! Wake up! You're having a nightmare."

But she could not stop screaming.

Sixteen

Maggie wept. Paul watched her, reminding himself that these were tears for things that had happened a long time ago.

Eventually the shoulders stopped writhing—the face stilled.

"I'm sorry," she told him.

She looked exhausted, old.

"I guess Henry and I never really had a chance," she said abruptly, at last. "I remember something Kelly once said to me—I think it's very true. She said that in order for love to last, respect has to be there." She tapped herself on the chest. "I've always respected Maggie. Sometimes I think she's crazy as all get-out, but I've always respected her."

"And Henry?"

"No. That went away. It started to go right after we were married, when I saw how completely he was under his mother's thumb." She sighed. "He was simply too weak a man for me. By the time Alexis was a year old, I was completely out of love."

Her eyes narrowed.

"It's curious. I remember the exact moment it happened—the exact moment I knew."

She paused.

"It was Halloween. We were going to a party some neighbors were giving. I thought it would be fun if Henry and I didn't tell each other what our costumes were going to be.

"I decided to go as Huck Finn." Maggie shook her head. "Let all those other actresses dream of playing Hamlet—for me, it's always been Huck Finn.

"I got a marvelous costume together. Ragged shirt, an old straw hat, a bundle on a stick. I even had a bandanna to tie around Huck's stubbed toe.

"Right before we were to leave for the party, Henry came out of his room and we met in the hall.

"He was Julius Caesar, wearing a Roman toga made from a sheet—with his dress shoes underneath.

"So there we were—staring at each other. Him wanting to conquer the world, me wanting to escape down the Mississippi. In that one moment I knew it was all over."

After a long silence, she began to speak again.

"When Alexis was two, *Life* magazine wanted to do an article on me. Old Mrs. Avery hated the idea, of course, but I said yes anyway. A little blond reporter— I'll never forget her—came to the house and interviewed me all day.

"A few months later, the article came out. I was alone when I read it. I remember running around my bedroom, thinking I was screaming; but no screams were coming out."

She looked at Paul's uncomprehending face.

"Basically, the article said that I was the luckiest woman on the face of the earth, and that I had nothing left to wish for."

He nodded. "I suppose the worst thing was that it should have been true."

"Yes," she told him. "That was it, exactly. I would wake up every morning in my beautiful lace nightgown in my beautiful antique French bed. I had all the security I wanted, all the money, a husband, a child—and then this crushing weight would come. I think emptiness is the heaviest weight in the world, don't you?"

She looked as if she were in physical pain.

"Except for being with Alexis, my life was deadly—absolutely deadly. That idiotic round of lunches, parties. The charity events. The endless gossip, the small talk." She shrugged slightly. "At first, I tried to fit in; I tried to make friends with those women. But we were just too different. They had never been anything but rich. All they talked about was shopping and tennis. And I told you what my first memory was—the man at the church social blowing the schoolteacher's brains out. We really didn't have a lot in common.

"And it was the same with Henry," she went on rapidly. "After a year or so, we simply had nothing left to say to each other. He was at work most of the day, and when he did come home, we were *polite* to each other. It was awful. As if we had just met for the first time. And naturally his mother was always there. Three or four times a week, we'd go out for business dinners, and on the nights we stayed home, Henry would sit in his library and listen to opera and I'd go upstairs and be with Alexis."

"Do you think your husband considered the marriage a success?"

She was silent a moment. "I do, actually. At least at that point. Henry was a bright man, but not especially intuitive. Philip would have known in an instant how I felt; Henry, no. He was too self-absorbed. And too happy. Henry had everything he wanted in his life—the big house, the big job, the glamorous wife—even a new baby. I'm sure the thought never crossed his mind that I wasn't as happy as he was."

"Didn't you tell him how you felt?"

She hesitated. "Those were the fifties. Things were very different then. We didn't have all the things we have now—the relationship counselors and the talk shows and the self-help books. In those days, you got married and you just made the best of it."

Paul frowned. "That doesn't sound like you."

Maggie raised an eyebrow.

"And who exactly are you to judge what sounds like me?"

"I'm sorry."

Instantly, she relaxed. "But you're right, of course. What you're forgetting, though, is that part of me wanted that security. Wanted it very much. And I had a child now. Besides, I've always known which fights to pick—I knew what Henry was, I knew what he wanted out of life; he wasn't going to change, no matter what I said. And in many ways, the little blond reporter was right—I was very lucky."

"But not in the ways that mattered."

"No," she said. "Almost every night I would dream I was onstage again."

She grimaced.

"I remember, one afternoon at some amateur charity theatrical, I had a few too many sherries. After the last ghastly scene was performed, I got up onstage, uninvited, and launched into 'The quality of mercy is not strained . . .' "

"Everyone must have been very impressed," Paul told her.

"Well, impressed is putting it nicely. Stunned would be a better word. Actually I bombed."

There was a long silence.

Paul broke into it.

"You said Alexis was the bright spot in your life."

Maggie's face grew soft. "Yes."

"Were you able to spend much time with her?"

"Every moment I could. Of course, the day she was born, old Mrs. Avery had a trained nanny waiting to look after her, but that was one fight I managed to win. We kept the nanny, but I raised Alexis."

"Did Alexis's birth make a difference in your relationship with your mother-in-law?" Paul asked.

Maggie laughed.

"I'll say it did. Alexis became our main battleground. From the moment she was born, old Mrs. Avery and I argued over absolutely everything. What she should eat. Where she should go to school. Who she should play with. And there were endless fights about her behavior. Old Mrs. Avery wanted her to be some prim little doll, and I simply wasn't going to let that happen.

"I remember one awful day. It was Alexis's birthday party, and I'd bought her a piñata. I let her have as many turns to hit it as she wanted—it was her birthday, for Pete's sake—and afterward, all hell broke loose." Her mouth tightened. "That woman told me I wasn't fit to raise a child."

"And your husband?"

"Oh, Henry just sat there. I assume his silence meant consent.

"A few weeks later, they sent Alexis to a prissy girls' school—no doubt to counteract my influence. But I kept on." Her lips tightened. "It became a sort of mission with me—come hell or high water, I had to save my child from becoming an Avery."

"How do you do something like that?"

"I tried to show her what real life was like. I showed her the way most people live. I took her to places like Harlem and the Bowery."

"Didn't that frighten her?"

"Yes, but it was important that she see it. And of course, we did fun things, too—the park and the beach and the zoo. And naturally, I took her to every matinee in town."

She rolled her eyes. "Old Mrs. Avery hated my taking her anywhere. And she made sure that she got equal time. She'd bring Alexis into her room and they'd have their little tea parties together," she said sourly, "and do work for committees." Then she paused. "The truth was, Alexis liked all that, too. And that made me work all the harder to sway her *my* way."

She sighed.

"I can just imagine what the child psychologists would have to say about all this. I'm sure they would find it terribly unhealthy. But I do believe that one thing is safe to say," she told Paul with a strange smile. "The way things turned out, if I *hadn't* made Alexis my whole life, I would have been a much happier woman."

Maggie rose abruptly. She started to walk around the room, adjusting a bowl of flowers, a cushion, a picture.

"Do things being out of place drive you crazy?" she asked Paul lightly. "It does me. Even when I'm in a hotel room, I go around straightening all the pictures on the walls."

He watched, saying nothing. Finally she slowed, stopped. He watched as the last picture she had straightened moved on its hook and dropped at an angle once more. Maggie saw, but did not reposition it.

She sat back down on the sofa, lit a cigarette.

"So our lives went on," she said. "The same way for eight years. I didn't think anything would ever change."

She stared at the bowl of roses on the table in front of her.

"And then, in one day, it *all* changed." She took a deep breath. "It was a day in June—a beautiful day. I decided to take Alexis into New York. We went to the Metropolitan Museum, and had lunch there. We always loved doing that. Then we went onto Bloomingdale's, and did some shopping. Isn't it funny—I can still see the little doll I bought her. As we were leaving, I remembered that there was an antique store just around the corner. I was looking for some chairs, and I asked Alexis if she minded going. She said that would be fine. Then we were going to get ice cream afterward."

When Maggie looked up again, her eyes were black with confusion.

"Going over things this way can drive you mad. You think, if I hadn't remembered about the antique store—what would have happened? If I had taken a different exit from Bloomingdale's?"

The room was still, waiting.

"We were walking down the street—and then I looked up and there was Philip. He crossed the street and came over to us. He was just the same. Exactly the same.

"I introduced Alexis. He stooped down next to her and held out his hand. But she was very shy and wouldn't let go of me. You know, it's strange—that was the only time they ever met. I doubt if she would even remember.

"I wanted to get away from him, but Philip kept on talking. He told me everything I didn't want to know. He said he was in New York shooting a film—and that he would be there for some time. And then he told me which hotel he was staying at."

She smiled at Paul.

"I think that's the one deliberately cruel thing he ever did to me."

A crease deepened between Maggie's eyes as she began to play with the tassel on the sofa pillow.

"Alexis and I went on to the antique store, and then we got our ice cream. I pretended nothing had happened, but I think Alexis knew. She was usually so curious, and yet she never once asked me who the man we had met was.

"By the time we got home, I had such a headache I could hardly see. I gave Alexis to the nanny, and I locked myself in my room.

"Three days was as long as I could stand it. Finally, I called Philip at his hotel." She looked steadily at Paul. "And of course, we met."

She picked up the fringed pillow, held it against her, rubbed her chin along the top.

"It was strange and sad—and wonderful—being with Philip again.

"I didn't think of Henry at all," she said offhandedly.

* * *

It was growing dark outside. Maggie's face looked strained.

"I did think about Alexis. I didn't feel guilty, though; I didn't think that anything I was doing could possibly hurt her. She would never know; for that matter, Henry would never know. And it would all be over in a few weeks.

"The truth was, I couldn't look beyond the moment. I only knew I had to be with Philip. Do you think that's very selfish?"

Paul was taken by surprise, could not formulate an answer in time. Maggie coiled.

"You do," she said coldly. "Well, you've obviously never been married to someone you don't love."

"No—I do understand."

He watched her uncoil.

"It was a very difficult time," she went on bleakly. "Philip would call me at the house, in the morning when Henry was out. If a servant answered, he would say he was Mr. Banicek—a little character we had invented—an antique restorer. And we would arrange to meet.

"Each time, I told myself I wouldn't go. And each time, I would watch myself get dressed, do my hair, get in my car, and drive to Philip.

"And then when I left, I would swear to myself that I wouldn't go back ever again.

"I took it one day at a time. I knew it had no future. I didn't even ask about his wife."

She closed her eyes.

"Then one day, I came into the hotel room and

Philip said to me—as if it were the most casual thing in the world—that he was going to leave her."

Maggie's eyes, when she opened them again, looked bruised.

"I pretended I hadn't heard him. I couldn't let myself go through that hell again.

"But this time, he did leave."

Paul was taken aback by her calmness. Again he was reminded that all these things had been lived out many years before.

"That must have been very gratifying," he said, groping for the right word.

She raised her eyebrows at his choice.

"It was heaven. For two, three weeks, I was in heaven. It was like a miracle. It meant I could escape from everything. Philip and I planned the whole thing out. He would go back to France. I would stay another few months, then tell Henry I wanted a divorce. He would never even have to know it was because of Philip. Alexis and I would move to France, wait a few more months, then Philip and I would get back together. And then it would be the three of us, Philip, Alexis, and me, living in Paris—in our little eighteenth-century house on the river. Philip making movies. Alexis learning French. Me acting again."

She exhaled shortly. "Well, the little fantasy didn't last very long. Henry found out."

"How?"

"His mother, of course. One of the servants mentioned 'Mr. Banicek' to her and she got suspicious. She had me followed by a detective. When I came in one night, I was 'confronted by the evidence,' as they say."

"It must have been horrible."

"It was one of the worst nights of my life. Henry, I

must say, behaved with dignity. He told me he hadn't realized how unhappy I must have been. He even said he supposed he was in part to blame."

"And Mrs. Avery?"

"She told me to pack my things and go.

"Henry sent her up to her room. Then we went into the library and talked all night." Maggie rose again and strode around the room. "I said I was leaving, that I wanted a divorce; he said to think of Alexis, how much that would hurt Alexis. He told me how selfish I was being. He said I would ruin her life." Maggie ran her fingers restlessly through her hair. "I couldn't do that to her. So I agreed. I said I would stay and we would keep on with the marriage. For Alexis's sake.

"I called Philip, with Henry in the room, and told him what had happened. I said that I couldn't see him anymore. When I put down that phone, I knew my life was over."

She sat back down on the sofa.

"Henry and I went on for four more months. We both tried. He'd come home from the office a little earlier, so we could spend more time together. I went out and watched him play golf. I even listened to opera with him. But of course, it didn't work. How could it?

"We both knew it was hopeless. We started to fight. In all our years of marriage, we had never fought. Alexis would hear us—I know it frightened her."

Her face was set. "One night Henry came home, and he'd been drinking. He didn't usually drink. He wanted to make love. I tried to go along, but it had gotten to the point where I couldn't bear his touching me. I told him to stop, but he got angrier and angrier."

She paused.

"Like your first husband."

"Yes," she said, surprised. "I've never connected the two.

"In the morning, he apologized. He cried; I don't think I'd ever seen Henry cry before. He said he had been desperate. I completely understood.

"A few days later, the phone rang. It's funny the way destiny works—nine times out of ten, the butler answered the phone, but that day, for whatever reason, he didn't. So I picked it up. It was Philip. He was back in New York again for a few days. He told me he was going to spend the weekend in Southampton, and asked me if I would go with him—be with him one last time.

"I said yes."

She put down the cigarette.

"I behaved like a complete coward. I told Henry I was going into New York for the day, to see a show. I didn't take a suitcase. I left another note in his den, where he would find it when he got home from work. I told him I had gone away with Philip—but just for the weekend, just to say good-bye. He'd be livid, of course, but I was beyond caring at this point. Things couldn't get any worse than they were.

"But I did worry about Alexis. I didn't want her to come home from school, and find me gone like that. So I left her a note, too, saying that I would be away for the weekend. I remember going into her closet, and holding up her dresses and smelling them. I think I loved her in that moment more than I had ever loved her in my life." Tears came into her eyes.

"There were two things of mine that she had always wanted—one was a scrapbook from my acting days, and the other was a crown I'd worn when I played

Gertrude. I got them from my closet and I put them next to the note.

"And then I left the house."

Her voice was so low Paul could hardly hear her.

"I don't think it ever occurred to me that I would never be back. Or that I would never see Alexis again."

Seventeen

Alexis went through the week, feeling as though she were moving to music—the dark underpinning chords of a film noir. The woman going up the steps, suspecting nothing—and the audience, alerted by the music, knowing someone is waiting at the top of the steps, but unable to warn her. Alexis felt as if she was both audience and victim—and the music never left her head. She knew it was all nonsense. Nothing had happened. Nothing was going to happen. But ever since the moment in the coffee shop with Richard Fredericks, the uneasiness had been with her

She was annoyed and embarrassed to find how often she thought about the tall, dark-haired man. His words moved in and out of her mind: "I've wanted to meet you for thirty-five years." For a day or two after the meeting, she had half expected him to call. Then she thought he might write—that a letter in the strange handwriting would come in the mail. But there was no letter, no call. Of course not—how could there be? She had not given him her phone number or her address.

A week went by, but she could not forget their encounter. The following Tuesday, when she arrived at Brian House, Alexis was half prepared for Steven Wheelhouse to come out of his office, pull her in again, and reintroduce her to the dark man with the intense eyes—but the door remained closed. And when she entered her classroom, the children were not chattering about how a big Hollywood documentary maker was going to make them all stars. Richard Fredericks was forgotten—it was as if he had never been.

Alexis came home tired that afternoon. She made herself a cup of tea and settled down at the kitchen table to drink it. As she sat, her glance wandered around the bright room to a little copper pot filled with silk daisies—something Sylvia had bought her years ago at an antiques fair.

It had been a while since she'd talked to Sylvia, and Alexis decided to call her. It was four-thirty now—a perfect time. Sylvia would have finished her round of golf, and she would be back home.

Alexis pictured Sylvia moving about her Florida bungalow, its airy rooms filled with wicker furniture and tropical print pillows. After Henry died, Sylvia had taken none of the Avery furniture, nor any of the things she had lived with during their life together. That had been a surprise—Alexis had supposed Sylvia would have wanted to keep as many memories as possible. But perhaps it made her too lonely.

She dialed the number.

"Alexis!" Sylvia cried. "I was just missing you."

"And I was missing you."

They chatted for a few minutes, about Sylvia's

health and her golf game, and Alexis's spread in *Architectural Digest.*

"And how's your grandmother doing?" Sylvia asked.

"Much better. I talked to her this morning, and she told me she'd been playing bridge till eleven last night."

"Good for her."

"Sylvia," Alexis said suddenly, "I have a question for you."

"Yes, dear?"

"It's something about my—mother."

"Yes?"

"Did she—when I was a child—do you remember anything about a room that was fixed up for me in Paris, and—filled with toys?"

Hearing herself say it, it sounded insane.

Sylvia paused.

"No, dear," she said. "I don't remember anything like that. But you might try asking your grandmother. She was the one who always dealt with your mother."

"That's all right—it isn't important," Alexis said quickly. "I don't want to worry Grandmother with anything at the moment."

They talked a few minutes more, and said goodbye. After she hung up the phone, Alexis paused. Sylvia had said that her grandmother was the one who had always dealt with her mother. But hadn't her grandmother told her, years and years ago, that there had been no contact with Maggie since Alexis was eight years old? Alexis frowned. Then she pushed the thought aside. What did it matter, anyway? It didn't matter at all.

*   *   *

The following morning, Alexis was walking up Park Avenue when she heard a voice calling excitedly behind her.

"Mrs. Donleavy! Mrs. Donleavy!"

She turned, and smiled at the plump figure hurrying along the street.

"Hello, Mrs. Lawson—how are you?"

"Just on my way to have my teeth cleaned."

"And how's your beautiful apartment?"

"Everyone who sees it absolutely loves it. What's that terribly ugly shade of green?"

"Puce?"

"That's it. They're puce with envy."

Alexis laughed. "Good for us."

Mrs. Lawson clasped her hands together. "I'm so looking forward to the Designer's Showcase this weekend. I can't wait to see your room."

"I'm afraid I didn't do one this year," Alexis told her. "The invitation came a little late, and I was already booked up."

"Well, if you're not in it, then I'm not going," Mrs. Lawson said stoutly.

"Oh, but you must. I appreciate your loyalty, but believe me, there are some marvelous decorators doing the showcase. I wouldn't miss it for anything."

Mrs. Lawson replied that she would think about it, and they said good-bye.

The following Tuesday, Alexis arrived at Brian House a few minutes early. Steven Wheelhouse's door was closed, and she tapped lightly.

"Come in!" he called.

"Ah, Mrs. Donleavy," he said with a smile as she entered. "Good to see you."

Alexis was surprised by his warmth.

"I'm glad you came by—there's something I wanted to ask you. But first, let me say congratulations on the way your class has been going—it seems to be one of the high points of the week."

"Thank you," she said.

"What I was wondering was, maybe starting in September, if you're still interested, we could increase the class size—I've asked around, and there are quite a few other kids who'd like to join."

Alexis smiled. "That would be wonderful," she assured him. "I'd be happy to do it."

"Great. I'll set it up. And now, what can I do for you?"

"Have you ever heard of the Designer's Showcase?"

"I can't say that I have."

"Well, it's a yearly charity event. They have them all over the country. The idea is that a group of different interior designers do a makeover on a mansion. It's a sort of movable feast, with different charities participating, and different houses being used. This year, there's one being held at Hempstead House out in Sands Point. I went out to the show this weekend, and it's absolutely wonderful. With your permission, I'd like to bring Linda, Tamara, and Greg out to see it this Friday."

There was a pause.

"But Mrs. Donleavy, isn't Sands Point out on Long Island?"

"Yes—it's an hour away."

"I'm afraid that's too far."

"It isn't a hard trip," Alexis told him. "And it doesn't take that long to see the house. I would pick the kids up at nine-thirty and have them back by four."

He shook his head. "I don't think so. Something like that—there are just too many variables. And we don't allow the kids to go anywhere without a staff member."

"Couldn't a staff member come along?"

"Not for that length of time. I'm sorry."

Alexis sighed. "Please think about it," she said. "They would benefit so much from seeing these rooms. And this isn't an opportunity that's going to come up often. In fact, it will probably never come up again."

She could see he was starting to waver.

"Look," she told him. "I know these kids. I have a good idea about what they can or cannot handle—and believe me, they can handle this. When Linda and I went to the Met, everything worked out just fine—this would, too. I promise you."

He sighed.

"You'd have them back by four?"

"Yes."

"Well—all right."

Alexis smiled at her class.

"We're going on an outing this Friday."

She was unprepared for the tumult that followed her words.

"Oh, my God!"

"Where?"

"Will I miss my math test?"

"What are we supposed to wear?"

"Is it just for us?"

Tamara and Greg were dancing around, giving each other high fives. Only Linda seemed rather subdued. Alexis wondered if the girl could possibly feel a little jealous—if she preferred it when the outings were just hers and Alexis's.

Briskly, she laid the scene before the class.

"On Friday morning, I'll pick you up here and we'll go out to Long Island, to a place called Sands Point. We're going to see a Designer's Showcase. What that means is a series of rooms, each one decorated by a different designer. It'll give us a chance to see some of the elements of style we've been discussing, and the ways in which different decorators have incorporated them. And I think you'll enjoy the place," she said, "Next to the house itself, there's an actual castle that was—"

"A castle!" Tamara shrieked. "Oh, my God—you're taking us to a castle?!"

Pandemonium returned.

For the rest of the week, the outing stayed poised on Alexis's mind. Carefully, she planned it all out. She had thought about driving to Sands Point, but then she imagined how Ron would react to having the kids in his Mercedes, so she had decided to take the train instead. She would pick everyone up in a taxi—the kids had their instructions to be ready and waiting with a counselor in front of Brian House at nine-thirty—they would go to Penn Station, take the train to Port Washington, and get in around eleven-thirty. They would see the showcase, have lunch, and then come home. Nothing too daunting in that.

Alexis smiled, imagining how much the kids would love the day. She could hardly wait to see Greg's expression when he saw the huge stone fountain in the middle of the living room—or Linda's reaction to the way Arliss Glatt had chosen to decorate the library. Or Tamara's face when she saw the gift shop.

On Friday morning Ron and Alexis were sitting at the kitchen table, having breakfast.

"How does your day look?" Alexis asked.

"Pretty busy. I've got a closing today. Jacobson swears he's made sure the funds are available, and the money's transferred, but on that Colgate deal . . ."

Alexis nodded politely as he talked on.

He finished his cereal and was starting to leave the table.

"And what about you?" he asked. "Any exciting plans?"

Something in the way he was rising from his chair, not even waiting for her answer, made Alexis flush.

"Oh, yes, big plans," she said deliberately.

"Really?" He was half out of his seat by now.

"Those kids I tutor—I'm taking them out to Sands Point for the day."

Ron was listening a hundred percent now. He had stopped rising. He sat down again. Alexis regretted hugely what she had just said.

"That's out of the question," he told her flatly.

And he went on to inform her at great length how, if anything happened to these kids, she could be legally liable, and how psychologically dangerous it was to involve herself more and more in the lives of children who were going nowhere.

Alexis waited for him to finish.

Then a wounded note crept into his voice. "And you've obviously forgotten we're having dinner with my clients from Chrysler tonight. It's an important dinner—and if you spend the day gallivanting around Sands Point, you're not going to be up to it."

So that was the reason for the outburst.

"I promise you, I can handle the clients from Chrysler," Alexis told him. "And I didn't forget about the dinner. I even bought a new dress to wear for it."

That was a lie, but Ron would never notice.

He ended up wishing her good luck on her outing.

Alexis got ready to go. But she found that the scene with Ron had depressed her—it was as if something of the innocence had been drained from the day.

She left the apartment building in good time, and the doorman called her a taxi. When she got in, she gave the driver the address of Brian House, and suggested the least congested route.

The traffic was terrible; by the time they reached Brian House, it was nine-forty. There was construction in front of the building, and the street had been torn up. There was nobody waiting outside.

"Stay here a minute," Alexis told the taxi driver. "I have to pick some people up—I'll be right back." She jumped out of the cab.

"Lady, I can't wait here!" the driver yelled after her.

Alexis pretended she didn't hear him.

She hurried into the lobby of the building. Tamara, Greg, and Linda weren't anywhere in sight. Neither was Dara, the receptionist. Neither was Steven Wheel-house.

A furious flurry of car horn erupted from the street. Alexis went back outside to the taxi driver.

"Lady, are you crazy or something!"

"Can't you go around the block," she asked. "I promise you—we'll be out in a minute."

"Forget it," he said.

Alexis paid him, and he drove off.

She went back inside Brian House, and a few moments later, Dara appeared.

"Oh, Mrs. Donleavy," she said, "The kids were wondering where you were—they're in the classroom."

Annoyed, Alexis rushed down the hall. But when she came into the room and saw them, her irritation vanished.

They looked absolutely wonderful. Tamara was wearing a peasant skirt and top, and her hair was festooned with matching colored bows. Greg was in a suit only slightly too small, and was resplendent in a purple bow tie. And Linda had recklessly plundered her collection of vintage thrift shop regalia.

"You all look just fantastic," Alexis told them.

As they hurried down the hall, Tamara and Greg circled Alexis, chattering, childish, but Linda seemed oddly tense. She kept hanging back, glancing around, as if waiting for something. Alexis wondered what was wrong, but there was no time to ask.

They left Brian House and emerged onto the torn-up pavement.

"We need a taxi," Alexis called over the noise of

the jackhammers. "Let's get away from this construction."

They hurried down the block, and waited at the next corner. The minutes went by, but no taxi came. Anxious, Alexis kept checking her watch. It was nine-fifty. Then it was nine fifty-five.

"Mrs. Donleavy," said a voice behind her. Alexis jumped and turned around. It was Raoul. He looked embarrassed, his words sounded heavy.

"I just wanted to tell you—I have a free day today. I thought maybe I could—go along—with you."

He was staring at Linda. She was staring back at him.

Alexis didn't doubt for a second that Raoul was lying.

"I'm sorry, Raoul, but this outing is for my class only. I don't have the authority to take anyone else."

It was as if he hadn't heard her. He waited in humble silence.

"And surely, if you have a free day, you have plans for it."

"I was supposed to see my brother—but this morning he called to cancel."

"Well, what did Mr. Wheelhouse tell you to do instead?"

Raoul shrugged. "He didn't tell me anything. He isn't in today."

The pleading on his face was horrible.

Alexis shook her head.

"Raoul," she said firmly. "I'm sorry. But there's no way I can take you with us. Surely you can see that. And you know you're not supposed to be wandering around like this. Please go back to Brian House; just pretend it's a regular day. I'm sure Mr. Wheelhouse will reschedule your free time."

A hardness glazed over the boy's eyes. Alexis knew that he had no intention of going back.

Frustration filled her. She would have to take him back herself.

She saw a taxi turn the corner toward them. She waved it down.

"Raoul," she said again. "Please go back to Brian House."

"No way," he told her. "I have a free day. I don't have to be there."

"Yes, you do—until other plans are made," she said firmly. "I'm bringing you back to school now, and you can talk to Dara about it. Maybe she can arrange something."

"But that'll be too late!" Raoul's voice rose. "I want to go with you."

"You know you can't."

"Then fuck it—I'm not going back there," he said. And Raoul started to walk in the direction opposite to Brian House.

Alexis was furious. She couldn't physically haul him back to school, and free day or no free day, she couldn't have him wandering the city. Nor could she miss this train; it would throw the whole day off schedule. As the taxi pulled up to the curb, she remembered the phrase about the lesser of two evils.

"Raoul!" she called sharply.

He turned.

"I want the truth. Do you really have a free day?"

"Yes," he told her soberly. "I swear it."

Alexis found herself looking at Linda.

"Yes, Mrs. Donleavy," Linda said, "I swear it, too."

She did not drop her eyes.

"Tamara? Greg?" Alexis asked. "Would you mind if Raoul joined our outing today?"

They shrugged.

"All right, Raoul," she said tightly. "I really resent the blackmail, but you leave me no choice. You'd better come with us."

She saw Linda's face. All the tension was suddenly siphoned off, leaving it dewy with joy.

They got into the taxi—Alexis in front with the driver, the four kids squeezed into the backseat.

When they reached Penn Station, Alexis called Brian House from her cellular phone. The connection was terrible, but she managed to make out that Steven Wheelhouse still wasn't in. She told Dara that Raoul was with her, and that she would bring him back with the others at four o'clock.

It was an hour's ride to Port Washington. They managed to get seats on the train, but Tamara and Greg did not remain in them long. They raced the length of the car, shrieking and laughing, as if they were six years old. Alexis could only control them for a few minutes at a time, and a part of her did not even want to try.

Linda and Raoul sat next to each other. Her head was on his shoulder, and he was stroking her hair. Alexis could not help watching; she found herself once more remembering Jimmy Craig, and the night she had slept by his side, his arms warm around her.

At last, the train slowed for its final stop. "Port

Washington!" the public address system announced in a muffled voice. "Everybody off."

They got off the train into the peaceful spring-smelling little station. The kids walked quietly, as if bewitched by the silence around them.

"How come it's so quiet?" Greg asked a little anxiously.

"It's the country," Tamara told him. "Haven't you ever been out in the country before?"

Greg shook his head.

"This isn't really country," Alexis said. "Sands Point is only eighteen miles from New York. It's really almost a suburb."

"It's the country," Tamara corrected her.

Alexis smiled. "I guess you're right," she said.

They found a taxi at the station and started off to Hempstead House. As they drove, Alexis told them about Sands Point.

"An author called F. Scott Fitzgerald wrote a very famous book about this area," she said. "It's called *The Great Gatsby.*"

Tamara gasped.

"Oh, my God! We read that! We read that for English!"

Greg looked around the huge houses they were driving by, and whistled.

"Man, I'm going to Gatsby's house," he said happily.

* * *

At last they reached the huge wrought-iron gates of the estate, and turned down a long wooded drive. Alexis pointed to a turreted stone building which could be seen through the trees.

"There's the castle I told you about—Castle Gould."

The kids crowded the window.

"It really is a castle," Linda breathed.

"Yes, it is—from Ireland. It was taken apart, stone by stone, brought over here, and completely reassembled."

Alexis pointed in the other direction, across a large, rough meadow.

"And that's Hempstead House, over there. That's where we'll be seeing the showcase."

The kids seemed considerably less impressed by this sight.

"It's pretty glamorous, too," Alexis reassured them. "Hempstead House is used for a lot of movies—in fact, they filmed the new version of *Great Expectations* here."

"Do you think they'll be making a movie today?" Tamara demanded. "Do you think I can be in it?"

Alexis started to smile, and then she was reminded of Richard Fredericks and his documentary. The taxi pulled up in front of Hempstead House.

The kids got out slowly from the taxi, staring in awe at the stone structure surrounded by its Sleeping Beauty blanket of trees. Alexis let them wander around the front yard while she waited in line for tickets.

"We're ready!" she called at last, but the kids didn't want to come.

"Couldn't we stay outside just a minute more?" Linda begged.

"Please!"

"Please!"

"Oh, all right," Alexis told them.

They continued to walk around, quieter than Alexis had ever seen them. Ignoring the crowds of people, they stared at the meadow and up into the dark trees as if dazed by the loveliness.

"Well, are we ready to go see the rooms now?" Alexis asked at last.

The kids went inside the house, as if to imprisonment. They walked quickly around, looking only briefly at the rooms. Alexis did her best to point out the high points, but even Linda, she could see, was not very interested. At every window, they would stop and gaze out at the sky and grass.

Finally, Alexis gave up.

"Why don't we go outside again?" she suggested, and the kids dashed for the exit.

Alexis stood by the front of the house and watched them, the warm wind blowing her skirt. Somewhere, a radio was playing, and Tamara and Greg were dancing to its beat, moving in happy unself-consciousness. Raoul, showing off for Linda, was doing handsprings and back flips on the spongy grass. He was surprisingly graceful. Alexis wondered where he had learned to do tricks like this.

After half an hour, she announced that it was time for lunch. She took the kids across to the cafeteria in the castle. They ate rapturously, and she was pleased with their company manners. Then they went to the gift shop, which was an even greater success. Alexis bought them each a book of postcards, and a catalog of the decorator exhibits they hadn't seen.

"Anybody interested in going back to the show-rooms?" she asked.

No one was interested. So they walked through the meadow and looked out over the water for a few minutes, then called a taxi and caught the next train back to New York.

During this ride, the kids sat quiet, tired. Tamara and Greg looked out of the windows, watching as, stop by stop, the countryside of Port Washington and Plandome and Great Neck gave way to the congestion of Queens. Alexis also watched Long Island sliding by, and she thought of her growing-up days.

"Mrs. Donleavy?" Linda was saying softly to her as the train pulled into Penn Station. "It's not even two o'clock yet. We don't have to be back to Brian House till four. After we get to the city, could we please go to your apartment?"

"Yes! Yes!" came the insistent chorus.

Alexis felt uncomfortable, and angry. Linda should not have mentioned the apartment; that was a secret she had promised to keep.

"I'm sorry—it's out of the question," she told Linda firmly.

She saw the eager expectation in the girl's eyes turn cold.

Alexis ended up taking the kids to the Museum of Modern Art for an hour.

"We'll stay in a group," she told them. "and if we should get separated, we'll meet at the entrance."

"Mrs. Donleavy," Linda said pleadingly. "I'm not feeling very well." She pointed toward the sculpture garden at the back. "Couldn't Raoul and I just sit there instead?" Even under the white makeup, she looked pale.

"I promise we won't move," she said.

Alexis hesitated. "Well, all right."

Linda and Raoul started toward the garden and Alexis took Tamara and Greg around the museum. Greg had a wonderful time; he found Picasso's "Guernica" almost immediately, and hovered by it, shaking his head and whistling. "Man, this is Bugland."

And Tamara was equally content. The paintings themselves didn't interest her much, but she spent a rapt fifteen minutes in the bookstore looking at their reproductions on postcards. Alexis bought her a set—and a poster of "Guernica" for Greg.

When Alexis went out to the sculpture garden, she found Linda and Raoul sitting on an iron bench and kissing. Uncomfortably, she went up to them.

"It's time to go back," she said.

They found a taxi and set off for Brian House. Tamara and Greg clowned around during the drive, making paper airplanes of their museum fliers, until finally the driver yelled at them to stop. But Linda and Raoul were solemn and quiet.

The taxi pulled up at the brick building, and the kids got out. They all thanked Alexis for the day.

"It was my pleasure," Alexis smiled. She watched until they were safely inside, and then she had the driver take her back to her apartment.

* * *

When Alexis got home, she realized she was very tired—tired almost to the verge of tears. And then she remembered—the dinner with the clients from Chrysler.

By the time Ron came home, she was bathed and dressed for the evening ahead.

"Hey, you're all ready!" Ron said when he saw her. "And you look beautiful—nice dress. So how did the big day go, anyway? Lose any kids in Sands Point?"

"No, it went very smoothly. Not quite according to plan, but we adjusted. I think it was a success."

"Well, that's great," he said, and went off to take a shower.

Alexis sat down on the couch with a glass of wine. The phone rang and she picked it up.

"Mrs. Donleavy—" It was Linda.

"Yes, Linda. What is it?" Alexis asked. She drew out the question because she knew that there was something very wrong.

There was only silence.

"What is it, Linda?" she asked again.

"It's Raoul," Linda whispered. "He—we—weren't telling the truth this morning. He didn't have a free day."

Oh, God, Alexis thought.

"We didn't think Mr. Wheelhouse was going to be in at all," Linda rushed on, "but he came back—and . . . when he found out Raoul had gone, he—he was so angry." She began to sob, bitter, harsh sobs. "He's said he's going to send Raoul back to court—and recommend that they send him away." Alexis could barely hear the final words. "To a locked facility."

Alexis closed her eyes.

Why had she let it happen? She had known all along that Raoul and Linda were lying.

"I'm so sorry," she said. "It's my fault. I never should have let him come."

"Oh, Mrs. Donleavy," Linda said, her voice trembling, "the reason I called . . . please couldn't we—one last time—meet at your apartment? We could sneak out of here," she went on quickly, "I know no one would tell on us—"

"No, Linda," Alexis told her. "Absolutely not."

Linda sounded stunned.

"But—but why? You let us before."

Pain settled onto Alexis's shoulders, and the sense of racing down an unpaved road.

"I know I did," she said. "And I shouldn't have. It was very wrong of me." She took a breath, forcing herself to sound even. "Listen to me, Linda. It's really not such a tragedy. Very soon, you and Raoul will both be adults. You'll be free to make—"

"Fuck you," Linda whispered.

And she slammed the phone down.

Ron came smiling out of the bedroom.
"Well, we'd better get going," he told Alexis.
Mechanically, she stood up.

Alexis got through the evening, unaware of anything that was going on around her—all she could think of was Linda and Raoul and the whispered,

"Fuck you." The dinner was a long one; when she and Ron got home, they went straight to bed. Once Alexis was sure Ron was asleep, she went into the living room and sat awake on the sofa for the rest of the night.

At seven-thirty in the morning, Steven Wheelhouse called to tell her that Linda and Raoul had run away, and that no one knew where they were.

Then he told Alexis that her services were no longer wanted at Brian House.

Eighteen

The door opened, and the butler came in.

"It's six o'clock, Madame."

"Ah—thank you, Pierre."

Paul could hear other voices in the hall, an increase of activity—but Maggie's tone remained unhurried, almost remote.

"I don't remember much about the next few months of my life," she told Paul. "Those months after I left Alexis. It's marvelous, isn't it, the way that Nature anesthetizes us when we need it.

"Philip had to go back to Paris to finish his film, and I decided that I would go with him. It was supposed to be temporary—a—what's that word? It starts with an R.

"Recognizance?"

"A recognizance trip. I would go for a month or two, just to get away from New York and the nightmare with Henry. Then I would have time to decide what I wanted to do next.

"Three weeks after we got to Paris, I was sitting at Fouquet, waiting for Philip to join me. All of a sudden, everyone started shouting—I didn't speak French, and I didn't know what was going on. But then someone turned on the television. President Kennedy had been killed." She grimaced. "Philip was absolutely shattered. He thought this meant the end of American civilization. He said we should stay in France and not go back at all. I didn't take him seriously; I had to go back for Alexis—but time went by, and we still didn't go back. And then we never went back," she added abruptly.

Paul knew this already, but the tone of her voice made the tragedy fresh.

"I wonder if, on some level, all along, I knew that we wouldn't. When that plane took off from New York, I cried in a way I have never cried before and I hope never to cry again. Philip was angry with me for crying," she added. "He could be a very jealous man.

"When we first got to Paris, we stayed at the Ritz, but Philip wanted something more permanent. We ended up renting an eighteenth-century apartment on the rue de Luxembourg. I insisted on getting a place with a short lease. But what is that word—inertia? When it gets harder and harder to make a move?"

She was silent.

"I've seen pictures of that apartment," Paul broke into the silence. "It was beautiful."

She nodded. "Yes—wasn't it."

"And pictures of you when you first lived there."

"How did I look?"

"Happy."

She considered. "In many ways I was very happy."

"You were with Philip."

"Yes. We were never apart. For over twenty years, we almost never left each other's side."

She looked at Paul.

"People are so surprised when I say this. They always want to know if we ever got tired of each other. Don't you think that's an odd question? Or were you about to ask it, too?"

"No," he said. "I wasn't."

"Good for you," she told him. "I think it's ridiculous. Do you get tired of being with yourself? Of course you don't. And I didn't get tired of being with Philip."

She stood up, went to the mantel, and brought over the picture that Paul had already looked at.

"He was a handsome man, wasn't he?"

"Very."

"And so alive. So creative. He could be cruel at times—in many ways he was a lot like my father—but I guess some part of me needed that. Yes," she said emphatically, "we had a good life. Terribly disjointed, of course. Full of drama, feeling—maybe too much feeling! Variety." She took the picture back, spoke to the smiling Philip. "God knows we were never bored."

"You enjoyed living in Paris?"

"Oh, yes. We were very happy here. We lived through it all—general strikes, student demonstrations, winters when the heating went out—but we loved it. Philip was at home here; he had spent a great deal of time in Paris as a child, and then of course he had lived here again with his—wife."

"Did you ever miss America?"

She raised her eyebrows.

"Only every day of my life. The most trivial things,

too—trashy newspapers—Chasens' chili—Lord and Taylor's. My dry cleaners on Lexington Avenue."

"Didn't you ever go back, even to visit?"

A spasm crossed her face.

"No. That part of my life was behind me."

"Even—Alexis?"

Paul was sorry he had spoken. Her head snapped up, betrayed.

"Even Alexis," she said deliberately. Then the anger damped out, and her voice was like ashes.

"The first thing I did when we moved into the apartment was decorate a room for her for when she came," she said. "I did that even before I finished Philip's and my bedroom. I found a lovely toystore called Le Nain Bleu, and I bought the place out. I filled her room with toys and dolls—even a little puppet show. And I put in the most beautiful antique iron bed you've ever seen."

There was a long silence.

"I still thought that Alexis would grow up in that apartment. Sleep in that little wrought-iron bed. I thought Philip and I would raise her and that Henry and the Averys would be somehow—just blotted out."

With a sort of puzzled defenselessness, she looked at Paul.

"I wonder at myself now—how I ever could have believed that would really happen.

"When the lawyer's letter came, it was a total shock."

She swallowed with difficulty.

"Give me just a moment," she said.

She fixed her eyes on Philip's picture.

"Philip was wonderful during that time. More wonderful than I'd ever seen him. He promised me I'd get

Alexis back. He spent a great deal of his own money, a great deal of time. We tried every avenue, but we lost.

"The court awarded Henry full custody of Alexis. And until she was twelve, I was allowed to see her at his discretion only. Which meant never.

"It's funny, the things you remember." Her voice was very detached. "I remember what I did when Philip told me the news. I ran around the apartment—completely berserk. Just kept running and running."

Her face was a mask.

"When we first came to Paris, I wrote Alexis almost every day. I tried to explain that my leaving had nothing to do with her. I promised that one day we would be together. But she never wrote me back."

"Are you sure she got your letters?"

"I'm not sure of anything. I know Henry wouldn't have kept them from her—he would never do anything like that. But that mother of his—absolutely. At least that's what I'd like to think. That the reason Alexis didn't write back was because she never got my letters.

"After we—heard the news, I couldn't stand to look at her room anymore. So I took those toys I had bought and started sending them to her. The room grew emptier and emptier.

"Finally I gave away the little antique iron bed.

"It was easier after that." Her smile was a grimace. "Besides, I told myself that once Alexis was twelve, she would be free to come to me. And our life together would start.

"But that didn't happen. She chose to stay with her father."

She put her hands over her face. Paul made a motion toward her, but she drew back. She took her hands away.

"Looking back on it," she said. "I wonder why I should have even been surprised."

"But didn't you call? Didn't you try to get in touch?"

"I couldn't have stood it," Maggie said.

"Are you sure she didn't want to come?"

"It had been a long time—Alexis was no longer a little girl. And that old woman had had four years to poison her about me." She swallowed. "Or maybe she hadn't even needed to do that. Maybe just telling Alexis the truth was enough."

Maggie took a deep breath. and continued more calmly. "Also Henry wrote in his letter that she was happy, doing well in school. I thought maybe the least selfish thing I could do at this point was to leave her alone."

There was a long pause.

"And perhaps I understood that she was the price for my being with Philip."

She sat back, folded her hands, and addressed Paul with formality.

"So. You make your choices in life, don't you?"

"I read something recently," he told her. "That you can have anything in life you want, but not everything."

She nodded thoughtfully.

"Yes. That's very true. And I got Philip, but not Alexis.

"Actually," she said after a moment, her voice deliberately lighter, "as things turned out, I did get to have a child of sorts. Philip's son, Richard. I think I told you about him."

"The little boy who used to steal your memo pad."

"Yes. Richard lived with his mother in Philadelphia—she was always very bitter about Philip leaving—

but he did come to Paris occasionally. I loved Richard," she said slowly, "but it was hard having him in the house."

"He wasn't Alexis."

"No."

She tapped her hand on the arm of the sofa.

"Enough," she went on briskly. "That's all very much in the past." She was silent a moment. "So Philip and I continued to be together. I lived for him, he lived for me. Though of course, he had his work as well—it's different for a man."

"I'm surprised the government let him work," Paul said. "I've heard Americans usually have a terrible time."

"Oh, but Philip wasn't an American. He was given American citizenship when he came over from Hungary, but his mother was French and he had actually been born in Marseilles. So there was no problem."

"And what about you—could you work?"

"At first I didn't even want to. I never wanted to do another movie again. But after a year or so, someone came to me with an idea I absolutely loved. They said I should start a little theater, an English language theater, where American and English actors could perform. Philip got his lawyers to set everything up; since I was an American, it had to be all nonprofit. I know people said that I paid myself a huge salary, but that's ridiculous. I did it for the sheer fun of the thing. We put on some marvelous shows."

"So I've heard. And you even acted in a few of them."

She nodded. "I was Amanda in *Glass Menagerie*. And a very sexy Auntie Mame. And the *Antigone* you asked about before. But mainly I directed and produced. We kept going for quite a few years—I'm proud of that. But times change—the audience started to drop off. And it was getting to be too much work. So I let it go."

"That must have been hard."

"A little. But it was nice to spend time just with Philip. We found this apartment, and moved into it. And we went around Paris together; we explored everything. He was passionate about Fin de siecle art, and we'd go looking for it in the most out-of-the-way places. We'd go on little trips, too, Deauville and London, and Switzerland. My favorite was Biarritz— have you ever been there?"

Paul said he had not.

"Lovely town—all those pink buildings.

"We had many wonderful years together. Truly wonderful years. And then, quite suddenly, Philip became ill. His throat had been bothering him for some time—I thought it was just allergies. But he went in to the doctor and they did some tests. We got the results the day after Easter."

She shivered.

"It's terrible how quickly cancer can spread.

"I asked Philip if there was anything I could do for him—and he said yes. That he wanted to see me make another movie."

Maggie shook her head. "I'd never quite realized how much my talent meant to Philip," she said. "In some strange way, I think it fulfilled him even more than it fulfilled me."

"Was it hard, getting started again?"

"Not really. By this time I'd been in France so long I had resident's status. And Philip had so many connections, we were able to get over any legal problems. In fact, almost overnight, I was set up with a joint venture production."

"*Le Montre.*"

"That's right."

"It's one of my favorites."

She seemed pleased. "Mine, too—I loved playing that woman—but what a nightmare it was to make. It had been such a long time since I'd worked—I was scared to death that I'd lost my talent. And the director they gave me was a complete imbecile."

"Renard?"

"Exactly. It was his first film, and he didn't know what on earth he was doing. Directed me all over the place. I paid no attention to him, of course, and by the end of the first week, when the rushes came in, it was obvious to everyone, the imbecile included, that I was the best thing in the film. So he let me alone, after that."

She laughed complacently.

"The movie was a smash; won the Palme D'Or at the Cannes Film Festival. The idiot Renard went on to other glories, and I was offered a second movie." The smile softened. "Philip was so proud. His health improved overnight; it gave him a reason to live.

"And then after that, there was another movie, then another.

"But I never finished the last one," she said abruptly. "The cancer returned. Worse than before."

The words came with great effort. "The hospital sent Philip home, and I never left his side for nine weeks."

She stared at the coffee table.

"It was almost a happy time, strange as that sounds. We played cards and I read him Modesty Blaise novels. And he looked so ridiculously elegant," she said lightly. "Lying there in his silk pajamas and scarf, and smelling of Royalle Lyme cologne."

Her mouth trembled.

"On Christmas Day, I was in the kitchen. I heard him call, 'Maggie! Come look!' He sounded terribly excited. I ran into the bedroom—he was sitting up in bed, pointing in front of him. There was nothing there. Then he fell back—and he was gone within an hour."

The room was darkening around them. She seemed very small against the sofa.

"Philip died in 1985," she said slowly. "That's one date I will never forget. After he died, I decided to stay in Paris. I planned on moving to another apartment, but didn't—I wanted to be where Philip had been."

Her voice came, cool, from the shadows.

"It was a strange time after he died. I didn't have the energy to do much of anything. I walked around Paris, read, got his papers in order. I tried to decide what I would do with the rest of my life; I didn't want to go back to America, but I wasn't sure I wanted to stay here. And without Philip, I had no desire to act anymore. So I didn't. For a long, long time.

"Then one day, about six years ago, I got a phone call out of the blue. It was from a woman named Charlotte Chandler; she was a film buff from Los Angeles. She told me she had seen one of my old films at the Cinémathèque Française. Apparently, she ran a little art movie theater called the Golden somewhere in Los Angeles, and she wanted to screen the film there. The Golden was about to go under, and she thought my movie might attract some business. I must admit, I felt a certain kinship with that little theater," Maggie smiled. "Well, the movie was shown, and the critic from the *Los Angeles Times* gave it a rave, and the next thing you know, they're lining up around the block to see me. Suddenly, all the old films are in demand again and I'm in distribution all over the world."

"And the Golden is still in business. I pass it on my way to work."

"It still is, and so am I. A star again, after all this time. It's downright indecent!"

She laughed, gloriously.

"And the offers still come in. I don't do much—I don't need to—but occasionally I'm tempted. In fact, I'd say I've made some of my best movies these last few years. I prefer to do European ones—at this point I feel more comfortable here—but I did go back to Hollywood a few years ago, to appear at a retrospective of my work. You wouldn't believe what they paid me! And to top it all off, I was asked to put my handprints in the cement of the Chinese Theatre."

"I know. I've seen them. Was it strange, being back in Hollywood again after all that time?"

"Actually, I enjoyed it more than I thought I would. It's changed so much that I could enjoy it like a regular tourist. Downtown's unrecognizable, and I couldn't believe what's happened to Rodeo Drive. But they do still have the flannel cakes at Musso and Frank's. Some things never change."

"And the rumor is that you're scheduled to start a movie in the spring."

"The rumor is correct."

"It must be wonderful to be you."

She leaned forward, hands clasped.

"Yes, it is. I absolutely love it. I love being famous. I love being stopped on the street, and being asked for autographs. And I love the film festivals. It's such fun sneaking into those—some of my old performances really hold up—some I could absolutely throttle myself for. But I enjoy them all.

"And I adore the retrospectives—hearing what the critics have to say about my 'technique.' It's all the most delicious hogwash, of course. I never had any kind of technique. But please don't tell the critics!"

They both laughed. Paul felt his heart grow light within him.

Then her voice lowered intimately.

"One thing that does bother me, though, are the posters—have you seen them? All of a sudden, they seem to have sprung up everywhere. Every time I pass a souvenir shop, there I am in the window. Marilyn Monroe, naturally. James Dean, well, of course. But me? I don't know."

The noises from the hall became louder. There was a discreet tap on the door.

Maggie sighed.

"I'd really best be going now," she said. "These days, it takes me quite a while to look smashing."

Paul felt a sort of desperation.

"Just three more questions," he said. "Do you often look back?"

Maggie considered.

"Who doesn't? Yes, I guess I look back a fair amount. Sometimes when I do, I can only seem to remember the bad times; and believe me, there've been plenty. Other days, the whole thing seems pure magic from beginning to end."

"Do you have any regrets?"

There was a long pause.

"Yes," she said abruptly. "And what's the last question?"

"What have you learned?"

At first she laughed.

"You must be kidding! That's an impossible one."

But then her face suddenly softened. In the twilight, in her husky voice, she sang the last lines of the song "Nature Boy."

"The greatest thing you'll ever learn, is just to love and be loved in return."

She gave a little shrug, smiled radiantly at Paul. "That's about it."

Slowly, he put away his notebook, turned off the tape recorder.

"I've enjoyed this," Maggie said. "And I hope I've given you what you wanted."

"You have," he told her.

They rose. He took a last look at the room, a last listen to the sounds of the draperies blowing, a last whiff of the lemon furniture polish and the flowers.

"Wait," Maggie said. "Take this with you."

And ceremoniously, she handed him a peony from the bouquet on the table.

They reached the hallway.

"Well, I just can't tell you—" Paul faltered. "This has been . . ." He could only shrug.

She laughed, almost shyly.

"Good-bye," Paul said.

Maggie clapped her hands over her ears.

"Oh, no!" she cried. "Never say that word. It's the saddest word in the English language. Say 'Until soon' instead. It's so much happier." She smiled at Paul. "And I haven't forgotten—the next time we meet, I'll make you my grilled cheese sandwich."

Bouyantly, foolishly happy, he left.

Nineteen

The morning passed. Alexis filled in her time with appointments and work. She checked her messages five, ten times, but there was no call from Steven Wheelhouse, no news of Linda.

The girl was ever-present in Alexis's mind. The delicate pale hands. The nervous brushing of her hair. Her face flushing pink under the white makeup. The sudden force of her hug.

Alexis sent out little golden letters into the Universe, COME BACK. COME BACK. COME BACK. But Linda did not answer.

"Sylvia." She tried to make her voice sound normal.

"Alexis, dear; how are you?"

Her warmth made Alexis start to weep.

"Not very well," she said.

"Why? What's happened?" Sylvia asked briskly.

Alexis told her about Linda, and there was a silence.

"Where is she now?"

"Nobody knows. Somewhere on the streets."

There was a pause. "None of this is your fault, Alexis."

"It's all my fault."

"This girl had problems long before she met you."

"I'm the one who let Raoul come."

"You couldn't have known what would happen."

"I let them break the rules."

"You were only trying to be kind."

Alexis closed her eyes.

Sylvia, so simple, so loving, did not understand at all.

"You've got nothing to reproach yourself with," Sylvia went on. "You gave this girl opportunities. You built up her self-esteem. You did so much for her. No matter what happens, you must always remember that."

After she hung up the phone, Alexis sat numbly. *You did so much for her.* But that wasn't true, was it? She remembered something Ron had said, the day she started tutoring. "You're not doing this for the kids, you know—you're doing this for yourself."

She had hated him for saying it, but it was the truth. It had all been for herself—she saw that with such clarity now. All those things she had done to help Linda—taking her to the museum, buying her the ring, commissioning her to paint the box for Mrs. Lawson, bringing her together with Raoul—these things had not been done for Linda at all. They had been done for Alexis.

She had had no power as a child, so she had given power to Linda. She had not been allowed to be an artist, so she had triumphed in Linda's work. She could not be with the boy she had loved, so she let Linda do it for her. For her.

Sick with self-loathing, Alexis put her hands in front of her face.

By midafternoon, there was still no word. Alexis left the apartment, hurrying to lose herself in the world outside. But she couldn't be lost. One eye was always looking out for a slim girl, dressed in raggle-taggle finery. She kept checking her messages, thinking surely Linda would call her.

But when dusk came, there was still nothing.

Alexis raged at Linda. Linda had never cared about her—she had only used her for the meetings with Raoul. Then, no, Alexis thought. No. That wasn't the truth. The girl had cared about her. But where she had gone wrong was in supposing that Linda needed her. When it was now so obvious that it was she who had needed Linda.

Alexis closed her eyes. What a cliché she was. The little girl who had lost her mother. The mother who had lost her little girl. Of course she would have found a Linda. A Linda through whom she could rewrite her own past. A Linda through whom she could resurrect her own daughter.

Except that it was all illusion.

Linda wasn't her childhood self. Linda wasn't Elise. Linda was Linda—a girl who, because of Alexis's meddling, because of Alexis's arrogance, was now lost.

And Alexis understood that she was never going to call.

Ron came home. He gave Alexis a quick kiss, then hurried into the den. She could hear him on the phone, talking business. She went into her dressing room, and changed into her nightgown. When she came out again, Ron was off the phone. He looked at her in surprise.

"What's the matter? Are you sick?"

"No," she said. "Just tired."

He made a calculating little sound, and she knew he was mentally reviewing the evening's schedule. There were no parties to attend; no one was coming for drinks. So he nodded. It was okay for her to be tired.

She looked down at the floor. She spoke as though the air were very brittle, and might shatter at a word.

"Ron," she said, "one of the kids I tutored has run away."

"Nothing to do with your class, I hope," he joked. Then he saw her face.

"I'm sorry," he said quickly. "I'm sure they'll find him soon."

"It's Linda."

She stumbled a little over the name. For some reason, she found herself suddenly picturing the shoes Linda always wore—those absurd little ballet slippers.

Ron was looking at her with concern.

"Well, don't get too upset. I'm sure she's fine."

"I think she's dead."

"Oh, come on! Why should she be dead?" he asked. "These are street-smart kids, Alexis. They know what they're doing."

But she was not listening. She was still thinking of Linda's shoes.

At seven forty-five the next morning, Alexis was awakened by the ringing of the phone.

"Mrs. Donleavy," Steven Wheelhouse said. "I think it's only fair that you should know this." There was a long pause. "They found Linda this morning. She OD'd."

"Is she in the hospital?" Alexis asked carefully.

"Yes."

"Which hospital?"

"Mrs. Donleavy," he said, "she died a few hours ago."

As she had known.

Alexis put her hand before her face.

"Was it—on purpose?" she asked at last.

"We're not sure."

"I see," she said evenly. "Is there going to be a memorial service of any kind?"

"Yes—this Thursday at two o'clock, at the school."

She was silent for a long moment.

"May I come?" she asked at last.

"If you want to."

"Thank you," she told him, and hung up.

With the click of the phone, the world faded to black around her.

Alexis stayed in her apartment for most of the next three days. Ron came and went. They talked little, and only about surface matters. When she told him the news about Linda, he was very kind. Alexis ate meals and made occasional business calls—but mainly she sat on the sofa and thought about her life.

It was amazing, her life. Amazing how, when you really came to examine it, when you really plied it for answers, how so many things turned into smoke. All the things she spent her time on, and her energy—the daily trivia, her whole professional world—even Ron and her marriage—all these seemed to fade as gently and inevitably as overexposed film. Getting paler by the moment, becoming less and less relevant.

But a few things did manage to keep their brilliant colors. Her daughter was the first. Linda was the second. The last one was her mother.

And all of them gone.

Thursday was very hot. It reminded Alexis of the first time she had ever seen Brian House, when the pavements had steamed in the sticky heat. The front door was closed; there was a picture of Linda taped to the upper panel, the rest of the door serving as a great frame. Alexis knew Linda wouldn't have enjoyed that display. It would have made her shy to have her picture on the front door.

The memorial service was held in the dining room, the tables laid flat against the walls, the chairs arranged in rows. At the front of the room was a lectern, surrounded by little bunches of flowers.

The kids sat in the chairs, stiffly, awkwardly, poised to leave. Alexis stood at the back of the room next to some restless boys, boys who had been friends of Raoul's.

"Do you know where Raoul is?" she asked one of them.

He looked at her suspiciously, and shrugged.

"Raoul's not here," he said with finality, and turned away.

A man and woman came into the room and were led by Steven Wheelhouse to the front row. Linda's father had a slight, dazed smile on his face, her mother wept beneath a black veil. Alexis could see the shape of Linda's face on the one, her hair on the other.

The service began. The sermon was delivered by a minister from a nearby church. He had never met Linda, and he used the occasion to rail against teenage drug abuse. Steven Wheelhouse spoke briefly, exhorting everyone to remember Linda's joy, her talent, her uniqueness. Two of her friends got up and spoke bashfully about how nice Linda had been, and how they had always thought she would be famous someday. Then they played Linda's favorite song—an Elvis Presley ballad. It hurt Alexis that she did not know Linda had liked Elvis Presley.

When the service was over, Alexis went down the hall, to Linda's room. Another girl had taken possession, and had ringed the wall over the bed with her orbit of rock musician posters and photographs. All traces of Linda were gone.

As she was coming back down the hall, she caught sight of Tamara and Greg and called out to them.

They came over warily. Alexis wondered what had been said between them about her—if in their minds, as in hers, she was the reason Linda was dead.

She asked them how they were. They told her formally that they were fine. She said she wouldn't be coming back to Brian House, and that she would miss them. They seemed embarrassed.

"How's Bugland?" she asked Greg. The reserve cracked slightly.

"I got a great new idea for sending them into space." Alexis nodded.

"Sounds very promising." She looked hard at Greg. "Keep up with Bugland," she told him. "I would feel very sad if I thought it would ever go away."

He scratched his ear, looked down at his feet.

Alexis turned to Tamara. She touched the girl's arm, and was surprised by how babyishly soft it felt.

"Good luck, Tamara," she said. "I hope I'll be on a plane someday and a beautiful flight attendant will show me to my seat—and it will be you."

Tamara smiled slightly.

"Yeah. Okay," she said. And she and Greg walked away.

Alexis looked after them for a long moment, her eyes burning.

As she was nearing the front door, she saw Linda's parents standing over to one side. She went up to them.

"I just want to tell you," she began. "I just want to tell you how much your daughter meant to me."

They did not know who she was. They nodded.

"Thank you," Linda's mother said.

Alexis saw Steven Wheelhouse standing by the front door. He looked very old. Their eyes met, and Alexis left the building.

As she was crossing the street, she heard her name. She turned and, for a moment, did not recognize

Richard Fredricks. She found herself unsurprised to find him there—as if he were a necessary element in a dream.

He told her he was in town for a few days, on business about the documentary.

"I seem to have come at a bad moment," he added. "Did you know the girl who died?"

Yes. No.

"She was one of my students," Alexis finally told him.

They walked along for a few moments in silence.

"Would you have coffee with me?" he asked her.

"All right."

It also seemed a part of the dream. And why shouldn't she have coffee with him? She had nothing else planned. Linda was dead.

They went to a fluorescent-lit health food restaurant. Richard did nearly all the talking; he spoke lightly, broadly, as if this were the first encounter he and Alexis had ever had. He never once referred to that other time.

And then, right before they left, he cleared his throat.

"I hope you've forgiven me," he said to her.

"Oh, yes," she told him offhandedly. "And anyway, there was nothing to forgive. It was just the shock of what you said—having her name brought up. You see, I've tried so hard not to think about my mother for years." Ruefully, she smiled. "But as it turns out, you were only the beginning."

The image of Maggie came into her mind as she

said it—one of the three vividly colored objects that remained in her black-and-white universe.

"Yes; things do conspire to catch up with you," Richard said.

Silently, she drank the last few bitter drops of her tea. When it was finished, it was time for her to go. A part of her was regretful.

"You resemble your mother," he said suddenly. "You didn't when you were a child, but you do now." And then he added, "You ought to go visit her, and see for yourself."

Alexis found herself smiling.

"Oh, I don't think so," she said lightly.

He smiled also.

"Will you see me again?"

"I don't think so," she repeated in the same tone.

"You never know. Maybe you'll change your mind."

Alexis went home. She took down a box of photographs from her closet, and began to sort through them. She remembered that she had started to do this once before, but she couldn't remember why she had stopped. Well, it didn't matter. She was finishing the job now.

She tipped the pile of pictures onto the carpet and picked them up, one by one. She looked at all the people, all the places. A little girl standing beside a horse. A woman weeding. A man and woman wearing bathing suits. A girl with Kabuki makeup standing beside a Christmas tree. A baby wearing a pink-and-white smocked dress. All the photos of her life. Yet a stranger seeing them would have no idea who any of these people were. He would not know Maggie. Or

Molasses. Or Ron and Alexis on their honeymoon. He would not have recognized Linda or Elise.

Amazing, how insubstantial a life was.

When Ron came into the apartment that evening, Alexis was still kneeling by the box of photos.

He came over to her.

She showed him a photo of Maggie, pushing her as a baby on a swing.

"I remember that swing set," she said.

He sat beside her. "Are you all right?" he asked.

"Not really."

"Is it—this girl who died?"

She did not answer for a moment.

"The thing is," she said slowly, "the thing is that there doesn't seem to be anything left. One day it was all real, and the next, it was all gone."

He was taken aback.

"Well, there's us," he said. "We're real, aren't we?"

"Are we?"

"Alexis, what's the matter with you? Things have never gone better. You're happy," he challenged her. "You always told me you were happy."

"I've never told you anything, Ron. I'm sorry," she added.

His voice became suddenly a lawyer's voice. "So what is it you're saying, exactly?"

"I'm not sure I'm saying anything." She paused. "No, I am. I'd like some time to think everything over."

He sighed. "I can't take any vacation days now."

She said nothing.

"Oh, I see." His voice was tight. "You want to go alone."

"I need to figure things out."

"I thought things were already figured out."

"I'm sorry," she said again.

There was a silence.

"How long do you plan on this taking?"

"I don't know."

His voice rose. "What are you telling me, Alexis? Will you be coming back?"

The question shocked her. The possibility of not coming back shocked her even more. But then the idea became suddenly, boundingly, familiar, as if it had been in her mind the entire time.

So there was the choice. It was hers.

"I don't know," she said, bewildered.

He grew white.

"Don't you love me anymore?"

"I do," she said slowly, "but not very deeply."

He looked as if she had hit him.

"Oh, Ron," she said quickly. "I don't know that I meant that. I'm just very confused."

She went toward him, but he stiffened.

"Well, do whatever you want," he said, and then added distinctly, "but if you go away, keep this in mind—I may have plans of my own."

This she had not expected—but surprisingly, the knowledge did not frighten her.

"Well," she said almost brightly, the way one would to a child, "we'll just have to wait and see what happens, won't we?"

She went into the bedroom, and sat down on the bed. She felt completely, utterly, numb. She wondered if her marriage was ending. Whether she would leave

Ron, or he would leave her. Or whether they would somehow continue, business as usual, after the hiatus. Or whether, somehow, they could soar, impossibly, above all this and manage to make something unsuspected and marvelous and real out of their lives together.

She didn't know.

A few minutes later, Ron came into the room.

He sat down on the bed.

"I want you to be happy," he said.

She reached over and squeezed his hand.

"Go on your trip," he told her heavily. "Figure out what you need to. And who knows? Maybe your doing this—maybe it will end up being good for us, too."

"Maybe it will."

They sat in silence.

"Can you at least tell me where you're going?"

"Actually," she said, "would you think I was crazy if I told you I was going to Paris?"

He paused. And then he smiled.

"No. I'd say it was about time."

Alexis looked down. She was still holding the picture of Maggie pushing the swing.

"Make sure you tell her about me," he said.

"I will."

It was a gusty morning, very blue, and Alexis decided to take a walk. As she walked, she tried to think about her life, but she couldn't get it straight, and the voices kept floating past her.

Mother, I'm marrying her.

Are you at Wellesley?

I'm Ron Donleavy, by the way.

It'll be the greatest love of your life.

Is that your daughter? Oh, sorry. I somehow got the idea she was.

Come back. Come back. Come back.

Until soon.

But she kept mixing up who was who, and the faces, the blond boy, the white-faced girl, the golden-haired child, and the woman with the jade green eyes kept changing into one another.

But it didn't really matter, did it?

She remembered a song—something she had learned a long time ago, and she started to sing it under her breath. "When I was just a little girl, I asked my mother, 'What will I be?'"

It was getting very hot. Her feet started to hurt. She stopped at the corner of Madison and Sixty-fourth Street and took off her shoes. Then she continued to walk in her stockinged feet, down the street, humming, swinging her shoes.

Epilogue

R on walked Alexis to the boarding area. That was as far as he was allowed.

"You're sure you'll be all right?" he asked her.

"Yes," she answered carefully. "Thank you so much for taking me."

"Not a problem."

There was a pause.

"Give me a call when you get in."

"I will."

"And keep in touch."

"Of course."

She smiled at him, kissed him on the cheek, then started toward the gate.

The take-off was smooth.

As the plane climbed up through the sky, an odd image came to Alexis. She imagined all the ties that held her to earth snapping—ping, ping—one by one.

Another thousand feet higher, another tie that simply couldn't make the stretch. Ping. Ron was one of the first to go, Linda, one of the last. Even her daughter, as they passed through a mass of cumulous clouds, finally snapped and left Alexis free.

The captain's voice came on, saying that they had reached cruising altitude, and that the passengers were allowed to move about the cabin.

Alexis unbuckled the strap of her seat belt. It was the last constraint of all.

How strange, she thought. *When this plane lands, I will be a person without a past, a present, or a future.*

She wondered what would happen.

At dawn, they landed at Charles de Gaulle Airport. Alexis went through Customs, Immigration. At last, the doors to the lobby swung open. Crowds of people were waiting for the passengers—waving, crying.

Alexis looked around. For a moment, she saw nobody—and she wondered if her letter had not reached its destination. But then, toward the back of the room, she saw her at last. The small, red-haired woman in the jade green dress, waiting.

Alexis picked up her bag and moved slowly toward her.

For a sneak preview of
Mary Sheldon's next novel,
REFLECTION
coming from Kensington Books
in April, 2003
just turn the page. . . .

Prologue One

June, 1956

It was seven o'clock in the morning, and the Los Angeles sunshine was already heavily dosed with smog. The princess telephone on Zoë's bedside table rang.

"Damn!" said Zoë sleepily. She groped through a tangle of pink satin sheets and finally found the receiver.

"Hello?"

When she heard the voice on the other end, she was no longer sleepy.

"Yes, Max?"

She edged out from under the sheets and sat down on the pink satin comforter and listened in eager silence for a few moments. Then she frowned, picked up a cigarette, and lit it. The tip smoldered and glared.

"Well," she said abruptly at last. "I see. No, don't be silly—not your fault at all. It obviously wasn't meant to be. Anyway, thank you for putting in a good word for me."

Slowly, she put down the receiver. Then she sat back on the bed and finished the cigarette.

From the next room, there came a high, whimpering cry. Zoë sighed and crushed out the cigarette stub.

"I'm coming, baby," she called. "I'm coming."

Zoë arrived at Nat and Al's a few minutes before noon. As she sat in the booth, she caught sight of Hans Lasky coming into the restaurant. He looked thinner, grayer, but Zoë was touched to see how elegantly he had dressed himself for their lunch.

She settled her face into a pleasant smile as he approached.

"Dear Hans," she murmured, and kissed his cheek.

"Something's wrong," he said instantly. His accented voice was anxious. "What has happened?"

"I don't get the job," she told he flatly. "Max called this morning. They decided to go with someone with more experience."

Hans frowned. "I'm sorry. I know how you wanted it. But I think maybe this isn't a bad thing."

Zoë shook her head. "It would have meant Europe. Not to mention the prestige. It would have set me up for life—a few years over there, then I could have started my own agency."

"And why can't you start your own agency now?"

Zoë's laugh was bitter. "Do you have any idea what that would take? You have to have a hell of a track record to get anything like that off the ground. And I've got nothing."

The older man shook his head and smiled. "Ah, but I have a track record, my dear."

Zoë started to say something, but he held up a hand. "I'll tell you what you do. You see a client you want, you tell these prospective Mamas that if they sign with you, Hans Lasky will photograph their little darlings free of charge."

"Hans!"

He beamed at her. "And I'll put out the good word for you. 'Zoë Andrews—she's young, but believe me, she's the best children's agent in town.' You'll see—before you can turn around, you'll have all the big business you want." He patted her hand affectionately. "This call you got this morning, trust me, it's a blessing."

He picked up a pickle with a delicate hand and started to eat it.

"Think of Caroline," he added. "If you had gotten the job, what would have happened to her? She couldn't have gone with you."

"No," Zoë admitted. "I guess Barton would have taken her. He's planning on moving back to New York as soon as the divorce is final." Seeing Hans's look, Zoë added rather acidly, "I wasn't planning on giving up my child, Hans. It would have been for just a year or two."

"But it never would have worked like that," he told her. "Barton would have wanted her to stay with him. No, it's far better like this. Babies belong with their mothers. So you will have Caroline and your agency as well. You wait and see."

Zoë put her hand on top of his and squeezed it.

When she got home, Daphne, the teenaged babysitter was sitting on the flowered sofa, watching television.

"Everything okay?" Zoë asked. "Caroline behave herself? She didn't throw any wild parties?"

The girl laughed. "She was perfect. I put her down for her nap a few minute ago."

When Daphne left, Zoë went into the nursery. She walked over to the crib and touched the sleeping child.

"Well, baby doll," she whispered, "it looks like you're stuck with me. So let's make it into something grand."

Caroline opened her dark blue eyes, and looked at Zoë.

$\mathcal{P}rologue$ Two

It was seven o'clock in the morning, and the Los Angeles sunshine was already heavily dosed with smog. The princess telephone on Zoč's bedside table rang abruptly.

Zoč groped through a tangle of pink satin sheets and finally found the receiver.

"Hello?"

When she heard the voice on the other end, she was no longer sleepy.

"Yes, Max?"

She edged out from under the sheets and sat down on the pink satin comforter. She listened in eager silence for a few moments, then smiled, picked up a cigarette, and lit it.

"Well, hurray," she said lightly, at last. "That's wonderful news. Tell them I accept. And thank you so much, Max, for putting in the word for me. I just need to get some things settled, and I'm all yours."

She said goodbye, and hung up the phone. She sat back down on the bed and slowly smoked.

From the other room came a small, high cry. Zoë stubbed out her cigarette.

"I'm coming," she called.

Caroline was lying in her crib, her face puckered and wet. Zoë picked her up and held her against her shoulder.

"It's all right," she told the baby. "Completely wasted tears. Zoë's here."

Zoë was the first to arrive at Nat n' Als. She waved at Barton when she saw him enter the restaurant. She could see he had dressed with special care.

He kissed her cautiously on the cheek and sat down.

"You're looking well."

"Thank you," she smiled at him graciously.

They talked idly for a few minutes, ordered coffee.

"So," Barton said at last, "why did you need to see me?"

Zoë took a breath.

"Are you still planning on going back to New York when all this is over?"

He seemed surprised by the question. "I don't think there's much point in my staying out here."

Zoë nodded. "Well," she said lightly, "You might not be going alone."

He drew in a breath, tensed. She realized that he thought she was referring to herself.

"What are you talking about?"

"Caroline," she said quickly. She strained to keep the light tone. "It looks like you'll be taking care of her for a while."

Barton blinked. "What?"

"I got a call this morning from New York. The

Dawson agency is starting an overseas branch—they want me to head it. It'll mean the next few years in Europe."

Barton started to say something—Zoë cut him off.

"It's a great opportunity, but it means that I can't take care of Caroline for a while."

There was silence. "Why can't she go with you?"

"I'm starting up an agency, Barton. It's going to mean working round-the-clock, constant travel. I can't do that to her. And I want this job."

She smiled at his face.

"It'll be great," she said lightly. "You won't even know she's there. You'll get one of those penthouses on Park Avenue, and you'll find a wonderful housekeeper." Her smile become a little sour. "Who knows—you might even get married again."

"I don't think that's going to happen," Barton said. "Listen, Zoë—are you serious about this? You really want me to take Caroline?"

"Well, I don't want you to," she said sharply, "but I don't see that I have a choice at the moment."

"And what happens after Europe?"

"I'll take her back, of course."

Barton shook his head. "No. That's not fair. I can't have her for a year or two, and then just give her up."

"Well, we'll worry about that later," Zoë told him hastily. "We don't have to work out every detail this second. I'm sure we can come up with a compromise."

"Maybe so. But we need to talk to the lawyers. Everything must be made absolutely clear."

She sighed. "All right, all right."

The waitress brought the bill. Zoë reached for her purse, but Barton stopped her.

"Let me," he said. He brought out his wallet, flipped it open.

"Congratulations on landing the job, by the way," he told her.

Zoë looked at him thoughtfully. "You know something? You're really quite a handsome man. I can see why I fell for you."

When Zoë got back to her apartment, Daphne was sitting on the flowered sofa, watching television.

"Everything okay?" Zoë asked her. "Caroline behave herself?"

The girl laughed. "She was perfect. I put her down for her nap a few minutes ago."

When the babysitter left, Zoë went into the baby's room. She reached through the slats of the crib and touched the tiny pink hand.

"Zoë's little star," she whispered. "Zoë's little star." She blinked back tears. "I've worked so hard for this, baby—and you'll have a great time in New York. But it won't be forever. I promise you."

Zoë picked the baby up out of the crib and held her. In the mirror, she saw the two of them, the woman and the baby, reflected together. Her mouth tightened and began to tremble. She hugged Caroline so hard that the baby woke and began to wail.

Caroline

Caroline's first memory is of stealing the television set.

She is four years old. It happens on a day when her father is away on a business trip. He is away a lot—this will be the third time in six weeks. He is an architect: Caroline has seen his name—Barton Andrews—written in the lobby of many buildings. She cannot read the words, but she traces the letters with her fingers.

Caroline is proud every time she sees her father's name—he must be almost as famous as President Eisenhower. She goes up to passersby, and points and tells them, "That's my daddy." But she doesn't understand why he has to be away so often. New York has everything: the zoo, the park, the smiling doorman at the front of their building. And their apartment has everything, too: a toy closet in her room, a big television set in the den, and a balcony that lets you see a tiny, precious Central Park far below. But her father still leaves New York to go on his business trips.

* * *

Caroline is always sad to see him go. She likes having her father near her. He is neat and handsome, and his smell is safe and lemony. She likes going into his den and playing with his brass paperweights and his ivory chessmen. She likes it when he laughs, and when he tickles her before bed. She even rather likes it when he plays spelling games with her at dinner, though not as much as he does. But when he goes away, that's all right, too. In a way, it's even more fun. Because when her father is gone, she can spend more time with Laura.

Laura has been with Caroline always. She is old and very dark and smells like things kept secret. Laura is the most important person in the house. It is Laura's face that shines over Caroline every morning. It is Laura's hand that decides how much brown sugar Caroline will get on her oatmeal. It is the state of Laura's bones that determines whether or not there will be a trip to the park that afternoon. And it is Laura's mouth, comforting, which gives the last kiss before bedtime.

When Barton is away, dinner is not served in the dining room; Caroline and Laura sit on stools in the kitchen, eating lovely easy meals like creamed corn and canned peaches—not the fancy foods that Barton always wants Caroline to try.

"What if you grow up to be the ambassador to China or Mexico someday?" he asks her. "You'll have to eat everything you're given, or you'll let down the whole government."

Caroline doesn't want to be the ambassador to China or Mexico. She just wants to sit at the kitchen table, eating creamed corn forever.

After dinner, she and Laura play cards—they play Old Maid for so long sometimes that when Caroline closes her eyes afterward, she can still see the cards shimmering against the backs of her eyelids. She always wins the game.

"Not again! Boo hoo!" Laura pretends to cry. And Caroline rushes over and hugs her and comforts her and loves her, loves her.

Then, at bedtime, Laura tucks Caroline in bed and tells her scary stories about the Virgin Islands, where she came from. She tells Caroline about men who wear wooden masks and dance in the firelight. Caroline is frightened to death of these masks—she imagines the eyes, huge and dripping—but she doesn't tell Laura she is scared, because she doesn't want the stories to stop.

Often, Barton is away on weekends, and these are the best times of all.

"Can we go to your house tomorrow?" Caroline asks Laura every time he leaves on a Friday night. "Please, please!"

Laura doesn't always say yes; she isn't sure that Caroline's father really likes their going. But every so often, she agrees.

It's an adventure to get up extra early and walk down the street to the subway. Then there is the thick warmth of the train to be enjoyed, and all the noises, which might be scary if Caroline weren't holding Laura's hand. And finally there is stepping off into a whole new place—a street very different from the one Caroline lives on.

There are no doormen in front of these buildings, and no flowers, but there are a lot of stray dogs and people sitting on the steps of their houses. Laura and

Caroline walk down one street, then turn the corner, and there is Laura's house, blue and faded, and there is Laura's daughter Dale, small and big-haired, and there, best and worst of all, is Yvette.

Yvette is Laura's granddaughter, and she is six. Before Caroline met Yvette, back in the days when she had only heard her name, she thought Yvette would look like a special car she had seen on a television commercial. But Yvette turned out not to be curvy and red. She was as dark as Laura, with hair in tiny corn-rows, tied with ribbons.

"Can I have hair like Yvette's?" Caroline had asked Laura.

Laura had laughed. "I don't think it would suit you."

"I don't care."

So that night, Laura put Caroline's hair in tiny blond braids all over her head. Caroline pretended she thought it was pretty, but she secretly knew it didn't look right. She asked Laura to take the braids out.

Everything about Yvette was interesting. She had a gerbil in a little cage. She had been to the Automat. She knew someone whose father had gone to prison. And she could hula hoop.

But the most exciting thing about Yvette's life was Playland. She got to go there twice a year, once in the winter and once in the summer. Playland sounded like the most wonderful place on Earth, bright as the cards from Old Maid, with licorice as long as your arm and pink spun candy like an old woman's hairdo.

Caroline could never hear enough about it.

"I went on the roller coaster last time I was there," Yvette tells her.

Caroline is awed. "The big one?"

"Yeah, that one."

"Did you go on the Tilt-A-Whirl?"

"Sure."

"And the elephants?"

"Oh, yeah. Though they're getting kinda babyish for me now."

But the greatest thing about Playland is the throwing game.

"You go up to this booth, and a man gives you these three rings, and you've got to throw them over the tops of milk bottles. And if you do it, you get a big prize!"

Caroline tenses. She knows what's coming next.

"Wanna see what I won?"

Caroline nods.

They go into Yvette's room. And there in the corner is the huge pink plush teddy bear, bigger than Caroline, bigger than Yvette, with a red ribbon around its neck, and a satin heart stitched onto its chest.

Caroline sighs with envy.

Yvette sees her face and chuckles.

"Well, maybe you'll win one too, someday."

Caroline nods, a little hopelessly. She has mentioned Playland over and over again to her father, but so far he has shown no signs of wanting to take her there.

"Anyway, we can practice," Yvette says brightly.

They do this every visit—they make their own "throwing game." They take all Dale's empty milk bottles and put them in the hall and try to toss cardboard rings around them.

As Caroline throws the rings, she dreams of the bear she will someday win at Playland. She won't choose a pink teddy bear, like Yvette's—no, hers will be turquoise, and she'll name it Rajah. She won't let go of Rajah for a moment. She'll take him with her on the Ferris wheel. He will be her partner on the giant slide. Rajah will feel fear along with her on the Tilt-A-Whirl.

She rings her third milk bottle, and smiles.

GET MORE OF THE BOOKS
YOU WANT FROM TODAY'S
HOTTEST AUTHORS

Kensington Profiles:
The Rich and Famous